The Eternal Sea

ANGIE FRAZIER

SCHOLASTIC PRESS / NEW YORK

Library of Congress Cataloging-in-Publication Data
Frazier, Angie.
The Eternal Sea / by Angie Frazier. — 1st ed.
p. cm.
Summary: Realizing that the magic of Umandu, the stone that
grants immortality, is not done, seventeen-year-old Camille
accompanies Oscar, Ira, and Randall to Egypt, where all their
lives are in grave danger.
[1. Adventure and adventurers — Fiction. 2. Supernatural — Fiction.
3. Love — Fiction. 4. Egypt — History — 19th century — Fiction.]
I. Title. II. Title: Everlasting two.
PZ7.F8688Evm 2011
[Fic] — dc22
2010027432

ISBN 978-0-545-11475-2

10 9 8 7 6 5 4 3 2 1   11 12 13 14 15

Printed in the U.S.A. 23
First edition, June 2011

The text type was set in Garth Graphic.
Book design by Lillie Howard

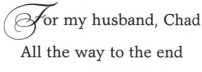For my husband, Chad

All the way to the end

ONE

1855 PORT ADELAIDE, AUSTRALIA

*D*ark soil gathered under Camille's fingernails as she dug at the earth. A midafternoon shower had dampened the ground, but rain couldn't keep her from the broken-down garden. She'd needed a task. She'd needed to do something more than sit idly by, restless and waiting. Camille knelt in the overgrown herb bed beside her mother's home and tugged at the tangled remnants of winter savory and chives, lemon balm and oregano. Camille's mother had once tended this same plot, but weeds and neglect had destroyed it. The garden had died, and so had Camille's mother.

Camille threw aside a clump of dirt and roots, and stopped to think about what she was doing. This wasn't her garden. She turned to the house beside her, to the white paint flaking off the clapboards and shutters. This wasn't her home. It had been her mother's, yes, but never Camille's. She didn't belong here. Her home was half a continent and an entire ocean away. And she wasn't sure she belonged there, either.

The front gate squealed and feet sounded up the brick walk. Camille smiled at the trill of a lighthearted whistle she knew well, and brushed back a lock of her sun-streaked raven hair. The whistle broke off in the center of a note.

"Don't tell me you've gone all domestic," called a voice from the walk. "Maybe tomorrow you could have a batch of muffins hot from the oven waiting for me."

Camille twisted around and watched her friend Ira Beam saunter inside the sorry excuse for a garden. She squinted into the blinding sun as it settled over Port Adelaide's tidal river and the marshy swamplands beyond.

"Sorry, Ira, but tearing weeds out of the ground is about as domestic as I get." She turned back to her work and attacked a dried-out knot of thyme. The plant hadn't been tended for years. According to every law of nature, it should be dead. Yet the thyme's pungent scent still took to the air when Camille rustled it. This should have amazed her, but recently Camille, too, had discovered a way around the laws of nature. Things that were dead didn't necessarily have to stay that way.

Ira slid onto the stone bench beside the herb bed. The brim of his hat cast a shadow over his pale blue eyes. Thin white lines webbed out across his temples. Though Ira couldn't be a year or two past twenty, the Australian sun had weathered his face. The rest of him, though, his bouncing step and playful humor, was just as youthful as he was.

"Why are you bothering with this place?" he asked. "I thought you were heading back to California."

Camille released the handful of thyme when the roots resisted. They were still strong. Worth saving.

"I am going home. Eventually." Her fingers tensed around the brittle limbs of some winter savory as the person she'd been waiting for, the person who had promised to take her home, came to mind. Oscar Kildare. A painful stab twisted deep inside her chest. She tried not to think of him constantly but usually failed. Most of the memories she had of Oscar were made of velvet. Soft and warm. Indulgent. Lately, however, nearly every memory of him pricked like thorns.

She yanked the roots from the ground. "I don't know how much longer Oscar will be working the wharves to earn enough for our passage home, and honestly I'm bored out of my skull. We've been in Port Adelaide two weeks now, and I've spent the whole time cooped up in this house."

Ira couldn't possibly understand. He'd been out at the taverns playing — and cheating — at poker every night.

"I've already told you, love, you can come with me any evening. It'd be a real life experience for you."

Camille threw a handful of soil at him.

"I've had my fill of life experiences for now, thank you." She got to her feet and brushed clumps of dirt from her skirt.

The dress had belonged to her mother. Lavender silk, embroidered with thin vertical stripes of a darker shade of purple. It was one of many Camille had found in her mother's closet. Her own dress had gone through months of turmoil. When at long last Camille had peeled off the filthy and torn homespun, she'd imagined she was stripping away the last four months as well.

"So, listen." Ira rubbed his hands together. "I won a nice round this afternoon and thought we'd celebrate with dinner."

Camille instantly felt bad about throwing dirt at him. Ira had been a constant companion these last weeks. He refused to let one day pass without visiting.

"Really? Ira, that's sweet. I know how hard you cheated today, and you want to spend some of those spoils on me? I'm touched." She held back a laugh as Ira's lips puckered.

He hiked up one of his golden brown eyebrows. "Yeah, you *are* touched, especially if you think I'm actually buying you dinner. If my pockets remind me correctly, you still owe me big."

Camille's good humor fell flat. The money she'd promised Ira when she hired him as her guide three months ago in Melbourne remained unpaid. She'd been penniless then, not knowing how Ira would get his compensation. Not much had changed since. But she'd made a promise, and she would keep it.

"I'll get you your money, Ira." The solemn vow took him by surprise. His hiked eyebrow smoothed out.

"Hey, I'm only joking with you, love. You don't owe me nothing, anyhow. Just a ride to Sydney is all. Though I admit, I'd be hesitant to leave off from there." He grinned deviously. "What would you do without me, right?"

Camille looked away, hoping to change the subject. Ira was too good to her. "So then you *are* going to take me out to dinner?"

He shot up from the bench and tipped the brim of his hat to her. The suede was aged with dirt and sweat, and completely lost of any firmness.

"I'm sweeping you away to a quaint little shack on a rocky cove."

Camille crossed her arms. "You're taking me to Monty's? What kind of dinner is that?" She recalled Ira's irritable friend. Monty could hardly keep himself clean, let alone his home or cookware. "Sweaty sock stew? Fried potatoes seasoned with river salt?"

Ira followed her as she walked to the garden gate. "Come on, he's not that bad. Sure he smells like a whiskey barrel, but he *did* sober up long enough to sail you up Spencer's Bay to that cursed —"

Camille spun around and glared at him.

"Sorry, I forgot," Ira said softly. "You don't like talking about it, and I don't blame you, but, you've gotta face it some —"

Camille cut him off a second time by hurrying away, up the brick walk to the front door.

"I'm going to wash my hands. Wait here." She disappeared inside, shutting the door behind her. Camille leaned against it. Her heart rapped against her breastbone.

Face it. How could she? Four months ago, her father, Captain William Rowen, had died when his ship sunk to the depths of the Tasman Sea. Any typical seventeen-year-old girl would have grieved and tried to move on. But Camille wasn't a typical girl.

She had not simply lost her father — she'd survived the shipwreck that had claimed him. Camille had also learned that the mother she'd always believed dead was living in Port Adelaide, Australia, and was the keeper of the coveted map to Umandu, the legendary stone of a mythical immortal race. However, the stone was not just a silly story for drunken sailors and treasure hunters. It had the very real power to do what Camille wanted most: bring someone back from the dead.

No. Camille had not been a typical grieving daughter.

She blinked back tears at the thought of her father. Camille had set out across Australia to bring him back to life, but she'd failed. He was still dead.

Camille hastily wiped away a tear that had rolled down

her cheek, and went into the kitchen. Wide plank floor-boards bowed underfoot on her way to the water basin, where she dunked her earth-coated hands. The single window's white lace curtain flipped and fluttered in the breeze, which was heavy with the scent of rain. A shiver of gooseflesh raced up her arms. Her mother's kitchen was of the no-frills sort. Its rustic cabinetry, wood slab countertops, and worn woven rugs gave it a dreary feel. Against the opposite wall was the big iron cookstove that Camille's brother, Samuel, had been trying to teach her to use.

She loved the way that sounded: *her brother*. Having a sibling was still fresh enough to bring on a wide smile each time she remembered she had one. Before finding her mother, she'd been an only child. Camille distractedly wiped her hands and forearms on a linen towel. How odd it felt to know that for sixteen years, there had been a second half of her on the earth and yet she'd only just learned of him.

Ira gave a short greeting to someone out on the brick walk, most likely Samuel back from town. The front door opened just as Camille saw her reflection in the shine of a copper bowl beside the water basin. Dirt from the garden smudged one of her cheeks and her forehead, too. She reached back into the bowl and splashed her face as heavy footsteps pounded up the stairs to the second floor. Camille patted her face dry with the linen towel, checked her reflection one last time, and then went into the sitting room. The stairs rattled with her brother's descent, just as Ira came inside and slammed the door behind him.

"What has Samuel in such a hurry?" she asked Ira. But the person who came out of the stairwell and into the sitting room was not Samuel.

Camille froze midstep, stunned by the sudden sight of him. The gentle slope of his broad shoulders, the lean cut of his waist, his grown-out, dark blond hair. Oscar Kildare came down off the last step and fixed her with an unreadable stare. It had been two full weeks since she'd seen him. Camille wanted to go to him, burrow deep into his arms and kiss him as much as she wanted to shout at him to leave. But she knew her anger would not win out. Because try as she might, Camille could not look at Oscar without seeing him as he'd been the morning she'd finally found the magical stone — vacant-eyed and ashy-lipped, in a pool of his own blood. Dead.

"So you decided to visit, did you?" Ira asked, his usual good nature gone.

Oscar reached into his trouser pocket, ignoring Ira's sarcastic question. He took out a small, string-tied leather pouch and without a word, set it on the arm of the horsehair sofa. The contents settled with a metallic, chiming noise. Coins?

"What is this?" Camille looked from the pouch to Oscar. It was then that she noticed the bag in his other hand. It was the burlap bag she had so carefully hidden away in the closet upstairs in her mother's room. Inside it was the stone of the immortals. *Umandu.* How had Oscar known where to find it? He'd gone straight upstairs to the closet, as if he'd been watching her the day she shoved it in there.

"What are you doing with that?" she asked. She hadn't touched or even looked at the stone since the morning she'd found it. As soon as she'd laid her hands on it, the stone had read her heart's desire. It had determined who Camille most wanted alive again. And her heart had left her father behind.

Oscar's eyes, fringed by thick golden lashes, slid to the bag of coins. "It's the money I've earned on the wharves. There's enough there for your passage back to San Francisco. Both you and Samuel." He glanced toward Ira without meeting his eyes. "And enough for you to get to Sydney."

Ira snorted instead of thanking him. Oscar wasn't exactly one of Ira's *mates* any longer, not since Oscar had disappeared without a word, without any excuse whatsoever. But Camille knew why he'd left her. At least she thought she did.

Oscar turned his eyes to her. For a moment, the hard, empty gleam was gone and he seemed himself: the sailor her father had asked her not to associate with, the friend she'd needed when she'd been determined to reach Port Adelaide and Umandu. The man she'd finally let herself fall in love with, despite the reality of a perfectly suitable fiancé waiting for her back home.

Randall Jackson. Thinking about him tangled Camille up inside.

"You mean there's enough for me, Samuel, and you," she corrected.

In the minutes after bringing Oscar's lifeless body back from the dead, it had become clear that they would return to California together, as a couple. It had to her anyway. But then Camille had made a mistake. She'd told Oscar the deep secret she'd been keeping: Randall Jackson's money was the only thing floating her father's shipping company. Not marrying him would mean Randall's departure and Rowen & Company's ruin. It would mean Camille would be bankrupt. She'd lose everything.

She pressed her lips tightly together, remembering the look of horror on Oscar's face after she'd told him her secret. And shortly after, everything she thought she'd known about Oscar had fallen to pieces.

"It's enough for you and Samuel," Oscar repeated, the hard gleam returning. "I'm not going back with you."

The ache in Camille's chest felt like corset strings cutting off her air supply. She stared at Oscar, openmouthed.

"No. You have to come back."

He fixed his grip on the burlap bag. "That's not something I can do right now."

The sitting room seemed to tilt, tipping her off balance. Camille leaned against the secretary desk.

"But, what about . . . I thought if you had some time to think, to plan . . . I thought we'd still be . . ." She closed her eyes and took a breath, hating that she'd been so caught off guard that she couldn't finish a single sentence.

"I know what I led you to believe, and I'm sorry for it." Oscar didn't so much as fidget. He stood rigid, as if he'd rehearsed these lines for a perfectly cold delivery. "The truth is, I can't be with you. Not here, or in San Francisco. It's impossible."

Camille shook her head, and pressed the heel of her palm to her temple. "But you said you loved me. I chose you, Oscar. My heart chose *you* and not my —"

"Father. I know." He finally showed some level of discomfort by tightening the muscles of his jaw. "You made a mistake. *I* made a mistake."

He started for the front door, the burlap bag still clenched in his fist. Ira drew back his shoulders and held up his hand to stop him.

"Now hold on, you bloody idiot. Who do you think you are, treating her that way? What the devil's gotten into you?"

Camille took advantage of Oscar's momentary distraction and dove forward, tearing the burlap bag out of his hands. She backed up, out of reach.

Oscar's chest expanded with a long, impatient breath. "Give me the bag, Camille. Now."

She drew the bag closer. Her hurt and shock gave way to anger. "Why should I? What could you possibly want with the stone now?"

Her pulse raced. Her hands and arms throbbed intensely. And then Camille became aware of a strange heat spreading through her stomach where she held the bag against her.

"It doesn't have anything to do with you," Oscar said.

Camille fumbled for a retort, but her attention tore between the pulse of the burlap bag and Oscar's callousness. He made a sudden grab for the bag, almost freeing it from Camille's hands. She hung on to one of the straps and Oscar only succeeded in pulling her toward him, slamming her against his chest.

Camille's eyes widened as a pale white beam of light cut through the bag. The woven burlap split the beam into scores of smaller rays, casting out a kaleidoscope of pearly white light. She ripped the top back. White luminescence hit her square in the face. The heat dashed a prickling sensation over her skin and spiked the small hairs on her arms. This simply couldn't be happening. The legend of Umandu was supposed to be done. Over. She parted her lips and stared up at Oscar. He didn't look half as surprised as she felt. *He'd already known*, she realized.

He'd already known Umandu wasn't finished.

TWO

"Did you know about this?" she asked, dazed over the glaring light and Oscar's intentions to leave with the stone. To leave *her*.

She reached in and touched the stone. It throbbed, licking her fingers with such heat that at first the heat felt like ice. The stone shouldn't be doing this. Camille had already tapped it of its power.

Umandu had been hidden inside a massive dome of boulders for centuries — possibly millennia. Camille had outmaneuvered Stuart McGreenery, her rival for the stone, and had reached Umandu first. She'd been the first to touch the stone, and in doing so, she'd been the one to wield its power.

"It didn't shine like this before," Oscar said.

"Before?" Ira asked, his widened eyes staring warily at the burlap bag.

Oscar sighed, as if he'd said something unintended. "On the *Lady Kate*, on our way back here. I took a look at the stone one night while you were on watch. I felt it beat like that, like a heart, but it didn't give off light like this."

He shielded his eyes as Camille pulled the stone from the bag. Ira cursed under his breath and took a significant step backward. The heat still crossed between ice and warmth, but it didn't hurt. She held it out, away from her body.

"Didn't you think that was important enough to share with us?" she asked, the stone's pulse stronger now. The way it settled into the same throbbing rhythm of her heart disconcerted her. She returned the stone to the bag. While inside, her fingers brushed against the leather map that had led them to the stone. Like Umandu, the map had been a magical entity. She hadn't touched or unrolled the map since the dome of boulders either. She'd wanted to forget about it entirely.

Oscar crossed his arms. "The stone brought me back to life. That makes it my concern."

"It makes it *our* concern, or have you forgotten the part about my heart choosing you?"

Camille went to the sofa and lowered herself onto one of the timeworn cushions. Perhaps Oscar remembered too well. He was alive at the expense of her father. It was an enormous burden. At least it was for her.

She looked to Ira. Her friend's face was still screwed up in consternation. "Ira?"

Ira gathered himself enough to notice her eyes rolling a few times toward the front door. He cleared his throat.

"You sure, love?" He sent a threatening glance Oscar's way.

She nodded, and Ira grumbled something incoherent as he stepped back outside.

As soon as the door shut, Oscar went to the fireplace. He turned to face her, his expression rigid. Camille tried not to stare at where the top undone buttons of his shirt revealed smooth, tanned skin.

He spoke softly. "I want you to go back to California." It still came across as a command.

"Without you," she said.

He nodded once. "Without me."

Her nose stung, tears forming.

"And do what once I arrive?" she asked. *Don't say it. Don't say it,* she pleaded in silence.

Oscar turned away, showing her his profile. "There's a reason your father wanted Randall to be your husband. Maybe I misjudged Randall. Maybe William's reasons were sound."

Camille stared at him, his words twisting all the things she'd come to rely on. That Oscar wanted to be with her. That he loved her.

"You don't really believe that," she whispered. "You're only saying all of this because I told you about Randall's investments holding Rowen and Company together. But I've already told you, I don't care about his money. I don't care about money at all."

Oscar uncrossed his arms and left the fire-warmed hearth. His eyes locked on Camille.

"Well, you should. It makes a difference, Camille." He held out his hand. "Give me the bag."

Camille shot to her feet. What had happened to Oscar? Who was this person in front of her?

"Why? What are you going to do with it?" she asked. Stuart McGreenery had been planning on selling its power to the highest bidder. Oscar couldn't possibly want to do the same thing now, could he? But then, he'd changed so drastically as soon as he'd learned Camille's fortune was gone.

 13

"There's just something I need to take care of," he answered vaguely.

The stone's value would be unimaginable if it still had power. No amount of money could have tempted Camille from parting with it, though. Not if there was the possibility of the stone granting more than just one resurrection.

"You can't have it," she whispered.

Oscar spoke through clenched teeth. "Camille, *please*."

"I found it and that makes it mine."

It was the claim of a spoiled little girl, but she didn't know what else to say or do. She hated Oscar right then almost as much as she loved him.

"You don't even know what all of this means," he said.

She dug into the bag and ignored the icy heat of the stone as she pulled it out, still brilliantly lit. Camille's ears rang with adrenaline and fury.

"Then you should tell me what it means. Whatever it is, I should be a part of it."

Oscar came within inches of her. "Give me the stone, Camille."

She expected his spicy sweet scent that had so often intoxicated her. She'd missed being close enough to smell it, though now her nose traced nothing but sea salt.

She dropped the stone back into the bag, then glared at him as defiantly as she could without giving away her true longing and pain. "If you want it, you'll have to fight me for it."

The side of his mouth twitched, and for a second he seemed amused. But then his grin fell.

"I'm being serious," he said.

Camille held the bag closer, wrapping both arms around it. He'd never lay a hand on her. Oscar was her protector. He always had been. But this Oscar, this heartless Oscar, made her uncertain.

"So am I," she said.

He balled his hands into fists. His stare burned through her, his indecision over what to do palpable. But then he swept past, leaving a chill breeze against her shoulder as he stormed around the sofa.

The white light and icy heat of the stone weakened at the slam of the front door. It extinguished before Oscar smacked the front gate closed as well. Only a warm pulsation remained, constant as a heartbeat.

"I guess this means dinner's off," Ira said as he tried to keep up with Camille's fast pace toward St. Vincent Street and the wharves.

"I can't think of food right now, Ira."

She carried the burlap bag with her, too afraid to leave it back at the house alone.

"What did Oscar say about the stone?" Ira asked. "Did he know why it kicked back to life like that?"

Camille didn't want to tell Ira all of the things Oscar had said. She simmered with humiliation and anger. How could Oscar do this? How could he be so cruel?

"Let's just find my brother," she said.

Caroline's China, pinched between other buildings along a village side street, sparkled tastefully in a port filled with copper smelting factories, cargo stores, warehouses, sailmaker lofts, and chandleries. The china shop had been her mother's livelihood. And it had been there, inside the narrow storefront with shelving displays of crystal, fine china, and porcelain, where Camille had discovered the truth of why her mother had abandoned her.

Ira pressed his face up against the glass window of the shop.

"What's Sir Prim Pants going to know about it?" he asked. Camille pushed open the door and set off the small brass bell above.

She wasn't sure Samuel would know anything at all, but she needed to tell him. He was her brother. He'd been there when Oscar died and when Camille brought him back.

"Be nice, Ira," she whispered and then closed the door. Ira rolled his eyes but kept quiet.

Her brother's back was turned to her as she walked toward the counter.

"Please, if you want to see something, ask for assistance," he said.

It was the same way they'd met. Samuel had turned around that first time, as he did now, and Camille had stared her mother's infidelity in the face.

So many of Samuel's features, his black hair, green eyes, and even the hump along the bridge of his nose, were the replica of hers. But the deep, handsome cleft in his chin and the high structure of his cheekbones were striking resemblances to his father. It was too painful. Camille turned her eyes away. He was her half brother, yes. But he was also the son of the man Camille despised most in the world: Stuart McGreenery. He had been the root of so much pain. The fact that McGreenery was dead didn't lessen her hate for him one bit.

"Oh, it's you." Samuel sounded disappointed that he wouldn't be making a sale. The shop's inventory was mostly packed in crates, anyway, ready for shipment to San Francisco.

Samuel checked the hands on the cut-crystal wall clock. "I suppose you're hungry. Camille, really, I've shown you how to light the stove a dozen times." He sighed. "That's it. I'm officially giving up your housekeeping lessons as a lost cause."

She leveled him with her jade green eyes. "Ha, very funny. I'm not here for that reason. There's something I need to speak to you about."

A delft vase inside one of the open crates on the floor drew Ira's hand. His fingers ran over the smooth blue and white glaze.

"Ah, ah, ah." Samuel hopped to Ira's side and removed his hand from the vase. "That is seventeenth-century transferware. Please don't paw at it."

Ira coughed something rude into his hand and backed up to the door. Samuel had been at the shop for days on end clearing the shelves, wrapping and folding and packing and then rewrapping and repacking. He'd told Camille that leaving Port Adelaide was the only option for him — he didn't want to stay now that his mother was dead. There was the whole world to see, after all. But instead of exhilaration over the move to California, he'd seemed irritated and distracted. She glanced at the stacks of crates, wondering if they had really required so much attention and time, or if they had provided her brother with an excuse to sequester himself away.

"What is it, Camille?" Samuel asked, covering up the transferware crate.

She slowly opened the top of the bag, unsure how to tell him. Perhaps she just needed to show him. But when she gripped the stone and brought it out of the bag, it was its normal dull amber color. There was no white light or icy heat.

"Is there something the matter with it?" he asked. Samuel didn't wait for an answer but came over and plucked it out of her hand. He turned it over carefully, his hands accustomed to handling expensive and irreplaceable objects.

"It looks fine to me," he said.

"You can't feel it?" she asked.

Samuel peered at her. "Feel what?"

Camille gestured to the stone. "The pulse. It has a pulse. And heat. Ira saw it back at the house. Oscar, too," she added, wanting to hurry past his name. She turned to Ira for confirmation. "The stone shot out light, didn't it?"

Ira whipped his hand away from a stained-glass sun catcher.

"It did. And I swear I haven't had a sip of rum today," he answered.

Her brother gave the stone another wary inspection. He put both hands on it, waiting to feel the pulse and heat. Camille could tell from his expression that he felt nothing. She took the stone back. The throb and warmth were there, against her skin, though it was still its normal amber color.

"I don't know, Camille." Samuel searched her face carefully, as if trying to detect some sort of illness. "So Oscar finally decided to make an appearance, did he? Did he say where he's been keeping himself these last weeks? Where he's been staying?"

Camille shoved the stone back into the bag, defenses rising. "No, he didn't. And I'm not making any of this up about the stone."

"I didn't say you were," he answered.

Ira's knee bumped against a massive urn. The base lifted and tipped dangerously. Ira caught it, but not before Samuel shot more daggers with his eyes.

"Fine, I'm leaving." Ira swung open the door. "You coming to Monty's, love?"

Camille shook her head. "Not tonight, Ira. Will I see you tomorrow?"

Ira winked at her. "'Course you will. I force my pleasurable company upon the willing and unwilling alike."

The bell's chime rang itself silent as she watched Ira shut the door, pull his long leather coat tighter around his chest, and head toward the wharves. The harbor's sparkling light had faded. Dusk rolled in quickly, along with the usual night winds off the tidal river.

"I wish I could show you what the stone did," Camille said, still gazing out the window.

"You've already used it," Samuel replied. "Maybe this pulse you say you feel is a side effect? Something that only you can feel because you're the one who found it?"

And Oscar, too. He'd felt it.

"You're probably right," she sighed, turning back to him. "Will you come home soon?"

Her brother ran his hands through his long black hair. He seemed to take in the enormity of the shop's mess, and leaned against the counter.

"I'll be there later," Samuel said.

Camille didn't know her brother very well. They'd

only been acquainted for a little less than two months. But she did know his work ethic, dogged and restless.

"I suppose it'll be jam and bread for me again tonight?" she asked, trying to smile. It was difficult. All she could think about was the pouch of money, still on the arm of the sofa. It would be the first thing she saw when she walked in the house.

"Jam and bread is safer than you attempting to light the stove," Samuel answered. But then his smooth cheek rose into a half grin. "Really, I'll try and be there within the hour. I promise."

Camille left the shop and started back. She'd show Samuel the money when he got home. And then she would have to explain how Oscar wasn't coming with them. How he'd cast her off. The shame of it all warmed her cheeks and drew the sting of tears. What had happened to the Oscar she knew, the one she'd fallen in love with? He'd been so determined to take the stone and send her home. Samuel longed to leave Port Adelaide, and so did Camille. But not like this.

She reached the house and entered the dim sitting room, taking a moment to light the oil lamp by the door. It illuminated the furniture and the leather pouch on the sofa. Camille plucked it up and threw it into the burlap bag. Samuel and Oscar might not agree, but she didn't care.

San Francisco would just have to wait.

THREE

The wharves along St. Vincent Street were at their usual bustle when Camille arrived late the next morning. She was finished being housebound and bored to tears. Finished waiting for Oscar to show up and tell her what was happening. She had questions for him, and she was determined to get some answers.

The flow of bodies, the calls of the wharfies and crews, made Camille feel less alone. Oscar's behavior had kept her awake all night — that and the soothing pulse of the burlap bag she'd kept at her side. The stone was now inside the secretary in her mother's sitting room, the closet no longer a viable hiding place. Though needing to hide it from Oscar in the first place was preposterous.

She didn't want to believe he cared about her lost fortune enough to abandon her. Perhaps it was something else entirely. Her heart had chosen his life over her father's, and she was certain Oscar was struggling with it. But he wasn't the only one. Besides, if the stone's new life hinted to any sort of possibility, if there was another way to reach her father, there was no chance she'd return to San Francisco before finding out.

The tidal wind lifted the ivory lace collar of her mother's mossy green, layered linen dress as she walked down the wharf. She was embarrassed to admit it, but when Oscar had not come to visit her at the house, not even once since they'd been back, she'd gone down to the harbor to see him. She'd hid behind the corner of a chandlery and watched him work, trying to think of a way to approach him without feeling or sounding needy.

"What are you doing here?"

Camille spun around. Oscar stood over her, yet another storm in his eyes.

"I'm looking for you." She wished it hadn't come out as a whisper.

"Well, you found me."

Yes, she had, along with the dull ache inside her chest. She had to get on with it before she lost her nerve.

"Why do you want the stone so badly?"

Oscar lowered his chin and watched a few wharfies haul a barrel past them before answering.

"I need it for where I'm going." His short, emotionless sentences were starting to crawl under her skin. "And I'll be needing the map, too."

The map? Oscar moved around Camille, but she caught up to him before he could pick up a crate to load.

"Quit being so vague and just tell me what's happening with the stone."

"Isn't it obvious?" He lowered his voice and reversed his direction, stepping closer. "It's not over. It never was. I don't know if it ever will be."

Camille expected him to storm away again, but instead he stared beyond the new cutter ship that he and the others were employed to load, watching a grand East Indiaman brig three wharves down. She wanted to know why he wasn't more eager about what a still-active Umandu might offer. Oscar was intelligent, his mind as sharp as his mouth could be at times. He just *had* to be imagining the possibilities.

Camille hesitated. "Isn't this a . . . good thing?"

He cut his eyes from the new ship to her, searing her with them. "There is nothing good about any of this, Camille. I need to get back to work."

Tired of him turning his back on her, Camille caught the crook of his arm.

"Camille?" A voice from the head of the wharf caused her to her drop her hand. "My God, is that you, Camille?"

Shock warmed her neck and prickled her ears. That voice. It tunneled all the way inside her head, where at last she placed it. Her stomach flipped and knotted. Without inhaling a single breath she turned and saw the very person she'd been dreading for months.

Randall Jackson's flushed pink lips turned up into an endless smile. "Thank God, it *is* you!"

Randall pushed by the swarm of workers and crushed Camille against his chest in an embrace.

Camille blinked. Once. Twice. A third time, as her fiancé pulled away and gripped her by the shoulders, taking her in fully.

She sucked in a sharp breath. "Randall?"

He laughed and took her cheeks into both of his palms. "Camille, I can't believe this. You're here. You're really here!"

She attempted to ask him what he was doing in Port Adelaide, but he silenced her with a kiss. It was strong and brimming with relief, like one long sigh. Stronger than any kiss they'd shared back in San Francisco. The kiss startled her as much as his sudden presence in a world empty of him for so long.

"I've missed you so much," he said when he at last drew back. His name ricocheted through her mind. *Randall, Randall, Randall.* What was he doing here?

"I don't understand," she finally said, stealing a glance at Oscar. He looked as if he'd like to rip off Randall's lips and toss them in the harbor as fish bait. Though it wasn't the right moment for it, Camille took heart in his reaction.

"How did you . . . when did you . . . ?" She gasped. Her letter. She'd sent him a letter as soon as she and Oscar had come ashore at Port Melbourne. She'd told him about the shipwreck and their rescue, and about her mother being in Port Adelaide. But she had definitely not asked him to come.

Randall smiled widely again, the grin accentuating his perfectly chiseled chin and the healthy flush of his cheeks. He grasped her hands and pulled them close to his chest.

"The morning after I received your letter I found a ship heading to Australia and booked passage. I was so worried about you. And your father." The joy in his smile faded. "I'm sorry, Camille. I still can't believe he's gone. I can only imagine what you must have been going through here, all alone."

Oscar took a step forward. "She wasn't alone."

Randall inhaled evenly and rounded on his heel to acknowledge Oscar.

"I see that. I am glad you survived the shipwreck, Oscar." Without another ounce of salutation for him, Randall turned back to Camille. He took her in from head to foot.

"I've been looking forward to this moment for so long," he said. "Your letter mentioned that your mother was in Port Adelaide, and knowing just how adventurous you are" — he ran his finger down the slope of her nose — "I knew you'd come here to find her."

Randall had anticipated that? He couldn't possibly know her that well. They'd been nothing more than childhood acquaintances until a few weeks before he'd proposed.

"You mean you came all this way, spent months on a ship . . . Randall, you couldn't even stand being aboard the *Christina* while she was moored in the harbor."

He made a show of breathing in Port Adelaide's fishy harbor air. He exhaled loudly and pressed his hands against his gray and black striped tweed vest.

"It's just as your father always said: I found my sea legs in time. Besides —" He took her hands in his once more. His skin was warm and dry, while hers was damp and hot. "I had something important waiting for me across the Pacific."

A false grin labored its way across her cheeks. She hadn't been waiting for him. She'd been falling in love with the very person Randall couldn't stand.

Her father had pleaded with her to find happiness with Randall so that Rowen & Company could thrive again. Randall's investments had been floating the shipping company for a while, though Camille had only learned of his vital importance just before her father died. But now, holding his hand, being under his earnest gaze, Camille remembered something else — he loved her. Randall Jackson truly loved her, and had apparently struggled through his fear of the sea and paralyzing sickness to come to her aid. Her neck broke out in new beads of sweat.

"I'm not sure what to say," she whispered.

He gave her a soft peck on the forehead. "I'll only accept a complete account of everything that's happened since you arrived here in Australia."

Her throat ran dry and her tongue felt as if it had transformed into a piece of ancient driftwood.

"There's, well, a lot to tell you. I can't even think how to begin."

He squeezed her hands. "You've been through too much."

If he only knew the half of it, she thought.

She hadn't bargained on having to explain everything to him this soon. She hadn't even worked out what she might say, or how the conversation might flow. But here he was, standing before her on the crowded docks expecting answers.

"I think we should go someplace else to talk," she said. The harbor workers were bumping and brushing against them as they tried to work, giving Camille and Randall annoyed glances as they went.

"I'll take you to our ship." Randall stepped aside and swept out an arm toward the East Indiaman brig a few wharves down.

Our ship. A ship to take the both of them home, back to the life Randall still believed they would have together. Her knees quavered.

"Actually, Randall, I . . ." She swallowed hard. "I'd love to show you my mother's house. It would give you a break from the ship."

Randall clasped his hands behind his back. "That sounds like heaven. Lead the way."

He held out his arm and Camille took it in reflex, stunned at how open and loving and thrilled Randall was acting. It was as if he had everything he wanted right there, in her. It made her tremble.

Camille turned. "Oscar, will you be able to —" But the dock was clear of him. He'd gone off already, leaving her to do all the finessing with Randall.

"He's working as a dockhand?" Randall's lips turned downward, though it was still somehow a smile. "Quite a tumble from first mate, I'd say."

Camille ignored the statement, still stinging from Oscar taking off without a word. Her father had made Oscar first mate at the ripe age of nineteen, which was completely unheard of in the world of merchant shipping. Stooping to the level of a harbor lackey would injure any first mate's pride. Oscar had managed it without so much as a blink of an eye.

Randall's hand grasped hers confidently.

"Shall we?" He urged her to move from the dock, out of the way of the wharfies.

The chaos of the harbor filled up the first few minutes of their walk, requiring nothing more than "watch out" or "over here." Randall dodged two boys racing through the street, and then they were suddenly out of the fray. The seashell dust settled and she caught Randall inspecting her.

"What is it?" she asked, curious about the amused look he was giving her.

"You look changed. Your hair, it's lightened." He reached out to curl a lock of it around his finger.

She pretended to be distracted by something, and moved her head just enough to unravel the curl from his finger.

"Oh, that's from all the sun," she said. "It's darkened my skin, too, but it will lighten once I'm indoors more."

Why was she making these wretched excuses? She liked her bronzed skin, and the streaks of gold through her black hair.

"I think you look well, considering what you've been through these many months," he said. "Tell me, how long have you been in Port Adelaide?"

She'd anticipated these kinds of questions but had expected to have the entire voyage home to California to think of answers. This wasn't fair. Randall's surprise arrival had thrown her passive plans completely to the wind.

"In total?" she asked, calculating in her mind and trying to buy some time. Should she tell him about Umandu now? Later? Never? "Well, we were here a few days, then left for about three weeks, and then have been back for a few more weeks."

He slowed his pace up the hill. "You left? What have you been doing?"

"I, well, I was . . . you know, it's really a curious thing, what I've been doing these last few months. Sometimes I can't even believe it myself," she said, twittering a laugh. The laugh stalled out and Randall still waited, even more intent. Marvelous.

They arrived at the brick path leading up to her mother's house. Camille unlatched the gate for them.

"Listen, I'll tell you everything, I promise," she said. "But it's complicated and long and I'm not sure you're going to trust my state of mind when I'm through."

He arched an eyebrow, looking at her as if she were attempting to be charming. She pulled her arm out from under his.

"I'm being serious, Randall."

He stopped her from walking up the brick path. "I can tell," he said, still amused. "I honestly can't wait to hear this."

And Camille honestly didn't know how she was going to explain it. The front door opened and saved her. Ira slapped his hat on his head of sandy blond hair and charged down the brick path, looking up just in time to avoid trampling them both.

"Whoa there!" Ira skidded to a stop. "I came by, but Sir Prim Pants said you'd already . . ."

Ira slowly stopped talking as his eyes fell upon Randall. Blankly, he took him in from head to foot. Randall mirrored him, looking at the Australian with shocked confusion. Camille cleared her throat.

"Ira, this is Randall Jackson." Ira frowned without recognition. Camille quickly added, "My fiancé."

Ira's mouth parted into a wide circle. "Oh. Right, your *fiancé*."

Camille cringed. Ira adjusted the collar of his worn shirt and stuck his calloused hand out to Randall. "Just so we start off on the right foot, I want to make it crystal clear that pawning the sapphire was her idea, and not mine."

Ira grabbed Randall's hand without waiting for Randall to extend it. He gave it a vigorous shake and let go.

Randall flexed his fingers. "Yes, well, it's very . . . interesting meeting you. Did you just say you pawned Camille's engagement ring?" He glanced at Camille, trying to spot the sapphire ring on her finger that was very plainly not there.

Ira pulled the brim of his hat down around his eyes just as Samuel appeared in the doorway. He saw Randall and stepped forward.

"Is there something I can help you with?"

Camille exhaled with relief, wanting to put off for as long as possible the explanation of why she'd let Ira pawn the engagement ring back in Melbourne. She hadn't cared about parting with it at the time. She and Oscar had needed to fund their trek to Port Adelaide. But seeing Randall's face fall with the news stirred up a dose of guilt.

She took Samuel by the arm and held him close to her side. "Randall, I want you to meet Samuel McGinty. My brother."

Randall took Samuel's hand cautiously, looking from Camille to Samuel in bewilderment. He gave his hand a brief shake.

"Brother?"

Samuel joined in on the confusion. "Randall . . . ?"

Her face flushed with heat and the fire reached the tips of her ears. She hadn't told Samuel about Randall at all. She'd never even told him she was engaged!

"Jackson," Camille finished for her brother. "You remember, my fiancé?" She looked up at him in silent pleading and squeezed his arm as inconspicuously as possible.

He didn't catch on as fast as she'd have preferred, but she watched as the ploy finally dawned on him.

"How could I forget? Your name comes up in conversation so often," Samuel said. Camille hoped Randall couldn't hear the sarcasm that was all too clear to her.

"You see? There's a lot to tell you, and explaining it all

might take a little bit of time," she said to Randall. "We should probably go inside and sit down, and maybe you'd like a cup of tea, and —"

Ira sliced through all of her stalling.

"Her mum had an affair with that McGreenery bloke, then took off pregnant with him." Ira jerked a thumb toward Samuel. "She had a map that led to a stone that could bring someone back to life, right? So we got the map, raced that bloke McGreenery up Spencer's Bay, beat him to the stone, and now, much to everyone's pleasure, he's dead."

Ira brushed off his palms, pleased with himself. Camille stared at him, horrified.

"Stuart McGreenery's dead?" Randall asked.

Samuel tugged Ira's arm with a disapproving shake of his head. They went back indoors, forgetting whatever they had been about to do before she and Randall showed up.

"What was McGreenery even doing here? Racing you to a stone? And what's all this about a map?" Randall asked.

Camille stepped backward over the threshold. "I told you, it's complicated. Ira just has a fast mouth."

Randall followed her into the sitting room and shut the door loudly behind him.

"Is this some sort of amusement? Stuart McGreenery — *dead*? A map, a stone . . ." He gestured irritably to the kitchen from where Ira's and Samuel's voices drifted. "Was that Ira person trying to play a joke on me? Because if so, it certainly isn't humorous."

"I wish it were, but no. It's real, even if it sounds insane. So insane, I wasn't sure I was going to tell you once I got home."

She wrapped her arms around her middle, holding herself tight. This was not how she'd wanted things to unfold.

"You planned to lie? Camille, if we're going to be married, I want you to always tell me the truth, even if . . . even if it doesn't make a whole lot of sense."

Randall rapped his knuckles against the back of the sofa. He'd said the panic word: *married*. Camille took a step away.

"Perhaps the stone and map aren't what we need to talk about right now. There are other things." She took a breath to continue, but expelled it as the door whooshed open without so much as a knock. Oscar filled the entrance, unwittingly saving her.

Randall focused on him. "The harbormaster won't like that you've taken off in the middle of the day."

Oscar slammed the door. The reverberation shook the front wall of the house. "I don't care what the harbormaster likes. I quit."

Randall removed his jacket and laid it on the back of the sofa with a soft snort. The sound perfectly illustrated the contempt the two men had always displayed for each other.

"Of course you did. I suppose you're ready to go home, pick up where William left off. What have you been hoping for, Oscar, the position of captain?"

Camille's neck grew hot and her eyes watered. Randall's comment was miles out of line. No one could ever take her father's place. She hated Randall right then for even suggesting it.

The only signs of Oscar's fury were in the taut, ropy muscles of his neck.

"I'm not picking back up in San Francisco." His sight never once settled on Camille, making her feel invisible and unimportant. "You get what you want, Jackson: You're rid of me."

Oscar crossed the room to the secretary. Camille held her breath as he threw open the top cupboard and extracted the burlap bag. How in the blazes had he known it was there?

"You can't!" She rushed over and latched on to the bottom half of the bag.

The explosion of white light stole the breath from her lungs, as it had the evening before. Beams cut through the burlap, illuminating Camille's skin, Oscar's clothing, and bleaching the color out of the braided rug beneath them.

Randall's cheeks paled a notch as he ogled the bag. "What in Christ's name is that?"

Camille let go of the bag. The white light washed out to a dull pearlescent glow as soon as she did. At any other moment, she would have wondered at that. But not right then. There could be no more procrastination now. She had to tell Randall the truth.

"It's . . . it's the stone I found," she whispered. "The one Ira spoke of."

Randall tilted his head sideways, as if he hadn't heard her correctly.

"A stone that can bring someone back to life? Impossible." Randall frowned. "It's nothing but a myth, if it's even the same myth I'm thinking of."

Camille started to object, but stopped. "Wait — you've heard of it?"

Randall sighed. "Hasn't every child? I can't count how many times my nursemaid told me that bedtime story. But that's all it is. A story."

Every child did *not* know of the stone. Camille's father had banned storytelling and tales aboard his ships, and had only talked in hushed tones by her bedside about the construction of a solid ship, the elements of a fine wind, and how to tie knots, until she drifted off to sleep.

"Oscar, show him." She gestured to the softly glowing bag. He made no move to comply.

"Let him believe what he wants. It doesn't matter. I'm taking the stone and the map, and you're going back home." Oscar finally looked at her. "Back home, where you'll be safe."

Camille opened her mouth to protest, but Randall interrupted.

"Do you mean to say my fiancée has been in danger here?"

"Swimming in it," Ira butted in from where he stood in the kitchen entrance. He held a jar of raspberry preserves and popped a spoonful into his mouth. "But it was her own fault, seeing how she cursed us when she blurted out the stone's name."

Ira shivered and crossed himself with the preserves jar in hand. He and the others still didn't like hearing the stone's name aloud, and would never speak it themselves. Samuel came to stand beside Ira in the threshold. Her brother stared in awe at the glowing burlap bag.

Oscar moved for the door, looking as if he might mow down Randall, who stood tall against him. Oscar stopped just before impact.

"What kind of danger is she in? Camille told me that you both left Port Adelaide for a time. Does the danger stem from that? Where exactly have you been, Kildare?"

Oscar smirked. A quarrel was not far off. Randall always started calling Oscar by his last name when he'd scraped his last reserves of patience.

"We've been up Spencer's Bay, inland of a harbor called Talladay," Camille answered.

Oscar tried to move around him, but Randall blocked him again.

"What business did you have dragging Camille there?"

She inserted herself between them, shoving them apart. "*I* dragged *him*. And we went for the stone, Randall." All she had to do was nod toward the glowing burlap bag. "We followed the map and found the stone of the immortals. It's not just a bedtime story."

Camille successfully wrenched the bag from Oscar's hand and dug inside. She gripped the stone, caught the scroll of rolled leather under her thumb, and brought both objects out. Hushed silence absorbed the tense air inside the sitting room. The icy heat and the twisty feeling of her stomach were too much for her. Camille set the stone gingerly on the low parlor table but hung on to the leather map. The surface of it was enchanted, yes, but at least it didn't have a pulse.

"It's a glowing rock," Randall said, observing the rippling amber with skepticism. He crouched beside the table to inspect it closer. "There must be some explanation."

"Yeah. Magg-ick," Ira said while dragging his tongue over the convex curve of the spoon.

Randall glanced up at him, his hazel eyes bright. "Magic? I'd first believe in sea monsters and mermaids."

Randall would believe in sea monsters? He was just trying to butt heads with Oscar, most likely.

"How about spiders the size of cannon shot, and beasts that look like human dogs?" Ira asked. Slowly, Randall stood.

"Beg pardon?"

Ira raised his eyebrows. "You should see the claw marks those nasties left on her —"

Camille snapped open the map, not needing to sidetrack into the preternatural beasts that had nearly torn her apart on the way to the stone. She could only imagine how Randall would react to *that*. The crack of the leather shut Ira up nicely. A storm cloud of dust from the unfurled map billowed across the sitting room. Swirls of opal, sapphire, and gold sparkled in the sunlight shining through the window.

Randall stared at the dust, shook free from the enchanted surface, as it drifted toward the floor. He reached his fingers into the cloud and turned his hand to catch some in his palm. He marveled as the dust caked into the eddying lines of his fingertips, and then asked for the map with a hesitant gesture of his hand. Camille gave it to him.

The creases around Randall's temples smoothed. "This is . . . I mean, this is . . . I can't believe it."

He then did something Camille hadn't seen anyone do, and never thought to do herself. He brought the leather map to his nose and sniffed it. She remembered the way he used to sniff the fruit in the Saturday morning markets back home. He had the best nose, able to tell when the flesh beneath the rind of a melon was at the perfect height of ripeness. He'd always given her the best fruits, too, taking for himself the ones that still had a day or more to sit and mature.

"What is it?" she asked when his lips parted with a smile. He went back in for another sniff.

"It's faint, but it's still there. Do you smell it?" He nearly shoved the map against her nose. Instead of the expected scent of dry hide, she smelled something sweeter. Earthy and aromatic, and a fragrance she'd smelled not so long ago.

"It's myrrh," Camille whispered. The chill wind that had entered her cabin on the *Christina* and fanned over her had smelled of myrrh. She was impressed Randall had thought to smell the map, and a little surprised she had not after having had it for so long.

Randall brushed a finger along the map's surface. "And what are these, hieroglyphics?"

Camille's smile fell. There were no hieroglyphics on the map. Oscar sighed and dipped his head. He ran a hand through his newly trimmed hair.

"Hieroglyphics?" Samuel asked, stepping closer.

Ira peered over Randall's shoulder. "Hiero-whatics?"

Oscar made for the map, but Camille snatched it away, her hand the strike of a viper. She turned the map over, expecting to see the path they had followed, the lustrous ocean brilliant as sapphires and the forested hills sparkling like emeralds.

But the map didn't show those things at all.

Camille blinked long and hard, and then refocused. The magic of the map wasn't gone. It was just *rearranged*. The sapphire ocean was to the right instead of left. The emerald hillsides had all but vanished, replaced by ripples of fine gold. The silvery shimmering vein had new twists and forks, leading to three coal black drawings of what looked like flagpoles. And instead of English words, hieroglyphs now labeled the map.

The familiar flash of amber light that only her eyes could see rolled over the surface. She held the map away from her. Before, the flames had burned a riddle into the hide that had helped her figure out how to use Umandu's power. No one else had been able to see it. But now, there wasn't a riddle to read: There was a series of unintelligible symbols. It still looked as if the illustrations should by all logic dislodge and fall away if held upside down. But this wasn't the same map.

"Oscar." Her voice was willowy and forgetful of the vowels in his name. "You knew. The map had already changed and you knew."

His rueful expression told all; he'd seen the new map on the *Lady Kate* the night he'd held the stone. She watched Oscar turn in a tight circle, kneading the back of his neck until she was certain he'd inflict a bruise. He came out of his final loop and faced her.

"It's Egypt."

She gripped the leather so tightly, brown pulp rubbed off onto her thumbs.

"Egypt?" Camille looked back down at the sapphire body of water, narrow and reminiscent of a once-graceful finger marred by arthritis. Oscar came up beside her.

"I know it by the shape of the shoreline. That's the Red Sea. And this" — he reached over so his fingertip traveled above the golden dust to another, thinner line of blue — "is the Nile River."

Camille didn't question him. He was a sailor and knew the shape of the world and all its ports. Back in San Francisco Oscar might have been just another working-class drudge, but she'd always seen him differently. She'd seen the things that had lain invisible to those who didn't deem him worthy of a second glance.

"You should have told me," she said, the wonder of the new map wearing to resentment. "Why didn't you?"

Randall shifted toward them, reminding her that he was there.

"What is going on?"

The question irked her. Granted, he had no clue what was happening. He'd come expecting a happy reunion, and had instead been greeted with this mess. But Camille didn't know what was happening either, and that made her angry. Oscar had deceived her.

"The map has changed?" Samuel asked, pulling down a corner in order to see for himself. The symbols that had burned into the leather were now gone, just as the previous riddle had only remained for a minute. But other strange pictures covered the map instead of English words — birds, feathers, snakes, squiggly lines, ovals, and squares, and other things that made no sense. It was a language of symbols. Egyptian hieroglyphics.

"Why would it now point to Egypt?" Samuel asked.

Stunned, Camille let her brother have the map. She recalled Oscar's demands for the map. *I need it for where I'm going.*

"That's where you're going," she said. "You're planning to follow it."

Without me. Her feelings were beyond hurt. They were crippled.

"Would someone please stop and tell me what's happening? The map has changed? What did it first point to?" Randall asked.

With evaporating patience, Camille faced him. "The stone. The first map pointed us to —" She glanced at Ira, whose eyes had bugged out. "I shouldn't say its name."

"Umandu?" Randall asked, one eyebrow pressed down in amusement. Ira crossed himself again.

"I wouldn't say its name out loud again, if I were you," Oscar muttered, but then cocked his mouth into a grin, no doubt as he remembered the curse. "Or on the other hand, be my guest."

Randall looked to the ceiling beams. His hand covered a mocking smile.

"Of course, the cursed stone that brings people back to life." He fixed Camille with pleading eyes. "You're asking me to believe the impossible."

Believing the impossible, putting faith in the unknown, was something she'd rapidly adapted to.

"If this legend is real, as you claim," Randall continued, "well, then, where is your father?"

Camille stared at him, her breath clotted in her chest.

"If you risked your life to find this Umandu stone," Randall said, "then your father's would be the soul you'd wish to restore, isn't that right? So tell me, where is he?"

Her heart gained speed as she waited for Oscar to speak. Waited for an answer to burst into her mind. If she told Randall the stone really had worked, that it had brought *Oscar* back from the dead, he'd know. Without having to say the words outright, Randall would know she loved Oscar. And with Oscar having snubbed her, with his deceit about the stone and map, Camille would look like a fool.

"My father is still dead," she answered. She *was* a fool. Fury roiled inside her, clamoring to be turned loose upon the man who'd turned her into one.

Randall pinched his lips together and nodded, his point successfully driven home. Ira and Samuel flicked their eyes from Camille to Randall, and then to Oscar, waiting. Surely, they expected Camille to set the record straight, explain that another, unexpected soul had been restored.

"But the map and stone, Randall. You can't deny them," she said instead. Ira and Samuel exchanged a bemused glance.

Randall's gloating faltered. "No. I suppose not. It's clear they both have special properties. You say the map actually rearranged itself to show Egypt?"

Ira swirled the spoon around inside the jar, clinking silver against glass. "Why Egypt?"

Camille looked to Oscar for the answer, but Samuel chimed in, still inspecting the map. He held it out for her to see.

"This looks like the end point of *this* map. Just like the boulder dome was the end point of the first." He pointed to the three flagpoles glittering like a black lava beach. Their outlines shifted with the charmed, breezy swells of the golden sand. "What if we have to go there?"

Oscar held up his hands. "Stop right there. Not we — *me*. I'm going, not you." He focused on Camille. "And definitely not you."

Randall took up his coat from the back of the sofa. "Oscar, I completely agree with you. And trust me, you will never hear me say that again."

He extended his arm toward Camille, expecting her hand. If she took it, if she went with Randall, leaving Umandu and Oscar behind, she'd be bound. Her path would be chosen. Not so long ago, after emerging victorious from the boulder dome, Camille had promised herself that whatever path she followed, she'd follow it only by her own choice.

"I'm sorry, Randall," she said, refusing his hand. "I won't let Oscar make these decisions for me."

"You can't be serious." Randall took a conspiratorial side-glance at the others. "Camille, whatever that stone and map is about, I don't want you a part of it."

"I already am." She admired the strength in her voice. She *was* a part of it. Oscar's turning away from her didn't change that. And his and Randall's attempts to steer her in the direction that suited them only lent her more courage. "I *am* going to Egypt. So, Oscar, you should tell me what we expect to find there."

FOUR

esigned, Oscar lowered himself to the sofa and rubbed his eyes a long moment. "This is only one of the stones stolen from the gatekeeper to the Underworld. There is a second stone —"

Camille interrupted, recalling the legend. "The gate-keeper was able to retrieve only one of the stones the goddess stole to create her race of immortals. Together, the two stones gave her the power to turn a living human immortal, and they also allowed her to reclaim any soul she chose from the Underworld."

Randall exhaled dramatically and tossed his coat back down.

"So if this is only one of those stones" — Randall gave an exasperated gesture toward Umandu — "you think you need the second stone, the one the gatekeeper took back to the Underworld, in order to carry out the legend's promise of a resurrection?"

A pregnant pause ensued. Someone had to answer. Someone had to tell him that a resurrection had already been granted. Camille parted her lips to speak.

"That's what I think," Oscar cut in. Ira, Camille, and Samuel all snapped their heads in his direction. "They need to be joined together."

Randall took Camille, who was baffled by Oscar's response, by the elbow.

"This is outrageous. You do know that, don't you?" He breathed deeply and ran his fingers through his glossy brown hair. "Do you really believe this stone was stolen from the Underworld? The *Underworld*, Camille. As if such a place actually exists."

"But the map, Randall. You saw it. And the stone —"

He let go of her arm and stepped back. "I know. I know what I saw and it's . . . it's fantastical. It's unexplainable." He glanced to Ira and Samuel but ignored Oscar. "And all of you seem so convinced."

She and Oscar exchanged a brief meeting of the eyes as Randall struggled to push aside his disbelief. They could easily prove to Randall that it was real. All they had to do was explain about Oscar's resurrection. Yet neither Camille nor Oscar parted their lips to do so.

"I'm not for this," Randall finally whispered. "I think it's a fool's errand and in the end nothing will come of it except for wasted time and effort. However, it's clear that I'm not going to be able to convince you to come home to San Francisco just yet. So, if this is what you truly want" — he nodded toward Umandu glowing dimly on the the parlor table — "then I suppose I have no choice but to help."

Camille swallowed hard, her throat dry. His concession sounded so miserable. She didn't want him to feel forced into accompanying them.

"You don't have to help, Randall, not if you don't —"

"Of course I do. What do you think I'm going to do, sail home while you take off to Egypt?" Randall bowed his head in a funereal manner. "I left the company in able hands. I'll send back a letter telling them not to expect me home for some months."

She hoped he would change his mind. How was she going to get to the bottom of Oscar's behavior with Randall hovering about?

"How could you help?" Ira asked Randall.

He craned his ear to him. "I'd have to sort that out a bit more."

A sharp, sardonic laugh rumbled deep in Oscar's chest.

"Is this what you want, Camille?" Randall asked, giving her one last chance to back down. But Camille realized it didn't matter what she wanted. She'd been the one to begin this mess with the stone. It was her responsibility to finish it.

"I don't know if it's what I want, but I know it's what I need to do," she answered.

Randall released his pent up breath. "I was afraid you'd say that. Very well, then, I'll be back later for you."

He kissed Camille so quickly she barely felt his lips. He darted out the front door. A wet dot from his kiss remained on the corner of her lower lip. Covering her hand with the lace trimming of her sleeve, Camille wiped the trace of it away as Oscar looked on.

"You have a *fiancé*?" Samuel asked. He rolled up the map and tied it off, glancing from her to Oscar. "So you two . . . you've been . . ."

Oscar fixed Samuel with a rigid stare. Camille could see his silent warning for Samuel to be quiet. Her brother, however, did not. Samuel turned back to Camille, his curiosity replaced by irritation.

"Scolding our mother on her deathbed looks a bit hypocritical of you now, wouldn't you say?"

The heat of shame burned her cheeks. When Camille's mother had admitted to having an affair with Stuart McGreenery, Camille had been hard on her. Maybe too hard.

"It's not the same," she said. "I'm not married like she was."

"But you're *engaged* to marry, and you've just lied to him," Samuel snapped at her.

"Enough," Oscar said. Samuel pursed his lips and bit back whatever else he'd wanted to say. He held out the rolled map to Camille. She took it, surprised by the similarities he'd quickly drawn between her mother's deceit and her own. Without a word, Samuel took his jacket down from a peg near the door and left.

Camille stared at the map in her hand. She was engaged. Not married. There was a difference — a big difference.

"Why didn't you tell Randall the truth?" she asked Oscar.

"Why didn't *you*?" he retorted.

Ira stepped up behind Camille in a show of solidarity. "It wasn't just her job to spill the truth. You should have said something. You should have stuck to the promises you made to her back at that bloody dome of boulders, you great big, good-for-nothing —"

Camille turned around and gripped both of Ira's tensed arms. She only had to level her eyes with his to persuade him away from his tirade. Ira exhaled and, biting the inside of his cheek to keep quiet, made for the front door.

"There. We've driven everyone away. Are you happy now?" she asked.

Oscar sat forward on the couch, resting his arms on his thighs. "I'll be happy if you tell Randall that you've changed your mind. That you want to go back to California."

Camille dropped her arms from in front of her chest, stunned. "I'm not like you. I won't change my mind so easily."

He got to his feet. "And I won't let you make the mistake of choosing me again."

Camille dug her nails into her palms, ready to scream at the top of her lungs. Ready to hurt him as much as he'd hurt her.

"Was my heart's choice really my mistake, Oscar? Or was it telling you that my father had lost everything and that we'd be poor? Was my mistake believing you truly cared about *me* and not the fortune attached to me?"

His eyes searched her face, his lips pressed taut and chin shifting from side to side, as if in thought.

"You may not believe money matters, Camille, but it does," he finally replied. He cast his eyes away from her, wincing as he grit his teeth. "I'm sorry you had to find out this way."

Tears hazed her eyes and clogged her throat.

"What happened to you?" she whispered, voice quavering. "Whatever it was, it made you weak, and scared, and a coward."

Camille grabbed the stone from the parlor table and fled up the stairs before she burst into sobs in front of him. She reached her mother's room and heard the slam of the front door. She rivaled it with the slam of her bedroom door, furious with Oscar and the way he'd deceived her. Terrified all over again at the idea of being Randall's wife. Inexplicably annoyed with Umandu and the second stone, and the way the two rocks seemed to be ruling all sides of her life.

Camille's legs folded beneath her and she dropped to the threshold just inside the doorway. Umandu's amber light faded again, curiously lost of its brilliancy. She drew her knees to her chest and lowered her head. One loud sob escaped, followed by another, and then a deluge, and for the life of her she could not understand how she had managed to cross to the other side of the world and end up in the exact same place.

FIVE

amille!"

She jerked her head up and opened her eyes. Camille pushed herself up from the bare wooden floor and realized she must have sobbed herself to sleep. *How pathetic*, she thought as she rubbed her stiff neck.

"Camille, are you up here?" Samuel's voice carried from the stairwell and his feet pounded the steps.

The bedroom was cloaked in shadows. She'd apparently slept the afternoon away. Camille opened the bedroom door just as her brother reached the threshold.

"You've got to hurry," he said breathlessly. His chest heaved as if he'd been running a distance.

Another pair of feet climbed the stairwell to the cramped upstairs. Ira came around the corner.

"Tell me there isn't more magic underfoot," he said.

Camille brightened at the sight of him. "I thought you'd left."

Ira leaned against the plaster wall and made a show of rubbing his stomach. "Got hungry. Monty didn't have a scrap of food at his place."

Camille bit back a grin. Ira could bluff at the poker table, but not with her. He'd come back to make sure she was okay after her quarrel with Oscar.

Samuel ushered Camille back into her room. "Pack everything you need. We've been invited aboard the *Eclipse.*"

She grabbed the edge of the bureau before she fell from all of his prodding.

"The *Eclipse*?"

Samuel rolled his eyes. "The ship your fiancé arrived on." He looked at her from under a furrowed brow.

"But how? Why?" she asked.

"The captain, Camille, he's amazing. Pure generosity. You see, when Randall spoke to him about our need to reach Egypt, the captain threw in his support."

Camille shot a dubious glance toward Ira, who had followed them into the bedroom.

"Why would he do that?" Ira asked.

"Ira's right. We haven't so much as met." Camille didn't even know where the *Eclipse* made berth.

"Pack, Camille," Samuel said again, and then went to his own room to do the same.

She chased after him. "But why are *you* packing?"

He looked at her as if she were speaking a foreign language. "Because I'm coming with you, of course. I've already closed up the shop."

She sagged against the door's frame, wishing she could still be asleep on the floor of her mother's room.

"Samuel, I don't even know what to expect in Egypt. I can't read hieroglyphics, so I have no idea what the map wants us to do, or why Oscar is so intent on finding the second stone. The whole thing is a complete mystery, and it hasn't anything to do with you. If it's anything like the search for the first stone, it could be dangerous. You should stay with the plan to go to San Francisco."

His dark brows slanted together as he looked up from stuffing his suede rucksack. "Do you think I'm a coward?"

"Of course not!" Camille felt as if all her sisterly concern was spiraling into a fast mess of misunder-standing. "It's nothing like that. It's just that you didn't find the stone. You didn't touch it, I did. If you don't want to involve yourself any further, I won't think less of you for it."

He crossed to his bureau and slammed the two open drawers shut. "I would have thought you'd want your brother with you. But it seems you want to be rid of me instead."

She shook her head, exasperated. "It isn't that at all."

He opened a third drawer in his bureau and turned away from her. "Then we should finish packing."

She threw up her hands in defeat and went back to her room.

Ira lounged in the doorway as she selected three of her mother's more modest, manageable dresses from the closet. A navy twill skirt, a white blouse and Zouave jacket; a deep ruby linen dress, fitted throughout the waist and sleeves; and finally, her favorite lavender silk dress. Camille pulled open a bureau drawer and removed a few pairs of silk stockings and an extra pair of pantalettes. Ira whistled.

"There's no reason why I can't be better prepared this time," she said. The dresses, stockings, belts, and a cloak all folded easily and fit into a leather case, with plenty of room left over for the burlap bag.

She bit her lip as she snapped the leather case shut.

"Ira," she said, unable to look at him. "I know I haven't paid you yet for everything you've done for me, and I know there's absolutely no compensation in it for you, but I was hoping you might consider . . . if you might just *think* about . . ."

"You want me to go to Egypt with you?" he finished for her. She nodded, but Ira met it with silence.

Samuel had already finished packing and could be heard downstairs, opening and closing cupboards. Camille reopened her suitcase, still on the top of the bureau, and dug inside the burlap bag for the money Oscar had given her the day before.

"I'm sorry, I shouldn't have asked. You want to go to Sydney, and that's where you should go." She held out the small drawstring bag. "Take it."

Ira's aquamarine eyes inspected the proffered bag a moment before he uncrossed his arms and accepted it. He bounced the bag from hand to hand, weighing the contents. He then joined Camille at the bureau and shoved the money back inside the burlap bag.

"What are you doing?" she asked as Ira snapped the latches shut.

"I'm not going to Sydney, love." He slid the suitcase off the bureau and held it for her.

"But, Ira, Sydney is all you've been talking about. I know you want to go." She tried to take the suitcase from his hand, but he held it away.

"And I'll get there eventually," he replied. "But do you think I'd give up the chance to see Egypt first?"

He winked at her, but she saw beyond the ploy. Ira's

soft side had surfaced recently, and all because of Oscar's indifference.

"Ira, I don't want you to feel like you have to come," she said, secretly warming to his newfound protective side. "I can take care of myself."

He moved past her, taking her suitcase with him. "Noted. But I've made up my mind. Besides —" He bashfully rubbed his palm over the rough whiskers on his cheek. "Whether you want to admit it or not, you need someone who won't run out on you."

Camille shook her head, smiling just as bashfully as Ira was.

"All right, I'll admit it. But I don't need a porter." She took the suitcase from his hand and sighed. "What happened to Australia's most notorious con man?"

He rolled his eyes. "Yeah, yeah. Let's get moving before my entire reputation gets ruined."

She followed Ira into the sitting room where Samuel stood waiting by the open door.

"Do you have everything you'll need?" her brother asked, his voice tight. He was still injured by her suggestion that he stay behind.

Ira started down the brick walk, and Samuel closed the door behind them.

"Yes, but the captain's offer doesn't make sense, Samuel. Surely, he must have a route to adhere to, a schedule to keep."

Her brother's quick pace was hard to match as he raced down the lane, toward the harbor where late afternoon sunlight flashed off the green water. His excitement was peculiar, especially after spending the last weeks brooding and anxious about San Francisco. Perhaps all this new vigor was due to the fact that he *wasn't* going to San Francisco. Maybe he hadn't wanted to go there in the first place. The notion struck with a sharp edge.

"The hold was emptied in Auckland and the captain says he has no pressing matters to attend to," he explained.

Camille suspected the captain's crew might feel otherwise. Egypt was a two-month sail, and they probably had wives or families somewhere waiting for their scheduled return. How could a sea captain not have any pressing matters to attend to? Randall had been the one to convince this captain. Had he offered to pay some insane amount of money? He'd have closed up his wallet immediately had she told him the truth about Oscar. And she had to tell him. She knew she did. She would find him aboard the *Eclipse* and explain everything.

The three of them made their way past the first few brick warehouses along the beginning of the harbor road. Samuel stopped so suddenly Camille trod on his heels. She regained her balance and saw Samuel stare pointedly to the left where the road dead-ended at the wrought-iron gates of a cemetery.

Their mother was beneath one of the headstones there, the dirt so freshly turned that seedlings of grass probably hadn't even sprouted. At first, Camille wondered if Samuel wanted to stop in before leaving Port Adelaide. But as she peered through the encroaching dark, along the smutty gray maze of headstones and craggy-limbed trees, she saw a shadowed outline standing in the center of the graveyard.

She'd know the shape of his body anywhere.

Camille held her suitcase in front of Ira to keep him from walking ahead. "Oscar's in the cemetery."

Ira came back to her side. "Now that's just plain creepy."

"What's he doing there?" Samuel asked. He didn't wait for a reply. "Go fetch him, Camille. We've kept Captain Starbuck waiting longer than I expected. I'll run ahead and tell him that you're on your way."

He continued on up the harbor road past a row of taverns and grog houses as Camille and Ira headed slowly toward the cemetery gates.

"What's he doing?" Camille asked as one of her boots sunk in a muddy rut. Oscar stood, unmoving, beside a giant tree, its bent limbs reaching toward the ground.

"Visiting your mum?" Ira suggested. That didn't make sense, but nothing else did, either.

An evening harbor mist had settled around Camille's feet, the gray and blue haze playing tricks on her eyes. Ira opened the gates and the hinges squealed. Camille edged closer to him, bumping his shoulder as they neared Oscar's inert figure behind a row of angelic statuary and slanted grave markers. He didn't turn to look at his company, though he knew they were there. The damp, rusty hinges of the gates had announced them well enough.

Ira rocked back on his heels, looking genuinely aghast. "You got a real interesting way to blow off steam."

"I wanted to be alone," Oscar replied without so much as a glance in their direction.

She'd called him such horrid names: a coward, weak. Here he stood, alone in a cemetery, looking like he agreed.

"Yeah, I guess." Ira cleared his throat, clearly not sympathetic. "Can we, you know, ditch the crypt and head back to the ship?"

Oscar turned suddenly and rushed past them.

"Ship? What ship? I already told you I'm doing this alone." Barbs stuck out from each word.

Ira hurried to follow him. "If by alone you mean with me, Camille, Sir Prim Pants, Lover Boy, and the captain and crew of the *Eclipse*, then yes. You're on your bloody own."

Oscar halted abruptly. He turned with a ferocious stare. "The *Eclipse*?"

"Lover Boy got its captain to take us to Egypt," Ira answered.

Oscar breathed in deeply and picked up his speed through the open gates and into the silent, muddy street. Camille wanted to rip out Ira's tongue. Randall was *not* her lover. Just the thought, the mere image of it . . . Camille ran to keep up and stumbled into another rut, causing her to bump against a member of a small crowd gathered outside a warehouse.

"Oh, excuse me," she said, quickly regaining her footing. An aching chill surfaced on her arm. She reached up to touch it, alarmed by how cold that one spot was.

The small group of men stood huddled together, their faces cast in shadows. They wore hats and jackets and trousers, just the same as every other man in Port Adelaide. No one spoke a word.

Rubbing her shoulder again, the cold pain started to ebb. It was nothing, she decided. The harbor fog rolled past the wharves, bollards, and lading cranes. Tendrils of white reflected the flicker of the gas lanterns stationed at the beginning of each wharf. Oscar and Ira had disappeared into the fog ahead. Snatches of their heated argument made their way back to her.

Camille considered calling out for them to stop and wait for her, but sealed her lips. It was only fog. As long as she could hear their voices, she could follow them just fine.

A slick-coated harbor rat squealed and flashed in front of Camille's boots. It scurried away, its claws scratching along the cobblestones. She held back the gasp in her throat. She hurried forward, a tremor shaking her cool facade. Oscar's and Ira's voices had grown surprisingly softer, the unwieldy fog having devoured their argument. Catching up to them didn't feel so simple anymore. Why hadn't they noticed she wasn't with them? Men.

A figure hurried off one of the docks and slammed into Camille. She cried out as the impact flung her to the side. Her suitcase flew from her hand and skidded along the cobbles.

"Camille?" Oscar shouted from up ahead.

The figure turned to her. "Jesus, watch where you're . . . wait. Camille?"

A face parted through the fog and she recognized it. Unfortunately.

"Lucius Drake," she said.

Oscar's second, frantic shout was nearly on top of them. "Camille! Where are you?"

Lucius groaned. "Not him again . . ."

Oscar broke into sight just as Camille felt the old, familiar desire to kick the only other survivor of the *Christina* in the shins.

"It's just Lucius," she muttered.

Lucius Drake had lived through the shipwreck and been rescued by the *Londoner* just as she and Oscar had, but their similarities ended there. Caring only for himself, Lucius had not only joined Stuart McGreenery's crew but had then agreed to lead three of the deadliest bushrangers in Australia to Camille, Oscar, and Ira with orders to have them killed. After settling back in Port Adelaide, Camille had been more than happy to part Lucius's company.

"What are you still doing here?" she asked as Ira reached them. He saw Lucius and swore under his breath.

"The answer is no," Ira said, directly to Lucius.

Lucius puckered his eyebrows. "No, what?"

"No, you can't come with us," Ira answered.

"He's *not* coming with us," Camille and Oscar said at the same time. They nearly smiled at each other but quickly abandoned it.

"Fine by me. I don't want to go anywhere with you anyhow," Lucius said. He paused, and then dropped his arms from their crossed position. "Unless you're going back home. Are you?"

The keys of a piano inside one of the harbor hotels pealed to life. The bubbly rhythm was ill suited to the chilled, soggy night. Oscar scratched at the back of his head in aggravation.

"We are most definitely not heading to California," he said, and then resumed walking back toward the wharf where they had seen the *Eclipse* docked earlier that day. "Good night, Drake. Come on, Camille."

"In that case . . ." Lucius brushed past Camille and walked toward the bustling hotel. She watched him disappear into the fog, so thick it masked the brick and iron-framed warehouses and sail lofts along the harbor road.

She turned to follow Ira and Oscar, but then noticed her empty hands. The suitcase. It had gone sailing to the side. Camille stopped to search for it, crouching to the ground to see under the fog. A moment later she had found it, but by then Oscar and Ira had once again moved ahead, out of her field of vision. They were arguing again, too.

Camille started forward, enveloped by the soupy haze. She wanted to get off the harbor road with all its mist and shadows. The sound of scuffling feet behind her stirred the hair on her arms. She told her feet to keep moving, but they didn't. She ordered her head not to turn and look, but it did.

Through the fog, tinged a dull yellow from the wharves' lantern light, came a rippling, dark movement. Three wharves back, a group of men took shape. It was the same group of men into which she'd stumbled, with their slouchy hats and odd silence. They walked three abreast, their strides identical, their arms cutting forward and back like crazed pendulums. They marched with evident purpose — and were headed straight toward her. The three men passed the second wharf lamp, less than thirty feet away.

Camille took a few clumsy backward steps and slammed into something solid. She whipped around, startled, and saw Lucius in front of her.

"Blast it, Lucius, where did you come from this time?"

Piano music phantomed through the night. He'd been walking in the opposite direction, for heaven's sake. How had he come to be in front of her?

"What do you want?" she asked.

Lucius wore an impassive expression on his pointed, arrow-shaped face.

"Oscar told you the truth. We aren't going home yet," she said.

Lucius said nothing. He simply stared at her, each of his arched eyebrows looking permanently arrogant.

"Well, good luck, Lucius." She stepped to the side, ready to pass him.

"Good luck with what?" said a voice from behind her.

She swiveled on her heel and watched as a second Lucius Drake appeared through the fog. Camille gaped at him, but he didn't seem to notice.

"Listen, I'm willing to make a deal with you and Kildare. Wherever you're going, it's got to be better than this marsh hole. What if —"

Lucius quit speaking as his eyes rested on his double. "What the . . . ?"

Camille whipped back around in time to see the other Lucius's face flicker. It rippled and shifted and melted angle by angle until the face no longer belonged to Lucius. Within a handful of heartbeats, a man with a short nose and wide, defined cheekbones was standing in front of her. His thin lips pulled south into a drooping crescent, and his eyes . . . they were two flat, black saucers without rims of white.

The skin on her arms iced over as he grabbed hold of her. The suitcase slammed onto the cobbles once again.

"Who are you? What are you doing?" Her words splintered on their way out, the frigid grasp on her arms slicing her to the marrow. The chill seeped through her, penetrating her skin, her veins.

"Oscar." She'd whispered it, though it had been intended as a scream. Her throat wouldn't allow for anything more.

Coldness fogged her mind, clouding out Lucius's demand to let her go. She noticed a glimmer around the man's throat. A round, golden pendant, strung upon a chain, peeked through the first few undone buttons of his shirt.

Camille opened her mouth to try to scream again. Just then the man opened his colorless lips and emitted a high-pitched scream. A woman's scream. *Her* scream.

"Oscar! Help!"

Hearing her voice pour out of the man's mouth shocked Camille into focus, though only momentarily. He'd used her voice, but she had no idea how. As Oscar shouted her name in return, his voice so far away, Camille forgot to care.

She shivered, the current of ice leeching her of her senses. Oscar's voice drew fainter as black spots mottled her vision. Her body grew so cold she barely felt it when the man holding her finally tossed her aside. Her shin slammed against something immobile, and her hand scraped along something jagged and metal. Her hearing and vision returned. Lucius stood with his lips parted in shock, his feet scrabbling backward. When he turned, he stopped and swore.

The three men that had been so strangely marching toward her were now right behind Lucius. All of them wore the same golden pendant around their necks. Her heart beat out an erratic cadence.

"Camille!" Oscar screamed. She looked away for one moment, toward the direction of his voice. When she glanced back, the men were gone. Lucius was still turning in circles.

"H-here," she said, but not nearly loud enough.

The bottoms of Oscar's shoes scudded to a stop beside her.

"What happened?" he asked as Ira arrived, huffing for air. Oscar pulled her up with a strong tug.

"It was a man. Four men, and he was Lucius, and then he ch-changed, his face . . ." She stopped, certain she sounded like a drunkard who'd just tripped out of one of the hotel taverns.

"You're freezing." Oscar's hand stiffened around hers. "You need to get to the ship."

Lucius sidled up next to them, pale-faced. "I'm coming with you."

Still holding her hand, Oscar picked up the suitcase and pulled her along at a fast clip. "No, you're not, Drake. Find your own way home."

Camille rammed into Oscar's side as he came to a standstill. The man who'd spoken with her voice advanced out of the mist. Oscar let go of Camille's hand and shoved her behind him.

"It's him," she whispered into Oscar's shoulder. The other three men appeared at their sides, flanking them.

"What do you want?" Oscar growled.

The man grinned. "The stone," he answered, then pointed a pale finger toward Oscar. "And you."

Camille grasped Oscar's arm with one hand, her other groping for the suitcase's handle. Her fingers met Oscar's firm hold. These men — if they were even men at all — knew about the stone, but how? And how had his face changed like that?

"We're bringing you both back," another one said. His voice was a high whisper, sharply edged.

"Back where?" Oscar asked.

"Where you belong," yet another man answered.

Camille glanced over her shoulder for Ira, realizing

he'd been too silent for his mouthy nature. She only saw Lucius in a state of shock. Where had Ira gone? Camille clutched Oscar's arm tighter as a new person, though only a shadowy figure, came through the fog.

"We'll take the stone first," the crescent-lipped man said, holding out his hand expectantly.

The shadowed figure advanced quickly and rammed into him. The man lurched forward as he was hit, and Oscar used the opportunity to bury his fist into the man's stomach. Just then, Ira stormed out of the fog behind Camille and wailed his fist into another man's jaw.

"Camille!" the shadowy figure screamed. It was a *female* voice.

A woman? It couldn't be real, just as the creature beckoning Oscar with her voice hadn't been real. But then a hand was on her, pulling her sideways. Camille wrenched free and turned to face a fright of a girl. A tangle of hair framed her smudged face and the whites of her eyes flashed bright. She was shorter than Camille, though she looked to be about the same age. A strong odor of sweat and filth reached up Camille's nostrils.

"Who are you? How do you know my name?"

But before the girl could answer, another cold hand grasped Camille and yanked her backward. She clawed at the man with her free arm. Her fingers caught on the pendant around his neck and the chain snapped with a quick *tink*. She fell to the ground, the pendant locked inside her palm. The man was pawing his chest in a wild search for the pendant when Lucius tackled him.

They struggled on the street, arms interlocked. A dark mist wrapped around them as they fought, and impossibly, the mist seemed to reach right through the man's body, turning it translucent. He rolled on top of Lucius, pinning him down, and then rent the air with a coarse scream. The man's legs and torso swirled away, becoming a part of the black, roiling mist. The wisps of dark smoke reached the man's chest, spread down his arms, and engulfed Lucius as well. Both men screamed now as the mist reached their heads — and then twirled away.

They were gone. Both Lucius and the stranger. Vanished.

The strange girl came to Camille's side once more and pulled her to her feet.

"Come with me!"

Camille tore out of her grasp and rushed toward Oscar, who was a few yards away. He had just kneed one of the other men in the gut. Camille darted forward and snapped an identical pendant from that man's neck.

"What are you doing?" Oscar shouted. But like the first man, this one, too, whittled away into black smoke. She didn't understand it. There wasn't time to.

As one of the two remaining men slammed into Oscar, Ira jumped onto the man's back and pummeled him with his fists. Before Camille could help, a frozen hand clamped around her wrist. The teeth-chattering chill instantly set in as the man twisted her arm behind her. Before the chug of her brain could run out of fuel, Camille crushed her heel into the bridge of his foot. He growled, sounding more annoyed than hurt, and shoved her to the road. Camille crawled backward, her legs unable to lift her. The man followed, slowly, intently, enjoying the pathetic chase.

Camille's hands slid over the moss-slimed edge of the harbor wall, the water slurping below. She could go no farther. The man drew back his arms preparing to either strike or shove. But then someone flew into his side and catapulted him over Camille's head and into the harbor below. Her eyes focused and she saw her rescuer.

"Randall!"

He knelt beside her, taking rattling breaths. "Are you hurt?"

Randall helped Camille to her feet before she could answer, her legs suddenly composed of the finest grain of sand in the world. She'd completely forgotten about Randall, and right then he shone bright with wonder.

"What's going on?" he asked. But the last man was still battling Ira and Oscar, and somehow winning.

"No time. I have to get the pendant off his neck."

Randall held her back. "The pendant? Tell me what's happening!"

The last man struck Ira hard in the spine, felling him, and then grabbed hold of Oscar's throat. The chill must have immediately seeped in, for Oscar's knees buckled and his arms lost their grip. The man wrapped his fingers around his golden pendant, his other hand still firmly around Oscar's throat.

"No," Camille whispered, remembering how Lucius had also swirled away into the mist. "No!"

The man pulled the pendant free. Smoke plumed and hissed at his feet. Just then Camille saw her discarded suitcase on the street in front of her. She picked it up and ran forward, slicing the case through the air. She severed the vanishing man's grip, and Ira, having recovered, rammed into Oscar and threw him aside. The man screamed in rage as the black mist spiraled up from his feet, where Ira had stumbled and now kneeled. The man, fast smoldering

and fading, latched on to Ira's coat collar. The smoke destroying the man engulfed Ira as well.

"No! Ira!" Camille screamed and rushed forward.
Randall snagged her arm and pulled her back. "Let me go!"

Ira stopped struggling. His eyes darted down to his
nonexistent legs. They shot up, landed on Camille, and
with a look of pure horror he opened his mouth.

The smoke swallowed him before he could scream.

SIX

The cabin aboard the *Eclipse* smelled of camphor and nettle. Camille sat perched on the edge of a bunk, knee to knee with Samuel. Her hand rested palm up in her brother's lap. The long gash on her hand was deep enough to show the white of muscle beyond the torn, red flesh. The cabin swayed, her stomach clenched, and Camille closed her eyes.

Oscar and Randall had rushed her to the waiting ship as soon as the last swirl of black mist had cleared from the harbor road. The black mist that had taken Ira from them.

With a warm cloth, Samuel cleaned away the dirt. Pain seared up the length of her arm.

"Sorry," he said, though he didn't lessen the assault on her hand. He was still upset about her suggestion that he continue on to San Francisco as planned. Camille would tell Randall the truth as soon as she saw him, and then perhaps her brother would have someone to sail back to California with. She didn't want Samuel involved if things were going to be this dangerous.

Samuel sighed. "For the last time, stop moving, or I'll never be able to clean it properly."

She opened her eyes and took the warm cloth from him. "I'll do it myself."

He held up his hands in defeat. "At least be thorough. There could be dirt in there still. My God, Camille, I can't believe this. They took Ira?" He rubbed his eyes and the bridge of his nose. "My God."

A knock rattled the cabin door. Flustered, Samuel got up and opened it. Randall stepped inside the cramped cabin. There was room enough for two narrow bunks, perpendicular to each other, a wooden chair, and a chest of drawers. Camille hadn't taken in much else of the *Eclipse*. Her arrival had been rushed and the deck had been veiled by nightfall.

"The tide is in and Captain Starbuck is sailing out on it." Randall closed the door behind him.

Camille leaped from the edge of the bunk. "What? No!"

The floors moved beneath Camille's feet as the *Eclipse* pushed into the bay. She gritted her teeth, annoyed. It hadn't just been nausea making her head swim. The crew had been releasing the ship from her mooring lines.

"He has to, Camille. He doesn't want to risk another attack," Randall replied.

But she hadn't meant to set sail aboard the *Eclipse*! She'd intended to confess to Randall and then leave. Either that or be *told* to leave.

Camille pressed on her wound too hard. "You have to tell the captain to stop. We have to go back."

Randall came forward and slid his hands down her sleeves. He closed his fingers lightly around her wrists.

"There is no point. Your friend won't be there." Randall pulled his brows together, his gaze heartbreakingly earnest. "I'm so sorry. I can tell that you care for Ira. Camille, if there were a way, I'd do whatever it took to get him back."

Randall's misinterpretation for her need to return to shore caught her by surprise, as did his gallant avowal for a man he'd just met earlier that day.

"But I can't let you go back there, not after those . . . those *creatures* attacked you on the harbor road. You're safer at sea, Camille."

He pulled on her wrists slightly, bringing her closer. Randall rested his forehead against hers, Camille's breath trapped in her throat. Samuel coughed to remind them of his presence. Randall stepped away.

Samuel held out a small glass bottle, the cork pitted with use. "Pour it on your hand and try not to cuss."

Camille took the bottle, thinking she'd give anything to hear a good cuss word from Ira right then. He should be there in the cabin, cracking jokes about her frequent misfortunes with injury. Ira had been with them from the start. He'd stuck by them, even knowing it would be dangerous. And now Ira was gone — alive or dead she didn't know. Camille sank to the bunk, her throat knotting off once again.

Randall hovered near the door after Samuel left. How could she tell him the truth now? The way he'd gazed at her, so worried and sincere. The way he'd pressed his forehead to hers, as if he'd longed to reassure her that she was safe. But it wasn't supposed to be Randall doing that. It was supposed to be Oscar.

"Did you want help with that?" Randall nodded toward the bottle of camphor. Help meant touching. Camille shook her head and popped out the cork. The liquid stung down to the bone.

"What did you say to the captain about the attack?" she asked, her eyes watering.

Randall threw up his arms. "What could I say? I still have no idea what happened out there, or what those things were." He exhaled, trying to regain his composure. "I just said we'd been attacked and it was urgent we leave immediately if he wanted to insure his passengers' safety."

As much as Camille didn't want to be on the *Eclipse*, she also didn't want to risk another encounter with those creatures. Randall swung the chair around and sat in it backward. He wrapped his arms around the back and straddled it with his legs. She tried to remember if he'd ever seated himself so casually before.

"Explain," he said.

"I don't know what they were, either, Randall."

She reached inside her skirt pocket. The weight of the golden pendant surprised her. Camille had been able to pluck it from the road and slip it into her pocket before Oscar had hauled her to the *Eclipse*. She wriggled the pendant free. An oil lamp swaying on a stretch of chain link gave off plenty of light for her to see it by. The surface glinted, and Camille stared at it, openmouthed.

A skeleton face.

Ridges built the cheekbones and forehead, hollows for the eye sockets and nose. A series of carvings created the grimacing teeth, the lines cut deep into the gold. The same face had appeared before each stroke of bad luck on her way to Umandu: in a chartreuse wave, in the soapsuds of a bath, out of thin air, smoke, even sand. What was it doing here, on this pendant?

Randall drew back at the sight of the skull. Camille told him about the apparitions on the way to Umandu.

"They've come here for the stone, then?" Randall asked. "These creatures that took Ira?"

Camille flipped open the latches of the suitcase beside her on the bed. She then opened the burlap bag and put the pendant inside, next to Umandu. One of the creatures had said that. But it had also said something about needing Oscar as well. That they were going to take the stone and Oscar back to where they belonged. Camille's fingers brushed against Umandu. She stroked the stone once, its pulse gentle and rhythmic. She wanted to keep her hand on the stone. At the first touch of it, her nerves had instantly settled. Its odd warmth had crept in under her skin and spread to the rest of her body.

"Yes, they said they wanted the stone," she finally answered. She ignored the fact that she was omitting half of the truth. They wanted Oscar, too, and she suspected it had something to do with his resurrection. A resurrection Randall didn't, and couldn't, know anything about. Not now that the *Eclipse* was nearing the mouth of the tidal river that would empty them into the Great Australian Bight and beyond that, the Indian Ocean.

Randall got up from the chair and sat on the bunk beside her. The mattress dipped to the side, rocking Camille closer to him. Had she not feared an attempt at a kiss, she would have rested her head against his shoulder and closed her throbbing eyes.

"Do they want to stop you from reaching the other stone?" he asked.

"I don't know," she answered, and was glad at least that was the truth.

Something was wrong. She knew it even in her slumber. The cabin . . . it shouldn't have been so cold. Camille shivered and tried to pull the bunk's blanket up to her chin, but her fingers grasped nothing but air. Frigid air.

Confused, she opened her eyes — and sat up with a start. A white, ice-covered land stretched before her instead of the dark cabin on the *Eclipse*. And instead of her bunk, she sat on ice, its bitter coldness reaching through her dress. Scrambling to her feet, she saw the blinding terrain softly undulated toward massive ice cliffs in the distance.

This couldn't be real. It had to be a dream.

Camille remembered snuffing out the lantern and settling under the covers in her bunk not long after Samuel, her roommate, had returned with a promise to introduce her to the captain the next morning. And yet, what felt like only moments later, Camille found herself standing on a milky blue and white ice cap. She inspected the skin on her arms and saw the rise of gooseflesh. She touched her skin. Felt it. People didn't feel things in dreams. Wind whistled in her ears.

What was this place? She turned with caution. Far behind her was the frothy gray of a winter sea. She wrapped her arms around herself. Even her eyelids were freezing. She closed and squeezed them tight. When she opened them again, everything was gone — the icy tundra, the sea — replaced by the dark, beamed ceiling of her cabin.

Camille jolted up, tangled in sheets that were just as chilled as her brief dream had been. The air in front of her clouded when she breathed. The silver breath hung before her. She reached underneath her pillow for the burlap bag she'd stored there. She felt the rough fabric, the warmth of the stone and its gentle throb. It put her at instant ease. Her breathing slowed, no longer forming clouds of frost.

The cabin door burst open. Camille jumped as corridor lamplight shone on the figure of a girl. She darted inside and closed the door behind her. Camille swung her legs over the side of the bunk.

"Who are you?" Camille demanded. "What are you doing in here?"

Samuel snorted awake.

"Shhh," the girl said. A match was struck and the wick of a candle leaped with flame. The glow brightened the girl's face. It was the same girl who'd come to their rescue on the wharves. Sweat and grit covered her skin and her chest heaved with quick breaths.

Samuel's feet twisted in his blanket as he tried to push it off. "What's going on?"

The girl held a finger to her mouth and hushed them again.

"You have it," she said. A grin spread across her filthy cheeks. Her sweaty, sour odor crossed the cabin and Camille fought the instinct to pinch her nostrils tight.

"Who are you?" Samuel asked. The girl paid no attention to him. Her eyes were trained on Camille.

"You're Camille, and you've found the stone. Haven't you?" The girl took a step forward. Camille's hand went to the burlap bag shoved under her pillow.

"How do you know that?" She stole a glance at the girl's neckline. No golden pendant.

Samuel calmly moved between the girl and Camille. "I'm going to fetch the captain if you don't tell us who you are this instant." This time, the girl acknowledged him.

"You don't have to worry. I'm a friend." She leaned her head to see past Samuel and met Camille's eyes. "And I'm here to help you."

SEVEN

A shout rang out on deck. The girl darted around Samuel and came at Camille. "Where is the stone?"

Camille balked at her. "Why should I tell you that?"

"You don't need to worry about me, Camille. I'm not here to take the stone. I want to help you. It's my duty. My destiny." She whispered the last words, her pointed chin tucked into her neck, her eyes boring into Camille's.

"What exactly are you talking about?" Camille asked. The girl sighed dramatically.

"I don't *expect* you to understand." Camille bristled at the way she'd stressed *expect*, as if Camille were dense. "It's obvious you have no idea what you're dealing with here. Good heavens, the *mistakes* you've made . . . but they're of no matter now. I'm here to set things to right, and all you need to do is trust me."

Camille laughed out loud. "Trust you? I don't even know who you are!"

More noise erupted from the galley. Too much noise for the middle of the night. Something was going on, and Camille suspected it had to do with this girl.

"I'm here to help you, to keep you and the stone safe," the girl said as voices bounced off the corridor walls.

She was certainly no warrior. She was petite and dainty-looking, and hadn't a single weapon on her. And why would her destiny be to protect Camille, someone she had never so much as met?

"I have enough protection already," Camille said crisply. "What is your name, and how do you know about me and the stone?"

The chaos outside their cabin blared to a halt. A fist came down on the door.

"Miss Rowen, Mr. McGinty? May I have a word?"

Samuel quickly tucked his shirt in, his hair matted to one side from sleep. "That's the captain."

The girl dove forward and clutched Camille's arms with small, birdlike hands.

"No matter what he says, I *am* here to help you. You can't trust him," she said, her wide eyes pleading.

The captain's fist shook the door once again.

"Come in," Samuel answered.

The door flung open. The young man who stormed into the cabin took Camille by surprise as much as the strange girl had.

"Miss Rowen, I must apologize." The young man leaned into a deep, though brief, bow. Two shipmates stood behind him, filling the doorway. "I had hoped to greet you in the morning after a full night's rest. Clearly, that rest has been disturbed." He cut a hard glance toward the filthy, odorous girl.

"I don't understand," Camille muttered.

"Captain, who is this girl?" Samuel asked.

Captain? Camille couldn't believe it. She'd imagined a rugged old salt as the captain of the *Eclipse*, not this young, dashing man. There was no chance he was over the age of twenty-five.

"This girl is my niece," Captain Starbuck replied, incensed. He flattened his nostrils as he no doubt picked up on her ripe smell. "You are a disgrace, Margaret. I should have guessed you'd do something as brash as stowing away on my ship."

The girl's cheeks pinked. "Uncle Lionel, you left me no choice. I had to —"

"Enough, Margaret. Look at you." Captain Starbuck called all eyes to her ratty dress and knotted hair. "What would your father say?"

Margaret lifted her chin. "Why are you pretending to care?"

Randall appeared from behind the two shipmates, frantic. He pushed his way through, probably fearing the ruckus had been another otherworldly attack.

"What's happened?" he asked. Starbuck's fierce glare didn't waver from his niece's face.

"We're fine," Camille answered, though she wasn't sure what had just happened at all. The cabin, filled with too many people, closed in around her. "But if you'll excuse me, I need some air."

Camille pushed her way past Samuel and the captain, avoiding Margaret's eyes.

"Let her through," Randall ordered. He placed a hand at the small of her back and guided her from the cabin. Margaret called after Camille as Randall maneuvered her past a new horde of sailors gathered just outside the door.

"I meant what I said."

"That is *enough*," Starbuck replied.

On deck, Camille closed her eyes and breathed deeply.

"What was all that about?" Randall held her close. She didn't try to free herself. At that moment, having a steady person to lean against was exactly what she needed.

"I don't know. That girl . . ."

"Who *is* she?" he asked.

"She's the one who helped us in the harbor-front attack." Camille stole a glance at Randall. "She's the captain's niece. And she says she's here because of the stone."

"Starbuck's niece?" Randall asked. "How did she get aboard the ship, and what could she possibly know about the stone?"

Camille wondered the same things. She questioned everything.

"I need to speak some more to her," Camille said, turning to leave. Even though Margaret unsettled her, she needed answers.

"Please, wait a moment." Randall stepped in front of the companionway.

Camille's eyes were level with the collar of his shirt. The first few metal buttons were undone, no doubt for comfort while sleeping. A few sprouts of brown hair hinted to more hidden beneath his shirt, and before she could stop herself Camille wondered what the rest of his chest might look like. Oscar's was smooth and defined, and the few times she'd seen his bare torso her lungs had lost all function.

Oscar. Where was he? He hadn't come to her cabin after the harbor attack, not even to say good night. And the shouting belowdecks should have caught his attention.

Randall's fingers touched the gauze wrapped around Camille's wounded hand.

"You gave me a fright tonight," he said softly.

Her back beaded with sweat. "Everyone had a fright," she replied. She didn't want to be in a hushed conversation with Randall. Too many things could work their way out into the open, honest air.

"But you're the one I care about, Camille." There he went again, laying his heart out on the butchering table. Why did he have to go and do those sorts of things?

"I've learned how to take care of myself these last few months," she said. "I don't need the cosseting other girls might."

Heavens, she sounded full of herself. Either that or unappreciative of the rescue Randall had performed out on the wharves.

He grinned widely. "That's clear, especially after seeing the way you fought tonight."

One of his top incisors turned inward slightly, giving his smile a crooked look. It was the first time she'd noticed the imperfection, and yet it didn't diminish his looks at all. In fact, for that one moment, that single crooked tooth made Randall Jackson look vulnerable. And completely real.

He kissed Camille on her temple, where her horseshoe-shaped scar from the *Christina* had settled into a smooth white arc. He'd noticed it without saying a word. How gracious.

"It seemed as if the captain wasn't keen on that Margaret girl being aboard. Maybe you should stay away from her."

Camille considered it, but only briefly. Margaret knew about the stone, about *her*, and Camille needed to know how.

An order rang out on the night-cloaked deck. "Kildare! Lay out the topgallant mast!"

Camille pulled away from Randall. "Kildare? Not Oscar?"

She couldn't see anything up in the rigging. The flickering lanterns hitched around deck were too weak to reach much higher than two yards up the mainmast.

"I thought he was going to tell you himself," Randall said. "Oscar's resigned from Rowen and Company. He's joined Captain Starbuck's crew."

The casual announcement struck her with the serrated edge of high treason. Oscar had joined another captain's crew? But he worked for Rowen & Company, for her father. He was first mate, for heaven's sake! It hit her then. Oscar had quit. He'd quit his job and he'd quit her.

It was over.

Early the next morning, Camille found Oscar at the bowsprit halfheartedly untangling a pile of bobstays thicker than his forearms. His eyes traveled over the slate blue sea as he worked the ropes, but she knew he wasn't seeing the waves. She walked across deck toward him, catching furtive glances from sailors as she passed. Camille looked up, away from them, and noticed scrolling woodwork along the ship's deck, helm, and even the masts. Copper plates had been hammered onto the rail every ten yards or so, and onto each mast, the image of a circle eclipsing another circle cut into each plate. Gazing up, Camille saw traces of a repeating pattern embroidered with golden thread on the billowing canvas. It was an extravagance a mere merchant vessel didn't usually employ. And merchant vessels weren't normally captained by someone as young as Lionel Starbuck. She knew she still had to formally meet the captain, but she'd first wanted to see Oscar.

Camille stopped just behind him. He wore a tattered hemp shirt, replacing the checked fustian one from which he'd ripped the sleeves in order to make a bandage for Camille after the beast attack. She remembered how he'd held her close that night in the beasts' cave. His arms sturdy and safe around her while she slept.

"Is your hand all right?" Oscar asked before he'd even turned to see her.

She ignored his question. "If you wanted to quit, you should have told me."

He looked away from the water. "I wasn't up for an argument, and Randall was more than happy to see me go."

She balled her hands into painful fists, the gauze still wrapped around her injured palm. "Why are you doing this?"

The only reason to work among the crew, to live, eat, and sleep among them, would be to remove himself from Camille and the other passengers aboard the *Eclipse*. A sailor's duty was constant, his work never complete. Being busy away from her was his motive, she was certain of it.

He coiled a length of braided rope neatly at his feet, then calmly started on another. "Those things are after me, Camille. You saw what they did to Ira." He finally looked at her — really looked at her. She didn't want him to stop. "I don't want them anywhere near you."

"Oh," she whispered. "I thought it was because you . . ." Camille stopped, aware of how pitiful the rest of her sentence would sound. She cleared her throat and changed the subject. "Starbuck is quite young to be a merchant captain, don't you think?"

Oscar raised his eyebrows skeptically and lowered his voice. "The crew says he delivers cargoes here and there, but mostly he's a gentleman captain. Sails around the world for the fun of it." He dropped his voice even lower and added, "Must be nice."

That explained why Starbuck had "no pressing matters to attend to," as Samuel had put it. Camille had never before met a captain of leisure, and she most certainly never expected to meet one so *young*. She wondered at Randall's luck at finding a gentleman captain in San Francisco's harbor the day after receiving her letter of distress. Or perhaps it hadn't been luck at all. On her journey to find Umandu, Camille had become accustomed to the idea of fate, and had even begun to believe in it.

Oscar looked her over, wary of her silence. "Are you feeling all right? That creature on the harbor road had you nearly unconscious last night."

It had been a long time since Oscar had asked how she was doing. He sounded so much like his old self that it hurt. Camille frowned. "I'm fine, except for a headache that lasted for hours."

Oscar's eyes hitched on something behind her. Camille heard a high, wispy voice.

"That's because they freeze you from the inside out."

Camille turned and dropped her jaw as Margaret came up beside her. Her hair, now washed, was a radiant blond. Her newly laundered dress flattered her petite frame. Her scrubbed face revealed delicately thin lips, a narrow, equally delicate nose, and a pair of startling topaz eyes. The stinky, filthy girl was gone, replaced by a beauty. Margaret's fingers laced in front of her ruffled celery-colored skirt.

"When they touch you and take hold, they're freezing you," Margaret explained. "It's how they incapacitate their prey. Your head ached because your brain was thawing."

Oscar lowered the rope. *"Thawing?"*

"How do you know about those creatures?" Camille asked. "Do you know where they took our friend Ira? Is he . . . is he dead?"

Margaret kept her attention on Oscar. "I'm Maggie."

"I thought you were Margaret," Camille replied.

"Only my uncle insists on calling me that," she said, and then quickly looked Camille over. "Do you have it with you? You shouldn't leave the stone by itself."

Camille tightened her posture, annoyed. Oscar cleared his throat.

"I'm Oscar."

Maggie pulled the corner of her mouth into a smile and sighed. "I know."

"You didn't answer me," Camille said with waning patience. "Do you know where Ira is?"

Maggie cocked her head. "Don't worry. Your friend's not exactly dead."

Camille's spirits soared, despite the way Maggie had used the word *exactly* and how she then drew herself a few inches closer to Oscar.

"How do you know that?" Camille asked.

"The same way I knew you'd found the stone," Maggie answered. "The same way I know you used its gift on Oscar."

He retreated a small step. Maggie laughed a small snort, but even that came out lovely.

"Don't be frightened. I'm not very happy that Camille went and used the stone's magic, but I'm definitely not a Courier."

"A what?" Camille asked. She hated how many questions she had when this girl was around.

"You really do have a lot to learn, don't you?" Maggie asked with a roll of her dazzling eyes. Camille grated her teeth.

Oscar let the still-tangled rope fall back to the deck. "If you have something important to tell us, say it."

Maggie took note of the sailors nearby. "Not here. My uncle's ears are everywhere. Let's go to Camille's cabin. Or, Camille, I should say, *our* cabin. Your brother has agreed to bunk with Randall."

This morning was going from bad to worse. The idea of having Maggie as a roommate was about as pleasant as the raw sting of the wound on her hand.

Oscar seemed to realize the attention the three of them were gathering on deck. "Go. I'll be there when I can."

EIGHT

Camille followed Maggie down the spotless, well-lit corridor belowdecks, hoping to evade Randall on the way to the cabin. She didn't want him to join their little rendezvous when the fact that Camille had used the stone would inevitably be discussed. It would be impossible to keep the truth hidden from Randall forever, but telling him now would only make for a very long and awkward sail to Egypt. Camille promised herself that she'd tell him before stepping one foot onto African soil. She wouldn't allow Randall to accompany them in ignorance from that point on. He and Starbuck could simply turn the *Eclipse* around and head back for home. Camille tried not to think about how horrible telling him the truth at that late point would be.

Maggie came to a brusque standstill and Camille rammed into her.

"What are you doing? Our door isn't —" Camille stopped when she saw Captain Starbuck standing just outside their cabin.

"Uncle Lionel," Maggie said flatly.

The exasperation the captain had displayed the night before was gone. He grinned widely, the sprinkling of freckles over the bridge of his nose playing up his youth. Starbuck ignored his niece and fixed his warm greeting on Camille.

"Miss Rowen, I just arrived to knock on your door and introduce myself properly. I'm happy to see you looking well rested." He spared Maggie a withering glance before focusing back on Camille. "Would you join me in my cabin for breakfast? Your brother is waiting for us."

Camille hesitated, taking a quick glance over her shoulder to make sure Randall hadn't stepped out of his cabin. She yelped when she saw a brawny sailor glaring down at her from not two feet away. He grimaced, his light-colored hair shorn nearly to his scalp to reveal uneven planes where his skull dipped and ridged. His ears sported black, circular piercings, and green ink tattoos peeked out from the collar of his tight-fitting shirt.

"Let me introduce my first mate, Mr. Hardy," Captain Starbuck said, then chuckled. "Don't worry. He's tame."

Hardy's eyes slid lazily from Camille's breasts to her ankles without shame. He coughed out a coarse laugh and added, "Most of the time."

Camille turned her back to him and found Starbuck stifling an amused grin. She didn't know what was so humorous.

"I'm sorry, Captain, but I find I'm not as well rested as I'd hoped."

Starbuck frowned and smoothed down his silken vest, clearly not having expected that answer.

"Perhaps another time." He opened the cabin door and extended his arm over the threshold. Camille passed through, eager to be gone from Mr. Hardy's disturbing presence. Maggie followed, but her uncle detained her with a firm hand on her elbow. "Remember what we discussed, Margaret. Do *not* disturb Miss Rowen."

Maggie jerked her arm free and closed the door, practically on Starbuck's nose.

"Well, that was unpleasant." Maggie sighed and crossed to Samuel's bunk. His paltry belongings had already been cleared from the cabin. "I knew Mr. Hardy to be a brute, but I had no idea how very ugly he was."

Maggie tested the bunk mattress with a few bounces.

"What do you mean?" Camille asked. "You've never seen your uncle's first mate before today?"

She longed to go to her own bunk and lift the pillow to find the burlap bag. Camille could practically feel the pulse and warmth of the stone against her fingers from where she stood by the bureau. How was that possible? *It isn't*, she told herself. She was just imagining things. She remembered how the stone had felt when she'd held it last.

"Uncle Lionel hired him just before leaving California," Maggie explained. "By then I was already stowed away. I heard Hardy shouting orders from where I was hidden the whole voyage, and I saw him briefly last night as my uncle was tossing me in the canvas storage closet. . . ." She lifted a silky handful of hair and sniffed it, then crinkled her nose. "But it was too dark to see just how repulsive he was."

"The canvas storage closet? Is that where you stowed away?" Camille asked, stunned Maggie had remained undetected for so long a sail.

"Ha. I wish." Maggie got up and headed for the bureau without explaining exactly where she *had* stowed away.

As Maggie opened the top drawer and peered inside, Camille realized it was of no importance, anyway.

"What did you mean when you said Ira wasn't exactly dead?" Camille asked.

Maggie pawed through the dresses in the drawer. "A Courier can't kill what isn't already dead. Meaning, if your friend's heart was still beating in his chest when they took him, he's alive in the Forelands."

Camille had never heard of such a place.

"How does one get to these Forelands?"

Maggie shut a drawer and opened another. She ruffled through the silk stockings and pantalettes.

"Why did you go searching for the stone if you knew absolutely nothing about it?" Maggie asked. She slammed the drawer and glared at Camille. "You weren't supposed to actually *use* the stone. Didn't anyone ever tell you that?"

Camille trembled, frustration and impatience coming to boil.

"Yes, someone did tell me. But he was my enemy and I had no reason to believe a single word he said."

McGreenery had laughed at her when she'd announced she was going to use Umandu to bring her father back to life. Now, with Maggie chastising her as well, she wanted to know exactly why it had been so wrong.

"If you know so much about it, why don't you tell me why using the stone was such a huge mistake?"

Maggie rolled her eyes and moved on to the third and final drawer. "You were supposed to wait until both of the stones could be joined together, so you could draw from an endless well of power, not a shallow puddle."

The impact of Umandu's magic had been stronger than anything Camille had ever imagined possible. And Maggie was likening it to a shallow puddle?

"If you're looking for the stone, you can stop. I'm not going to show it to you until you tell me what you're about," Camille said. She didn't dare glance toward her bunk and the rumple of blankets there for fear of giving away the stone's hiding spot.

"I've already told you," Maggie said.

"You've done nothing but confuse me!"

Maggie sighed and shut the bottom drawer. "Well, I'm sorry. I wasn't prepared for how little you'd know."

Oscar entered the cabin without knocking. He shut the door and stood sentry in front of it, crossing his arms and displaying the full bulk of his chest and biceps. He stared at Maggie, at first fiery and annoyed. But then something changed in the way he looked at her. Something softened.

"Tell us what you know," he said. It sounded less of a demand and more like awed curiosity. Camille's blood ran hot.

"It seems she knows everything," Camille muttered.

Maggie assented with a smug grin and arched her pale eyebrow. "When it comes to the stones of the immortals, yes, I do know just about everything."

What was she, perfection incarnate? Annoyed, Camille quickly checked her reflection in the glaze of the white porcelain pitcher on the bureau. Her cheeks and nose looked grotesquely wide, and sprigs of hair stuck out from her tangled bun. Lovely.

"Then why was Camille the one to find it and not you?" Oscar asked.

"I didn't have any control over who found the stone," Maggie answered with a dissatisfied look toward Camille. "If I had, I would have chosen someone more knowledgeable. Besides, it's my duty to be the guardian, not the discoverer."

Before Camille could ask why Maggie was the "guardian," Maggie had turned on her heel. She was at Camille's bunk in a millisecond, tearing back the covers. Camille and Oscar both stepped forward to stop her, but Maggie already had the stone out of the burlap bag. She held it up to her face, her color rising.

"Umandu," she whispered, apparently unafraid of saying its name out loud. "It's beautiful."

Camille wrinkled her nose. The stone's ragged triangular shape made it look as if it had been cut from a larger rock with a chisel.

"I've been waiting my whole life to see it." Maggie set the stone carefully on the bunk and unfurled the map. Dust glittered in the lamplight.

"How did you know to find me?" Camille asked.

"I heard you," Maggie replied, inspecting the face of the map. "The very first time you said the stone's name."

Oscar's eyes danced with Camille's for a moment, looking as confused as she felt.

"Heard me?" she repeated. "Impossible. I was aboard my father's ship. Alone in my cabin, and —"

"And then a whispering came, am I correct?" Maggie looked up from the map. Camille blinked, startled. "A shiver of fragrant air blew over you, and the chanting grew louder. Then it stopped, and when it did, peril followed?"

Exactly. Maggie knew what had happened inside Camille's cabin; she knew what Camille had heard inside her head when no one possibly could.

"That was you chanting? *You* cursed me?"

Maggie snorted. "No, of course not. It wasn't a curse. Haven't you figured that out? I was simply warning you that Domorius also heard you, and that he'd be trying to stop you."

The cabin rang silent. If Camille attempted to speak, she feared the words would tumble out as unintelligible grunts.

"I'd been waiting for someone to say the stone's name forever." Maggie ran her fingers along the map's hieroglyphs. Could she see the symbols that no one else could? Camille hoped not. But then again, as insufferable as it would be, perhaps Maggie would know how to decipher them.

"Most people who knew about the stone also knew not to say its name. Of course, that was good and bad. Good, because then Domorius didn't know someone was trying to find the stone. Bad, because I wouldn't know, either, and wouldn't be able to help them. So I suppose I can't really be upset with you about that," she said to Camille.

Oscar took a step farther into the cabin. Camille noticed with a hollow feeling that it was in Maggie's direction and not hers.

"How did you warn her with the chanting? And who's this Domorius guy you're talking about?" he asked.

Maggie inhaled and then blew out, fluttering the blond tresses framing her forehead. "I'm not sure how I sent the warning. It just . . . happened. My father always told me it would come naturally, and he was right. It did."

A wistful smile curved her lips. Camille wasn't satisfied one bit.

"What does your father have to do with any of this? And why has the duty of guardian fallen to you and not someone else?"

Maggie tossed the questions around in her head, literally bobbing her head from side to side as she got up from the bunk and paced the floor, rolling and unrolling the leather scroll.

"Well, it's a long story, and we have quite the sail ahead of us. I think I should first tell you what your biggest threat is."

Camille took the map from Maggie before she could snap it open one more time. Enchanted dust kept clouding the air.

"Vanishing men with golden pendants?"

Maggie nodded. "They're Couriers, Domorius's army of sorts. They were men at one point in time, but when they died and were about to cross over to the Underworld, they struck bargains with Domorius instead. They would do his bidding to be able to stay on earth, mostly as watchmen for the stone. As long as they wore their pendants, they wouldn't truly die, though they wouldn't truly be alive, either. When Camille found the stone and spent its powers, Domorius sent them to find it and take back the soul owed to him."

A shiver straightened Camille's spine. She took an involuntary step closer to Oscar. "Domorius . . . he's . . . ?"

Maggie seemed to know what Camille was trying to ask. "He goes by a lot of different names, depending on the culture. The Angel of Death, the Grim Reaper, the

Gatekeeper to the Underworld . . . of course, you might simply know him as Death."

Camille swallowed hard. "They want to bring Oscar's soul back to the Underworld."

Maggie nodded.

"Are more of these Couriers coming?" Oscar asked without a single tremor in his voice. How could he be so calm? They were after his very *soul*. And Camille was to blame. She'd used the stone and as good as invited the Couriers to come and attack. Camille finally understood what Maggie and McGreenery had meant about making an enormous mistake.

"How do I stop them?" Camille asked.

Oscar spun toward her. "You're not going near them."

"I'm the one who did this!"

Maggie tapped a finger against her lower lip and vaulted one of her thin, nearly invisible eyebrows.

"You can't stop them now," she said. "Not until the two stones are joined together."

Until they are joined together. It was exactly what Oscar had told Randall earlier. She stared at him, wanting to ask him how he'd known, but Maggie kept talking, making it easy for Oscar to ignore her.

"Think of the stone as one magnet, and Oscar's soul as another. When you touched the stone, you told it what you wanted most. It drew Oscar's soul out of the Underworld, where it was supposed to stay."

What you wanted most rang in her ears. It threatened to derail the conversation and send her into torment over having not chosen her father. Camille couldn't let it happen.

"So his soul returned to him, and now these Couriers want to take it away again? But why? The stone was supposed to bring him back to life fair and square," Camille said.

"There's nothing fair about Death," Maggie said. "Besides, Oscar's soul couldn't have returned to him, anyway."

Oscar took in a short, rasping breath. "What do you mean by that?"

"The stone drew your soul from the Underworld, but on its own the stone couldn't have had enough power to finish the job." She pinned Camille with her topaz glare. "That is what I meant about a shallow puddle instead of a deep well of power. I think when the stones are joined together your soul will finish the journey from the Underworld and return to you in one piece. Until then, the Couriers will keep coming, and there are only so many ways to fight them off."

Like ridding them of the golden pendant. Oscar stepped forward.

"If my soul isn't in the Underworld, and it isn't inside me, then where is it?"

Camille couldn't grasp any of this. She felt trapped inside a terrible and vivid never-ending dream.

"I said I knew *almost* everything about the legend. Almost," Maggie repeated. "If I'd been thirty or forty years old when Camille found the stone, I probably would know where your soul is — or the pieces of your soul, since it very well could have fragmented on its way out of the Underworld. Maybe part of it is inside you somewhere, I don't know. But I remember my father telling me fragmenting was possible. . . ." Maggie trailed off, tracing her lower lip with her finger in contemplation.

Camille shuddered with the idea of her own soul being somewhere other than inside her. Oscar shifted his footing uncomfortably. She wondered if he felt any different because of it. No one could feel their soul, of course — and yet, wasn't someone's soul the very thing that set them apart from everyone else? Wasn't it what made them *them*?

"How would your father know about any of this?" Oscar asked.

Maggie lifted her chin proudly. "He was the stone's guardian, too. He taught me everything he'd learned from his mother, who had been the guardian before him. And when he died . . ." Maggie paused to clamp down on the trembling of her voice. "When he died, I took his place."

Camille still wanted to know why Maggie's family line had been chosen, but she wanted answers to other questions more.

"So I'm assuming this map leads to the Underworld's entrance in Egypt? And that's where Death keeps the second stone?" Camille asked. Maggie bit her lower lip and nodded.

"And I have to take it from him?" Camille watched Maggie's sheepish nod once more and thought she might be sick.

Oscar stormed toward the door.

"Where are you going?" Camille and Maggie asked in unison.

"We're only one day from Port Adelaide. I'm telling the captain to take us back."

Camille hurried in front of him and knocked his hand from the knob. "Absolutely not."

"The Couriers want my soul, Camille, not yours. They took Ira and nearly took you trying to get to me. They used you as bait."

He reached for the knob and Camille batted his hand away again. "Going back to Port Adelaide won't change anything. Besides, you've already joined the crew."

His shoulders fell. "I can quit just as easy as I joined. You'll stay in Port Adelaide and *I'll* go to Egypt. I'll finish this alone, just how I planned."

Maggie coughed. "Ah, actually, you can't. You can go into the Forelands, but if you step one foot inside the Underworld, Domorius will keep you there. He wants your soul, but I'm pretty sure he'd settle for your body. Besides, finding the Death Stone is Camille's task, not yours."

Oscar backed off with a frustrated growl. Camille wanted to have all the answers stored away somewhere just like Maggie seemed to.

"Death Stone?" Camille asked.

"Umandu is the stone of life," Maggie explained. "This second stone is the complete opposite."

Still steaming, Oscar faced Maggie. "Where do they come from, these Couriers? Tell me they can't materialize out of thin air."

Maggie waved a hand. "Of course they can't do that. They might be partly dead, but they're real people. Men . . ." She walked to Oscar's side and tapped her finger against Oscar's chest. "Just. Like. You."

He seized Maggie's hand and lowered it to her side. "What do you mean by that?"

Maggie maintained her poise. "That they might be alive, but at one point before that, they were dead."

Oscar continued to hold Maggie's hand down at her side.

"Oscar isn't a Courier," Camille interjected. "He isn't anything like them."

Maggie waited a beat, still under Oscar's intense scrutiny, before replying. "No. He isn't a Courier. If he were, he would be wearing a pendant and, of course, in the process of freezing my brain."

Oscar let go of her hand and threw the door wide. He turned to Camille. "Just stay away. It's safer for you," he said, "and it's better for me."

The door creaked shut, and he was gone.

NINE

The pantry on the *Eclipse* smelled unusual. Camille searched the shelves, trying to find the source of the mystery odor as well as something halfway decent to eat. The food on Starbuck's ship was dreadful: cold salted beef, sludge for coffee, tasteless hard biscuits, mushy carrots, and thin soup. Morning through night her belly rumbled and her head felt like it would float away. Camille had finally decided to raid the pantry and produce something edible for herself.

Between barrels of salted pork and beef, Camille saw six quart-size glass jars on a bottom shelf. Each one was filled to the rim with grainy white powder, perhaps salt. The odd smell of the pantry strengthened the closer she got. Camille picked up one jar and twisted off the metal cover.

The odor exploded up her nostrils. She held the jar as far back as her arms would allow.

"Heavens," she muttered, and dared to bring the powder back to her nose.

"You do know stealing from a ship pantry is a punishable offense, right?"

Camille swiveled around and saw her brother standing in the pantry doorway. She relaxed and set the glass jar back on the shelf.

"I'm willing to risk a stroll down the plank if it means I can scrounge up something decent to eat."

Camille opened a tin can of crackers and stuffed a few handfuls of them into the pockets of her ruby linen dress. Samuel sifted through the jars on another wall and selected some grape preserves.

"Game for a picnic?" he asked, and they went up on deck into the breezy afternoon.

The full sails threw shadows over the scrubbed planks. As they took to the bow, Camille remembered all the things she loved about sailing: the fresh scent of salt on the air; the sound of wind filling the sails; being but a small dot on the ocean, like crossing a powerful beast's scaly, slippery back. It all gave her a sense of challenge and reward.

"I've hardly seen you this last week," Camille said as they found a private spot on deck.

"Captain Starbuck has been showing me the ropes around the *Eclipse*," Samuel replied. Camille had noticed her brother could always be found with the captain. Once, she'd even seen Starbuck instructing Samuel at the helm.

With Starbuck being such a young captain, perhaps her brother was taking to the idea of sailing, or even the business of the shipping trade. If that were the case, he'd get along well in San Francisco. Maybe he would even join her in Rowen & Company. They could use Samuel's contacts in the fine-china trade and build up the company again *without* Randall's money. Camille knew it was a long shot, but the ambiguity of it let her have hope.

"Have you started to figure out the hieroglyphs on the map?" Samuel asked as he scooped a glob of purple preserves onto a cracker.

Camille heaped an even bigger glob onto her own cracker. "They're impossible. I don't know how I'm ever going to figure what they say without the help of someone who actually knows how to read them." She stuffed the cracker into her mouth and, ditching all respectability, spoke with a full mouth. "I'm hoping someone in Egypt can help once we arrive."

Samuel took a handkerchief from his coat and, with a roll of his eyes, handed it to her. "You've got grape on your chin."

Camille cleaned up, feeling daunted by the reminder of the hieroglyphs.

"Perhaps Maggie could help. Has she said anything more about what it is you're supposed to do once we reach Egypt?" Samuel asked.

Camille narrowed her eyes and handed the handkerchief back to her brother. "The only thing Maggie bothers to talk about is how I've done everything wrong. She's acting as if I forced her to stow away and come to my aid. Like she's doing me some huge favor and I'm not grateful enough. I can't stand her, Samuel. I've never had many friends, let alone girl friends, but if the majority of them are like Maggie Starbuck, I'll be happy to keep it that way."

Her brother wiped a few crumbs from the corner of his lip. "I don't think the majority of girls are like Maggie at all. She's certainly unique."

Seawater misted up over the railing and spattered the narrow patch of deck at the front of the ship.

"Do you think she's pretty?" Camille asked. She knew the question was petty, but she couldn't forget the way Oscar and Maggie had stared each other down at their first meeting.

"Of course she is. She's stunning." Samuel twisted the lid back onto the preserves. Camille tried not to show her disappointment. "But forgetting Maggie a moment" — he took a quick look over his shoulder — "I want to know why you're still lying to Randall."

Camille threw the last bite of her cracker over the railing. "It's complicated."

Samuel crinkled his forehead. "And deceitful."

The word sliced through her. "Who are you to judge? It's my problem, not yours."

Samuel crossed his arms and used his height against Camille. He glared down at her. "What you're doing is wrong."

She took a step backward, his hostility surprising her once again.

"Don't you think I know that? I know I have to tell him the truth —"

"So what are you waiting for?"

"Stop being such a bully," she said. "I don't need you preaching morals to me."

He huffed. "You've had plenty of time to tell Randall the truth. What is it? Are you still sneaking around with Oscar?"

Camille balled her hands and itched to jab a fist into Samuel's shoulder. He looked down his nose at her with the same haughty stare Stuart McGreenery had mastered.

"For being the son of the most appalling man I've ever met, you manage to sit on a pretty high horse," she whispered.

Samuel's haughty stare flashed over to something even more arrogant.

"You should know, *sister*, that Randall has been asking me questions."

Camille didn't want to give him the satisfaction of taking his bait, but she couldn't resist. "About what?"

Samuel simpered, pleased with himself. "About you and Oscar mostly, a little bit about the stone. He's not as clueless as you wish he were."

Of course he wasn't. Randall was intelligent and intuitive. Why else would her father have trusted him so dearly with Rowen & Company? Having money to invest had been one thing, but to allow him such access to finances and securing other investors took trust in his abilities. He could zero in on a fraudulent associate just as easily as he could an honest one. And yet she'd been pretending he couldn't see through her just as easily.

A gust of wind surprised Camille and Samuel. She leaned against it and stood firm, but Samuel stumbled sideways. She caught his side. As she helped to steady him he didn't seem so much like his father. Instead, Samuel seemed like a sixteen-year-old boy with minnows for sea legs.

"Don't worry," she said, frustrated over their argument. "I'm sure with the sailing lessons Captain Starbuck is giving you, you'll grow your sea legs fast."

Samuel narrowed his eyes.

"We have two things in common, Camille. The same mother" — Samuel yanked his arm away, snagging one of Camille's chipped nails on a coat thread — "and both of our fathers were sea captains. So as for my sea legs, I'll get along just fine."

Samuel smoothed each of his sleeves at the wrist and then turned to leave. Camille shoved her finger into her mouth and tasted blood. The nail had torn down to the skin.

She leaned against a giant spool of rope. Why was he so offended by the way she'd screwed everything up? If Samuel knew her better, he'd understand that she did intend to tell Randall the truth. He'd understand that maybe things weren't so black-and-white.

How *could* he know her, though? She didn't even know herself lately. She had a plan to tell Randall the truth, but she had no plan whatsoever regarding the second stone. She'd had a plan right from the start with Umandu. But this second stone had her stumped. Or perhaps Oscar was the thing stumping her. She'd been concentrating so much on how he'd changed that she hadn't been able to focus on the task at hand — to save his soul and to find Ira.

It had to stop. She had to make things right, beginning with Randall.

The deck didn't so much as creak as Camille hurried to the companionway. The wood was perfection, caulked and scrubbed and gleaming in the early afternoon sun. Starbuck's meticulous ship, its spotless decks and sails festooned with embroidery, hit her as odd again as she traveled the corridor to Randall's cabin. She wondered what a gentleman captain transported. Though it had been emptied in Auckland, the ship's hold might give her the answer. She'd have to pay it a visit. But first: Randall.

Camille stood at Randall's door, her chest heaving, her pulse threatening to burst through her skin. As she lifted her hand to knock, she thought of how he'd braved a Pacific crossing to come to her rescue. Of the way he'd leaped to her aid yet again on the wharves, and of how he'd been intuitive enough to actually bring the map to his nose and detect its peculiar scent.

Her arm collapsed to her side. The peculiar scent. That's what she'd smelled in the pantry's curious glass jars of white powder. Myrrh.

The door to Randall's cabin swung wide, catching her off guard. Daylight from the cabin's porthole flooded her vision, and Randall rammed into her before noticing she was there.

"Camille?" He backed off of her toes. "I'm so sorry, I didn't hear you. Did you knock?"

She fished around for an answer, and suddenly remembered her decision to confess the truth. Terrified, she stood still and speechless.

"I've crushed your toes, haven't I? Here, come in." Randall swung his arm toward his single desk chair. "Sit down."

Camille sat in the chair and caught a glimpse of an extra pillow and blanket folded neatly on the cabin's only bunk.

"Which of you is sleeping on the floor?" she asked to buy more time.

Randall perched on the edge of the bunk. He sat with a relaxed droop to his shoulders. They were not anywhere near the breadth of Oscar's, but they still filled out his band-collared shirt nicely. Camille looked away. She shouldn't be noticing those things.

"Your brother is quite the diplomat. We're taking turns," Randall said.

Camille slid her fingertip over the torn nail. Drying blood rimmed her cuticle. Diplomat didn't sound like a fitting word just then.

"What's the matter?" Randall rose from the bunk and crouched in front of her. "You're biting the inside of your cheek."

Camille released her cheek from between her teeth. "What do you mean?"

Randall laughed and cast his eyes to the floor. "You bite your cheek when something is bothering you."

She did? She'd never noticed that before.

"Oh." Camille felt the inside of her cheek with her tongue. Perhaps it wasn't attractive. It didn't sound attractive.

He took her hand and held it without fidgeting. "So tell me. What's wrong?"

Tell him. Just tell him! she screamed to herself.

"It's, it's just that," Camille started, frantic over what to say next. She pulled her hand away. The cold sweat breaking out on her palms was not what she wanted to share with him when his hands were warm and dry.

"There's myrrh in the pantry." Camille cringed inside for being such a gutless coward.

"Myrrh?" Randall backed up. "I wonder why. It's hardly anything the cook should be using in his, ah, concoctions." He lowered his voice. "I can't exactly call it food."

Camille stood up as eight bells on deck rang out, signaling the change in watch. "I'm sure it's nothing."

A lie. Why was she lying to him again? Randall intercepted her as she tried to reach the door, taking her wrist in his hand.

"The map smells of myrrh, and now it's in the pantry? I wouldn't call it nothing."

Randall tensed his fingers around her wrist. Camille held her breath tight in her lungs, noticing how her skin was aflame where he touched her. She hadn't expected that. Not at all.

He let go of her. Camille clasped her hands behind her back and rubbed away the after-tingling of his touch.

"It looked like salt at first, but the smell set it apart," she said.

Randall pulled his brows together in contemplation. "Myrrh doesn't look like salt. It's a reddish brown clay. My father used to have an herb woman make pastes for his toothaches." Randall laughed to himself. "He did have horrible teeth."

The clamor of sailors trudging by Randall's cabin resounded from the corridor, some on their way up deck and others on their way below.

Randall took up his jacket from the back of the chair. "You think it's all connected?"

"Where are you going?"

Randall shrugged into his coat. "To the pantry. I'm feeling a bit hungry. You?"

Camille grinned. "Raiding the pantry is a punishable offense, or didn't you know?"

He opened the door to an influx of sailors, Oscar among them. Oscar stopped, jamming up the flow of foot traffic, and stared inside Randall's cabin.

"Kildare," Randall greeted without enthusiasm. He

probably expected Oscar to move along, but Oscar stayed put. He made the sailors go around his rigid frame.

"Is there something you want?" Randall asked.

Oscar standing there, staring as if he'd just caught Camille and Randall in some improper act, would most definitely lead to questions from Randall that she didn't want to answer. She started to step between them, into the corridor, but the next sailor bumped into Oscar's shoulder and he rejoined his watch heading to the fo'c'sle, the large, arrow-shaped cabin at the bow of the ship where all of the sailors bunked.

Randall closed the door behind them, exhaling heavily as he no doubt subdued a harsh comment about Oscar. As they walked to the pantry, Camille stole a glance behind them. Oscar stood halfway inside the fo'c'sle. He stared after them another moment before bowing his head and disappearing inside.

———

That evening, Camille and Randall ate supper in his cabin, carefully tasting the cold beef and hard biscuits softened to porridge for any hint of myrrh. Their trip to the pantry had done nothing more than determine the glass jars were filled with myrrh-infused salt. Randall had been brave enough to sprinkle a few white granules onto his finger and taste them. With a puckered-up face he'd twisted the cover back on and raced to the water cask.

"It's not in here." Camille dropped her spoon into the porridge. It tasted awful, but not of myrrh.

She sat on his bunk, trying to focus on the curiosity of myrrh and not the partly irritated, partly miserable expression Oscar's face had held hours before. Randall took her bowl and set it on the desk, and then held out his hand to her.

"Come on, I'll walk you back to your cabin."

She let him lead her into the corridor, sorry to be just a few steps away from saying good-bye for the evening. Randall's company was hand over fist better than Maggie's. The *Eclipse* cut through calm evening waters, the creak of the timbers light and soothing, in contrast to everything Camille felt inside.

"Have you spoken to Oscar since we set sail?" Randall asked. Camille tensed.

"Once or twice," she answered. Why did he want to know? Had he been questioning Oscar's tortured expression from earlier as well?

"It would be best if you didn't from now on. You know that sailors don't have the privilege of mingling with the passengers," Randall replied. "Besides, I think Kildare is finally starting to understand where it is he belongs. We should leave him be."

Camille brushed past him as they reached her cabin. "Why must you be so pompous toward him? You always have been. You might not like Oscar, but he saved my life. He helped me find the stone."

And I love him, she added to herself. *And I hate him.*

"You're right." Randall gave a decisive lift of his chin. "I don't like him. I never have. I get the impression that he feels . . . familiar with you." Randall cast his eyes in the direction of the fo'c'sle. Camille was thankful for it. Her rising color would have betrayed her.

"We did spend months together," she offered weakly. "With Ira, that is. The three of us. Traveling to the map. To the stone."

Yes, Ira had been there. It hadn't just been her and Oscar alone together the whole time, forgetting Randall and her father and everything real that waited back home in California.

"The map, yes," Randall said. He finally looked at her. "I've been thinking about the symbols on the map. Perhaps I can help you determine what they are."

"You know how to read hieroglyphs?"

Randall took her hand in his. Her fingers stiffened with uncertainty, her insides rolling into a bundle of conflicting emotions: excitement, fear, thrill, guilt.

"No," he answered. "But two confused heads working together are better than one."

He was right. She definitely did not want to figure out the map alone. Camille sighed and nodded, accepting his offer. "We'll begin tomorrow."

Of course, she had no idea how. But doing something about the map would feel better than puzzling over it.

Randall stepped closer. "I don't like leaving you alone."

"I won't be." Her smile trembled. "Maggie. Remember?"

The silent corridor seemed to encourage him. Randall leaned closer, his breath warm as he kissed her forehead, his lips soft. Camille stood inert. Did she even want this? This was Randall, for heaven's sake. The very person she'd dreaded marrying. He brushed his lips against her temple, then her cheekbone. She should step away. Remind him of the impropriety of it. But she did nothing as his lips reached the soft flesh of her cheek.

Lamplight cascaded over them as the door to the cabin whipped open. Randall drew back quickly. Camille turned to see Maggie standing in the doorway.

"Oh my. How embarrassing for me," Maggie said, obviously not embarrassed at all. She continued to stand there instead of closing the door. Randall cleared his throat and ran his fingers through his hair.

"Good night, Camille," he said, lingering in the corridor another moment before turning back for his cabin.

Camille went into her cabin and shut the door.

"That was extremely rude," Camille said as she sat on her bunk and started to untie her bootlaces.

"I heard voices." Maggie shrugged a shoulder. "Besides, what are you doing kissing him when you're in love with Oscar?"

The bootlaces fell from Camille's fingers. She looked up at Maggie, stunned. "What do you know about any of that? And not that it's any of your business, but I was not kissing him."

Maggie leaned against the bureau and gave a *tsk-tsk* sound with her tongue. "Does Randall not know you've used the stone? That you've brought Oscar back from the dead?"

Camille retied her boots with oomph. "That's not your concern."

She wished she could go somewhere, anywhere, away from Maggie. But there was no place to go.

Maggie sighed dramatically. "Oh, fine. But it's a dangerous line you're walking."

"If you don't mind, I'd rather not take advice from someone who insults me every chance she gets."

Camille turned down her covers. Sleep, at least, promised respite from her present company. Though sleep also threatened icy dreams. Camille shivered. A second dream had occurred not long after the first, and though it had been a handful of nights, Camille feared the dream's return.

Maggie peeled back her own thin blankets. "I can't help it. Your using the stone took me by surprise, and now I have to decide what to tell you and how, without completely overwhelming you. I've concluded that you'll learn more if I don't give you all the answers."

How considerate, Camille thought as she took up her cloak from the foot of the bunk and wrapped it around her shoulders. If the dream did return and Camille woke to frost in the air, she wanted to be prepared.

"It's warm in here already," Maggie said. "What do you need that for?"

Camille stuck her booted feet under the covers. "Still none of your business."

Maggie bit the corner of her mouth and squinted. Her eyes popped open wide. "You've been there." She pointed at Camille. "You've been going there in your sleep!"

Camille stopped pulling the blankets up. "Where?"

Maggie parted her lips to spill out an answer, but stopped herself. "No. No, I don't think I should . . . no. Never mind."

She turned back to her own bunk and got under the covers quickly, making a racket as she settled down with her back to Camille. Still sitting upright, Camille considered what Maggie had just said: *You've been going there in your sleep.* But they were just dreams. She wasn't actually going anywhere. She was on a ship in the middle of the Indian Ocean, for heaven's sake.

Entirely too warm with her cloak on, she put out the lantern and lay back onto the uncomfortable hay pallet. Instead of Maggie's strange comment, her mind reversed to Randall in the corridor. The warmth of his lips . . . the tightening of her stomach. She squeezed her eyes shut and turned onto her side. A hot poker of guilt twisted inside her. But not because she felt like she was betraying Oscar. It twisted and hurt because she felt like she was betraying herself. Camille reached further back, to the memories she'd been relying on for the smallest amounts of happiness the last few weeks: of Oscar lying beside her in her mother's house, holding her protectively to him, his lips pressed against hers. Camille stayed there, refusing to travel ahead in time. Refusing to open her eyes and remember that all of that was over.

A whistling wind convinced her to open her lashes a millimeter. Blinding white made her eyes water, and a rash of cold attacked her. Camille sat up. Her bunk was gone, replaced by a sheet of packed snow and ice. She pressed her bare hands against the ice and got to her feet, staring in fright at the barren landscape around her. The dream had returned, but how had she fallen asleep so quickly? The sheer cliffs of ice, closer this time, were streaked with twisting veins of pale blue, purple, milky white, and green.

A gusty wind ripped through her loose hair, biting at her scalp. Camille clutched her cloak tighter around her neck. Her cloak? Looking down, she saw she still wore it. And her boots! She'd taken them with her into her dream. Was it a trick of her subconscious? She didn't know. What was this place? The only definition of land were the ice cliffs ahead, and behind her, the gray stormy sea.

"Hello?" Camille called. She couldn't recall ever speaking in dreams before. Just like she'd never touched or felt anything in her dreams.

Standing there shivering, though not as cold as she'd been the last two times, wasn't the way to find out where she was. She walked toward the ice cliffs, the wind sawing through her cloak and stinging her bare fingers. A blur of white near the cliffs made her stop, but then it was gone. Camille studied the cliffs, certain something had just passed in front of them. Her eyes finally tripped over a different shade of white standing out against the ice: a four-legged animal. It watched Camille intently. She backed up a few hasty steps, slipping. Camille fell toward the hard ground and closed her eyes, ready for impact.

The soft pallet of hay caught her, and the darkness of her cabin swallowed the glaring white. She shot up in her bunk, the last breath of arctic wind letting go of her hair. Again, it felt as if the cabin were in a deep freeze. Camille lit the lantern, her hands shaking. Gooseflesh riddled her skin. The light caught Maggie, sitting up in her bunk wide-eyed and pale.

"Where were you?" she asked, her breath clouding in front of her. Maggie waved her hand through the silver mist.

"Right here, in my bunk," Camille answered, teeth chattering. She didn't wish to confide in Maggie. Her dreams were her own. And that's all they were. Dreams.

Maggie pulled her blankets up around her and rested on an elbow. "Of course you were," she said sarcastically. She threw the covers over herself and hunkered down into them, out of sight.

TEN

Camille lounged in her bunk for as long as she could the next morning. The ice dream hadn't come back, but she'd still had barely a wink of sleep all night. And Maggie's cryptic statement, *You've been going there in your sleep,* had kept Camille on edge, too.

Camille feigned sleep until the rustling sounds of Maggie dressing had stopped. She opened her eyes a few moments after the cabin door clicked shut just to be sure Maggie hadn't faked leaving to catch Camille in the act. Seeing the cabin empty, Camille sighed and rolled onto her side, snuggling the burlap bag closer to her under the blanket. The stone's pulse vibrated through her, the warmth a balm against the sleepless night.

Maggie had told Camille to keep the stone with her at all times, and Camille mostly followed that advice. Having the stone with her felt right, as if she were its protector of sorts. But if the captain or crew saw her toting around a burlap bag everywhere she went, they were bound to become curious about the objects inside. So Camille hid the stone the best she could whenever she wasn't with it, beneath the hay mattress, or in a notch in the timbers above her bunk where a lantern usually sat. She'd take it with her today, though, when she and Randall started their task of decoding the hieroglyphs.

She forced herself out of bed and away from the stone's persuasive warmth. Almost instantly, Camille felt weighted down by the burden of the hieroglyphs. She dressed, splashed her face with cool water from the basin, twisted her hair into a haphazard bun, and opened the door to the corridor.

Camille startled backward. First Mate Hardy had been walking past her cabin and had stopped in his tracks to face her. His leering grin revealed yellow teeth and wind-chapped lips. His bushy eyebrows hung like awnings over his deeply set eyes. She pursed her lips, noticing Hardy had blocked her way out of the cabin.

"Just roll out of bed, did we?" His gravelly voice grated her ears.

"Bad night's sleep. Excuse me." She tried to push past him and into the corridor. He slid to the side to prevent her.

"Aye, I've been having those, too. Bad dreams. Can't get rid of 'em," Hardy said. "They're about this prissy chit who's keeping secrets from the captain. And she's ignorant enough to think no one suspects nothing."

Hardy leered closer. Camille retreated back inside the cabin, but not before something potent on the first mate wafted up her nostrils. Not sweat or anything unclean. Something she'd smelled a lot of lately. Myrrh. He positively reeked of myrrh.

She looked over his clothing and his calloused hands, and tried to inspect his face, but it was hard to maintain eye contact with him. Maggie had been right: This man was repulsive. Camille swung the door to close it, but Hardy grabbed the edge and pushed himself inside.

Camille finally found her voice. "Get out of my cabin."

"It was *my* cabin, just so you know," he growled. "Hope my bunk's keepin' you warm at night."

Starbuck's first mate needed to be beaten back into line.

"Let me pass," she ordered. Hardy's coarse chuckle told Camille he wasn't about to do any such thing.

"First you're going to tell me —" Hardy's demand was cut short by a barking voice in the corridor.

"What is going on?" Randall entered the cabin. "What are you doing inside Miss Rowen's cabin?"

Hardy changed tack and started to answer that he thought he'd left something behind in his cabin.

"He's lying. He forced his way in here," Camille said.

Hardy's nostrils flared, his dark eyes thin slits as he glowered at her.

"Mr. Hardy, I respect your position on this ship." Randall advanced on the first mate and drove him back into the corridor. "But if you set foot in this cabin again, I'll be forced to forget your ranking. Am I clear?"

Hardy seethed in silence but didn't cause any more of a scene. He moved on toward the fo'c'sle, and Camille released her pent-up breath.

"Are you all right?" Randall took her cheek into his warm hand. Lost for words, Camille nodded.

"I need to speak to the captain about this," he said, and darted into the corridor. Camille kept his pace, staring up at him as they headed toward the galley.

"What is it?" Randall asked. Camille smiled.

"You're intimidating." She'd never known it. And brave, too. Hardy could have squashed Randall flat with one solid punch.

"Of course I am. How do you think I've helped grow your father's business so quickly?"

The mention of her father and the company wiped her smile clean. Randall seemed to realize the blunder and changed the subject.

"I don't like Hardy," Randall said, his voice lower. "There's something wrong about him. The whole sail across the Pacific, I kept expecting to wake up in the middle of the night with him standing above me with a knife to my throat."

They crossed the rest of the galley. Straight ahead was the dark, wood-paneled door, stamped in the upper center with a bloodred circle of stained glass. She'd only been inside the captain's cabin once, having had no excuse the second time Starbuck had asked her to breakfast and take tea with him.

Randall, still fuming, only paused to knock once before twisting the ivory knob and sweeping inside.

Camille came in behind him and met with an empty cabin, save for her brother riffling through the four-leveled bookcase. Samuel staggered back from the shelves.

"What are you doing?" Camille asked. He looked like he'd been searching for something, which only piqued her curiosity.

Samuel shoved the book he was holding back into its proper place. "It's no concern of yours."

"Don't worry, I'm not going to tell the captain you're in here." Camille closed the door quietly behind Randall.

Starbuck must have been on deck. Samuel lifted his coat from a velvet balloon-back chair.

"Are you implying that I've broken into his cabin? He knows I'm here."

But Samuel had looked much too stunned when she'd come in to have been in Starbuck's cabin by invitation.

"You don't need to lie to me," Camille said.

Samuel threw his coat on with as much force as the winds pushing the *Eclipse* west. "I don't need to tell you everything either."

Quiet rage rounded his eyes into glistening pools. He rushed from the room, slamming the door behind him.

"He seems a bit . . . on edge," Randall commented softly as he crossed to the bookshelves. He craned his head to read the titles embossed on the spines. "Samuel could have been telling the truth, you know. He and the captain do seem to get on well."

Camille stared after her brother, her eyes on the stained-glass circle of the door. Randall was right. She shouldn't have assumed he'd been lying to her.

Randall ran his fingers along the books.

"What are you looking for?" she asked.

"A good book. Seafaring is starting to get dull, if you ask me."

Camille ran her fingers through the tasseled fringe of a sea tapestry. "I happen to love it."

He glanced up at her and smiled. "I know you do." Randall's fingers stopped on a green leather-bound book. "Look at this."

He forced it from its spot, wedged between two thick texts. He held it outward, gold letters stamped deep into the cover. Above and below the title were the same kinds of symbols emblazoned on the map.

"I think our captain must have a similar interest." Randall read the title aloud: *"The Use and Meaning of Ancient Letters."*

Camille took the book from his hand and opened it. Inside, a number of pages, covered with both hieroglyphs and English text, had been dog-eared. Passages had been underlined, notes scratched into the side margins in different colored inks.

"This seems like too much of a coincidence," she said. It looked as though Starbuck had been studying this book for some time.

"But it could be." Randall gestured to the books stuffed throughout each nook and cranny of the cabin. "He seems well read."

A captain of leisure would most definitely have the time for it. Voices built and ebbed in the galley. If the captain found them snooping in his cabin, Randall's complaint about Hardy would hold little merit.

"Let's go," she said, putting the book under her arm. "You can talk to the captain about Hardy later."

They made their way back to Randall's cabin, stopping briefly in hers to fetch the map.

"Now what?" Randall asked once they were at his desk. He unfurled the map for them, again lifting it to his nose. Camille smiled and took the map from his hands.

At once, the wave of amber light rolled across the upper right hand quadrant. The symbols seared into the leather and gave off sparks and smoke.

"You don't see those, do you?" she asked, pointing to the glowing symbols. His arched eyebrows questioned her sanity. "That's what I thought. I'll draw the symbols so you can see them, too. And you" — she handed him the heavy tome — "get to read."

Randall took a deep breath and sat heavily on his bunk. Camille uncorked the bottle of ink.

"If this doesn't work, at least we'll be able to have stimulating conversations about the use and meaning of ancient letters," he said, propping a pillow against the headboard.

Camille dipped the pen nib into the indigo ink. "Oh yes. Stimulating."

She caught his grin out of the corner of her eye. She stifled her laugh before letting loose completely.

It was the first time her cheeks had ached from smiling for as long as she could remember.

Camille worked to copy the hieroglyphs all afternoon, drawing on the parchment Randall had brought with him for correspondence with San Francisco. She'd crumpled up piece after piece, either not satisfied with her copy or because she'd made a mistake. The hieroglyphs, unchanging each time she opened the map, only remained burned into the leather for a minute, at the most, before dissolving. Camille had to close and reopen the map to be able to view them and check her progress. It was tiresome to say the least.

Besides, art was not her best talent.

Back home, girls were schooled in all sorts of subjects, like music and art, neither of which had ever held Camille's interest. If it hadn't been for her father's indifference over whether she learned in school or aboard his ship, she might have been subjected to such proper learning. She'd never wanted for it in any subject — until right then.

Before leaving for supper, Camille had completed four measly symbols: a feather, a seated figure, a dingo head on a stick, and some strange object she couldn't even recognize. By the time she settled down in her bunk that night, her eyes burned from the flashes of amber light she'd subjected herself to.

"Where were you all day?" Maggie spoke around a few pins clenched tightly between her teeth. She sat on her bunk in her ivory chemise and lacy petticoat, mending a torn ruffle of her dress hem.

"With Randall." Camille closed her eyes and stretched her fingers one by one.

"He seems very taken with you."

Camille opened an eye and peered at Maggie. Her comment reeked of false sincerity. "I should hope so. He proposed to me."

"That doesn't mean a thing. You weren't taken with him when you accepted his proposal," Maggie replied.

Camille sat up onto her elbows. "How would you know who I was and wasn't taken with before this Umandu affair happened?"

Maggie took the pins from between her lips and smiled condescendingly at her. "It's a little obvious."

Camille couldn't be that transparent. Randall wouldn't be bothering with her if she exuded love for Oscar.

She lay back down and wrapped herself up in her cloak, uncertain. If she hadn't been taken with Randall in the beginning, perhaps he hadn't been taken with her, either. What if Randall only proposed because of his ties to her father, and the business? It had worried her before, while she'd been in San Francisco. Now the idea of it did more than just worry her. It hurt.

"A lot of things have been changing since I found the stone," Camille whispered. Maggie stuffed the pins into a silky pincushion, and then primped the mended pale green skirt ruffle.

"I know you don't want to go after this second stone," Maggie said. "You thought everything was over. You thought you had Oscar back for good."

Camille blushed into her pillow. She hated that this girl knew something so deep and private about her.

"How do you know about the stone and what I need to do?" Camille asked.

"I told you. It's my destiny to help you. It's what I've been learning since I was old enough to understand my father's lessons. We were both Firstborns, and the Firstborns are always the guides."

"So, is that it? You help me find the stone, Oscar gets his soul back, and we finally get to go home?" Camille asked.

Maggie let out a heavy, long-winded sigh, fraught with disappointment. Camille wanted to chuck a pillow at her.

"Did you really believe one resurrection was all the stone had to offer? That it would cease being as coveted as it has always been by people who want control of their fate? Even you, Camille. You weren't willing to accept the fate of your father. Or Oscar. Did you think you could walk away from such a gift without having to pay for it?"

Yes, Camille thought. Yes, she did, and now she felt unbearably stupid.

"What are you?" Camille asked, tired of not having an answer to that.

Maggie slipped out of her petticoat so that all she wore was her long chemise and ankle-length pantalettes. She drew her knees up toward her chest and wrapped her arms around them. Her slim frame, pale skin, and flaxen hair made her look fragile and innocent. Camille already knew looks were too often deceiving.

"You can't understand what I am until you know more about the immortals," she replied.

"Well, then, why don't you enlighten me?" Camille said, exhausted by this high-horse routine of hers.

Maggie set her mended skirt to the side and settled back in her bunk. "For some reason, I don't think you'll be shocked to hear the whole mess started as a love story."

Camille ground her teeth in annoyance, but made no comment.

"It started when an Egyptian goddess of rebirth, Uma, and the gatekeeper to the Underworld, Domorius, fell in love. But Domorius was fickle and soon dismissed Uma, telling her he could only truly respect someone whose power mirrored his own. So to avenge herself, she stole the two stones of the Underworld. The stones were the symbols of Domorius's power over the living and the dead, and Uma fled with them to the icy northern tundra to build her kingdom. To prove to him that he'd misjudged her and made a mistake."

The barren, ice-crusted land of her dreams came to Camille's mind: the angry, whitecapped ocean in the distance, studded with glaciers; the frozen cliffs streaked with the colors of the aurora borealis; the swift-moving, four-legged animal.

"You know about my dreams, don't you?"

Maggie smoothed and folded her mended dress, and brought it to the bureau. "Even if I did, I can't help you there."

"I thought you were supposed to be my guide," Camille said. Maggie turned from the bureau and faced her, eyes bright.

"I'm your guide here, in this world," she said. "Not there. I'm sorry."

Camille frowned at the way Maggie had said "this world." As if Camille had been visiting another one altogether in her dreams.

"You haven't explained what you are yet," Camille reminded.

Maggie held up a thin, perfectly manicured finger to put Camille's impatience on hold.

"Joined, the stones not only gave Uma the power to grant others immortality, but the ability to resurrect the dead," she said, continuing on with her story. "Domorius didn't like that Uma could reach inside his realm and remove souls at her whim, that someone else's powers matched his. Besides, mortal men, born with a preordained amount of years to live, were choosing to become immortal, and therefore cheating Domorius of his duties: to escort the dead to the Underworld and to their new level of existence. The only way to overcome the immortals would be to rid them of the magic sustaining them. And so Domorius sent his Couriers to retrieve the two stones and put an end to Uma's kingdom."

The mere mention of the Couriers brought the hairs on Camille's arms on end. Domorius's army. Walking corpses. She rubbed her arms, trying not to look too rapt by Maggie's story.

"Knowing her immortals would soon fall, and that she would face Domorius's punishment, Uma took the stone of life and wrapped it in leather. With a single touch, she enchanted the leather into a map that would allow the one person seeking it — the one who, like Uma, had equal measures of passion, love, uncertainty, and vengeance in their heart — to find the stone. Uma gave the map and stone to one of her people and sent that person away before the Couriers could arrive."

"Uma," Camille whispered.

Maggie nodded. "Umandu."

"And the immortal she sent away with the stone and map?"

"My ancestor," Maggie answered. "The legend says my ancestor hid the stone and left the map with a stranger so it could begin its journey out into the world. Though before parting with the map, she took with her a helping of the enchantment and passed it along to her firstborn mortal. Who then passed it on to the next firstborn, and so on."

Until one generation the enchantment passed into Maggie Starbuck.

"Satisfied?" she asked Camille.

"I don't think 'satisfied' could be used to describe anything regarding this situation," she answered. "What about the Death Stone? Why didn't Uma send that one away to be hid as well?"

Maggie's expression slackened, as if she'd never considered that question before. "I don't know. Perhaps Uma cared more for the stone of life. She did, after all, focus on giving life, not death."

Camille wasn't sure what to believe. It sounded like a fantastical tale, not reality. Though the lines between what

Camille knew to be real and what she never imagined possible had been blurring.

Maggie extinguished her lamp and nestled under her covers. Less than a minute later, Camille heard dainty snores. That was quick. Sleep was probably easy for people who didn't need to fear it.

ELEVEN

The next week, Camille continued to sleep in her cloak and boots, though each night she considered not putting them on. To be so eccentric and anxious bothered her to no end. But unlike normal dreams that quickly faded from memory, this one kept its grasp. She couldn't forget the frigid wind or the pain of her bare feet on the ice.

She couldn't deny that it was more than just a dream.

The bell on deck signaled the change in watch. Camille listened from her bunk in her dark cabin as feet paraded past her cabin. The men let loose a host of bodily functions as they passed, too. None of them were Oscar, though. She'd calculated that his watch was at sunrise and again at evening. After breakfast and before dinner each day, Camille took a walk on deck, the fresh air revitalizing after being cooped up below. And though she always caught Oscar's attention, he would then proceed to ignore her.

She missed Oscar's voice. She missed being able to tell him things, like the so-real-she-might-develop-frostbite dreams. She wanted a "good morning" or "good night" from him, even if he didn't smile when he said it. It might have been his soul that was lost, but it had started to feel as if Oscar was disappearing altogether. It scared her more than anything else.

The change in watch finally came to an end, and after all the men had shuffled past, Camille sat up in her bunk. She wondered how long she'd been lying there awake. An hour? Maybe two. She kept thinking over the hieroglyphs she and Randall had been trying to decode, and how they were getting nowhere with them. Hardy bothered her as well. He hadn't tried to speak to her since the debacle in her cabin, but she still wondered why he'd hinted to her secrets and why he'd smelled of myrrh.

Maggie snored softly, every now and again snorting as she turned onto her side. She taunted Camille even when unconscious.

The last handful of nights, Camille had toyed with the idea of sneaking down into the hold, curious about what kind of goods the captain had transported to Auckland. Randall had told her a few crates had been drawn from the hold, but he hadn't known what was inside them. Camille swung her legs over the edge of the bunk and slipped the burlap bag from underneath her pillow. She shrugged on the shoulder straps, the stone inside resting against the center of her back. It pulsed its usual welcoming and soothed her nerves. Camille took up the unlit lantern and a box of phosphorous matches. There was no need for them as she walked the corridor to the ladder leading into the belly of the ship, but she'd need the light in the hold.

Camille opened the door a few inches and slipped out. She slowly shut it, the creak of the hinges piercing in the night. She turned and stepped forward. Her nose smacked into something hard and Camille leaped back. The stone against her back hiked in heat and pulse, and the white beams, dormant for so long, cut through the woven bag and lit her from behind.

She gasped loudly. "What are you doing?"

A corridor lamp flickered, lighting one side of Oscar's face.

"What arc *you* doing?" he replied.

Camille's heartbeat chugged back to normal. Umandu continued to throb.

"I'm —" She stopped and looked around, not wanting any of the crew to hear her answer. The corridor was empty.

"Oh. Never mind." Oscar nodded toward the shining burlap bag. "You take that with you to the head, too?"

Camille wished the stone would dim. If any of the crew were to see it, she wouldn't know how to explain.

"I'm not visiting the head. I'm going to the hold." Camille walked past Oscar, but then hesitated. She turned back to him, hoping she had the courage to ask. "Will you come with me?"

To her surprise, he started to follow. "What do you expect to find? The hold's empty."

The ladder that led into the cavity of the ship was cold and damp. The deeper the ship's levels, the more moisture in the wood. The odor of a hold was usually a mix of nose-tickling mildew, stale runoff water in the bilge, and whatever the ship transported. For her father that would have been wood, freshly sawed and stacked, still green and tacky. It could have also meant the sweet ripeness of Mission grapes, still clustered on vines and packed in sawdust.

Camille stepped off the ladder into the pitch-black hold. The inviting scent of scrubbed wood and salt held an undertone of manure and hay. The stone inside the bag gave off light, but more would be needed. She opened the lantern door while Oscar took the tinderbox and lit the wick. The glow brightened a small circle of space around them. Camille could hear the cluck of chickens and laying hens. The heavy breathing of pigs came from the far right, where the animals were most likely encaged and stamped with numbers, counting down to their slaughter.

"Have you learned anything about the *Eclipse*?" Camille asked as she hurried over the bilge-planks to the other end of the hold. The lamp dashed light over tall crates and barrels.

"Like?" he asked.

"Like what port it hails from, what the crew thinks of taking a bunch of strays to a far-off land, if each mate needs to be roughly the size of an ox to be taken on?"

The lamp flashed over the transom timbers of the stern, but she saw nothing pointing to any specific load of goods.

"An ox?" Oscar asked, humor in his voice.

"You can't tell me you haven't noticed the bulk of his crew."

"I've noticed," he answered. "But it's not just their size. There's something off about them. They look like a bunch of old salts, they know the ship, and their duties, but . . . I don't know. It's almost as if they're still green somehow."

Oscar had been around sailors since he'd been a boy, and was an old salt himself, despite his age. An experienced sailor could easily tell when another sailor hadn't been long at sea. If Oscar sensed something was off about the crew, he was definitely right.

"And Starbuck?" she asked. He shook his head, his lips drawn into a frown.

"He's got money. Old money, the others have said. Plenty to waste on this ship, I suppose."

The floorboards of the deck above them creaked with the weight of feet. She and Oscar hushed and waited for the creaking to pass. Once it did, Oscar leaned to the side to see the burlap sack.

"You don't trust your bunkmate enough to leave that behind?"

Camille had forgotten the warmth of the stone against her.

"I feel better with it close," she answered. It was true, too. Having it with her felt natural. "I'm starting to wonder if Maggie isn't the only Starbuck who knows about the stone. Randall and I found a book of hieroglyphs in the captain's cabin, and its condition makes me think he's been studying it for ages." She saw Oscar pause with the mention of Randall.

"Randall's helping me decipher the map," she explained, struck with guilt when there was no reason for it.

"I don't think you should be sneaking around the ship like that," Oscar said, stepping up on a barrel to slide back the top of a large crate.

"Isn't that what we're doing right now?" she asked.

He took a look inside. "Yeah, but this time is different."

Camille gave him the lamp, and he lowered it inside the crate. "And how is that?"

"Because this time, you're sneaking around with me." He brought the lantern out of the crate and hopped down. "It's empty."

She reached for the lantern. "Oh, and sneaking around with you is so much safer, is it?"

Oscar held on to the lantern's handle. The stone's pulse picked up more speed and increased in brightness. Why did it always do that?

"There are only two people aboard this ship I trust."

"Randall isn't going to harm me," she said.

He tugged on the lantern handle, pulling Camille closer to him. "But is he going to protect you?"

Umandu crossed over from hot to burning. Camille let go of the lantern and stepped away. The stone's energy plummeted. She couldn't think of how to respond to Oscar. The stone's baffling autonomy stole away her attention.

The ceiling creaked again, this time with more than one pair of feet. The ladder to the hold rattled. Oscar quickly snuffed out the wick. He grabbed Camille's hand and hauled her with him up and into the crate. Her boots scuffed the bare base of the container as he slid the top into place. The pigs and chickens snorted and clucked loud enough to muffle any noise the two of them made.

The other end of the hold brightened with a pair of lanterns. Pressing her eye up to a slit in the wood slats, Camille saw the rugged, yet graceful, figure of Lionel Starbuck, and — she pinched her brows together — Samuel.

"I don't know if any of this makes sense," Starbuck said, his tone strangely soft as he led her brother into the opposite side of the hold, out of Camille's limited view. She could hardly hear what they were saying.

"I've noticed, too . . ." She picked up on her brother's response.

"Don't try to . . ." But Starbuck's words were lost as the caged animals broke out in another ruckus. What were they doing down there?

Oscar had managed to silence his breathing. Without the light, the warmth of his body near her, or even the sounds of his breath, Camille started to doubt his very presence. She'd witnessed Ira dissolve into thin air with one of the Couriers, and a creeping fear forced her to reach her fingers out beside her. Each millimeter her arm stretched without contact, her eyes grew wider, her panic spiking. But then her fingers brushed against cloth and flesh. Oscar's hand grasped hers.

She was so relieved, she didn't care that the stone burst to life again, lighting up the space inside the crate. Oscar stripped the shoulder straps from Camille's arms and gently rolled the burlap bag into the far corner of the crate. The light extinguished, but he kept his hands on her arms. He drew her closer, his fingers slipping to her hips.

He raked his hands up her back and even though they were cold compared to the stone, they spellbound her. Sparks kindled in her stomach, between her hips, and then, without warning, her mouth was on fire with his. He crushed her against his chest, his hold urgent, his fingers lost in her hair. Oscar pushed hard against her mouth, but his lips were no longer moving with hers. His soft kiss had turned into something else. It was angry and rigid. Forced. Camille tried to back away, but his grasp wouldn't allow it.

"That is a last resort, of course."

Starbuck's voice pierced their kiss, and Oscar at last peeled his lips from hers. Camille opened her eyes and saw the yellow glow of the captain's lamp filter inside the container. Patterns of light rippled over Oscar's face, his eyes sharp and bright as he leveled her with a disappointed stare. Camille couldn't remember how to breathe. She met his frustrated gaze and felt something inside her break off and shatter.

"I hope it doesn't come to that," Samuel said as the ladder rattled under their feet once more. Step by step, the lantern glow disappeared, leaving Camille and Oscar alone in the dark.

She pushed against Oscar's clamped embrace and freed herself, her blood hot and swollen in her veins.

"What game are you playing?" she whispered.

He made a breathy sound with his throat and, after a momentary pause, slid the top off the container. "You think I'm playing a game?"

He shoved the top harder than necessary. Camille cringed, certain Starbuck and Samuel had heard it.

"You can't tell me to marry Randall and then kiss me."

Camille picked up the burlap bag and slipped on the straps. The pulse of the stone encouraged her to stay angry. She gripped the lip of the crate and struggled to pull herself up. Oscar took her hips in his hands to help her, but she shook them off and heaved herself up and down onto the other side.

"It was pretty clear you didn't want to kiss me," she said, trying to forget his dissatisfied expression. "Do you think I couldn't tell you were forcing your way through it?"

He swung over the side and landed, bowing the planks under the tips of her toes.

"You don't understand —"

"You're right, I *don't* understand!" she said in a whispered shout. "I can't figure out what I did to make you feel this way. Tell me it's not just about my father's money." *Or lack thereof,* she added to herself.

The stone's light lit up a brief, derisive grin on Oscar's lips. "It's not about money. It never was."

The confession should have relieved her more than it did. "Then tell me why," she whispered.

He shook his head, his lips a straight line once more. "I can't."

She backed away from him, furious. "I don't want you to kiss me again."

Camille rushed toward the ladder steps, knowing it was a lie, and instantly regretting it.

TWELVE

Camille watched the storm blow in from her cabin's porthole. She leaned her head against the cold circle of thick glass as the clock on the bureau ticked softly toward the end of Oscar's watch. For several days she'd waited in her cabin for her breath of fresh air until she knew for certain he would not be on deck. Her stroll now had less of a view of the ocean, what with the darkening clouds and sun having set, but it was a price she was willing to pay to avoid him.

Camille checked the clock. Three minutes until the bells. She turned back to the charcoal clouds and the white-capped waves. She'd spent the day in Randall's room copying hieroglyphs and with much better success. The lines of the falcon's beak had turned out shaky, but passable. Each time she looked to see where Randall was in the pages of his research, he'd been watching her instead. He'd made no attempt to mask it, either.

If Randall knew what had happened between her and Oscar in the hold, he'd be livid. He'd be hurt, too, and she couldn't bear the idea of wounding him. These last few days Randall had revealed himself to her in ways he'd never managed back home. He knew to offer her something to drink before she even mentioned that she was thirsty; he knew when to suggest a break, or when to leave and take one without her. He knew not to bring up anything having to do with Samuel, who now seemed to be avoiding Camille.

The bell clanged eight times up on deck, signaling the new watch. Camille waited through the hubbub of the changing watch, and then threw on her cloak. On deck, she met with a wet wind. The clouds were solid and gray, and frothy white waves spilled over the rail and crashed on deck. She didn't feel like getting soaked, so she knew it would be a brief breath of fresh air.

She turned to walk starboard when cries of alarm drew Camille's eyes upward. About fifty feet in the air, sailors rode the swells of the sea while balancing precariously on ladderlike ratlines, and the horizontal yards from which the sails hung low and full. A rigging line slipped through one of the pulleys and past a sailor's grasping hand. The stray rope fell toward deck, caught on the wind. The rope whipped at her, thrashing close enough to leave a taste of its sting against her cheek.

"Ho there!" Captain Starbuck's deep voice shouted from behind her. The line quivered and lashed out again, blown by the strong headwind. Camille threw up her arm to fend off the renegade rope. With a burning, almost unintelligible pain, the rough hemp coiled around her forearm and tugged her forward, off her feet.

Starbuck broadsided her and grabbed hold of the line. The wind sawed at them both as he struggled to unravel the rope cutting into her arm up to the elbow. His coat sleeves slid back and exposed his wrists. Deep green ink colored the underside of his left wrist — a tattoo. Her mind flashed to Hardy and his skin drawings, and then, in the ages it seemed for him to free her from the line, Camille registered Starbuck's tattoo.

It was of two triangles, one turned on its base, and the other flipped onto its pointed crest. The underside of the enchanted map had the same symbol.

The rope released her and Camille fell back, her arm stinging beneath her sleeve. Starbuck ordered his sailors to heave up the line before turning back to her. "That could have been costly. You aren't injured, I hope?"

Camille shook her head, her attention still stuck on his exposed wrist. He followed her eyes, and pulled down the sleeve of his coat. He kept his head lowered, his wide-brimmed tarpaulin hat shielding his copper blond eyebrows. Starbuck slowly lifted his pale brown eyes to her.

"You recognize my marking." His stare was as abrasive as the wild rope had been. "Tell me, have you and Randall deciphered any of the hieroglyphs yet?"

He knew they'd taken his book. Of course he knew. *Samuel.* He'd betrayed her yet again. But this . . . Starbuck had the mark of Umandu permanently inked on his skin! The clouds darkened and the sails drew fuller with the wind.

"What do you want with the stone?" she asked.

Starbuck lifted the corner of his lips, but the smile was patronizing. It was the way he looked at Maggie.

"Just because I am not a Firstborn doesn't mean I'm ignorant of the stones. My brother was a good teacher. He was more like a father to me. Those first ten years he taught me everything he knew about the legend, about our family's destiny — until Margaret was born." His lips pinched together with the memory.

"So you're jealous of your niece?" Camille asked, rubbing her arm. "You want to be the one to guide me to the second stone?"

He snorted a laugh. "*Guide* you? Hardly. I'm not restricted to the role of guardian like my brother was, like Margaret is. But I do know more about the stones than you ever will, so I've decided to do you a favor. I'm taking over for you."

Camille took a nervous glance around deck, at the sailors who were no doubt picking up on their conversation.

"Why would you want to do that?" she asked. She had set out to find Ira and bring him home, and to see Oscar's soul fully returned to him. Those things could be of no importance to Captain Starbuck.

"Let's face it, Camille. You're not equipped to handle the stones' powers. They're dark. They're dangerous. And you're just a girl who doesn't know what — or *who* — she wants."

It was difficult to rise above his haughty insult, but the allusion to the stones' powers intrigued her enough to stay focused.

"So instead of letting me do it, you want to take the stone and go into the Underworld?" Camille asked.

"Not at all. Only you can fetch the second stone." Starbuck stepped closer. "Once you have both stones, I'll relieve you of them."

The rain had drenched her cloak and hair. Her black locks clung to her cheeks in the gusty wind. The goddess Uma had used the stones' collective power to build her kingdom of immortals. That couldn't be what Starbuck wanted . . . could it?

"I *can't* give them to you. I need both of the stones to get Oscar's soul back."

Starbuck frowned and then gave a small shrug. "I don't care about Oscar's soul."

Camille recoiled from him. "I think I'm going to have to say no to your offer." She started for the companionway, appalled, but Starbuck grabbed hold of her bruised arm and tugged her back.

"It wasn't a proposition, Camille. Do you think I went to all this trouble to get you aboard my ship only to bid you farewell and a safe journey once we docked in Suez? I don't think so."

His remark sunk in like a pair of lead weights. Right then the handsome Captain Starbuck, so boyish and hospitable, appeared even more like a viper than Hardy — or Stuart McGreenery.

"You will give me the stones," Starbuck repeated. She tried to yank free, but he only put more pressure on her injured forearm.

"Why would I do that?" she asked.

"Because you are an obedient and considerate girl, who not only values her own well-being, but the lives of those she loves." His pupils enlarged as he spoke, soaking up each iris.

The back of her throat closed off. "You wouldn't dare."

"Your brother is very trusting. Like a puppy, rather, searching for approval. And your fiancé, he is on the hunt for something much along the same lines. But Kildare," Starbuck said. "Next to you, he might just be the most dangerous one of you all. I'm very happy he decided to join my crew, where my men can keep a close eye on him."

Camille ground her teeth so roughly she feared they might cave. "You won't touch them."

Captain Starbuck nodded, obviously pleased with her reaction. "You're right. I won't — as long as we have an accord. Forget Oscar's soul. Forget your friend Ira. They're both gone, and you'll soon see they should stay that way."

He knew about Ira. Only Samuel could have told Starbuck about him.

"Giving me the stones will be a painless transaction," Starbuck added. "Unless of course you break our accord. If you do that, there will be plenty of pain to go around."

Camille winced as he gave her arm one last squeeze and then shoved her away. She held her arm close to her chest, trembling. If she gave him the stones, what would he do with them? What kind of power would she be handing over to Lionel Starbuck? But to deny him now meant jeopardizing the others.

"Fine," she said. "Though it's not so much of an accord as it is coercion."

He stepped aside and gestured toward the companionway, all conviviality now returned. "See it any way you like. Enjoy your evening."

A last look around deck revealed each and every last sailor watching her, even while doing their duties. Oscar was the odd man out among Captain Starbuck's crew. The one they were all instructed to keep tabs on. And she now feared for him.

She swept down the corridor to Randall's cabin. As soon as he opened the door to her pounding knock, she hurried inside.

"Camille, what's wrong?"

She realized she was biting her cheek and stopped.

"I knew finding the book on hieroglyphs in Starbuck's cabin wasn't a coincidence. He wants the stones, both of them."

Randall shut the door behind her. "Wait, wait. How do you know this? He's been nothing but generous with us."

"That was how he wanted it to look. He used you as an excuse to find me. And if I don't give him what he wants, he says he'll harm you and Samuel . . . and Oscar." She said the last name fast and soft. Randall squared his shoulders and stalked to the door.

"I need to speak to our captain."

Camille stepped in front of him. "No, that wouldn't help." She wasn't sure what exactly *would* help. Randall grasped her arm.

"I won't allow him to threaten you." The injury from the renegade rope burned. Camille flinched.

"He didn't harm you, did he?" Randall pushed up her sleeve. The skin was chafed and red, with bruises already forming. He swore under his breath.

"No," she said. "It was a line that came loose from the rigging. It's nothing. What's important is that Starbuck designed this entire voyage, right from the start. Even before he arrived in San Francisco."

She watched Randall consider this a few moments, her exposed forearm still in his palm. He gently traced the swollen track of red lines with his fingers. Like before, her skin prickled and warmed where he touched her.

"But how would he have known to come find me? And to get the timing so perfectly." Randall shook his head. "It's impossible."

He pulled her dress sleeve back down to cover her arm, but continued to hold her hand in his.

"I think he's been using Maggie," Camille said. "She said that she knew when I had spoken the stone's name on board the *Christina*. It was some sort of magic; I don't understand it, but she knew where to find me. What if she told her uncle, and then he tried to leave her behind?"

Waves writhed outside, sloshing against his porthole as the winds produced an awful howl.

"I shouldn't have trusted him," Randall said, his head bowed. "I've put you in danger."

Camille lifted his chin with her fingers. "This isn't your fault. You had no way of knowing."

Randall forced a smile, but obviously wasn't pardoning himself.

"And you didn't hear me correctly," she added. "I'm not in any danger. Captain Starbuck only threatened you, Oscar, and Samuel. He needs me to get to the stone."

He laughed at that. "Oh, well, thank you, that makes me feel much better."

Camille started to laugh, too, but before she could, Randall's lips were on hers. He'd moved fast, not giving her the chance to back away. His lips were warm and had the thinnest trace of sea salt. The initial shock of his feverish kiss wore off and her eyes fluttered closed. An unexpected hunger built inside, rising from the bottom of her stomach, scorching her chest. Dangerously parallel to the yearning she felt when in Oscar's arms.

She pushed against Randall's chest and broke free. He took a breath and backed away.

"I took you by surprise," he said, but didn't tack on an apology. He wasn't sorry. She saw it in the way he bit back a sly grin. "Next time I won't sneak up on you like that."

Next time. He was planning on kissing her again?

A part of her wanted him to.

She didn't understand it. For the first time since she'd known him, she wanted him to kiss her again. But at the mere thought of Oscar, Randall's lips felt wrong and improper, even though he actually *was* her fiancé. What was wrong with her?

"You . . . you won't say anything to anger the captain?" she asked. The throbbing of her lips bothered her. They weren't supposed to be doing that.

"For the moment I'll stay silent," Randall answered, the dark, defending gleam returning to his eyes. "But we should think about how we're going to break away from the *Eclipse* when we come ashore in Egypt."

A catlike wind yowled through the masts and yards, snapping the canvas loud enough for them to hear below. Camille felt for the knob, her back still pressed against the door.

"I need to speak with Samuel," she said as she recalled his suspicious visit to the hold. Was Samuel being tricked into thinking he was the captain's new confidant? Or was he truly? Camille couldn't exactly discuss it with Randall. He'd want to know why she had been in the hold, and with whom.

"I'll tell him when he comes in for the night," Randall said. "Perhaps you should stay in your cabin more now. I'd feel better, at least."

He might, but Camille suffered a mild case of claustrophobia just thinking about it.

"Of course," she said anyway, and thought of the other person to whom she needed to speak.

Randall offered to walk her to her cabin, but she promised she'd be fine alone along the short length of corridor. She even went so far as to go inside her cabin — thankfully empty of Maggie — and shut the door behind her, in case he was listening. He did care, didn't he? She smiled as she counted to ten, opened the door, and scuttled toward the fo'c'sle.

As the bow of the ship narrowed, the timbers ate up the width of the corridor. The fo'c'sle shone with dim lamplight. Oscar's watch would be resting, their bellies full from dinner and bodies exhausted from preparing for the coming storm. Camille stepped lightly toward the open threshold. A woman entering the fo'c'sle was considered an indecent act, even among rogue men. And, of course, she didn't want to come across Hardy. Snoring emboldened her to step forward and peer inside.

Hammocks swayed from ceiling beams. Legs hung down from them, with trousers hiked to kneecaps. Bunks were stacked three high, with hardly enough space in between for a sailor to turn onto his side. None of them were Oscar, though. Careful not to set the planks creaking, Camille started back for her cabin.

A murmur of whispering distracted her as she passed the closed door to the canvas room, where spare canvas, rigging, random tools, and equipment were all stored. Pushing her daring to the limit, she pressed her ear to the door. It opened an inch. A lamp lit the corner of the room. She closed one eye for better vision in the other, and focused.

Maggie stood inside the room, her dress as luminescent as the wings of a lunar moth. In her small, cupped hands was the hand of another whom Camille could not see. With her lithe fingers, Maggie caressed the palm of the hand she held, her eyes fluttering closed. Camille had done the same thing a few minutes earlier, enraptured in Randall's kiss. She felt like an intruder, witnessing a private moment between Maggie and . . . who? Could it be Samuel? Perhaps she was the reason her brother had been so chummy with Captain Starbuck.

"I won't tell her," Maggie whispered. "But if you decide you want to —"

"I don't," the second person interrupted. The voice spiraled through Camille's ears. That was most definitely *not* her brother.

Camille shoved the door aside and barged in. Maggie dropped Oscar's hand. They both looked at Camille in horror, Oscar rubbing his palm on the side of his trousers.

"What are you two doing in here?" Camille asked.

Together, she added to herself. *Alone!*

They both stumbled for an answer, but Maggie was faster to piece something together.

"Oscar came searching for you," she said.

"I heard a stray line tangled around your arm on deck," he said, catching up. "Are you all right?"

"Do you really think I'm gullible enough to believe you two have been in here discussing that?" Camille peered around the room. Nothing but shelving and boxes and smaller crates. A fine place to meet secretly, just as the pantry had been on the *Lady Kate*. Her throat clenched tight.

Oscar and Maggie glanced meaningfully at each other.

Camille couldn't believe it. They weren't even trying to play innocent.

"I came looking for you, Oscar, to tell you not to trust anyone on the crew. I came looking for you because I was worried," Camille said, certain she was waking the slumbering sailors nearby. She didn't care.

Oscar took a step forward, but Camille backed away. With daggered eyes, she looked at Maggie.

"You were right, Maggie. I can't trust your uncle. And I can't trust you." She then pointed her blistering gaze at Oscar. "Or you for that matter."

Camille slammed the door behind her as she left. She made it down the corridor and inside her cabin just as Randall's door opened.

She pounded her fists into her thighs. Damn Maggie! Camille should have known this would happen. The way Maggie had looked at Oscar, and the way he'd looked at her . . . The girl was human, after all, and Oscar was handsome, and Maggie was beautiful, and he'd kissed Camille in the hold and hated it. She didn't want to be on the *Eclipse*, didn't want to have to see Oscar holding the hand of another girl.

For a moment, Camille considered taking the map and stone and tossing them both at the feet of their captain. *Take them*, she'd tell him. *I don't care anymore.* But Starbuck wouldn't have taken them. He couldn't do anything with them, without her. She was stuck.

Trapped.

THIRTEEN

The ice cliffs were closer this time, the hues of purple, blue, and green striking in their depth and vividness. Camille stood on the ice, thankful she hadn't forgone her boots and cloak even after nearly two weeks without one of the ice dreams. The wind gathered speed over the flat terrain and seared her exposed skin, her eyes tearing. Again, the land was barren and white, and again, she felt the reality of this place as equally as she did the decks of the *Eclipse*.

Ribbons of twilight hung in the sky, and the lonely whistle of wind crept in under her cloak's hood. The air was thin and Camille's head swooned as she breathed it. Altitude? Her dream had altitude. She thought of the ice tundra Maggie had told her about: Uma's land of immortals. Could this place have something to do with it?

A sliver of white caught Camille's attention near the frozen cliffs. A four-legged creature was at the foot of the cliffs, standing out against the mantles of dusky color. The distance between the animal and Camille allowed only the black definition of eyes and nose, and tufts of silver, pointed ears. A wolf.

The animal watched her, its body as frozen as the ice cap beneath them. Camille held her breath. The predator was a mere two-hundred-yard sprint away, and could spring at any moment. Even at a distance, the wolf was enormous, its paws bulbous.

This is a dream, just a dream. The wolf took a step forward and sent Camille's heart and lungs up into the base of her throat. *A dream. A dream.* The wolf's front paw lifted and scratched at the ice. *Wake up!*

The wolf streaked forward, its teeth bared and ears flattened to its skull. Shocked into motion, Camille stumbled backward. Behind her the land held no respite, no shelter. No escape. She heard the sound of the wolf's rough grunting as she ran — truly ran with her heart thumping, breathing choppy, unlike running in other, lesser dreams. Stealing a look behind her, Camille saw the wolf close in, strings of saliva whipping off its incisors. Her boots slipped on the ice and she floundered forward, onto her side. Camille cracked her elbow on the hard surface. She rolled over, throwing her arms over her face and neck to protect herself from the wolf.

The bright white glare of snow flashed over to darkness, and a hay pallet cradled her backside instead of sheer ice. Camille bolted up in her bunk, heaving for breath. As always, it puffed and clouded in front of her face.

"Nightmare?" Maggie casually asked from across the cabin.

"A wolf," Camille answered, still gasping for air.

Maggie's blankets rustled as she shoved them aside and sprang up.

"What did you say?"

Camille pulled the blankets up around her and wiggled her stiff toes inside her boots.

"A wolf was chasing me. This huge, white wolf," she explained before she remembered she wasn't, in fact, on speaking terms with Maggie. "Never mind. It was just a dream," Camille lied.

"Are you certain about that?"

Camille squeezed her eyes shut and wished she could do the same with her ears to block Maggie out altogether.

She turned onto her side. Her elbow smarted with pain. With her cold fingers, Camille prodded the sharp joint. The skin was tender and likely bruised. She'd fallen in her dream, and had taken her injuries into reality.

For several days, Camille barely ate or slept. A persistent, gnawing ache lived in her. Every time she pictured Maggie's eyelids fluttering shut, Oscar's hand in hers, Camille's stomach twisted. And not only that, but her elbow was still healing from the dream-inflicted bruise. There was no mistaking the yellow and purple discoloration as a hallucination. Camille didn't even want to think of what would have happened had the wolf reached her. Each night she fought sleep, terrified she'd be taken back to the tundra.

All Camille could manage was to move from her cabin in the morning after waking, to Randall's cabin to work on the map, and then up on deck for a constitutional stroll well after Oscar's watch had gone below. Learning hieroglyphs was a tedious and grueling task. So far they'd only deciphered a handful of words, including *gates*, *row*, *snakes*, and *power*. They'd also learned that connecting words like *and*, *the*, and *of* were hardly used in the Egyptian language. Putting the words together to form their correct meaning might be more like a guessing game. But Camille welcomed the work. The only place she didn't have to think about Oscar or Maggie, or suffer the biting sourness she'd come to realize as jealousy, was inside Randall's cabin.

She propped her chin in her palm and worked on another hieroglyph. Some were simple: squiggly lines stacked three high or a sharply drawn, horizontal oval. Others, like this eye-shaped symbol with a sickle-like blade atop of it, were complicated.

"This is torture," Randall muttered from the bunk. He pushed himself up from the pillow on which he'd been reclining, and closed the thick tome in his lap. "Let's take a break and talk more about how we're going to escape Captain Starbuck once we dock in Suez. Did you talk to Maggie about our idea?"

Camille dropped her pen and stretched her neck, avoiding Randall's eyes. "Not yet. I wanted to wait until we had a solid plan."

That was partly true, at least. She and Randall had been trying to formulate how all five of them — Camille, Randall, Oscar, Samuel, and Maggie — could get away without Starbuck or his crew catching them. There was no possible way Camille was going to hand over the stones, sacrificing her chance to set things right. Oscar's soul *would* be returned to him, and Camille *would* find Ira and bring him home. Starbuck wasn't going to stop her.

"I think it's a good plan so far," Randall said. "A diversion will draw the crew's attention away from you long enough to disappear into the port city."

Camille shook her head, tired of arguing with him. "No. You might be able to divert the crew's attention by picking a fight with Hardy, but you'll also get locked up. I'm not leaving you behind."

Randall started to object, but just then a cry rained down through the decks. "Sail ho!"

Camille and Randall froze, staring at each other as if they might have both heard incorrectly. But then it came again, this time from the fo'c'sle.

"Sail ho!"

A barrage of feet filled the corridor, and when Randall opened the door, Camille saw the men off watch rushing up on deck. She threw the burlap bag onto her back, and she and Randall joined them, eager to see what ship the sailor in the crow's nest had spotted. A handful of other vessels had been seen in the last weeks through the captain's glass, though none growing larger than a speck of white on the horizon.

Like any other captain, Starbuck wasn't going to miss an opportunity to greet another ship and exchange whatever news each brought from their corner of the world. Camille saw the grand billowing sails of the three-masted brig as soon as she came on deck. She peered at the oncoming ship. The brig struck her as familiar and her mind raced to figure why. On the quarterdeck, Captain Starbuck lowered his glass and announced the passing ship's inscribed name.

"The *Stealth*. Bare poles! Send up the signal to hail-to!"

Camille parted her lips and stepped backward as if someone had just lashed out at her. She trod on Randall's toes and he grasped her waist to steady her.

"The *Stealth*? That's Stuart McGreenery's ship," Randall whispered into her ear.

Camille swept her panicked eyes over the decks and found Oscar. He and a half dozen other sailors were in the rigging lashing the sails to bring the *Eclipse* to a standstill. Oscar's focus on his work slipped as he stared at the *Stealth*, sidling up next to Starbuck's East Indiaman.

McGreenery had headed on foot into the Australian wilds to search for the stone with a small band of his sailors, leaving the *Stealth* moored in Talladay's harbor. Neither he nor any of his men had returned. Camille could only assume that one of the remaining crewmen had commandeered the ship and set sail. And here the *Stealth* was, like a ghost from the past come to haunt her.

Oscar saw her where she stood near the companionway and gave a barely perceptible shake of his head. *Don't say anything*, it read. Camille didn't think any of the *Stealth*'s crewmembers knew what she or Oscar looked like, but they would know Samuel if they spotted him. Her brother had traveled with them up to Talladay, and if they recognized him, they were sure to come aboard with demands to know what had happened to their former captain and mates.

Before Camille could begin to search the decks for her brother, Samuel was at her side, his face pale and tense.

"I think it would be best if I go below," he said quietly. "I don't want to cause Captain Starbuck any trouble."

He hurried past her and descended the companionway ladder. Once he was out of sight, Camille said, "I wouldn't mind causing Starbuck trouble, but not with the *Stealth*."

Randall murmured in agreement as the sailors threw out the grappling hooks to pull McGreenery's ship alongside the *Eclipse*. The hooks held the vessels about ten feet apart: close enough for the captains to eventually shout to each other, and yet far enough apart to keep the two ships from chafing.

"You never did tell me how McGreenery died," Randall said. Camille squirmed, remembering the moment well — too well. She wished she could forget.

"Oscar killed him," she answered. "He did it to save my life." What she didn't say was that Oscar had also killed McGreenery to avenge his own murder.

Randall had no response for something so clearly heroic of the person he disliked most. In the silence, a flutter of movement amidships on the *Stealth* stole her attention. Out of all the bustling sailors on the *Stealth*, there was one person who moved across the decks in a strange fluidity. He almost seemed to glide along the decks, heading toward the railing of the stern where there weren't any sailors working.

"I can thank him for that at least," Randall said, frugal with his praise.

But Camille was unable to look away from the finely suited sailor moving smoothly toward the deserted stern. A flash of red around his waist spiked the pace of her heart. A red sash.

"I mean it, Camille. I *will* thank him," Randall said again, but just then the odd sailor at the rail of the ship turned and faced her. He met her stare and Camille sucked in a sharp breath.

"Impossible," she whispered.

Stuart McGreenery stared at her from the rail, his lips twisting into a smug grin. He wore the same navy slacks and jacket, the egret white silk stockings, and the same red sash tied at the waist. The very clothes he wore the day Oscar killed him inside the boulder dome.

"What do you mean, *impossible?*" Randall asked. "I'm being sincere."

McGreenery couldn't be there on the *Stealth*. He was dead. But his flinty black eyes locked with hers, and he looked as real as any of the other men aboard the ship.

"Camille? Are you even listening to me?" Randall asked.

She wanted to gesture toward McGreenery, she wanted Randall to see it, too. But when she tried to speak, nothing more than a rasp escaped. A swell of the ocean caught her flimsy legs off guard. Randall steadied her again but by the time she'd refocused, there was no one at the stern's rail. The space was empty.

"He can't be —" Camille swept her eyes over the rest of the *Stealth*'s decks. McGreenery was gone.

Captain Starbuck and the *Stealth*'s new captain were exchanging greetings, their destinations, and news. Sailors from the *Eclipse* made quieter talk with the *Stealth* boys so as not to disturb their captains. Camille scanned their faces, but none of them were McGreenery.

"What's happening, Camille?" Randall stepped into her line of sight, blocking the decks of the *Stealth* completely.

"It was —" she started. But what could she say? She'd just seen a dead man aboard the *Stealth*.

That evening the winds turned wicked. The seas had started to run high while the *Stealth* was still stuck fast to the *Eclipse*. Randall, who had urged Camille below to rest when she'd been unable to explain her baffled trance, had come back to the cabin with news that the *Stealth* had departed without incident. Camille had been relieved, but only slightly. There had been an incident, namely her terrifying hallucination of Stuart McGreenery.

She had been more than willing to get back to work with the map and lose herself in the task. A handful of hours later, though, the eagerness had faded.

"Do you ever dream of the parties back home?" Randall asked. He took from Camille's hands the finished sketch she'd been working on, and gave her the one he'd translated in return. It was the letter *M*. All that work for one measly letter? "The quail's leg, pâté, caviar." Randall listed foods that would never be found on a ship at sea. "Champagne and ice, cheeses and fresh bread. And the smoking room . . . I'd give anything to just breathe the air of a smoking room right now."

Camille set the translation down, smiling. "I was never much for parties. But champagne and ice does sound refreshing."

"How about some warm rum instead?"

She thought he was only joking, but his brow remained crinkled, waiting for an answer.

"You're serious? Passengers aren't rationed rum."

Nor prisoners, which was what they really were. Randall swung his coat on.

"Something tells me the captain wants to keep his prized passenger content. I'll be back. Stay thirsty," he said, and slipped into the corridor.

Camille closed her eyes as she unraveled the map one more time before quitting for the night. It was just after five o'clock, and even though supper would be tasteless, she did have to eat something to keep her strength. She'd never worked so tirelessly on anything before. Crossing the Victoria highlands on horseback and on foot had been physically taxing, and yet somehow this task was just as difficult. It left her as exhausted as their Australian trek had. She had been keeping her eyes closed through the sparks and flashes of amber light. It helped cut back on the headaches she'd been getting. The sizzling sound of the map started to fade as the door opened behind her. Camille opened her eyes and turned in her chair. Samuel stood in the doorway. His expression was fierce, his cheeks a high crimson.

Camille swung out of her seat, rolled the map, and shoved it into the pocket of her navy twill skirt. "What's wrong?"

She was hopeful that Samuel had learned of Starbuck's coercive threat and had come to discuss it. She had tried to speak to him once about it, but as soon as Samuel heard *Starbuck* and *I need to tell you the truth about him,* he'd walked away.

Now Samuel stormed inside. " 'What's wrong?' You're planning to desert the *Eclipse* and you're asking me what's wrong?"

Samuel unbuttoned the two metal clasps at his collar with fervor and cast his hat onto the bunk.

"Who told you?" she asked.

"Maggie bombarded me on my way to the head just now," he answered, refusing to meet her eyes. "She said you and Randall were planning to sneak off once we arrived in Suez, and that I should join you."

Camille hadn't even told Maggie yet. How had she known?

"I have a reason to want to escape. It's what I've been needing to speak to you about. It's Starbuck. You have to know what he wants —"

Samuel held up his hand. "Stop. I know exactly what you want to say, and it couldn't be more false. Contrary to what you've come to believe, Captain Starbuck means to help us."

The stuffy chamber grew warmer as Camille stepped toward her brother.

"He doesn't want to do anything of the sort. He wants the stones, and he wants to be the one to join them."

"And why shouldn't he be the one to do so?" Samuel countered with a venomous scowl. "He's as educated about the stones and their powers as Maggie is. He'll know how to manage them. He'll know better than you."

Camille gaped at her brother. "And what about Oscar's soul? What about Ira? Maggie says I need to be the one to join the stones. *Me.* I can't give them to Starbuck, and I can't believe you'd encourage me to. Especially after the things he said. He threatened you, Samuel. He spoke horribly of you." She chose not to divulge the comments about Samuel being an eager puppy. It would only embarrass him and make him defensive.

"I don't believe he would threaten an earthworm, Camille, let alone me or you." He crossed his arms over his chest, his back straight, feet hip-width apart. He looked so proud. Older than when she first met him in the china shop back in Port Adelaide.

"Captain Starbuck is an honorable person. When he takes control of the stones, he'll have the power to restore Oscar's soul and bring Ira back."

Camille shook her head, hearing Starbuck's cavalier claim again in her mind: *I don't care about Oscar's soul.*

"He's fooling you," she said. "He's shown his true self to me, and it's not the generous, warmhearted man you think you know."

Samuel exhaled deeply.

"You are so very special, aren't you?" His question dripped with sarcasm. "Of course you think you've seen his true side. You think this whole excursion revolves around you."

Camille's mouth parted in astonishment. "What are you talking about?"

Samuel squinted though the light in the cabin was anything but bright.

"You found the stone, you brought Oscar back from the dead, you can see symbols on the map that no one else can, you are the only one who can access the second stone. You, you, *you.*"

"You think I'm enjoying this?" she asked. "That I'm flaunting whatever it is the stone needs me to do?"

He brushed past her. "Do you have any idea how self-important you sound?"

"Why are you saying these things?" she asked, staring after him.

He reeled around to face her. "Because I know what the stone did to my father! How it made him single-minded and ruthless. I know what it did to our mother, too. She only took the map from your father when she left the both of you to protect you. To protect you from monsters like my father. He used her to get his hands on it, and because of him, our mother went off and hid for the rest of her life. She hid herself; she hid me. . . . She was ashamed." Samuel took a shaky breath. "She was ashamed of me. Her *mistake*."

His misery seeped through the tremble of his voice and the quiver of his lower lip. He saw himself as a mistake. And when he looked at Camille, he saw all the ways their mother had done wrong. All the ways their mother had done *him* wrong.

"Even you, Camille," Samuel said. "When you look at me, you see nothing but my father."

She was ashamed to hear him say it, and to know that it was true. "I can't help it. You're so very like him."

"I am not!" he cried.

"Prove it to me, then," she said. "Just listen to what I have to say."

"You're my sister — I shouldn't have to *prove* anything. Captain Starbuck has never once asked me to prove my worth. For the first time, here on the *Eclipse,* I don't feel like a mistake."

Camille reached out to him. "You're not a mistake, Samuel. Our mother told me how much she loved you."

"Don't treat me like I'm stupid," he said, jerking his arm away from her. "Don't try and reassure me that she didn't regret my existence every day for the rest of her life."

Camille couldn't. She hadn't known her mother well enough to make such a reassurance.

"If the map and stone have brought you nothing but misery, why are you so supportive of Starbuck's claim on them? Why would you want anything at all to do with this?"

Samuel shifted his direction back to the door, his hands clasped behind his back. "Financial greed drove my father to search for the stone. You want it for your own personal reasons — *emotional* greed. With Captain Starbuck, no greed is involved. It's his family's responsibility to care for the stone. Responsibility, Camille. Not greed."

She breathed in deeply, trying to clear away a cloud of nauseating confusion. Samuel turned in a tight circle as if some great thought had just struck him.

"It's the stone. The stone has possessed you. It's dangerous. Captain Starbuck said it would do this if it weren't in the right hands. It has . . ." Samuel lowered his voice. "It has demonic properties, and I'm afraid you've already been exposed to them."

She stared at him, wide eyed. *Demonic properties*?

"What kind of nonsense is Starbuck feeding you?"

Samuel's open and eager expression closed down. "He might be close to us in age, but he is your captain. You would do well to call him by his proper title if you want to remain in his good graces."

The door to the cabin opened. Randall stepped in, holding a tin flagon in one hand.

"That man is not my captain, and his graces are of no value to me," she said.

Randall approached them with visible apprehension. "What's this about?"

Samuel ignored him. "You aren't seeing things straight, Camille. If it hasn't already, the stone will take over, blind you to what's real and what's not. My God, you're already paranoid! Look at what Captain Starbuck is doing for you, and you don't even appreciate it."

Camille couldn't believe what she was hearing. "I should appreciate that he'd harm you, Randall, and Oscar if I deny him the stones?"

He rolled his eyes into the back of his head and sighed. "It's just as I said. You're paranoid."

Randall reached out and laid a tentative hand on Samuel's shoulder. "Samuel, you should listen to what she has to say —"

He threw off Randall's hand and grabbed his hat from the bunk. "I won't be fooled as you've been." Samuel swung the door wide and stormed out.

Camille dropped her hands to her side. She'd been holding them out to him.

"That damned captain has convinced my brother I'm possessed by a demonic stone!" Camille blushed at her outburst. "Forgive me."

But Randall didn't seem to mind. He brushed a lock of her hair from her cheek. "I don't believe you're possessed."

It would have made her feel better if Randall knew of her ice dreams, of the McGreenery apparition, or of how she'd bonded with the stone when she brought Oscar back to the living world. Samuel had been right: Randall was being fooled. The time to confess all that had passed, though. The lie felt too big to approach now, especially now that they'd kissed. She felt guilty and scared and lost of any control.

Randall held the flagon of rum out to her. "I'll try and speak to Samuel. He and the captain seem to be close friends, though. It's as if Samuel is his confidant."

Camille took the rum. "Or his puppet."

"Don't worry. I hear brothers and sisters are supposed to fight all the time," he said.

Camille smiled into her flagon of rum, smelling the sweet liquid before taking a small sip. It burned her mouth and throat, overpowering the pain Samuel's visit had left.

"This doesn't change my mind about iced champagne, but thank you," she said, taking another small sip. It would warm her enough for a stroll on deck. "I think I just need some air."

"Want company?" Randall asked as she took up her cloak.

Camille handed the flagon back to him. "A few minutes alone might help clear my head. Will you guard the stone for me?"

He drew a sip from the rum, the muscles in his face relaxing. "Mmmm. Of course."

Then, as if he did it every day, Randall leaned in and kissed her on the cheek. He pulled away just enough to look into her eyes. He was close enough for her to trace the warm rum on his breath.

She recalled his last kiss, the way she'd enjoyed it more than she'd expected. Camille brushed her lips against his. Not really a kiss, more like a testing of the waters. The tips of their noses touched and danced, closer, farther away, and closer again. Randall ended the dance, pressing his mouth against hers. His kiss was gentle, unlike Oscar's forceful, needy one in the hold.

Scolding our mother on her deathbed looks a bit hypocritical of you now, wouldn't you say? Her brother's earlier accusation burned through Randall's kiss and stung her with its honesty.

She drew back, ashamed of herself. How could she do this? How could she let herself be kissed by two men on one ship?

"I'm . . . I'm sorry," she whispered, fumbling for the door. She left the cabin in a blur of motion, escaping before Randall could call her back.

FOURTEEN

amille climbed up on deck to see gray skies had shrouded the setting sun, turning the clouds to murky amber. Seven clangs of the watch bells, tossed around by the reedy sea wind, signaled a half hour left in Oscar's shift. She realized she'd lost complete track of the time. The midday nap, Samuel's visit, and the confusing kiss with Randall had disoriented her.

She gripped her cloak to her chin, the wind sending it behind her like a hawk's flapping wings. Oscar was up in the rigging, standing on the footropes beneath a sail yard, his concentration focused on raising the canvas. His body curved around the yard, his feet and back firmly braced. Kissing Randall had been wrong. Kissing Oscar had been wrong, too. She shouldn't be kissing either of them. Camille didn't want to deceive Randall — but she was. She didn't want to feel so torn up inside whenever she saw Oscar — but she did.

Seeing him at work reminded her of how he used to climb along the yards of the *Christina*, the quick work of his hands and agility of his legs. Up high, the swells of the sea were more pronounced than on deck. He'd always proven himself spry. Now as the winds forced the men up top even closer to the spars, which resembled arms sprouting out of the mast, she longed for what she'd had with Oscar before the *Christina*'s last sail. She'd been attracted to him, hoped he'd felt the same toward her. But there had been no danger in thinking about him, musing over what it might be like to touch him, be close to him. No danger of losing something she didn't really have.

Fronds of mist curled toward the whitecapped sea as the storm closed in. The humidity was high and the lightning and thunder would be severe because of it. Four men worked along the same yard as Oscar, two on the outer leeches, and two closer to the throat of the yard, near the mast. Their light-colored trousers were tucked into shin-high black boots. Their shirts, buttoned to the neck and belted around the waist with wide strips of leather, ruffled madly in the wind.

One of the sailors on the opposite end of the yard from Oscar finished securing a boltrope around the furled canvas. He gripped the waist-thick wood of the yard as a howling wind knocked him off balance. Camille gasped as his feet lost their placement on the footropes. He quickly recovered, and she exhaled. In the stormy light she noticed this sailor did not have his shirt buttoned to the top, like the others, as Captain Starbuck ordered.

As the sailor regained his balance, he craned his neck to look down the plane of the yard. Something slipped out of his shirt collar. A roundish object strung on a chain. A golden object. *A pendant.*

Camille's throat filled with acid as the Courier slid his feet along the footrope, toward the mast. He tucked the golden skull pendant back inside his collar, out of sight, never once parting his gaze from Oscar's back.

"Oscar!" The wind drove Camille's voice behind her instead of forward and up. A few of the crewmen near her on deck stopped to stare. "Oscar! Watch out!"

Her shouting was futile. She'd been in the rigging of ships before and if the wind was heavy, no voice could overcome it. The Courier kept moving, though his movements were slow and inexperienced. Even *she* would be faster than that. And then Camille knew what she needed to do.

She tugged off one boot, threw it aside, then tugged off the other. Rolling down her stockings and dismissing the men around her, she cast those aside, too. She needed bare feet, her soles safer than the tread of any boot. She dashed to the mast, grabbed the first metal rung, and pulled herself up.

"Miss!" one sailor cried from behind her, but she continued her climb with surprising speed. Rung after cold, wet rung she ascended the foremast, her legs burning.

The clouds let loose as she lifted her face to see where the Courier stood. Thick drops of rain pelted her in the eyes. The Courier had reached the mast.

"Oscar!" she shouted once more, but he still had his back turned, his hands busy with the reefing tackle. The other two sailors near the mast were also absorbed in reefing the canvas. But at her cry, the Courier turned his head. His shadowed eyes found her. His nose crinkled and his lips curled into a snarl.

"Stay away from him!" she shouted.

The Courier moved fast, shoving his fist into the chest of the unsuspecting sailor nearest him. Despite his bulk, the sailor toppled backward, lost his footing along the rope, and plummeted to the deck below. Camille screamed, watching in horror as the sailor thrashed until he met with the deck. She squeezed her eyes shut, then looked back up. The Courier was entangled with the second sailor.

She hastened her climb. The wind pounded at her back, throwing her cloak in front of her face. The cloak's chain clasp cut into her throat, choking her as she at last reached the yard. With one hand wrapped around the mast, she unhitched the clasp. The wind tore the velvet cloak from her fingers and it hurtled into the storm, a giant bird sailing away.

"Oscar!" she cried. This time, he turned.

The Courier kneed the second sailor in the gut, and hurled him forward over the yard, to the same fate of the other. The space between the Courier and Oscar was now frighteningly empty.

"Get down!" Oscar screamed at her before he ran along the footrope with practiced stealth and pounced on the Courier.

Camille looked for something, anything, to aid him. The wind pushed her skirts against her legs and she felt something solid press into her thigh. She reached into her skirt pocket. Her fingers wrapped around the map and her heart sank. She should have left the map behind in the cabin, safe with Randall and the stone.

The stormy sunset glow had been wiped from the sky, replaced by slate-colored clouds. Oscar pummeled the Courier in the mouth, who then threw his head forward, head-butting Oscar in the nose. The Courier reached for his pendant, his other hand tangled into Oscar's shirt.

"No!" Camille lunged forward without thinking to lower her feet onto the footrope — or let go of the map.

She balanced on the yard, her arms stretched out at her side, the map in hand. Her legs trembled with the swells of the sea and the snap of the wind.

"Goddamn it, Camille!" Oscar shouted after he tore free from the Courier.

Slowly, she lowered herself to the rope, blessedly taut from Oscar's and the Courier's weight. The running rigging at her waist seemed thinner than two strands of hair twisted together. Oscar pounded his fist into the Courier's kidney, and the Courier boxed him in the ear.

"Get back!" Oscar screamed to her again, but she couldn't. There had to be something she could do. She was only a few feet away from them now.

A gust of wind caught the edge of the rolled map and snapped it open. Her fingers clamped down as tight as possible, but the leather seemed to turn to water and before she knew it, was gone from her hand. The map flipped and landed open and flat between the shoulder blades of the Courier. He opened his throat to an inhuman scream, arching his back as the map ate away at his shirt, burning cloth and skin.

He flailed his arms, trying, unsuccessfully, to peel the map off as black smoke rose from his back. The Courier spun around and growled at her, his black eyes as hollow and wolfish as the animalistic scream still ringing in her ears. He bared a mouthful of grotesquely long and sharp teeth, and screeched again.

Oscar stripped the map off the Courier's back and shoved it safely away in his coat pocket.

The Courier growled and swung his arm out like a boom sweeping over a deck, connecting with Camille's shoulder. Her feet lifted off the rope and she fell backward, over the yard.

The world turned upside down and weightless, her scream cut short by the wind rushing into her mouth as she fell. A painful tug on her ankle jerked her to a stop. Lifting her head, she saw that her ankle was twisted in the running rigging. She also saw the Courier erupt into a plume of black smoke. The dark flames engulfed his body and whirled up to swallow his face. And then he was gone. His ashes trailed away in the gritty wind.

Oscar flung the pendant he'd seized out into the ocean. He bent down and clutched Camille's leg. With a hard tug he pulled her back over the yard. The blood rushed from her head and she swooned. Oscar held her against him, whispering in her ear to steady herself, to hold on, that she was safe.

"He . . . he was . . . going to . . ." Schools of black dots swam across her vision as Oscar guided her back along the footrope toward the mast.

"What were you thinking coming up here?" he asked.

She could tell he was trying to keep his voice calm.

"I had to warn you. I had to stop him."

"You could have been killed." Fury poked through every overenunciated syllable.

"You *would* have been killed!" she cried as Oscar stepped onto the first rung. She held on to the mast, pulling herself up onto the yard. No, *thank you*? No, *if you hadn't been there to warn me, I would have been Courier meat*?

Oscar took the recovered map and jammed it back into

the pocket of her skirt for her. "He couldn't have killed me, Camille. I'm already dead."

The *Eclipse* sloped into the lee of a wave, tossing Camille forward. Oscar steadied her with his chest and the cage of his arms. Her pulse beat madly. Rivulets of water coursed down her cheeks, and her hair was completely drenched.

"That's absurd. You aren't dead."

Oscar looked below, where a crowd of sailors stared up at them, waiting. How would they ever explain what had just happened?

His stormy frown returned to her. "My soul is lost. My *soul*."

She followed him as he dropped down the mast, her head still feeling funny from being suspended upside down. Her legs quivered, her ankle stung. They reached the deck and a throng of sailors encircled them. She scooped up her boots and stockings and held them to her chest, shivering.

Cold, hard faces stared at them, jaws and fists flexed. Sailing through the storm had seemingly lost any importance as the sailors pressed in on them. Oscar took a wary step in front of Camille. From around his shoulder, she saw Captain Starbuck part through the wall of rigid sailors. He wore his oilskins, a wide-brimmed tarpaulin hat shielding him from sea spray. His nostrils flared.

"What in Triton's fury just happened up there? Two of my men lay broken on the deck behind us, and I want to know why. Speak!"

Camille tried to step around the shelter of Oscar's frame, but he held her back.

"We were attacked by another sailor," he answered.

Saying the sailor had been one of Death's Couriers would have probably earned Oscar a solid punch in the gut by at least one of the men looming close.

"One of *my* men?" Starbuck narrowed his fevered eyes. "That's not possible. I gave my word to Miss Rowen that neither she nor her people would be harmed as long as she cooperated."

"He wasn't one of your men." Camille shoved past Oscar's arm. "He was a Courier. For someone so knowledgeable about the stones of the immortals, I'd think you'd know about them as well."

Starbuck sucked in a breath and swung his arm toward the companionway. "Not another word. Below! Now!"

Hardy slid into Camille's line of sight, along with two other menacing sailors. Oscar tugged Camille's arm lightly, and they went below, out of the rain and the drenching squalls of surf coming over the rails. Below, Camille felt the dampness of the wood with her bare feet.

"Camille? What's happening?" Randall called from down the corridor. He darted past the flickering lanterns strung along the hall.

"I need to speak with Miss Rowen immediately, if you don't mind," Captain Starbuck said impatiently from the entryway to his cabin.

"I do mind," Randall replied. "Whatever you need to discuss, you'll discuss with me as well."

Camille thought she heard Oscar groan. Captain Starbuck made a hasty gesture for them all to follow him inside.

"Close the door behind you," he ordered. As Randall did so, Samuel was revealed standing sentry behind it.

"What were you thinking, Camille, climbing up onto the rigging like that?" her brother asked before she could even register him being there, waiting for them.

"It's not as if I haven't done the same thing time and again on the *Christina*," she said. The way they were treating her, like a trained animal suddenly gone wild, infuriated her. And embarrassed her, too.

"You'll do nothing of the sort again while you're aboard my ship," Starbuck said from behind his desk.

"There was a Courier preparing to attack Oscar. What was I supposed to do? Be a useless ninny and watch from the deck?"

"A Courier?" Randall and Samuel repeated in unison.

"You will not speak of those creatures in front of my men," Starbuck warned through clenched teeth. His eyes flicked toward the door behind Samuel. Hardy stood outside, guarding their privacy.

"Why ever not?" she asked.

He pounded his desk, looking more like a petulant child than a captain. "Because I order it! Those creatures are products of the devil, brought here by the stone. My men will not be tainted by fear."

The door came crashing open and Maggie threw herself into the packed cabin. Hardy tried to hold her back.

"It's fine, Hardy," Starbuck said. "Shut the door behind you."

Maggie stormed up to her uncle as Hardy slammed the door with extra vigor.

"Why did I have to beat my way out of my cabin to find you?" she asked.

Starbuck sighed and rolled his eyes toward the ceiling. "We had an incident on deck, Margaret. I didn't need another female somewhere she wasn't designed to be."

Oscar turned to Maggie. "I thought you said the Couriers couldn't appear out of thin air."

"They can't," Maggie answered. Her shoulders drew up toward her ears. "Wait. What are you saying? There was a Courier aboard?"

Starbuck waved toward Camille and Oscar. "So they claim."

"Has it been aboard this whole time?" Samuel asked.

"No, it would have made its move before now," Maggie whispered.

The *Stealth*. The ship had been tucked up against the *Eclipse* for nearly an hour that very day. And the vision of McGreenery . . . the Courier might have taken on Stuart McGreenery's image just like the other Courier had taken on Lucius Drake's. He'd been taunting her.

"It climbed aboard this afternoon," Camille said, feeling vindicated that she hadn't simply been losing her mind. "From the *Stealth*."

And Camille had discovered another way to repel a Courier. The map itself was like a poison, having burned straight through the Courier's shirt and skin. But how? What was on the map other than enchantments and the odd scent of myrrh?

Myrrh. Hardy had been doused in it that time he'd leered close enough for Camille to smell him. There were jars upon jars of it in the pantry, too — enough for the whole crew to douse themselves with if they required . . . what? Protection? Yes, of course. The Couriers were repelled by myrrh.

"I don't understand," Randall said. "If these Couriers are after the stone, why was one up in the rigging after Oscar? I had the stone in my cabin all along."

The revelation about the myrrh subsided. The cabin hushed so that all Camille heard was the crash of the waves and the shrieks of wind.

"The stone isn't the only thing they're after," Captain Starbuck answered. She wanted to scream to stop Starbuck from finishing his explanation. "They've also been sent to recover Kildare's soul."

Randall's face contorted into a ball of confusion. Patches of heat and cold broke out on Camille's neck and back and chest.

"Go back to your cabins," Starbuck ordered before Randall could pose another question. "And not one word about the spectacle in the rigging. Or" — he found Camille — "our *arrangement* is off."

Camille turned and rushed from his cabin, fearful of what Randall would say next, the questions he would ask, the truth she would have to part with. She'd nearly made it to her cabin door before he caught up with her.

"I want to know what the captain meant by Oscar's soul."

His demand wasn't weak. It wasn't gently curious. It boomed through the corridor. She'd done this. She'd lied. Oh, why had she lied?

"Randall —" she started, but Oscar and Maggie came up behind him and she stopped speaking.

Randall stared, waiting for an answer, his chin tucked into his neck like a bull raring to attack the red flag.

"Why would they want Oscar's soul? You said they wanted the stones. Did you lie to me?"

Camille hated yes or no questions. If she said yes, Randall wouldn't listen to another word. If she said no, she'd be lying yet again.

"She didn't lie. I did." Oscar stepped up behind him. Randall took a sidelong glance at him.

"I let you," Camille said to Oscar, then changed the direction of her sentence toward Randall. "And I let you believe him."

How could she have done that? Of course she'd known it was wrong. Knew she'd have to tell Randall at some point. She should have told him right from the start. But he'd been tender and understanding. He'd been there when Oscar hadn't, and she'd needed that desperately. She'd been so selfish.

"Why Oscar's soul?" Randall repeated as Samuel slowly edged toward the fringe of their gathering in the narrow corridor. She and her brother exchanged a brief, knowing look. He'd kept her secret, even though he'd made his distaste for it evident. Why Oscar's soul? Randall's question lingered before her, clogging up the corridor.

"Because," Camille whispered, unable to look Randall full on, "he died."

Tears stung the backs of her eyes, surprising her with their sudden arrival. She hadn't expected them.

"I didn't hear you correctly," Randall said.

"Yes, you did." Camille dared to look at him. "We'd nearly made it to the stone when McGreenery and his men caught up to us. McGreenery put a spear through Oscar's heart." The confession rushed out like a great breath of wind. Her lips trembled. "He killed him. Right there, right in front of us. Oscar died."

Camille saw it all again, Oscar lying in the mess of his own blood. She'd never imagined blood could be that red, that startling and vivid. She'd knelt in it, her throat crushing with the knowledge that as the blood flowed from him, so went his life. She'd had no control over his death. No way to stop it, or save him.

"That's impossible," Randall finally said. "He's here. He's alive."

But by the way he said it, she knew that Randall already knew. He was simply grasping for any reason why Oscar would be alive instead of dead, other than the fact that she'd used the stone to resurrect him. Camille parted her lips to speak, but sealed them, thinking to let Randall come to terms with it himself. What could she say to soothe him, anyway? There was nothing that could mend the lie she'd spun and then ripped apart.

"You brought him back . . . instead of your father," Randall said slowly. "You chose Oscar Kildare over your own father."

Excuses congregated on the tip of her tongue. She swallowed them. Randall was right and she had nothing to defend herself with. That didn't stop Oscar from trying, though.

"You don't understand. William had already been gone for a few months, and Camille had just watched me die. The stone read her emotions. It makes sense why the stone thought I was the one she wanted back."

Read her emotions? The stone had read her heart. They were two different things. Her heart wouldn't have been swayed by a rush of emotions . . . would it?

"Do you think I'm a fool?" Randall whispered at the floor, his hurt coming to a boil.

A few swift steps brought him within inches of her, his chest heaving. "The way you look at him, the way he looks at you. They way you two have been avoiding each other this whole voyage. In Port Adelaide especially, when he tried rising up against me." Randall spewed words at a rapid clip, as if each example of her betrayal had been waiting for freedom. "I thought perhaps he'd shown you inappropriate interest. I even worried you'd returned it," he said softly, the muscles of his forearms tight from his balled fists. "But never, not once, did I imagine you'd favor Kildare — that you would *love* him — more than you did your own father."

You disgust me. He said it with the flare of his nostrils and his scornful gaze. Randall brushed past her. She was too stunned to try to stop him. A whimper escaped her as his door slammed behind him.

"He just needs time," Maggie whispered.

Camille held up her hand. She didn't want to be comforted. Everything Randall had said was true. She'd been cruel, when he'd been nothing but gallant and bold and loving. Camille opened her cabin door and practically fell inside. Her arms wrapped themselves tight around her middle as she slipped down onto her bunk, curling her legs beneath her. Right then she hated herself just as much as Randall did.

FIFTEEN

The burlap sack lay empty on Camille's bunk, its contents arranged in a semicircle around her: the map, the stone, the small bag of money Oscar had given her in Port Adelaide, and the golden pendant she'd found after the attack on the wharves. All of these objects had turned her life upside down and her heart inside out.

"Don't be an idiot," she whispered to herself. She'd done most of the destroying herself.

Had Ira been there, Camille didn't think she'd have gotten so far with her lies to Randall. Ira might be vulgar and obnoxious, but he also had a way of bringing out the honesty in her. He'd seemed shallow in the beginning, a card shark solely looking out for himself. But he hadn't turned out to be superficial at all. She missed his easy smile, his raunchy wit, and the way he somehow lightened even a dire situation.

Camille scooped the golden pendant into her palm and traced its grooves. Her fingertip ran along the angled jaw, the black voids of its eyes, the long, square teeth of its ghoulish mouth.

"Oh, Ira, where are you?"

Maggie snorted softly in her sleep, still covered to her ears in blankets. Dusky blue light came in through the porthole, filtered by the hues of ocean water. Camille guessed it to be just before dawn. Sleep had been sparse the night before, as it had the last four nights since Randall learned she'd betrayed him. He'd refused to speak to her, and had returned the burlap bag and the stone while she was on a trip to the head. Camille had knocked on his door and pleaded with him to at least do her the decency of opening it and telling her face-to-face to go away. She'd given up after a few of the sailors snickered at her in passing.

Now a knock at Camille's door coaxed her to put the pendant back in the sack, out of sight. She opened the door and fell mute. Randall stood there, a stack of papers in one hand, and a pen and inkpot in the other. In the days she'd spent away from him, she'd imagined him brooding behind the closed door of his cabin. The man standing before her didn't look brooding at all. Randall had a difficult time holding his eyes steady with hers, but he still managed to proudly hold his shoulders back. And then, without meaning to, Camille recalled their kiss. His tenderness and fervor.

"Good morning." His voice cracked as if he hadn't exercised his vocal cords in days. He extended the contents of both hands toward her. He seemed grateful to have something else to look at than her. "I should have brought these to you sooner."

Still unable to speak, afraid her own voice may shake if she tried, Camille looked at what he held. The top paper had a poorly rendered copy of the hawkish bird Camille had copied earlier. Randall had brought her the etchings of the hieroglyphs.

He was through collaborating with her, then. It hurt more than remembering his kiss. He no longer wanted her companionship. She shouldn't have been surprised. She didn't even want her own companionship.

"Oh." She took the papers, inkpot, and pen. "Thank you."

Think of something, she begged of herself. But she failed to.

"I thought it might be best if we worked in separate spaces," he said. Her pulse sputtered.

"You mean, you're still going to study the hieroglyphs?" she asked. "You're still going to help me?"

Randall lowered his chin, the bones in his cheeks defined by dark shadows. "I gave you my word that I would. And I don't break my promises."

He left her standing in the door, the pierced edge of his words so fine Camille didn't feel the pain of them at first. But then she realized he'd cut her, a stealthy reproach for the way she'd broken her promise to him.

"I believe he truly loves you."

Camille turned and saw Maggie, awake now and propped on an elbow. Camille slammed the door and opened her arms over the mattress, letting the contents spill onto her bunk. "Perhaps you could just mock me in your head and not aloud."

Randall didn't love her; he despised her. He had most likely spent the last four days debating whether or not to rip her copied hieroglyphs to scraps and feed them to the galley stove. He was a man of his word. Love didn't have an ounce to do with pledging his help.

"Fine, be blind if you choose." Maggie got out of bed, her chemise and pantalettes wrinkled.

Camille sat back down on her bunk, twisting the folds of her dress in her lap. The stone was at her side, and like always, her need to see and hold it was primal. Just picturing herself handing it over to Captain Starbuck made her shake with anger. She couldn't understand it. The triangular stone drew her hand to touch it, lift it from the hay mattress. Why should she feel such a sense of protection for this hunk of rock?

"Your uncle wants the stones," Camille said as she placed the stone back in the burlap sack. "It's why you told me not to trust him. What does he want to do, build an immortal kingdom like Uma did?"

Camille shoved the bag into the recess above her bunk. Maggie smoothed down her single dress, which hung from a peg driven into the wall.

"Of course he does," she replied blithely. "That's the point of retrieving the second stone. To rebuild what our ancestors lost."

Camille got to her feet and crossed the cabin to stand at Maggie's side. "I thought the point was to give Oscar's soul back to him."

Satisfied with her dress's condition, Maggie then went to the dresser and hunted down her corset.

"That's one of the points, yes." Maggie positioned the corset over her chemise and hooked the front busk together. The laces were still loose in the back. "Would you mind? I slept on my shoulder wrong."

Maggie rubbed her shoulder for emphasis. Camille groaned, though the idea of forcing the breath out of Maggie's lungs did hold appeal. She grabbed the top two laces and tugged.

"And the other points are?" She gave another agreeable tug. "Because you should know that I'm not going to be the leader of some immortal kingdom."

"You?" Maggie gasped for air. "I'd put that worry out of your head. There is someone much more qualified than you for that job."

Camille wished she could brace her foot against Maggie's back and yank.

"Would that person be you, by any chance?" she asked. Starbuck wanted the stones, why wouldn't Maggie?

But Maggie's incredulous glance over her shoulder said otherwise. Either that or Camille had just cracked a rib.

"I've already told you. I'm only the guardian." She turned her face away and waited while Camille tied the extra laces into a loop and threaded them through one of the eyelets.

"Then who?" she asked. Maggie shook out her petticoats.

"I think I'd rather surprise you with the answer," Maggie said with an infuriating smirk.

Camille went back to her bunk and organized the papers from Randall to keep from throttling her roommate. She picked up the inkpot and swirled the black ink inside to coat the beveled glass. She and Randall hadn't even finished arranging their escape from Starbuck.

"Then can you at least tell me how you knew about my plan to escape the *Eclipse*?" she asked as Maggie struggled into her petticoats.

"I stowed away on this ship for nearly three months," she answered, huffing. "I know all the right places to spy."

The nerve! Maggie had been spying on them. Camille wondered what else she'd heard.

"Uncle Lionel is anticipating an escape already, so you're going to need to do better than a distraction. Let's face it. You're going to need my help."

Camille set the inkpot back on the bunk and closed her eyes. Admitting to needing Maggie would be a blow to Camille's pride. But she had the sinking feeling the time had come.

———

Over a week later, the *Eclipse* sailed through the mouth of the Red Sea. Camille had been in the galley when Captain Starbuck walked through, announcing their progress to Samuel, his living and breathing shadow.

The two men hadn't seen her at the stove, scrubbing black ink from the pads of her fingertips quickly before the cook could return from the fresh water cask in the hold. She'd spent the morning copying hieroglyphs, the same as she'd been doing for days. Not once had Samuel come to check on her. It was for the best, probably. They'd only argue, anyway.

Samuel disappeared into the captain's cabin as the tepid water on the stovetop frothed with ink-stained bubbles. She searched for a linen towel to dry her hands, and found one beside a deep tray of knives and cleavers.

Camille's bruised elbow had healed, and since then not one of her dreams had taken her to the ice tundra. But she couldn't shake the fear each night before turning out the lantern that she'd return there. That the arctic wolf would be waiting for her. She'd lost her cloak in the Courier attack, so she'd been wearing her stylish Zouave jacket to bed each night, wrinkling it into a shameful state. If she had been able to take a cloak and boots into the dream, and had received a bruised elbow from another, could she carry in other things?

A paring knife with an ebony handle and a short, curved steel blade drew her attention. She plucked it from the tray and carefully pocketed it. It was inane. She'd probably only end up harming herself. But if she did return to the dream, she wanted something for protection. And having a knife hidden in her skirts aboard the *Eclipse* might not be a bad idea either.

The knife rested against the final pages of hieroglyphs copied just that morning. Camille left the galley, knowing she had to deliver them to Randall. She wondered if he'd want her help decoding them, or if he still wanted her to keep her distance. She walked to his cabin shivering with nerves. He opened the door on the second knock.

"Camille." Randall said her name as if he'd forgotten they were aboard the same ship.

"They're finished," she said, her hands clamped around the papers. She hoped he'd missed her. She knew she'd missed him.

Randall stepped aside and motioned for her to enter. Being inside Randall's cabin was uncomfortable now that he knew her feelings for Oscar.

"I've read the book twice. Certain chapters three times. I feel I have a grasp of the phonetics," Randall said. The wooden shape of his words reminded her of how he'd been before, back home. He acted as if the whole world were watching, judging, and he wanted to prove himself as a solid businessman.

"I'm sorry I took so long," Camille said. "The symbols

were small, and there were so many of them. I wanted to be sure I had them down correctly."

She put the papers on his desk. Outside the porthole, the sea rose up against the glass and then dipped down again. Randall took the stack of papers and laid them out across his bunk.

"That isn't the right order," Camille said. She stepped in to rearrange two leafs of paper, and bumped against him. The accidental contact derailed her a moment. She nearly forgot what she was doing. "There. That's it."

She had the symbols and their order memorized. The prospect of finally knowing what each symbol meant, what they made up as a whole, thrilled her.

"Do you want my help?" she asked, trying not to sound too eager.

Randall didn't turn to her as he began on the third row of papers, lined up side by side. "No."

Well, then, she thought, reaching for the cabin door. What had she expected?

"He stands outside your door at night," Randall said. She let go of the knob and turned.

"What?"

Randall faced her, but couldn't look her in the eye.

"He guards your door while you sleep," he explained.

Oscar . . . Oscar stood outside her cabin door at night? She pictured him there, leaning against the corridor wall, arms crossed.

"I didn't know that," she whispered. "He must be worried that a Courier will come."

All those times she'd woken from her ice tundra dreams, he'd been right outside her door. He'd been listening.

Protecting. He'd been acting like the Oscar she used to know so well.

Randall turned back to the spread of hieroglyphs. "I never thought to worry."

She wanted to tell him it was okay, that Oscar had always just been overly protective. But it wasn't much of a consolation, so she stayed quiet.

"Yesterday was the eighth." Randall finally glanced up at her. "Of August."

She wasn't sure what the date had to do with Oscar's personal sentry duties.

He sighed. "August the eighth, Camille."

August the eighth, August the eighth, August the —

Camille gasped. "The wedding."

Yesterday would have been their wedding day.

Randall looked relieved she'd actually remembered, though the corners of his mouth were still pulled into a frown. He picked up the heavy text of ancient Egyptian letters from where it lay on his pillow, and closed it.

"When I asked for your hand, I knew you didn't love me. How could you? You didn't know anything about me." Randall set the book down on the desk and tapped the cover a few times in thought. Camille balled the fabric of her skirt in her hot fingers, not prepared for this conversation at all.

"I thought perhaps we could come to know each other, and that one day I'd win more than just your hand." He didn't look at her as he spoke.

"I tried to feel the same way, Randall, I truly did —" He turned his back to her. "Please, listen! You're right. I didn't love you. I was terrified I never would."

Randall wheeled around to see her. "Then why did you accept my proposal?"

"If I hadn't, my father would have been furious. You don't understand. He was ashamed of me, of how I was different from the other girls. I'd always charmed him with the way I dismissed society while growing up. But when it came time to marry me off, I think he feared he would be the only one I could charm."

Camille's throat wound up into a knot as she spoke of her father. She'd been a disappointment to him back then, and even now remained one. Look how bungled up she'd made things.

"But I liked our trips to the markets," she added. "And here on the *Eclipse* . . . Randall, you've shown me how wonderful you are. I finally feel I'm beginning to know you."

He pushed back his shoulders and stood taller. "Do you think you could, possibly, come to have feelings for me . . . someday?"

The idea frightened her beyond anything else. She loved *Oscar*. She wanted *Oscar*. And yet, here this other man stood, still wanting her when she didn't deserve his forgiveness, let alone his love.

"I do have feelings for you," she answered, and it was the truth.

Oscar didn't want her anymore. He'd been pushing her away for the whole journey. If she didn't accept Randall, she'd end up alone. But that didn't seem a valid enough reason to say she loved him when she wasn't certain she did.

"But you also have feelings for *him*," Randall said. Camille nodded, her eyes closed.

"All right, then," he said. Camille opened her eyes, surprised by the change in his tone. He almost sounded chipper.

"All right, then, what?" she asked.

He walked to her, his chin high and his jaw set.

"At least I know I'm still in the running," he said. "Even if I'm late to enter the race."

SIXTEEN

The moment the bitter air stiffened the ruby linen of her dress, Camille was sorry she'd thrown off the cloak in the Courier attack. She opened her eyes to the blinding white tundra, her earlobes numb, her teeth already chattering. The Zouave jacket was too thin and completely inefficient.

The multihued cliffs had grown in height and mass, but only because she was much closer to them than she had been before. She wondered if the cliffs held some kind of importance.

A prickling sensation worked its way up her spine. She swiveled around, careful not to slip on the ice. Camille searched the windswept horizon for the white wolf whose memory haunted her. There it stood, thirty or forty yards to her left. Its black-rimmed eyes were trained on her, its silver tufted ears pointed toward her at full attention. Slowly, slowly, Camille slipped her hand into the pocket of her skirt. The shocking cold steel of the blade soothed her. She wrapped her fingers around the ebony handle and held it tightly. The knife was so small, and the wolf was so enormous. Fighting it off with a paring knife suddenly felt like sailing through a typhoon in a dinghy.

The wind slapped her skirt uncomfortably against the backs of her legs. The sky was slate blue and misty, and a hard, grating sleet showered down from the low-lying clouds. The wolf strode forward. Camille's pulse quickened. She steadied herself, tried to even her breathing, and slipped backward a few paces toward the cliffs. The wolf followed. A quick look at the ice cliffs revealed something Camille hadn't noticed before: a vaulted opening.

The wolf growled a wet, vicious warning. It crinkled its snout, bared its.teeth, and advanced into a canter. Camille started for the opening in the cliffs, but the sleet had drenched her, turning her dress to stiff canvas. Her steps were awkward and bumbling, her feet fast turning to blocks of ice despite the boots she wore.

The wolf moved into a sprint. Camille forgot all of the reasons why she ached and shivered, and ran, the knife now out of her pocket. A massive force thudded against her back. She sailed forward and crashed to the ground only feet from the entrance. The paring knife slid out in front of her and swiveled away. *No!* She lay motionless on her belly, listening to the sounds of wet breathing and of claws scratching against the icy floor. Camille closed her eyes, waiting for the wolf's teeth to sink into her flesh.

Something soft pressed up against her nose and mouth. Camille opened her eyes to find that her face was buried in her pillow. She lay on her bunk, still shivering and cold. And wet. She sat up, the sleet from her dreamscape still crusted onto the fabric of her dress. Unable to control the tremors of her hand, Camille reached into her pocket for the knife. She didn't know why she was surprised to find it missing, but she checked her other pocket with bated breath. Empty. An object from her world was still lying on the ice in some other world. A world Camille had access to because of Umandu.

Why did she keep going there? She had to find a way to stop before it happened again. Because next time, Camille worried she wouldn't be waking up in one piece.

A streak of silver stars sliced through the cloudless night sky. Camille breathed in the warm, salty air from the railing of the ship as it sailed up the Red Sea. She stood alone on deck, the night watch quiet and calm as the sailors worked around her. Maggie was asleep in their cabin, and if she weren't so afraid of sleeping, Camille would have been, too.

She'd spent most of the day in Randall's cabin, listening to him talk about how vowels were often omitted in hieroglyphic writing, why nouns were either masculine or feminine, and how determinative words didn't need to be transliterated. Camille had continually needed to force her mind back onto her work. Not because of the overwhelming task of learning a new language, or even because of her worrisome dream.

Randall wanted to be in the running; he wanted to compete with Oscar. Camille couldn't stop the thrill that coursed through her even now when she thought of his vow. But how dare she want Randall to fight for her? If Oscar had come to her that very second, his heart open, seeking her forgiveness and love, Camille would have given it to him without thought. But Oscar had changed, irrevocably she feared. She was afraid the man she loved was gone forever, no matter what.

A scream broke the silence on deck. Camille jumped as though someone had just tickled her spine, and she realized the scream had come from belowdecks. She raced to the companionway, and inside the corridor, sailors swarmed around the door to Camille and Maggie's cabin.

"What is this?" a gravelly voice shouted. *Hardy.* "What the devil is this?"

Camille pushed past one sailor, his body like stone.

"Camille!" Oscar's shout rose above the din. Then, "Get out of the way. Move it! Camille!"

She opened her mouth to speak, but an infuriated Maggie beat her to it. "How dare you come into my cabin? Sneaking in here like some thief! Uncle Lionel! Uncle *Lionel!*" Maggie's jagged voice split through the murmuring crowd.

"Where did she get it?" Hardy demanded.

At last, Camille elbowed her way through the men to her cabin door. Oscar grabbed her by the arm and brought her close to his side.

"Stay by me," he whispered as Maggie swiped at something in Hardy's hand. It was the Courier's golden pendant Camille had kept hidden in the burlap bag.

"You!" Hardy pointed at Camille. "Where did you get this?" He shook the skull pendant at Camille and it smacked off her cheekbone.

Oscar pushed Hardy's arm down. *"Back off."*

Randall appeared, pushing his way through the mass of bodies glowing in oil lamplight.

Camille reached for the pendant. "Give that back to me!"

Hardy hiked it up farther. "I know what it is! It's part of the legend," he said, his cheeks sweaty, the whites of his eyes yellow and streaked with red veins.

"She's made a pact with the devil!" he shouted to the others. An explosion of hollering assaulted her ears.

"I've done nothing of the sort!" Her protest was drowned out by the sailors' demands to throw the pendant overboard, and Camille along with it.

Oscar and Randall formed a blockade around her, shielding her from the riled crew.

"The devil has nothing to do with that pendant!" Maggie shouted, her voice too weak to conquer the crew's hollering.

A crushing silence fell upon them. Camille peeked between a gap in Oscar's and Randall's arms to see a few sailors step aside. Starbuck came through. In his hand was a pistol, his grip on it casual.

"Explain." His brief command jerked every hunched spine to attention.

"I went into *my* cabin to fetch my mending kit, and found this." Hardy held the pendant out as if to pass it along to Starbuck. But the captain waved the pistol in front of him, rejecting the golden skull.

"All this racket over a necklace?" he asked, forcing a flicker of his good humor. It snuffed out quickly.

"But it's from a Courier," Hardy said. "The chit's been keeping it with her this whole time."

"I knew that's what we seen up in the riggin'," said another voice from the crescent of sailors. The man pointed at Oscar. "The one fightin' Kildare. We all seen it, the way he burned up into the air!"

"It was a Courier!" someone else cried.

"Get rid of it! Get rid of her!"

The chanting for Camille's demise grew again. Randall pushed backward, pressing her against the corridor wall. The blockade of arms shielding her split apart and Oscar slowly joined the hollering sailors. He met her incredulous stare, looked toward Captain Starbuck, and then back at her. She relaxed, understanding. He wasn't abandoning her. He was going to try to help from the other side.

Starbuck raised his pistol above his head and cocked the hammer. The shouting ceased.

"Enough nonsense. There are no Couriers aboard this ship, not now, not ever! You —" He brought his pistol down and aimed it at Camille, ignoring Randall, who stood between them. "You have disappointed me."

He lowered the weapon to his side. "Mr. Hardy, take her to the tank compartment and lock her inside."

A second of silence followed before the men burst into cheers. Three sailors pounced on Randall, bullying him aside. Hardy seized Camille by the arms.

"Take your hands off me!" She pulled back, but his strength seemed equal to iron chains.

"Let her go!" Randall shouted just before a fist connected with his jaw. He doubled over and sank into the folds of the crowd. Hardy shoved her toward the ladder to the hold and the small room that held the ship's rum and water casks.

"It's about time I got you locked up," he hissed in her ear. "And thanks for the bit of coin I found with the pendant, too. That was a boon."

Camille twisted from side to side, trying to free herself, trying to search for Oscar. They stumbled through the hold until a door with black iron hinges materialized. Hardy swung the door wide and shoved her forward into the black pit of the tank compartment. The door slammed behind her.

"Which one of you's got the skull?" one sailor asked, his voice muffled through the door.

"Throw it overboard!" another rallied.

Camille rushed forward to pound on the door, but slammed into a pair of thick arms instead. *Hardy.* He pinned her arms to his chest.

"Listen closely," he whispered. Camille struggled to throw off Hardy's hands, tried stomping on his feet, but he seemed unfazed.

"I said listen!" he hissed into her face, his rotten breath and the odor of myrrh overpowering. "I know about your deal with Starbuck, and I'll be damned if I'm going to let you give him the stones."

Camille stopped thrashing and stared blindly through the darkness. "What did you say?"

"But you can't take off just yet," Hardy continued. "You have to stay right where Starbuck wants you, and I'm going to make sure you do. You see, Starbuck's a means to an end for me, and so are you. If you've got any brains at all, you won't make an enemy of me."

What on earth did he mean by that? The way he spoke, Hardy sounded as if he had an agenda of his own. He shoved her away as a slim ray of light shed over them.

"Contain yourself, Mr. Hardy," Captain Starbuck blithely said from behind them.

Hardy smirked and moved aside. Camille spun around, her face burning with humiliation as the sailors whistled and catcalled. She spotted Oscar in the crowd, his face contorted with rage. And yet he stood still. He wasn't going to storm up to Hardy and snap his neck like she knew he must be wanting to do.

"Well, Camille," Captain Starbuck said, sounding weary. "Welcome to your new accommodations. Luckily for you, we have only a handful of days before we arrive in the port of Suez. Until then, I'd like you to reflect on the terms of our agreement. You've already gone against one of my requests." The Couriers. Because of her and the pendant, his crew had burst into chaos.

Starbuck held out his arms. "You're now experiencing the punishment for it. Should you breach the core of our agreement — forming plans to find the stone without me, that is — the punishment will not be as . . . dainty as this." Starbuck took the edge of the door as Hardy strode easily out of the tank compartment. "You do understand my meaning?"

Camille looked at Oscar, knowing exactly what the captain meant. Oscar didn't see her, though. His eyes targeted the back of Hardy's head.

"I do," she answered.

"Excellent. Good night, then."

Captain Starbuck slammed the door and blackness swallowed her.

A last resort. The captain had said this to Samuel the night she and Oscar had spied on them in the hold. This was what he'd been speaking of. She leaned against the tank compartment's door, her cheek pressed to the damp wood.

"Father," she whispered. She hadn't thought of him for so long. She wanted him to storm onto the *Eclipse*, lead a mutiny against Captain Starbuck, free her from the ship's makeshift jail cell, and assure her with one of his firmly tender hugs that her heart hadn't made a mistake back in the boulder dome.

She listened as the waves washed against the hull, sighing and creaking with the gentle Red Sea current. The smell of rum and stale water inside the nearby casks made her stomach roll.

"Father, I need you," she said, her voice small. "I don't know what to do."

He'd said he would always be there to guide her, as long as she needed him. How could she not need her father? Even when she was wrinkled and bent with age she'd need him.

"I have to get away from Starbuck and Hardy, but how?"

The tightness of her chest loosened as she spoke. Her father wasn't there to answer her, but it didn't matter. In the dark, she could pretend he was there. In the quiet, she could imagine what he might say. He'd tell her that standing still wasn't going to get her off the *Eclipse*.

Camille jiggled the door's handle without success. If only she could see the rest of her prison to gauge how large it was, and if anything inside it might prove useful. Reaching her arms in front of her, she slid her foot forward. After a few, cautious steps, her toe nudged something hard. The object scraped against the floor. She bent down to touch it, and her fingers felt the edges of a steel box. Camille climbed atop the box with careful movements. In the dark, with nothing to hold on to, she swayed with the ship more than usual.

Once she stood at full height, she reached upward with one hand. It smashed against the ceiling, the beams much closer than she'd thought they would be. The pain lasted less than a second as she realized the beam had moved. She ignored the soft, mossy coating of the wood as she reached up again. The beam rose and fell with each push. She gave it one big heave, and the beam slid away, scraping as she shoved it aside. The dimmest ray of light filtered through. Camille's eyes focused, and she realized she was staring up at the floorboards of the second level of the ship.

Camille clasped her hands together and smothered a squeal of delight. She'd discovered Maggie's secret stowaway spot — and the way off the *Eclipse*.

SEVENTEEN

A knock on the door startled Camille. She slid the beam back into place and hopped off the steel box.

"Camille?" She heard a man's stifled whisper, and then another knock.

She sloshed through the rum and water runoff to the door and pressed her hands against it. "Who is it?"

She prayed it wasn't Hardy. She worried about him like she did the white wolf. They were both predators, and Camille the prey.

"It's me, Samuel."

Her chest ached with relief, but then hardened back up.

"What do you want?" she asked curtly.

"To give you something."

There was an iron-barred rectangular opening near her knees. She crouched and, in the light of an oil lamp, saw Samuel peering inside. He pushed a candlestick through the opening, followed by a pewter holder, and finally, a tinderbox.

Camille grasped the objects tightly. "Oh, Samuel, thank you, you have no idea how horrible it is in —"

Camille stopped. "Why are you giving these to me? Did Starbuck send you to draw me into his favor?"

Samuel closed his eyes. "No. I just didn't want you to be in there without light. Captain Starbuck is not trying to hurt you, Camille."

She forced the candle into the holder. The way he spoke made her feel like a child, scolded dozens of times for the same misdeed.

"Then why does he have me locked up in here?" she asked.

"To protect you from yourself!"

"The only danger I face is from him!"

Samuel growled in frustration. "You don't have any idea what danger you face. Maggie hasn't exactly told you everything you need to know, has she? Have you ever wondered why?"

With trembling hands, Camille struck a flame and lit the wick. Light, glorious light, filled the space.

"Because she wants me to figure it out on my own," she answered. "And because she's an exasperating, self-important imp. I know Starbuck is after the stones for the power it can give him."

The power of immortality. She didn't say it. Her brother already believed she was possessed by the darkness of the stone. Why toss more ammunition into his hands?

Samuel hung his head. Was he really so vulnerable? McGreenery had been anything but. Perhaps Samuel's gullible nature stemmed from their mother, who had fallen prey to McGreenery. Camille lowered the candle a bit. If that were the case, then she might very well share the same vulnerable nature.

"I'll bring you something to eat soon. And water, too," her brother said at last.

Camille listened to her brother walk away. Not even the welcome glow of the candle was enough to comfort her.

Camille propped herself up on her elbows and inspected the crawlway before her. The flickering light illuminated a swath of only a few feet, and the top of her head brushed the floor planks above. The narrow space smelled even more rancid than the tank compartment. She had the urge to abandon her idea altogether. Samuel might return with food and find her missing. If he discovered the crawl space, he'd inform Starbuck. This hidden level of the ship was her one chance at escape. Maggie must have used it to hide, and she'd been able to slip on and off the *Eclipse* unnoticed. It could work the same for Camille. She just needed to find Maggie and ask her how.

Camille pushed her hair from her face and moved the candle to the left. The light struck two sets of red, glimmering eyes. *Rats.* Taking a shallow breath, Camille looked up and saw a thin gap between two planks. Through the gap she spotted a lantern mounted to a wall. It looked like one of the corridor lanterns.

"I want someone on Kildare at all times. The same goes for Jackson."

Captain Starbuck! Camille ducked her head as the floorboards groaned under his feet.

"I don't want either of those men near the hold. You

know as well as I that the moment we make port she's going to try to escape." Starbuck's footsteps moved farther along the corridor. "If she did, your sister would be in grave danger. She's being led astray by the very forces bringing her to the Death Stone. The magic is using her, and she doesn't have a clue."

What rubbish was this about the magic using her?

"She's convinced you mean us harm, Lionel," Samuel said.

There was a pause. The deck creaked as their weight shifted on the planks. Her brother addressing his captain so informally sent her mind reeling. Oscar had addressed her father by his first name, but never at sea. Even Hardy, as the *Eclipse*'s first mate, would be flogged for such an offense.

"I've already told you, I *had* to threaten the others. It was the only way to make her cooperate," Starbuck replied. "You know I would never harm you, don't you?"

The kindness in his tone surprised her. And why were they whispering? They moved on toward the fo'c'sle, and then the corridor was silent. Camille needed to find Randall and make sure he was all right. She had a feeling Oscar was okay, but she still wanted to see him and be sure. And if she could find Maggie, she could ask her how to exit the ship via the crawl space. Getting locked up just might have been a blessing in disguise.

Camille set the candle near the opening of the crawl-way. That way, she'd know in which direction to return. Using her elbows, Camille pulled herself forward through the forgotten level of the *Eclipse*. If she had come up underneath the corridor, Randall's cabin had to be somewhere to her left.

She crawled along, peering up through gaps here and there. Dust and mold tickled her nose, and hard pebbles crunched beneath her elbows. Rat droppings. Perfect.

As she breathed in the silt on the floor and stifled a sneeze, Camille heard a soft voice echoing through the crawlway. She lifted her head.

> *"Early one morning, just as the sun was*
> *   rising,*
> *I heard a maid sing in the valley below.*
> *'Oh, don't deceive me, Oh, never leave me.*
> *How could you use a poor maiden so?'"*

It was singing. A female voice. Maggie!

Camille moved toward it, her back and thighs and elbows beginning to ache. The singing grew louder as she crawled.

> *"'How could you slight so pretty a girl who*
> *   loves you,*
> *A pretty girl who loves you so dearly and*
> *   warm?*
> *Though love's folly is surely but a fancy,*
> *Still it should prove to me sweeter than your*
> *   scorn.'"*

Camille came to rest just beneath Maggie's bright, clear singing and pounded lightly on the underside of the floorboard. The singing stopped.

"I thought I was going to have to sing my throat raw," Maggie said. "What took you so long?"

"I'm fine, thank you, and yourself?" Camille said, rolling her eyes. "I found your stowaway spot — and your spying spot as well."

Maggie could have easily hidden beneath the floors of Randall's cabin and listened in on their conversations about escaping the *Eclipse*.

"Well, I hoped you wouldn't sit next to the rum cask sobbing uselessly," Maggie replied.

"Just tell me how you snuck off the ship without being seen," Camille said, impatient to get back and avoid being caught.

"There is a second opening, but it's a bit tricky," Maggie answered.

Camille sighed, bringing up another cloud of moldy silt. Why must everything be tricky? Just once, she'd like to encounter an obstacle that was breezy and fun.

"It's in the fo'c'sle," Maggie continued. "At the very bow of the ship, just above the transoms. You'll feel a knot in the wood. You'll have to wait to emerge until all hands are needed on deck."

"Which will happen once the *Eclipse* is about to dock in Suez," Camille said. "But that still leaves me on the second level of the ship. How do I get away from there?"

She heard Maggie sigh. "That's where it becomes tricky. If we get to Suez at night, perhaps you could do what I did and simply sneak on deck, over the rail, and shinny down a mooring line without being seen."

Oh yes. Because that sounded so simple.

"And if it's day?" Camille asked.

"Then I think one of the men in love with you is going to have to sacrifice himself."

Camille stared at the planks above, lips parted. "What are you talking about?"

"I heard Randall's big plan to cause a distraction," Maggie replied. "It's a good plan, too. If he makes a scene in the hold trying to break down the brig door, there won't be a single sailor in the fo'c'sle for you to contend with, and perhaps only a few on deck. Oscar and I can even meet you there."

The idea of being with Oscar tempted her, but it felt wrong, too.

"And what about Randall? What happens to him?"

She couldn't leave Randall behind to face Starbuck's wrath alone.

"He gets to be the knight in shining armor and you get to be rid of him, just like you want," Maggie answered coldly.

Camille wished she could glare at Maggie instead of the floor planks. "That is *not* true. You don't know the first thing about what I want."

Did Maggie really believe her to be so callous and unfeeling? She checked back to her candle. It flickered dimly. Camille craned her neck at the faint sound of jiggling steps — someone was on the ladder to the hold.

"I have to go!" Camille hissed.

"I'll have the stone and map with me when we meet on deck," Maggie said hurriedly. "You'll hear me singing again when we're close to shore. And remember, wait for the diversion in the hold!"

Camille crawled frantically back toward her candle, still opposed to Randall's part in the plan, but without time to argue with Maggie. A burst of squawks and snorts came from the caged animals in the hold. Someone was heading for the tank compartment!

She reached the opening and dropped down onto the steel box, grabbed the candle, and slid the ceiling beam back in place. The iron door shook as a key cranked inside the lock. Camille leaped from the steel box and dashed to the bench just as the door swung wide.

EIGHTEEN

*O*scar darted inside the tank compartment and shut the door behind him. In his hand was a large iron key ring, holding keys to every lock on the *Eclipse*.

"Are you all right?" He studied her from head to foot. "Did he hurt you?"

Camille fought the urge to run to him and bury herself in his arms. She quickly gave up. Oscar met her halfway across the room and crushed her against him.

"I'm okay," she said, breathing in the salty sea scent of his shirt. "You're not supposed to be in here."

A light rumble of laughter resonated through Oscar's chest. He pressed his lips against the crown of her head and pulled away. "No, I'm not. I can only stay for a minute. Hardy'll wake up soon and discover his keys are missing. I just had to make sure you weren't hurt."

It was the first time he sounded like the old Oscar. The Oscar with a soul. He fixed his eyes on her, his expression one of torment.

"I thought I was protecting you," he said softly. He shook his head and looked away.

"I'm okay in here." Camille grabbed his arm to stop him from turning back for the door. "I really am. Oscar, I found a way off the *Eclipse*. There's a crawlway between the decks."

He glanced up and Camille realized the beam hadn't sealed completely. Oscar didn't need the steel box. He reached the beam with his fingertips and slid it back into place.

"Where does it lead?" he asked.

"To the fo'c'sle," she answered, and then recited the plan for their escape, at the cost of Randall.

"But there has to be another way," Camille said. "We can't just leave him behind."

Oscar hadn't moved far from her. They stood together in the circle of candlelight, Camille wanting to slide back into his arms.

"For this plan to work, someone has to stay behind," he said, confirming what she hadn't wanted to hear. "But Randall doesn't have to. I can do it."

He hushed her before she could protest. "Starbuck can't hurt me. I promise you, Camille. He can't. He won't."

How could he be so sure? She began to object again, but Oscar took her cheek in his hand. He brushed her lips with his thumb. His skin was rough from hard labor, and chilled from the damp air in the tank compartment. His lips were so close and inviting. Her own demand that he not kiss her again came back to vex her. Oscar seemed to have listened to her, though, and he didn't attempt it.

"The only important thing is that you get off this ship with the stone and map and find your way to Cairo. Maggie says it's where the map leads," he said.

He was touching her so tenderly, Camille didn't even care that he and Maggie had discussed the map without her.

"You have to find me," she whispered. "I'll stay in Suez until you do."

Oscar let go of her. "No. It won't be safe to stay. You have to get moving toward Cairo. I know you can do it, Camille."

His faith in her flattered her more than declarations of love ever could.

Oscar held up the round of keys. "I have to get these back to Hardy. And I'll tell Randall and Maggie the new plan."

Oscar lingered in the threshold a moment, clearly not wanting to lock Camille in again. She encouraged him with a nod of her head. The heavy wood door shut, and she stood alone once more. But Oscar had held her. He'd touched her and — and he'd decided to save Randall from sacrificing himself. So perhaps he still wanted Camille to be with Randall. Perhaps nothing had changed between her and Oscar at all.

The northern tip of the Red Sea tossed the *Eclipse*, clutching the ship in the fists of contrary winds. Camille clung to the nailed-down bench in the darkened tank compartment. She'd forgone the candle, finding it impossible to hold it and the bench at the same time. Before being thrown into the hold, she'd heard nervous talk about the shoals lining the coast, and the treacherous winds that could blow the *Eclipse* into them. Submerged well below water, the hold would be torn to shreds, Camille along with it. At least in the dark she wouldn't see it coming.

She pressed her cheek to the bench seat, her legs straight out behind her, arms holding on tightly. The stagnant water swooshed from side to side, splashing her hands and face. She'd had to use the chamber pot not too long ago, and she heard it now, sliding back and forth. Lovely.

The ship lunged and rollicked, and Camille was grateful the first few days of being locked up hadn't been this violent. Calm patches of time allowed her to drift to sleep before being thrown from the bench when another cloudburst hit. A desperate side of her looked forward to being transported to the ice-covered land just so she could be somewhere with light. It didn't happen, though, and each time she woke she was both relieved and disappointed. She wasn't in control of the dreams. Camille had no clue who — or what — was.

The days blurred together with the bells signaling on deck, until Camille didn't know if it was day or night, or if the food Samuel delivered to her was breakfast or supper. He didn't speak to her except to ask if she was sick or injured or needed something more to eat or drink. Oscar hadn't sneaked back to see her, and Randall had not been able to come at all. He must have been under intense watch. She missed them. She longed for them both. She knew doing so was wrong, but being stuck alone in the dark, she couldn't bring herself to care.

And then, one unknown hour, Camille noted the

gentle sway of the ship, the calm delight of her stomach. Then she heard something else. A faraway voice trickled through the narrow space between decks, hunting for the pair of ears awaiting it.

Singing. Maggie had started to sing.

NINETEEN

*C*rawling through the ceiling proved more difficult with a lit candle in one hand. Camille hadn't needed to mark the opening into the tank compartment this time. She wouldn't be returning to it.

She slid toward the bow of the ship at a slower pace, still hearing Maggie's singing every now and again. The nests of rats and vermin grew abundant as the ship's ribs narrowed in. The damp rot of the wood showed in patches of mushroom-shaped fungus, and the stench of mold and dust intensified until her eyes watered. Having light to view the crawling space should have been a welcome thing, but a rodent to her left, guarding a nest of at least a dozen babies, changed her mind.

She kept an ear open for Oscar's planned riot in the hold. Until then she'd be stuck between decks with the rats. *Find the knot, find the knot.* The candle illuminated the planks, and she soon came upon the blackened knot. She set the candle down.

Straining her ears, she heard the snorts and snores in the fo'c'sle above her.

"Rise up, you lazy clouts!" Hardy's voice spoiled the quiet. She startled and hit her head on the floor above. "Suez is in sight. All hands ahoy!"

The planks shook and bowed with feet, the hubbub scattering the vermin. Any moment now Oscar would make a show of trying to break down the tank compartment's door. He'd be able to put up a fight for a little bit, at least, and the sailors would all descend to the hold to join in the fight or witness the spectacle.

She positioned her hand inside the knot, prepared to give it a shove. Any moment. The fo'c'sle's racket thinned out as the sailors made their way into the corridor and toward the companionway. What was Oscar waiting for? Had something happened to keep him away from the hold? Camille held the candle out behind her. She could crawl back, try to find the opening and return to the tank compartment. But she'd never be able to escape then. This was her only chance. Perhaps the diversion in the hold was just taking longer to accomplish than she'd assumed it would.

Camille gave the knot a shove. The floor moved easily and quietly, and her dilated pupils took in the dim light of the fo'c'sle with comfort. The empty hammocks swung and a few lonely flames flickered behind the grates of a potbellied stove. With a flutter in her pulse, she climbed out of the crawl space. She slid the floor back into place, blew out the candle, and hurried toward the doorway. There she waited, hidden around the corner of the threshold, poised to run on deck as soon as shouting rose up from the hold.

But no shouting came. Only Maggie's singing drifted down the corridor.

"Beyond the red-stained sun, she finds a plane
of light,
so fragile the glass, to the waters below."

What was Maggie still doing in the cabin? Camille listened from the empty fo'c'sle as Maggie kept singing. The melody was identical to the song she'd sung before, but the words were new.

"Beyond the red-stained sun, she finds a plane
of light —"

"Shut up!" Hardy banged his fist once on Maggie's door.

"Maggot!" she shouted in return. Hardy chuckled. His steps grew fainter, heading toward the ladder to the hold.

He was going below, and he'd find the tank compartment empty. Camille peeked around the corner, saw the vacant corridor, and ran for Maggie's cabin. A heavy chain and padlock were fastened to the door handle, sealing Maggie inside. Something had gone wrong. Terribly wrong.

Camille knocked lightly. "It's me! What's happening?" she whispered against the door's seam.

Maggie's hushed voice answered from inside. "My uncle figured everything out yesterday. Randall thought he could convince your brother —" Maggie stopped. She didn't need to say more. Samuel had ratted them out.

"I stowed the burlap bag in the Chinese urn in my uncle's cabin before he locked me in here. You have to go! Don't worry about us, Camille. Get the stone and get off the ship!"

Camille took off down the corridor, toward the galley and the closed door of Starbuck's cabin. Her eyes locked on the stained-glass circle stamped in the center of his door. *Beyond the red-stained sun.* Maggie's new song lyrics had been giving her instructions!

"Escape!" Hardy's gravelly voice screamed from the hold. "She's loose!"

Camille sprinted toward the captain's cabin. She barreled through, slammed the door behind her, and cowered under the blaring light streaming through the series of lead glass windows along the farthest wall. *A plane of light!*

Hardy's plodding steps sounded from the hold's ladder. Camille flipped the lock and searched for the Chinese urn. She vaguely recalled it from the time she'd taken tea with Starbuck earlier in the voyage. It stood near his desk, a forest of palm tree fronds arranged inside. She parted the fronds and saw the soft rumple of brown burlap at the base.

Camille clutched the bag to her and soaked in Umandu's rhythm and warmth just as someone slammed against the captain's door. The knob jiggled but the lock held fast.

"Who's in there?" Hardy yelled, and then pounded on the door again.

Camille raced to the windows, etched with diamond-shaped leadwork. Maggie's song had said *to the waters below.* She had no choice. Camille had to go, with or without anyone at her side.

She searched for a way to open the tall windows, a hand crank or a sash of some sort. But there was none. The windows were permanently sealed. The chair behind the desk was solid wood, yet her strength in the moment surprised her. She lifted it up by the seat, and with a running start, hurled it toward the windows. The chair broke through and disappeared in a rainfall of sharp shards, leaving a jagged opening in the glass. Leaning out, she saw the peacock blue waters of Suez Bay far below. Camille's stomach twisted with nerves and doubt.

A fist punched through the door's red-stained circle and a tattooed and bloodied arm reached through, groping blindly for the lock. It had to be now, she knew, and she kicked around the jagged opening in the window to clear away pointed crags of glass.

The door burst open and the iron lock shot across the cabin. Hardy stormed inside, his tattooed arm bloody and torn by the slivers of glass left in the circle's rim. He lunged for her, but Camille took a deep breath and jumped.

Wind rushed at her, her skirts ballooning out and flapping up as she fell. The cold Suez Bay engulfed her. She plunged deeper, water filling her nose and stinging the back of her throat. She forced her legs apart and kicked toward the surface, the bag still in hand. Pulling it up was difficult. The water filled the burlap weave and weighed it down. Finally, eyes stinging from the salt water, Camille broke the surface.

"There!" She heard Captain Starbuck yell. When she gathered her bearings, she saw she'd hardly distanced herself from the *Eclipse* ten feet.

"The windlass! Weigh anchor!" Starbuck ordered over his shoulder. The massive iron hook unreeled from the cathead and splashed into the water.

The wake smacked her in the face, but Camille was able to use it as a starting shove to swim by. A thin, white-brown line of land peeked at her from over the waves, dotted by a village of square-looking homes.

Her boots were slowing her pace, weighing her down even more than Umandu sitting heavy in the bag. She couldn't cast them off, not if she needed to traverse the port city on her own. But they were so heavy, and the bag was awkward to hold as she sliced through the waves toward shore. Glancing back, she saw the hole in the stern's windows.

A body streaked through the opening, past the ragged glass, and splashed into the bay below. Damn that Hardy! He wasn't going to give up. Camille kicked harder, the warm, shore-bound waves pushing her along.

Choking on water, she heard a chugging thrum approaching from behind. A sputtering *slap, slap, slap* of something striking the surface hurt her eardrums, which were level with the water. Treading laboriously, she spun around and saw a steamer coming right for her. Instead of sails and wind, the boat splashed through the water with a round wheel sporting a series of wide, white paddles.

Just ahead of the steamer, Hardy's muscled arms cut through the waves, swimming toward her fast. He would reach her in less than a minute. Camille pushed on, but her body burned, and more water filled her nostrils and throat.

Men dressed in dingy white shirts and trousers swarmed the railing of the low steamer as it came along-side Hardy. They waved their arms and reached out to him, shouting in a language Camille did not recognize. Hardy fought off the helping hands, his focus solely on reaching her. The steamer began to pass him, and more men reached out to Camille instead. They plucked her from the water, and she landed in the vessel without an ounce of grace.

"Come back! Hey, help!" Hardy screamed, changing his mind and swimming for the steamer. The men went to the railing to fetch him.

"No! Don't let him aboard!" Camille got to her feet, her lavender silk dress sodden, her boots filled to the brim.

The men stared at her in confusion. Next to them, a huge pile of black rocks weighed down the stern. Camille shoved by the men and pulled a steel shovel from the base of the coal mound. One man was trying to bring Hardy up over the side of the steamer, but he was heavier than Camille, and arguing with them at that. As soon as Hardy found his feet aboard the coal steamer, Camille plowed the shovel into his stomach. He doubled over and she broadsided him across the head. Hardy stumbled over the rail and splashed back into the water.

"Go!" Camille handed the shovel to one of the steamer men. "Faster, please!"

Their voices rose up in their native tongue in excited pitches, furiously shoveling coal into a hatch. The paddles picked up speed, the rhythmic hissing and sputtering of the engine doubling in noise and pace.

The steamer men in their coal-stained clothes came back to her side without a single question regarding why she'd jumped ship — or why they'd left the other man behind. Hardy punched the surface of the water before turning back for the *Eclipse*.

"From where do you swim, miss?" one man asked, his English finer than she'd expected.

She nodded toward Starbuck's ship, moving under sail once more. "From there. Does this thing go any faster?"

He signaled for more coal to be thrown below, then showed his gleaming teeth and taunted Starbuck's ship with a wave. Camille gripped the burlap bag to her stomach and felt like smiling in victory, too. But there were people on that ship still in danger. Setting them free would not be easy.

TWENTY

*I*ra would have set off a small powder explosive. Her father would have organized a militia to storm the ship. Her mother would have turned and fled to another continent. As Camille disembarked from the coal steamer and stood tall on a dock in the port of Suez, the last option was the most tantalizing. It was also the most cowardly. She wanted to be rid of Captain Starbuck and his crew, but he still had something she wanted. Something she needed. Four things to be exact: Oscar, Randall, Maggie, and Samuel, even after everything he'd done to thwart her. Camille needed to figure out what *she* would do.

The men from the steamer surrounded her, asking her if they could be of assistance.

"I can escort you to one of Mr. Waghorn's hotels."

"A steamer is due this night to gather passengers for Bombay, if you care to secure passage."

The ruined silk dress clung to her, but the setting sun, the only object in the vast, blue sky was already working to dry it. Without a cloud in sight, the bay glistened. Rimmed by golden sand and the lush green fronds of palm trees, Suez harbor had a tropical feel. But she'd been to the tropics before, and this place was most definitely different. It felt urgent and confusing, the noise filtering through her ears in a mixture of different languages. She smelled the salt water, the heat of the sun rising up off the wooden dock, the sweat streaking the faces and clothing of the steamer men. And the sun . . . It burned her shoulders and the crown of her head.

"I have no money for either of those things," Camille finally admitted to the eager men, remembering how Hardy had stolen the small bag of money Oscar had given her. The steamer men backed away, their eyes suddenly catching on other things to tend to.

"But you can't just leave!" she cried. As soon as the words left her lips, she realized the absurdity of them.

Of course they could leave. They owed her nothing. As she looked into the bay and saw the *Eclipse*, panic flooded her. Starbuck's ship couldn't reach the docks; the sandy moles were too high to allow the ship's deep hull any closer. But he would be ashore soon enough, and Camille had no resources for fleeing him. No money, no papers, nothing. Oscar had believed she could find a way to Cairo, but it seemed utterly impossible.

The dock around her swirled with activity, and yet Camille felt apart from it. She watched with her dripping clothes and sodden, tangled hair as a small dinghy rowed toward the *Eclipse*, carrying the Suez harbormaster. Once he cleared the vessel, Captain Starbuck and his sailors would come ashore.

Behind her, a tall, sun-bleached stone wall encircled the town. She had to get inside. Camille walked to the end of the docks, curious eyes searching her as she passed.

Sailors, men in fine clothing and suits, harbor workers, women with parasols, even a smattering of children, both dark skinned and light, stared at her from crown to foot. She must have looked like a circus freak in her drenched silk, clinging to a burlap bag. These people were going to be able to give Captain Starbuck detailed directions right to her.

Inside the city wall, she wound along the narrow, dirt-packed streets. Instead of blending into the crowds of people and braying donkeys, Camille sorely stood out as the foreigner she was. She searched for a place to hide and wait, wanting to see if Starbuck came through the city gates with his prisoners or without them. If without, perhaps Camille could find a way back aboard the ship while it was lightly manned. Maggie had told her to forget them and continue onward, but Camille simply couldn't.

A series of thatched awnings spread shadows over portions of the street and in the doorways of shops. She needed to tuck herself away in one of those shadowed corners. With vigilant steps, Camille hurried from one storefront to the next, her eyes open to the people around her. Starbuck would send his sailors to search the streets, the hotels, the shops. Everywhere.

Beyond the shade of the thatched awnings, the air sparkled with dust set aflame in the sunset. It was beautiful, really, and had she not been running for her life, she might have taken time to admire the fact that she was in a new corner of the world. Her father had taken her to so many different places, and together they had explored them. There was no time for exploration now.

Her quick eyes faltered as they traveled over a familiar face across the street. Not only the face, but the way his stout legs stood slightly apart, his arms crossed over his paunch, even the backlit waves of hair — as if sea salt had stiffened each strand into a blown-about crest.

It was her father.

Camille stared across the street, her lips parted, her grip on the burlap bag slipping. William Rowen stared back, his emerald eyes dancing with amusement.

"Father?" Her voice cracked. This wasn't real. It couldn't be real. "Father?"

People rippled by in front of her through the street, her father cutting in and out of sight.

She forgot her plan to stay within the shadows and stepped out from underneath an awning. Camille swerved around a woman carrying a basket of fabric, and was nearly trampled by a donkey loaded with beaded silk lamp shades. She arrived at the corner where she'd seen him, but he was gone. There was no one there but an old woman sitting cross-legged on the packed dirt, shelling nuts and throwing them in a wide, wooden bowl.

Camille searched up and down the street, desperate. It couldn't have been her imagination. Her father had been there. He'd been real, as real as that time he'd come to her in the underground pool. A glimmer of indigo caught her vision up the street. It was him again.

"Father!" she cried. He smiled, his white teeth straight and gleaming. God, how she'd missed his smile. Her father turned and began walking away through the crowds, a cloud of foreign voices congesting her ears.

Camille started forward, fearing she'd lose sight of him again, then stopped. This wasn't real. She knew it in her soul, deep beneath the keen yearning to run after him. Her father's indigo suit became a pinprick in the distance, blotted out behind the masses of people hurrying to beat the last rays of the sun.

A sob lodged in her throat and her chin crumpled as she tried to hold back tears. He'd come to her in the underground pool; he'd helped her find her way out. What if he'd come here, to this bustling Suez street to guide her again? She did need help. Needed him to guide her.

Camille pushed her way between two men in front of her and raced forward. She hiked her dress hem to her shins and sprinted rudely down the street, catching the shocked attention of women clad head to foot in blue robes. They swung aside as she ran toward them, and men dropped their loads from their backs. Shoppers browsing kiosks swiveled around as she bolted past. Her eyes peeled through the fast-parting crowd for her father's suit. The dust entered her mouth and coated her teeth as she gasped for air. At last she saw him. He was at the entrance to another street. It ran perpendicular to the one on which she'd just become the center of attention.

"Father, wait!" This time, he obliged. He came to a halt and faced her. He wasn't real. She knew it just as she knew Captain Starbuck's men would find her easily with all of this commotion. But she still closed the last few feet between them, needing to touch him, needing to be sure. Camille reached her hand toward his weathered skin, the etchings of his life at sea on his temples and creased forehead.

"Camille, no!"

She snapped her head to the right at the sound of Oscar's shout. She couldn't see him. The new street was wider than the one behind her, and doubly packed. Her hand still outstretched, Camille turned back to her father.

Her vision gave a sudden flicker. Her father's blown-about hair wilted and thinned. His weathered skin smoothed out into a drab olive hue, and the pair of gleaming emerald eyes flashed over to hollow black. A Courier. Camille drew back her arm.

The Courier lunged forward and pinned Camille's arms to her side to prevent her from reaching for his collar. The coldness hit with a force more powerful than the time before in Port Adelaide's harbor. She instantly fell limp, a sharp ache erupting in her bones. It shot up her spine, throughout her skull, and fingered the sockets of her eyes. *They freeze you from the inside out.* Roughly, and unexpectedly, her head smacked off the dirt street. Warmth cascaded back into her as she gulped in a dusty breath. Oscar had the Courier facedown on the street beside her, the Courier's head locked in the crook of Oscar's arm.

"Get out of here!" he screamed to her.

Two of Starbuck's sailors hesitated nearby, their captain a few feet behind, shouting at them to grab Camille. The sailors frantically glanced from the Courier they feared to the girl they were ordered to retrieve.

Camille got to her feet and ran. Her limbs were still numb and she knew she wasn't running fast enough. A fist knotted itself in her loose curls. Her scalp burned and tears sprang to her eyes. She twisted herself around and swung the burlap bag between the sailor's legs. He doubled over with a grunt and released her.

The second sailor barreled toward her as the Courier hurtled Oscar into a nearby kiosk. Vendors and shoppers screamed and fled. The kiosk toppled to the side, a mound of cut-glass candelabras and chandeliers shattering onto the street. There was only one place she could go where the sailor would not follow. Camille ran straight for the Courier, passing him, certain the portion of her brain governing reason had been frozen solid. She reached Oscar, on his side in a heap of crystal.

Starbuck screamed at his sailor, who was stumbling away, his cheeks scarlet. Camille tore open the burlap bag and reached for the map, but her hand touched something unfamiliar. Cool and smooth, like glass. Taking it out, she saw it was a small jar of white powder, corked at the top. Even without smelling it she knew it was myrrh-infused salt from the pantry on the *Eclipse*. But how did it get into her bag?

The Courier leaped onto Oscar, but Oscar swiveled and threw the Courier into the kiosk's shattered contents.

"Now!" Captain Starbuck screamed. Oscar turned to confront the sailor, who'd lost his hesitation and unsheathed a knife.

At the same time, the Courier vaulted forward to attack Oscar from behind. Camille uncorked the glass jar and with a swift flick of the wrist, cast the salt into the Courier's face. His unearthly shrieks drilled deep into her ears. While he clawed at his face, Camille seized the pendant from around his neck and snapped the chain. The Courier's anguished scream took on new strength. Oscar swept Camille out of the Courier's reach as the creature spiraled into a crackling blaze of embers and smoke.

But then Oscar stumbled and grunted. Camille landed on her side in the street, the wind thumped out of her lungs. She brushed her hair from her eyes and looked up in time to see Starbuck's sailor extract the blade of his knife from Oscar's ribs.

The screams of the market shoppers and the grating screech of police whistles muffled into background noise. Flashing memories of Oscar writhing on his back in a bloody pool in front of the beasts' cave intercepted the reality of the Suez street. The sailor lifted the blade to his eyes, staring at the steel with a look of pure horror. No blood coated it. The blade was clean.

TWENTY-ONE

*O*scar pulled Camille to her feet, and they were off and running.

"Follow them!" Starbuck shouted as a white-clad policeman took him by the arm and wrenched it behind his back.

Starbuck and his crew had all been detained by the time Camille and Oscar rounded the corner, out of view. Dusk's blue light settled the winding streets into a murky maze. Sputtering lanterns and patches of candle- and lamplight spilled through windows. Their feet pounded the hard-packed dirt, only slowing once the blows of the police whistles faded.

"Keep walking," Oscar said, his hand a stone shackle around her wrist.

Camille fought her way out of his grasp and stopped in front of an alleyway the width of two people side by side.

"There was no blood," she said, her throat raw from running.

Oscar didn't seem winded at all as he looked behind them on the empty side street.

"He just grazed me. Come on, we can't stop. We have to find Randall. He and Maggie are with Hardy and four more of the crew."

Camille batted his arm away as he tried to urge her on.

"Oscar, he stabbed you. He sunk his knife right into your ribs. I saw it happen!"

Camille reached for his side, determined to find the wound. Her fingers brushed the tear in his shirt before he grabbed her hand and pulled her into the mouth of the alley, out of view.

"I don't have time to explain right now."

"Explain why you're not bleeding? Why you aren't even hurting from his blade?" Perhaps the evening light was playing tricks on her eyes. Much like the trick the Courier had played on her earlier.

"It's not important. We have to find the others and get out of Suez before Starbuck finds us. Before he finds this." Oscar gestured to the burlap bag still in Camille's hand. She lifted the bag and threw on the straps. If it had given off any beams of white light in the marketplace attack, she had been too distracted to notice. But now, Umandu glowed brilliantly.

"Take off your shirt," she said, not caring about Starbuck or the stone or finding the others.

Oscar's face grew darker in the dusky blue light. "Do what?"

"Remove your shirt. I want to see the wound."

Oscar turned in a circle, his hand rubbing the back of his neck. At last, he pulled his shirt over his head, exposing himself from the waist up. Camille cautiously ran her fingers over his skin, traveling over the old lashing scars

Oscar had received from his uncle when he was a boy. But other than those, his skin was flawless. Perfection. No gaping wound, bloody and black. Not even a scratch.

He threw on his shirt and faced her. "There, is that what you wanted to see?"

He tucked his shirt back into his trousers with angry shoves. Camille fell against the wall of the building lining the alley. She breathed heavily.

"You said Starbuck couldn't hurt you," she whispered, remembering now. "You said the Courier couldn't kill you because . . . because you were already dead."

Oscar, still agitated, grabbed Camille's hand and pressed her palm against his chest.

"What do you feel?" Oscar asked.

Under her palm she should have felt the thud of his heart. It should have been beating wildly after the encounter with the Courier, after running through the warren of streets. But his chest was serene as a windless day at sea.

"Your heart," she whispered.

"It doesn't beat." He dropped her hand. "I don't have a soul, and I don't have a heart."

He ran his hand through his hair and turned away from her.

"Not since . . ." she stumbled over her words. "Not since the resurrection?"

Oscar leaned against the opposite wall, both hands pressed against the stone. He hung his head. "You didn't bring me back to life, Camille."

She moved closer to him, daring to slip her hands onto his slumped shoulders.

"But you're here. You're breathing and talking and alive —"

He pushed away from the wall.

"I'm a monster!" he shouted. "Maggie said my soul was somewhere between me and the Underworld, but what she didn't say was that I wasn't even human anymore. I don't need food, water, sleep. I don't need air, Camille. I don't *feel* anything."

He touched her waist and followed the curve of her hip, rustling the front of her silk skirt.

"I remember what it was like," he said, drawing his hand away. "I remember knowing how you felt against me."

Camille's entire body flushed.

"I thought maybe I could get it back," he went on. "If I kissed you. If I held you. I thought maybe I could feel it again."

Like in the hold on the *Eclipse*, during the kiss he'd forced himself through. Oscar stepped back.

"But I'm dead, Camille. It doesn't matter if I'm standing here in front of you or lying in some shallow grave. My soul's gone. I'm dead. I can't give you what you need."

She curled her fingernails into the stone wall behind her. Oscar's heart no longer beat, it no longer pumped blood through his veins. His body was dead, his soul in limbo. So this was why he'd been treating her so horribly. This was the reason he'd abandoned her, hurt her, told her he didn't love her.

She repressed the meek words of comfort springing to her tongue as memories of the pain he'd caused struck her with physical reminders. How many times had she sobbed herself to sleep? How many times had she worried that her lost fortune was the thing that had turned him against her? All that pain, all those tears, and it was because his body had gone numb to her? To everything?

"You said you'd made a mistake loving me," she whispered.

"I had to say something to make you hate me. I'm sorry, I didn't want to hurt you, but —"

Camille shoved him in the chest with such force he slipped and fell. Oscar stayed on the ground, hands propping himself up for an incredulous moment. She leaned over him, her hands in fists.

"As soon as you didn't feel attracted to me, you decided loving me was pointless?"

Oscar jumped to his feet and brushed off the seat of his trousers. "I decided you deserved better than a walking corpse."

"That's not for you to decide!" She lowered her voice as a person shuffled by the alley entrance.

"Don't fool yourself, Camille. It's easy to stand here and claim the way I am now doesn't bother you."

"So, what, you'd rather me love someone else?" she asked.

Oscar peered around the corner of the alley to search the street.

"I don't know how long I'm going to be like this. Even if we find the Death Stone, I'm starting to doubt there's any chance of going back to the way things were."

A police whistle blared nearby. Camille considered arguing with Oscar, insisting that she could never love him any less, even if his veins were no longer full with blood.

But the words wouldn't come. She pictured Randall standing at the entrance to the alley, watching, listening.

She remembered the anguish in his eyes when he'd learned the stone had been used to resurrect Oscar. The quiet dignity of his promise to continue helping her with the hieroglyphs. The way he'd noticed she bit the inside of her cheek when she was anxious. Camille didn't want to hurt Randall again.

She remained silent as the police whistle faded in the distance.

"We need to go," Oscar said. "Starbuck told the others to meet him at the Nuance Hotel past sunset."

Camille nodded. Daylight would make things better. Once they moved on to Cairo, everything would clear. They started down the street, drenched in darkness and a cool, blue evening mist.

"Is Samuel with them?" she asked.

"Do you really think he wouldn't be?" Oscar replied. "I don't know how to put this. . . . I could be way off, but . . . it just seems like —"

Oscar never stumbled over his words.

"Come out with it," she said, worried.

They rounded a corner and saw a terraced building with brightened windows. The door to the building shot open and three burly sailors spilled out. Captain Starbuck stood in the doorway.

"Track them down." His voice carried to Camille and Oscar, who retreated around the corner, out of sight.

The door slammed on the grumblings of the men. Camille heard the words "Courier" and "bitch," the second setting her blood to boil.

Once the sailors were out of sight, Oscar darted forward. Camille followed him into the skinny alley next to the building. Oscar sidled up to one of the first-floor windows and peered inside. She leaned past his shoulder to see.

The green draperies were partially drawn. Beyond the crystal lamp in front of the window, a woman was sitting in a man's lap, her neck thrown back in a laugh, a glass of something fizzy in her manicured hand. She splashed some over the rim, and she and the man only laughed harder. The woman's skirt had a slit clean up to her thigh, exposing almond skin. Another woman with loose curls and bare shoulders passed in front of the laughing couple.

"What is it with us and brothels?" Camille whispered.

The side of Oscar's mouth lifted in a grin.

"I didn't see anyone at the front door standing guard. I'll try to get in."

He moved away from the window, a woman's high-pitched giggle coming straight through the glass.

"And you're going to stay *right here*," he continued. He brought his head down to her level and looked her in the eye. "Right here, Camille, don't even think of coming inside. I'll take care of getting Randall and Maggie."

She glanced up at the brightened windows above. "And Samuel," she added. Oscar exhaled and stood straight again.

"I don't think he's going to leave Starbuck. And I'm not going to waste time trying to convince him."

Oscar had been about to tell her something before Starbuck had sent his men out. He knew something about her brother that she didn't.

"Then take me with you and I'll convince him."

Oscar muttered something beneath his breath and turned around in a tight circle.

"Starbuck's men are afraid of you. They think you're a magnet for Couriers, and they're terrified of them. The captain may need you alive to get what he wants, but his men don't share the same sentiments. They can't kill me but they *can* kill you, and I know they want to."

His explanation should have settled with a knifing chill. But all Camille could do was think in awe about Oscar's indestructibility.

"Fine." She coasted over the shake of her voice. "I'll wait here."

"Okay. If I don't come back out in thirty minutes, you can assume something's happened." He paused. "If that's the case, get yourself to Cairo. Forget me, forget Randall. Just take the stone and the map and make your way there. Got it?"

Her belly flipped at the thought of doing that all by herself. Impossible.

"Got it," she said anyway. Of course, if Oscar wasn't back in thirty minutes, she was going in there after him.

He lingered a short moment, then hurried out of the alley. As soon as he was gone, Camille felt cold. Calm. It was Umandu. It had stopped the merciless thrashing, settling back into its normal rhythmic pulse. The stone only went wild whenever she was with Oscar. Camille wondered about that as she walked aimlessly down the alley, toward the back of the building. It was going to be a long half hour.

A back door drew her curiosity. If a half hour passed and Oscar hadn't returned, she wondered if she could get in through there. With light steps, she tiptoed over to test the handle. It turned. Satisfied, she stepped back, but her heels stumbled over something. A hand covered her mouth and another arm pulled her into a tight hold. She screamed, but the hand muffled it.

"Lurking in alleyways, eh?" The person's breath was hot in her ear. She expected it to be Hardy's, but it wasn't.

Her captor dragged her up the few steps to the back door, opened it, and threw her inside. Camille crashed against a shelf inside what looked like a storage room, and turned toward the stranger, the burlap bag still resting against the small of her back. She didn't recognize his face from the crew of the *Eclipse*. Even though she was still in danger, she exhaled with relief.

The man slicked back his dark hair and walked toward her.

"What are you? Some sort of beggar?" he asked. He spoke with a strange accent. Camille wanted to answer his question, assure him she was not a beggar, but she couldn't make use of her tongue.

"You want some food? Some money?" He came closer and she smelled an overpowering foreign spice on him.

"I'll see to it." His eyebrows arched. "But you'll have to work it off."

Camille shook her head as she slowly understood what he meant, but was too disgusted to respond. The man gripped her arm with a brutish squeeze and dragged her from the back room into a carpeted hallway. They entered an arched doorway leading to the front room, where at least a dozen men and women turned to see them.

"Look what I found!" her captor shouted. The room erupted in laughter.

"Let go of me this instant!" Her cry only caused the red-cheeked people around her to roar with more laughter.

She tried to pull away, but the man kept his hold. A string of brass bells above the front door pealed through the raucous laughter. Camille looked toward it, hoping to see Oscar. Instead, Hardy stood there, his thin lips twitching.

"Ain't she a treat?" Hardy asked.

Camille's captor leaned in toward her ear. "I said you'd have to work it off."

He shoved Camille into Hardy's chest, who then immediately dragged her toward a set of sweeping stone steps.

"The captain's a bit ticked with you," he said. "No little jar of myrrh's going to help you this time."

Camille lost her breath and stared at him. "You didn't . . . I mean, *you* didn't put it in . . . did you?"

At the top of the steps, Hardy gave her a purposeful shove into the stairwell post, knocking her thigh into the sharply carved edge. Pain seared through her leg as he yanked her down the hall.

"Shut up," he hissed. "Like I said before, you're a means to an end. That's all."

Hardy pulled her past a display column topped with the bust of a Romanesque warrior. With her free arm, Camille snatched the bust from the column and swung it toward Hardy's head. It connected with his nose, crunching bone and spurting blood. He yowled and released her, blood streaming over his lips.

Camille ran toward an open terrace, but an apartment door to the left opened, and two more thick-necked brutes slid into her path. She turned back around, but Hardy was already there. He thrust her through the open door to the apartment.

Captain Starbuck's voice startled her from inside. "And what of Kildare, Mr. Hardy?"

He approached from a silk-paneled room, making a show of ignoring Camille.

"He wasn't with her," Hardy answered. He ripped a handkerchief from one of the other sailor's hands and held it to his nose.

Starbuck threw his aloof expression Camille's way. "Where is he?"

Camille searched the silk-paneled receiving room. Two other doors led off into the adjoining rooms of the apartment.

"Tell me where Randall and my brother are first," she said. Reluctantly, she added, "And Maggie."

"You've disappointed me, Camille." Starbuck sat down in a velvet pocket chair.

"Embarrassed you in front of your crew is more like it."

Offending Starbuck was probably not the best course of action, but being kind and demure would also get her nowhere.

Starbuck waved her toward the table and a second velvet chair. "Sit."

Hardy rammed his fingers into Camille's back and pushed her forward. She glared at Hardy and at the two sailors on each side of her, but remained standing. Starbuck lifted a pitcher and poured a stream of clear water into a glass. She couldn't remember the last time she'd had something to drink. He held the glass out to her. Camille ditched her stubbornness and went to the table. She reached for the glass.

Starbuck retracted his hand. "Where is Kildare?"

She caught a small tremor of his hand and the surface of the water rippled.

"You're afraid of him," she whispered.

The young captain snorted. "I am not." For the first time that Camille could recall, Starbuck sounded juvenile.

"Oh, you aren't?" She met the eyes of the sailors on each side of her. One of them was the attacker from the market. She pointed to him. "You there. Did you tell the others how you ran Oscar through with your knife, and yet he got away, unharmed?"

The sailor's Adam's apple slid up and down with a gulp.

"Did you tell them how you pulled the blade from his ribs and not a drop of blood coated it?"

Captain Starbuck slammed the goblet of water on the table. It splashed Camille's skirt. "Enough! Bind her legs and wrists and get her out of my sight," he ordered Hardy. "Then make sure the others are still secure."

Hardy tugged her arms behind her back. "My pleasure."

"The closer to the stone, the thicker the Couriers will become!" Camille shouted. If she could instill fear in the crew, they might abandon their captain. If Starbuck's numbers dwindled, then perhaps she and the others could overtake him.

"Do you know how the Couriers kill? They freeze you from the inside out!" Camille said, her wrists burning from the rope Hardy cinched around them.

Starbuck's cool glare told her he knew her scheme.

"And gag her, too," he said before disappearing out onto the veranda. Toward the other apartments, she bet.

Hardy gurgled on a chuckle and spun her around to face him.

"Didn't specify what I needed to gag her with, now did he?" he said to the other sailors, waggling his tongue.

Camille jammed her knee between his legs, and bolted for the door. One of the other sailors tackled her, though, and held her to the floor. She kicked and thrashed as his fingers found her windpipe and squeezed. Oscar had been right. Starbuck's men did want her dead.

"No!"

Hardy severed the sailor's choke hold as he slammed into him. Camille coughed and rolled onto her side, the phantom squeeze of fingers still there.

"The captain needs her alive, you idiot!" Hardy buried his fist into the sailor's stomach.

Camille wormed across the diamond-tiled floor, her head woozy, her hands still bound. Someone seized her and hauled her to her feet. It was the second sailor. He yanked Camille's head back and pricked the underside of her chin with the tip of his blade. Hardy bashed his fist into the man's temple, grazing Camille's nose in the process.

The blade clattered to the floor as the second sailor and Hardy staggered away from her. Camille went for the knife just as the sailor who'd tried to strangle her pounced again.

"Camille!" Samuel rushed inside the silk-paneled room through the veranda doors.

Starbuck entered behind her brother, shouting for order as the sailor shoved Camille to the floor. The sailor picked up the blade and with an ear-piercing war cry, brought it down.

Captain Starbuck ripped the sailor's arm backward, allowing only the tip to glance off her chest. Samuel came to her side and rushed her through the open veranda doors.

"Where are Randall and Maggie?" Camille asked, her throat raw.

"I promise, they're safe." Samuel hurriedly untied the rope at her wrists. "But you have to go, Camille. Starbuck's men are turning. He feared they would. They want you dead."

Starbuck and Hardy were fisting it out with the rogue sailors. This was her only chance to run, and yet she couldn't. Not without her brother.

"Samuel, come with us." The rope fell away and she grasped his hand, pulling it toward her heart. "You're my brother, I need you."

Her brother's uncertainty spread clearly over his face as he looked to Starbuck, right then ducking out of the path of a blade. Camille felt her brother's resistance. So Oscar had been right after all.

"I wish you'd chosen me, Samuel," she whispered, and then darted back inside the apartment, running for the door.

"Stop her!" Captain Starbuck cried as she sprinted into the hallway and toward the stairwell.

She reached the top of the steps and saw Oscar at the bottom, Randall and Maggie at his side.

"Wait!" she cried, descending the stairs two by two to catch up.

The dark-haired man who'd taken her from the alley came into the foyer, blocking their exit. Not *again*.

Camille shrugged off the straps of the bag and swung her arm round and round, whipping the burlap into a blurring circle as she came to the last step. Sweeping by the others, she brought the sack into an upstroke and nailed the man straight in the jaw, sending him to the floor, out cold.

"You're going to need to work that off," Camille told him coolly before opening the front door.

Maggie nudged his leg with her toe as she walked by. "Hmmm. Very thorough."

Another set of feet stamped down the marble staircase behind them. It was Samuel, and he looked to be alone. Oscar shoved a hand into his chest, propelling him against the banister.

Samuel coughed and grasped the railing. "It's not what you think. I'm coming with you."

Overjoyed, Camille took Samuel by the hand and dragged him toward the door as a thundering of footfalls resounded from upstairs.

"I saw a stable on the way here," Randall said, patting the breast of his coat. Camille heard the chinking of coins inside. "I can hire us a way out of the city."

The five of them fled through the front door into the still, black night.

TWENTY-TWO

*R*andall tipped up Camille's chin and lifted the lantern to see better. His fingers caressed the painful bruises at the base of her neck.

"Hardy?" he asked. His touch set off a flurry of tremors inside her stomach.

They stood outside the city wall, the eastern sky opening with dawn's first blue rays. Randall's reserves of money had been able to pay for a pair of horses, a wagon, and a last-minute supply of water and food. Now they waited impatiently for it all to arrive. Maggie, who'd proudly claimed she had studied maps of Egypt since the time she could read, explained the three-day overland route to Cairo would be roughly eighty miles.

"No. Hardy actually saved my life," Camille answered, thinking also of the small jar of myrrh that had helped her and Oscar in the marketplace attack. The irony of it made her laugh. But it hurt her throat too much, so she stopped.

"You were supposed to stay in the alley." Oscar paced in and out of the lantern's light. They were all nervous that Starbuck and Hardy would find them.

"I didn't ask that man to drag me inside," she retorted.

Camille wanted him to inspect her neck, ask her if she was okay, give her something to press against the still-bleeding slice underneath her chin. She knew he still loved her, still cared. Why couldn't he get over himself to show it?

Randall pulled a handkerchief from the breast pocket of his suit coat and handed it to her. Camille took it, guilty for the disappointment that the gesture had come from him and not Oscar.

"Thank you," she whispered.

"Captain Starbuck will be searching for us by now," Samuel said quietly as he came to stand beside his sister. She wrapped her arms around her middle to ward off the predawn desert chill.

Choosing to go with her had been difficult; she could see it in the way his thick, black brows slanted into a frown. She could hear it in the way his voice allowed nothing more than a whisper. Perhaps he'd started to see Starbuck as an older brother. A brother he'd never had. Perhaps having a sister wasn't enough.

The clanging of chains, the snorting of horses, and the clatter of wheels caused them to stand and hush. The black outlines of two horses, a wagon, and a few livery-men stood out against the arched city gates.

Oscar took the lantern from Randall and extinguished the flame. "It's about time your money came in handy."

Following the overland route took little navigational exper-tise. Littered on the edges of the route, which turned out to be a visible depression in the sand, were the bleached bones and rotting carcasses of horses and camels that had not had enough fortitude — or water.

The wagon wheels plowed westward through the fine sand as the sun rose and warmed their backs. The three men sat together on the front bench but didn't speak to one another. Randall and Oscar had their obvious reasons, but they didn't say much to Samuel, either. Every now and again, from the rear of the wagon, where she and Maggie stretched their legs, Camille would notice Randall and Oscar glance suspiciously at Samuel. They didn't trust him, she figured. They'd seen his loyalty to Starbuck just as Camille had, but she had to believe that in the end, blood would always be thicker than water.

"You're doing nothing to help your bruises heal," Maggie stated as Camille rubbed her throat. Maggie was busy fashioning a brimmed hat out of a china plate and dinner napkin scavenged from the crates of supplies.

"I think that sailor damaged me permanently." Camille poked at her discolored skin.

"If you'd have hidden yourself a little bit better in the alley . . ." Oscar said again.

Camille dropped her hand from her throat. "Are you still harping on that?"

"I told you they'd try to kill you."

Camille looked to the sky, squinting against the sun. "Well, they didn't succeed."

He turned around with a harsh stare. "That's not the point. They could have. So forgive me if I get a little angry at the thought of one of Starbuck's men strangling you."

Oscar faced forward and crossed his arms over his chest.

"She got away safely," Randall cut in. "There's no need for you to argue with her."

"We're not arguing. We're discussing why she should have listened to me."

Randall leaned forward to see past Samuel, who was unluckily sitting between the two rivals. "She doesn't need to listen to you, Kildare. You're not her fiancé."

"No, I'm not." Oscar propped an elbow on his knee and leaned out to look Randall in the eye. "Do you really believe you still are?"

Camille pounded on the back of the driver's bench with her closed fist. "Stop it. I don't need to listen to *either* of you."

Oscar and Randall both turned in opposite directions and stared out into the desert. Maggie, oblivious to the quarrel, tied the dinner napkin into a knot at her chin and sat back happily, her eyes cast in a band of shade. Camille wanted shade, too, but had no desire to look as ridiculous as that.

She leaned out over the side of the wagon and breathed in deeply. *Was* Randall still her fiancé? She didn't know the answer. And now that Oscar had brought it up, Randall would probably want an answer, too.

The desert undulated with surprising patches of undergrowth, and on the hilly horizon, Camille saw a brown spot.

"What's that?" she asked.

"Rest house. There will be nearly a dozen of them along the road before we reach Cairo," Maggie said. Camille didn't question her knowledge.

"We'll push through this one," Samuel called back. He hadn't let the horses fall much below a canter. Sweat gleamed on the horse's flanks, but Camille didn't encourage her brother to slow.

The wagon sped by the rest house, which in their hasty passing looked more like an oversized outhouse crudely constructed by children. As they traveled on, the incessant shake of the wagon gave birth to a throbbing ache in Camille's temples. She rubbed them, her fingers tracing the horseshoe shaped scar.

That horrifying night in the Tasman Sea felt like an eternity ago. Her father had been gone for nearly half a year now. Yet whenever her mind tripped over a thought or memory of him, there came the unwanted pull in the back of her throat. She'd been so sure Umandu would bring him back. She then remembered what Maggie had said earlier: *Did you really believe one resurrection was all the stone had to offer?*

"Maggie," Camille said.

She lifted the brim of her makeshift hat. "Hmmm?"

"Do you want an immortal kingdom on this earth?"

All three men crooked their ears toward the back of the wagon.

"It doesn't matter what I want," Maggie answered with a tone of gravity. "It's my family's providence. It's everything our family line has ever stood for."

Their wagon stormed past a scattering of westward-bound camels topped with wicker seats. Billowing white canopies partly shielded the women and men riding in them, their hands high and waving. They shrank on the horizon at an alarming speed.

"But don't you think it's . . . I don't know . . . *wrong* to live forever?" Camille asked, not wanting to tread too heavily on Maggie's family honor. Camille understood what it was like to feel a duty to the family, even if that duty had been marriage and not leading a new civilization.

"Not necessarily," Maggie answered. "You only think that way because it's all you've ever been taught to believe in and accept. You're taught that death is a natural thing. But why must it be? Why must it be the *only* way, especially when the way of the immortals is possible?"

Maggie's philosophical reasoning seemed a bit far-fetched.

"But it's only possible when the stones are stolen from the Underworld," Camille countered. "To steal is wrong. It's greedy. And for as much as he claims it's not, it seems as if greed is the only thing driving Starbuck to be the one to lead this new way of life."

Samuel slapped the leather reins and the horses jumped a notch in speed, throwing Camille off balance. She straightened back up and glanced at her brother. His jaw was clenched, his ears red.

Maggie played with the napkin knot under her chin. "Greed. Revenge. Jealousy. You're right. His reasons are the wrong ones. That's why we can't let him have the stones."

If greed, revenge, and jealousy were the wrong reasons, then what did that say about Uma? She'd taken the stones from Domorius out of bitterness and vengeance. Maybe the stones would always be tied to such base emotions. If that was the case, Camille wondered if, in the end, the immortals hadn't gotten what they'd deserved.

"What happened to Uma?" Camille asked. "Did she become mortal as well?"

Maggie tightened the ridiculous-looking napkin chin strap. "Oh no, never. She was a goddess after all. But that doesn't mean Domorius didn't punish her for taking the stones from him."

Camille covered her eyes with the plane of her hand so she could see. "What did he do to her?"

The three men sat still with intrigue.

"All the stories I've heard tell of a transformation, a curse Domorius cast onto her that changed her into an animal for all time," Maggie explained.

Camille could still see Maggie, could still feel the sun baking her skin. But a spreading chill in her chest removed her from her place under the pale Egyptian sky, dropping her back inside the memories of her ice dream.

"An animal?" she repeated.

Maggie nodded and tipped her face up to the sun once more. "A wolf."

TWENTY-THREE

*C*amille woke with a start. The sun had fallen below the horizon, the desert now draped with a cool sheet of air. Camille could taste the sour relic of sleep on her breath, and took a deep swig of water.

She hadn't wanted to sleep at all. *A wolf.* Domorius had transformed Uma, the goddess of the immortals, into a wolf. The same wolf stalking her in her ice dreams? It wasn't plausible. It didn't make sense that Uma would want to harm Camille, the very person working to rejoin the stones. Isn't that what Uma wanted?

The wagon slowed, the horses overdue for water and rest. Maggie returned her napkin and plate sun hat to storage as they rumbled toward a timber-framed rest house. The horses jerked toward the water trough, paying no heed to Samuel's attempts to steer.

"We should leave before sunrise tomorrow," Randall said. He didn't have to voice his concern that Starbuck could catch up to them. It weighed on all of their minds.

Oscar stood and stretched, extending his hand toward Camille to help her down. Randall stepped into his path and did the same. Camille ignored them both and leaped off without aid.

Inside the rough dwelling, three rooms were open and spare, each with a few benches and a table. Sand coated the weathered floors. It filled the cracks between wide boards and crunched underneath Camille's boots. The odorous attendant grunted hello and indicated which room the men could have. Camille and Maggie were shown to the smallest of the three rooms.

They'd gleaned a few useful items from the wagon's crates, including blankets; jars of dates, honey, pickled eggs; a loaf of bread; and heavily preserved sliced ham. It didn't seem as if the rest house would provide much of anything beyond water and a place to shelter.

"Shall we dine with the others?" Maggie asked drolly, throwing her blanket over a hard bench. Camille tossed her blanket on top of the table in their room, claiming it as her bed.

"Splendid. I'll go powder my nose," she replied just as sarcastically, and headed for the well around the side of the hut.

She pumped the handle until a gush of water spewed out of the tap and into a waiting bucket. Washing away the grit and sweat, and feeling her parched skin suck up the water, helped clear the fog of her afternoon nap.

With water dripping from her chin, Camille searched the misty purple plains of the desert. The eerie quiet worried her even more than the busy Suez streets had. Camille shook the water from her hands and turned back for the hut's entrance. Holding a clean-looking cloth in his hand, Randall exited the front door and approached the well.

"You might want to hurry; the pickled eggs are going fast," he said with a forced grin. He wrung the cloth nervously between his two fists before handing it to her. She dried her face.

"What's wrong?" Camille handed the cloth back to him. He closed his fingers around her hand.

"I decoded most of the hieroglyphs before being detained on the *Eclipse*," he answered, his expression troubled.

"And?"

His thumb caressed the ridges of her knuckles.

"I'm not sure if you should go through with this." He licked his lips. It was difficult for Camille to focus on anything else.

"I don't have a choice. It's not about me. It's about Oscar, and Ira." She pulled her hand free from his hold. "What did the hieroglyphs say?"

Randall grasped the pump and pushed it down again and again until water cascaded from the tap. He splashed his face and drenched his glossy hair, which had grown to brush his earlobes. After toweling off, Randall reached inside his coat's inner pocket and took out a sheet of paper.

"I was able to write most of the passage down before Captain Starbuck's men confiscated the papers you'd worked on. I'd been writing the letters or words beneath each of your drawings. It was difficult, considering there were some that could be translated up to three different ways." He handed her the folded sheet of paper. "So unfortunately, Captain Starbuck now has the meaning of the hieroglyphs, too."

Camille unfolded the paper, anxious. Randall's pencil marks were scratchy, as if he'd been scribing the translation at the very moment the sailors were wrestling him into ropes. In the fading desert light, the words read with an ominous tone.

Discover the gates through the statue of snakes, visible at the eventide hour. Row through the river feeding on fear, and deliver yourself to the highest power.

Camille broke from the page. Deliver herself to the highest power. Domorius?

"That's it?" All that work, all those hours spent drawing symbols, reading mind-numbing text . . . all those head-aches for a single paragraph?

"There was a handful of symbols left to decipher, but I wasn't able to finish them." Randall kneaded his eyes with his fingertips. "I'm sorry, Camille."

She folded the paper into quarters. "For what? Randall, you're amazing. I could never have decoded half of the symbols without you."

Randall tossed the dampened cloth over his shoulder. "It's not enough. I haven't figured a way to get you out of this."

Camille didn't have a chance to tell him it wasn't his burden. Samuel appeared in the doorway to the hut, shouting that the station attendant had slaughtered a chicken and there would be meat soon. An hour later, Camille picked at the cooked fowl, the deciphered hieroglyphs settling into her memory. Oscar wasn't present, his need for food nonexistent. Her appetite was thin, too, the mere thought of a feast sickening instead of tempting. She and

Maggie retreated to their wicker bench and tabletop bed. With the lamp extinguished, and no window to permit moonlight, Camille stared into the dark space above her.

"Is there a reason why Uma would want to harm me?" she asked Maggie.

"Of course there isn't." Maggie paused. "Why?"

She considered telling Maggie of the ice tundra realm, of the white wolf there. Maggie had already felt the frost Camille brought back with her, had seen it firsthand. And yet, Maggie had chosen never to speak of it. Never explain it.

"No reason," Camille answered.

She's being led astray by the very forces bringing her to the Death Stone. She'd shrugged off Starbuck's earlier words to Samuel as rubbish. Camille hadn't even realized she'd remembered the statement, but there it was, sitting in her mind, filling her with doubt. *Was* the magic using her? Was *Maggie* using her? The only reasons she'd come this far were for Oscar's soul and Ira's rescue. Even if the magic truly was using her, there was no possible way she could refuse to follow it.

"That night I saw you and Oscar in the canvas room on the *Eclipse*," Camille said. "He'd just told you about his affliction. Hadn't he?"

How thin were the walls? Camille didn't want to be overheard.

"He sliced his palm straight to the bone. I watched it mend in a matter of seconds. I couldn't tell you; he made me promise," Maggie answered. "He asked me if he was the same as a Courier. He wanted to know if he were to let one of the Couriers take him, if your connection to the stones would be severed."

Camille sat up and turned toward Maggie's voice.

"I told him you would still be tied to the stones," Maggie continued. "That you would still need to join the two to free yourself. I told him he was your best protection, considering nothing and no one but a Courier could do him harm."

Oscar had considered letting a Courier take him? Camille felt like running to the next room and pounding her fists into his chest.

"It was a lie," Maggie whispered.

Camille straightened her spine. "What?"

"I lied. Not about him being your best protection; he really is that. But if the Couriers had taken him into the Underworld, his lost soul wouldn't have a body to return to. Ever. And with Oscar gone, your tie to Umandu would be broken. The Couriers would simply retrieve the stone for Domorius and be done with you."

Camille tried to comprehend this, but couldn't.

"Wouldn't Domorius be fearful of me evading the Couriers? Of coming after the second stone, anyway?"

"No. To enter the Underworld, Umandu must have a pulse. You and Oscar have both given it that pulse. If one of you were truly dead, the stone would fall dormant, and there would be no way through the gates."

Fact after new fact swirled at Camille and made her dizzy. Maggie hadn't seen fit to tell her any of this before?

"The stone's pulse," Camille whispered. She reached for the bag beside her. It radiated calm heat and a soothing rhythm.

Whenever she and Oscar were near the stone together, it rumbled with unbearable life and a luminous light.

"You two are connected through the stone," Maggie said. "Through it, you gave him a little bit of your own life when you chose him."

Camille recalled the throb of her fingers after Oscar's resurrection, the unsettling energy pushing outward from underneath her skin. Camille had given some of her own life to the stone, to Oscar. Perhaps that was why its pulse beat in harmony with hers. It was as if the three of them — Oscar, Camille, and the stone — were all pieces of a puzzle coming together.

Camille took the triangular stone out of the bag.

"You said the stone acted like a powerful magnet, drawing Oscar's soul from the Underworld and fracturing it."

"Yes . . ." Maggie's answer sounded wary.

"Could a part of his soul have splintered off inside the stone?" Camille asked.

She'd always assumed the life inside the stone was a form of magic, but what if it was something closer to human?

"I suppose it's possible," Maggie answered.

Camille threw off her blanket and got down from the table, needing to think, needing to move. In the dark, she slipped on her boots, forgetting the laces.

"Where are you going?" Maggie asked.

Camille felt her way to the door without giving an answer and walked up the hall, out the front entrance, and into the cloudless, star-strewn night. There was no wind, no chirping of insects, no thrumming of ocean waves. Just the stone in her hand beating its familiar rhythm, matching the rhythm of her own heart. Was the reason she felt so at home with the stone because she'd given a part of herself to it? And then Oscar . . . could a part of himself be inside it as well?

Or maybe she was just exhausted. Exhausted and confused. The desert's silence split apart briefly with a snort of a horse in the corral beside the hut. Knowing what to believe and who to trust had become so muddled. Had Maggie lied to Oscar for Camille's benefit, or for her own? Maggie, prepped since birth for rejoining the stones of the immortals, wouldn't want to risk losing her opportunity for greatness.

Everyone Camille knew had turned on her in some way. Her father had lied about her mother being dead; Oscar had pretended he didn't love her; Samuel had ultimately chosen to flee Suez with her, but had betrayed her many times before. Randall was the only one who had stayed consistent. Dependable.

A slight wind swept the sand. Camille listened to the minuscule grains skipping over one another, each racing ahead to be the first to get nowhere. She hugged her arms around her chest, holding Umandu closer. That's what this entire journey had been so far: a race to nothing tangible. Umandu and everything it represented was still such a mystery.

Camille startled as a dark figure stood up beside a corral post. The familiar shape of the shoulders calmed her.

"Oscar, what are you still doing up?" She then remembered sleep was something he no longer needed. The stone's pulse escalated as he walked closer.

Another moan of wind wriggled through her silk dress. Her skin flashed over with goose bumps. Oscar sat on the sagging front step, and Camille settled down beside him. She slipped Umandu into his lap.

"I think . . ." Camille didn't know how to say this without sounding outlandish. "I think I've found a fragment of your soul."

The stone's brilliant light revealed Oscar's furrowed brow. She removed her hand from it, and the stone returned to amber.

"Maggie said it would be close by, right?" Camille went on. "That your soul could have fractured when the stone took it from the Underworld. Well, what if the stone does this for us because we're *both* connected to the stone? I gave you some of my own life through the stone, and your soul . . . what if a part of it splintered off inside?"

Oscar exhaled long and loud, turning the stone over and over in his hands. Camille placed her palm over one of his hands to demonstrate again. The rhythm thumped to a heavy jog. She hardly noticed the ice of his skin as the pearlescent light illuminated his face.

"I knew where the stone was," he whispered. "I didn't understand how, but I knew you'd put it in your mother's closet. And then I knew you'd moved it to the secretary."

As if Oscar had been able to feel it, like an extension of his own body.

"And you knew that the two stones needed to be rejoined," Camille said. Oscar had said it to Randall back in Port Adelaide, and then Maggie had explained as much aboard the *Eclipse*. "How did you know?"

Oscar threaded his fingers through hers. He paused a minute before speaking.

"Do you remember how I said I was in that dory with your father? When I was dead, I mean. How I was suddenly sitting in a dory with William, and even though it was like a dream, I could still taste the salt on the air and feel the cold of the water?"

Camille nodded, tightening her fingers around his. She'd been envious of him. He'd been able to see and speak with her father, and she never would again.

"He'd just smiled at me and started talking. As if we weren't in the dory at all. As if we weren't both dead." Oscar stopped and lifted Camille's hand. He brought it to his mouth. His cool lips brushed her skin. "I told you that I couldn't remember what he'd said. That it was all bits and pieces that didn't make sense."

Camille held her breath, remembering how much she'd wanted to know what her father had said.

"I did piece it together. Pretty soon after we started back for the *Lady Kate*. William knew he'd be staying in the afterlife. He knew you'd choose me, and he said he understood, that it was okay. But then he told me that I'd be different. That to be myself again, you needed to find the second stone and bring them back together."

Oscar pressed his lips harder against Camille's hand. A shiver of cold raced up her arm.

"But why didn't you tell me?" Camille asked. "Why did you keep what my father said a secret?"

Oscar pulled his mouth from her skin. "I didn't want to frighten you."

"How could any of that frighten me?" If anything, it would have brought her relief. Her father had said it was okay; he'd already known what her heart would choose and it was *okay*.

Worry creased Oscar's brow. His eyes drifted over her face, her question left hanging. Camille knew Oscar well enough to know he was thinking fast, especially with the way his eyes darted from point to point on her face.

"I knew something was wrong with me, Camille. I knew it the moment I woke up in that boulder dome. But only when I pieced together your father's words did I realize just how different I was. That my heart wasn't beating. I didn't want you to be afraid of me, of what I'd become. William said you had to find the second stone, but I didn't want you to feel obligated. You were already giving up so much by choosing me. By not marrying Randall."

So the loss of her fortune had played a role, just not the one Camille had suspected.

"I didn't want you to go after this other stone, or put yourself in danger's way because of what was wrong with me. So that's why I lied to you — at first."

Camille sat back. "At first?"

He took another moment before explaining. "I should have told you on the *Eclipse*. The truth, I mean. I had a few chances, but Randall . . . he was taking care of you. And you seemed like you were doing better. Like you were surviving. Moving on. You didn't know the truth about me yet, and you didn't need me. If you did know the truth . . . what would it matter then?"

Camille let go of his hand. The light from the stone drained from his face.

"I wasn't doing better," she whispered. "I'd lost you. I'd lost my father. Randall was helping me, yes, and I was surviving, but that was *all* I was doing: surviving."

Yet he'd believed otherwise. He'd believed she was moving on. Oscar should have known her better than that.

The moonlight cast a white sheen over their clothes and boots as Oscar set the stone behind them. He slid closer, his hip and thigh connecting with hers. She shivered again. Even as upset as she was, she didn't want him to pull away.

Camille touched his knee, the hemp of his trousers softened with age.

"Can you feel this?" Camille asked, suddenly nervous to be close to him. To know Randall might step out and see them at any given moment.

He covered her hand with his. "I know what it's supposed to feel like, but . . . no. I can't."

"You can't feel things physically, but what about emotionally? I mean, do you miss things or people? Like my father?"

He turned his eyes toward her. "Of course I do. I missed you, too, on the *Eclipse*. I missed you the same way I used to when I'd have to wait all week for Sunday to arrive, just so I could come to your house for dinner with you and your father. When you'd stay behind for a voyage, and every day for months I'd have to look at William or walk past your cabin, remember you, and then try and pretend I wasn't dying to get back to San Francisco just to see you again."

She couldn't help but smile and lean against him. Camille had never liked staying behind on a voyage either, and for the exact same reason.

"I want a life with you, Camille, but a life involves actual living. If this is how I'm going to be . . ."

"Oscar, don't." Her eyes warmed with tears. "Once we join the stones, you'll be fully living."

Anger trampled his sadness. "And if I'm not? If there's yet another catch we don't know anything about, what then?"

"What exactly do you want me to say? You seem to have made up your mind already. Only if the stone puts you back to normal will you allow yourself to love me. But where does that leave *me*? It doesn't work that way. Do you honestly believe I'm going to stand waiting in the wings until you make up your mind, clutching my hands to my chest and praying you take me back?" Camille took a shaky breath and stood up. "For months now you've been telling me we made a mistake, that I should give Randall a chance," she said, her stomach balled into a knot. "Well, I did. Do you know what I found? He's not the man I thought he was. He's better."

Oscar's mouth formed a thin line. He lifted his chin and rose up onto taut legs.

"Randall was there for me when you weren't. He still loves me even though I betrayed him. The more time we spent together, the more I realized he'd only showed me a guarded sliver of himself back in San Francisco. The real Randall is so much more."

Oscar looked statuesque in the glare of the moon, tense and flexed.

"You love him." His voice sunk into the word *love*.

She didn't want to hurt Oscar, even though he'd hurt her. She couldn't lie to him, though. She wouldn't lie to herself, either.

"I think I might."

Her throat ached, but she couldn't stop.

"It's not as clear, or as quick, like it was with you. With Randall it's a bit slower. Something that builds."

Oscar leaned forward a little, as if he'd just been punched in the gut. "I shouldn't be this surprised. But I didn't think . . ."

He let the rest of his sentence slide off. He hadn't thought he'd had any real competition. Camille waited for the nudge of satisfaction over the way Oscar must be fumbling for footing, the rug pulled out from underneath him. She'd fumbled and fell for so long herself. But she could never take comfort in seeing him hurt.

"I haven't made up my mind about anything yet, Oscar. But I *do* know that I need someone who can stick it out, all the way to the end, with or without knowing what will happen."

Camille wanted to believe Oscar could be that person. It hurt too much to even consider he might not be.

He turned toward the corral. The moonlight brightened the planes of his back.

"Get some rest," he said. "I'm on watch."

"Oscar." She didn't want to leave their conversation mangled and frayed at the ends.

"Camille, please." He wanted to be alone, to be furious and broken. She knew those feelings well. She would never forget the way they had burned when she'd been the one drowning in them.

TWENTY-FOUR

*T*he color of the sky wasn't the same the next day. The bleached horizon and the impossibly blue dome had a yellow tinge to it, as if draped with a muslin sheet. Maggie didn't need her napkin and plate hat, and the apples of Camille's cheeks no longer ached from squinting.

Samuel, again at the reins, urged the two rested Arabian horses onward. The men's backs swayed in cadence with one another. Camille would have smiled, or made a joke about it, if the tension had been anything she could cut without a machete.

Oscar hadn't said a word since leaving the rest house hours before. He hadn't looked at Camille, hadn't acknowledged good morning greetings from anyone. He stared into the space directly in front of him and nowhere else. Camille knew his body well, the way he carried himself, the flexing of certain muscles when agitated, when relaxed, when prepared to fight. As he sat with overwrought posture, Camille wished she could see into his thoughts.

Did he despise her? Was he angry with himself? Did he want to rip Randall's head from his neck and chuck it far into the desert? Without one word or expression all morning, she didn't have a clue.

"Has anyone ever been in a desert before?" Samuel asked from the bench. He had been quiet, too. All of them had been, though now they muttered a disinterested, unanimous "No" and then immediately after, "Why?"

"Something feels off," her brother answered.

Camille huffed a laugh. The entire world was off.

"Camille," Maggie murmured. "Do you have the stone and map?"

"I looked at it again this morning," she answered, dragging the bag to her side. A pulse of warmth lit up the edge of her thigh. "As long as we're on the right route to Cairo we should be fine."

The enchanted path on the map wasn't complicated or twisted this time, unlike the one that had led to Umandu. Camille figured navigating the Underworld would be complicated enough.

"Wear it on your back so your hands are free," Maggie said.

Camille leaned her head against the rocking lip of the wagon and stared up at the strange yellow sky.

"What for? I think I might doze a bit. I hardly had any —"

"Do it now!" Maggie shouted, startling Camille to sit up straight.

Randall twisted around. "What's wrong?"

His eyes snagged on the horizon and Camille followed his stare. A massive black cloud rolled up into the sky far behind them. It spread across the horizon as far as Camille could see, gathering sand from the rippled desert floor with unnatural speed. As it grew in height, the crest of the cloud collapsed, only to grow higher the next moment, rising up and up, collapsing, and then shooting even taller than before.

"Samuel," Randall said. The trembling roar of the cloud was already washing out his voice. "Samuel!"

The wagon slowed. Camille's brother turned around.

"Holy Mary," he breathed.

Camille threw the straps of the bag over each shoulder, the burlap pouch resting snugly in the center of her back. She looked at Maggie, her guide's expression set by trancelike calm.

"We need shelter." Oscar's observation was as calm as Maggie looked, whereas Camille's heart rapped against her breastbone.

"There isn't a rest house in sight!" she shouted.

The cloud was getting closer, now less than a few hundred yards away. And the winds had an odd strength. They weren't just blowing. They were pulling, sucking them toward the cloud, where jagged splinters of lightning crackled in the center.

"Get out," Oscar said, still clear and composed. "Out of the wagon. Unhitch the horses. Now."

The sand moved under their feet like liquid. Oscar unhitched one horse while Randall and Samuel did the same for the other.

"What will unhitching the horses matter? The sand will suffocate us!" Randall screamed as the howling storm closed in. The world behind the wall of whipping sand was gone, the sky above them nonexistent. There was no possible way; they weren't going to make it.

A guttural cry joined the ear-prickling bolts of lightning. Oscar tilted the wagon onto its two left wheels. It balanced for a second, and then crashed over.

"Shelter," he said, his eyes narrowed against the shower of sand.

Camille had seen a twister of sand before, inside the boulder dome when something dark — perhaps sent by Domorius himself — had tried to beat out the magic and white light of Umandu. This vortex of sand and wind and lightning made the boulder dome twister look like a newborn lamb.

The sand slid out from underneath Camille's feet, and she fell. The wind sucked and slurped. Her fingers dug into the sand for traction, but she slid back, toward the cloud.

A thin hand clapped down over her arm and squeezed. Maggie held on to the overturned wagon with her other hand and tried to pull Camille to her. Camille dug her knees into the fluid sand, but it didn't help. Oscar hurtled over the wagon, past the spinning wheels, and dragged both Maggie and Camille out of the wind and under the wagon.

Her skin had gone numb from the pelting sand. Once that stopped, a burning sensation took over. The wagon's sides didn't run flush with the ground, so currents of sand and wind swirled around their heads.

"This won't save us," Randall said, crouching directly in front of her. The muddied light dimmed even more. Maggie knelt on one side of her, and Camille felt Oscar's cool body on her other side. Samuel covered his head with his arms, tucking himself into a fetal position.

The sand moved them, the wagon creaking and sliding toward the cloud. A small tug on one of her shoulders didn't merit attention as the storm howled. Camille's eardrums shook painfully. Her hands flew to her ears, but they still ached. The cloud had at last swallowed them. The burlap bag lifted and slammed down in the gusts of wind, once, twice, three times. And then the strap split apart.

The burlap bag flew off, the remaining strap sliding down her left arm, spinning wildly around her elbow. Camille fumbled to grab hold of the flailing bag that held the two objects she could not, under any circumstances, lose.

The strap slid to her wrist. Supplies that had crashed to the ground beneath the overturned wagon disappeared from sight as the winds sucked them out, and the bag, now loose, was also being dragged out. With all her strength, Camille tried to pull the bag back in. The wagon shuddered violently, lifting a few inches off the ground, and the strap slipped off her wrist. It sailed past her powerless fingers and toward the opening. Everything slowed, even the storm, as Camille's eyes locked on the burlap bag. A physical pain ripped through her.

Maggie sprung out of her crouch, stretching forward with a leopard's reflexes. Her dainty fingers clawed the last inch of the flailing strap before it disappeared. Maggie's hold on the thrumming sandy floor wasn't as solid. The bag, caught in the turbulent storm, began to wrench Maggie out with it.

Camille and Samuel, both closest, clutched Maggie's legs, her torso completely exposed to the sandstorm. Maggie screamed, and Camille closed her eyes with horror. The sand must have been slicing her raw. She opened her eyes, and saw both of Maggie's hands gripped the railing — in one of them was the bag.

"Take it!" Maggie cried, and Randall reached over to do as she ordered.

The wagon jumped and shook again. Maggie's legs slipped through their hands as if they were made of butter. And then, she was gone.

Camille screamed and Oscar's cool arm pulled her underneath him, protecting her with his body as the wagon trembled and rocked. Camille closed her eyes to the stabbing wind.

But then the wagon settled, the roar of the sandstorm faded into a hissing sigh, and sudden silence chimed through Camille's ears. Pure silence. She parted her sand-crusted lashes, crawled to the opening, and wriggled out. Camille turned in every direction.

"Maggie!" she shouted, sand lodged as far in as her tonsils.

The men climbed out from under the wagon, all of them matted with sand. Camille spotted the two stunned horses about fifty yards away. Unsteadily, the mounts rose to their hooves and shook their manes. If the horses were still in sight, Maggie should have been as well. But there was no sign of her in any direction.

Samuel hacked on sand. "Dust clouds don't just disappear like this."

The sky was clear, the dust cloud completely disintegrated.

"It couldn't have been natural," Camille replied. "He must have sent it."

None of the men needed to ask who *he* was. Camille reached for the burlap bag in Randall's hand.

"It took her," she said. Had the cloud been a Courier of unbelievable proportion? "She saved the stone. The map."

"She always made it clear it was her purpose," Samuel said. "To protect the stone. To protect you."

The reasoning wasn't enough to relieve the clamp around Camille's throat, the unexpected hollow of her stomach. It didn't seem fair that Maggie would sacrifice her own life for something Camille needed.

"The horses, Samuel," Oscar ordered, brushing sand from his hair and clothes. "We need to get moving before whatever that thing was realizes it didn't get what it came for. Randall, help me with the wagon."

The chassis groaned as the wheels crashed back onto the sand. The horses were hitched and traveling along the overland route before ten minutes passed. Crates, canteens, and shattered food jars littered the way.

"Slow down," Camille said to her brother after spotting something ahead.

The horses whinnied their impatience as Camille jumped over the edge and knelt to pick up a mint green bone china plate. Near it an ivory napkin lay twisted beneath the corner of a wooden crate.

"Camille?" Randall called anxiously. Without needing to look, she knew he was checking the eastern horizon, either for another storm or for Starbuck and Hardy. She wasn't sure which was more hazardous. Camille let the plate fall back into the sand, stood up, and climbed into the wagon.

"We aren't stopping until we reach Cairo," she said, leaving no room for objections.

TWENTY-FIVE

*T*he wall surrounding Cairo was higher than the one that encircled Suez, and stretched for miles around the city. They saw it on the horizon at dawn, having traveled the night through. Guards in white uniforms greeted their wagon, their lanterns raised to see what travelers were emerging from the desert at so early an hour. The last day and a half they'd covered the remaining miles of the overland route, stopping only for water for themselves and the horses. Camille was exhausted, starving, and furious.

Domorius had taken Ira and Maggie, both of her guides, both of whom had devoted themselves to helping her and Oscar. She should have been able to protect them somehow. Maggie had vexed Camille for months. Now, without her, Camille felt unsettled. Directionless.

Randall spoke in French to the guards — a language Camille had not even known he could speak. A moment later, the tattered and weary travelers were waved through. Unlike ragged Suez, the early morning light cast a freshness over Cairo, which looked in every aspect to be a civilized, European outpost. Shops lined a courtyard, front windows were sparkling clean, displays ordered and extravagant, doorsteps swept.

Their wagon threaded along the narrowing streets, each one seeming to have a theme. One devoted to cut glass, another to silver, gold, and other metals, a third to embroidery and fabrics of every fashion and value, and a fourth to the finest smelling sweetmeats and confections. This last street alone was percolating to life in the early hour. Camille's stomach kinked at the scent. She was so single-minded, she ignored the curious stares they drew on the cobbled sweetmeats street.

Randall, who'd been riding beside her in the back of the wagon, stood abruptly. His stomach had been cranking out hungry complaints for hours.

"Hold, Samuel." Randall leaped out of the wagon before it even came to a halt.

He disappeared into one of the shops that twinkled with lamplight and emitted the mouth-watering scent of mint, curry, and garlic.

Samuel peered into the shop's tantalizing windows. "What is he doing?"

Nets of cured meats, mounds of figs, slivered bars of dark chocolate, fat rolls of bread, and wheels of cheese . . . Camille couldn't take the taunting any longer and turned away.

"We'll find an alley to rest in," Oscar said.

"An alley in broad daylight? Couldn't that be dangerous?" she asked.

"I'll be awake," Oscar replied. *On watch*, he'd called it the other night. And he'd stood sentry outside her door on the *Eclipse*, too. Always watching. Protecting.

Randall exited the confectioner's shop, his hand closed

around a bulging muslin sack. He bounded back into the wagon. Camille swallowed hard at the scent of roasted meat and sage.

"Do you think you have enough money for a hotel, too?" she asked, imagining a down bed, soft blankets, and pillows. Glorious pillows.

Randall handed her the muslin bag. Camille hadn't been eating well at all. The lavender silk dress she'd worn well in Port Adelaide had grown too big around her waist, and she had to work harder to keep the shoulders from slipping down.

"Go ahead, Samuel, find a hotel," Randall said, and then motioned to the food. "Never mind your manners, Camille. Tear into it."

As Samuel steered the wagon slowly down a thatch-covered street, Camille tucked into the still-warm roasted lamb as if she'd never again see food.

"Saving some for you, Samuel," Randall said between a mouthful of bread and cheese. Samuel slapped the reins, inspired to find a hotel. Camille offered some to Oscar, but of course he declined.

The buildings in some quarters of the city were well crafted, and in others common and rough. They found a clean-looking hotel with verandas, windows with wide-slatted shutters, and thatch awnings. Walking inside, Camille became aware of how grimy and tattered they appeared to the hotelkeeper and the handful of early rising guests seated in a parlor room. The guests craned their pasty white Englishman and Englishwoman necks over their steaming cups of tea to see the scandalous display of three men and one lone, unchaperoned girl in the lobby.

Randall requested two rooms and paid for them promptly, then ordered a hot bath for each room. All of these things glittered like luxuries, when not too long ago they would have been ordinary, everyday necessities. Certainly the women in the parlor simply expected to eat, sleep in a bed, and have water to wash with whenever they required it. Camille had lived that way once, too. Fine hotels, bountiful plates of food, attentive service.

Standing in the lobby, her boots packed with sand, stockings damp from sweat, hair a tangle of knots and brittle from the sun, the chasm between Camille and those women seemed impossible to traverse. She'd lost those predictable comforts when she'd lost her father. Randall handed her the brass key to her own room, and she remembered the threat of losing those comforts had plagued her even before then. The money Randall had just passed to the hotelkeeper was the same source of comfort her father had sought for her.

The keen desire to be submerged in a steaming bath and lie in a down feather bed faded as she followed the hotelkeeper up the steps. The men were shown to one room and Camille to another, diagonally across the marble hallway. She closed the door behind her, wishing they'd stuck to Oscar's plan and found an alley for respite instead.

———

Camille sat on the divan at the foot of the bed, drying her hair with a thick towel. She wore a red silk wrap the hotelkeeper, noting their lack of proper luggage, had kindly offered when her bath was being prepared.

The rose oil was more elegant than anything she'd smelled in ages. She breathed it in but couldn't help but think of the cloying odor of myrrh instead. And how she never would have known the map had been enchanted with it had Randall not thought to smell it himself.

A soft rapping came on her door. Camille cinched the wrap tighter around her waist and went to answer it. She opened the door a few inches and peered into the hallway. Randall stood before her with a bowl heaped with olives and figs.

"I thought you might still be hungry."

Camille opened the door wider and let him inside. Her room was dark, the heavy draperies drawn to block out the morning sunshine. The four of them had planned to rest until evening — *the eventide hour,* the map had called it.

She laughed. "I think the bar of chocolate was the final straw, actually. But thank you. I'll save it for later."

Randall set the bowl on a sideboard. He'd already bathed, and smelled of musk oil instead of rose. She looked away from his still-rumpled clothing and damp brown hair, aware the silk wrap she wore bordered on scandalous. He didn't pay it any attention.

"Camille, I want to ask you something." Randall stepped toward the enamel tub filled with warm, scented water. Nervous, Camille watched his hand running along the rim, instead of his face.

"When Oscar asked if I still believed I was your fiancé, I didn't know how to answer."

Camille winced. She *knew* that would come back to pester her.

"I want to be," he continued as he passed the tub and slowly approached her near the divan. "But I don't think I am, am I?"

There was no point lying. Randall had already proven that he could handle a little heartbreak.

"No," she whispered, still unable to meet his stare.

"Then, in that case, I suppose it would be completely improper for me to do this."

Randall closed the final step between them and pulled Camille against his chest. He kissed her, his arms fixed tightly around her waist as if he'd predicted her to wrench away. But she didn't. She couldn't.

Camille parted her lips and kissed him in return, unable to stop once she had started. She unclenched her fists and curled them into his shirt, the clean musk of his skin a seduction all its own. Camille didn't resist as he pressed her closer. The thin silk wrap felt too warm as Randall wove his fingers through her damp hair, his lips more urgent than just moments before.

Her legs bumped into the divan, and Randall guided her down to sit, still locked in their kiss. He slid Camille closer, his mouth drifting to her neck, his fingers deftly slipping down one shoulder of her wrap to expose more skin to caress.

And that was the moment she knew he had to leave. Before anything more happened. Before she decided she *wanted* anything more to happen, because the possibility was real. Too real and too close.

"Stop," she said, the strength of her voice gone. Still, Randall heard her. He pulled back, his pleasure-hazed eyes showing understanding even before she said another word.

The corner of his mouth twitched into a satisfied grin. And ever the gentleman, Randall drew up the shoulder of her wrap to cover her. He got up from the divan, but Camille didn't trust her legs to follow him to the door. Her whole body felt flushed and faint. He turned back to look at her before opening it.

"I'll let you sleep," he said, still wearing his sly smile. "Though I don't think I'll be able to now."

He closed the door behind him. Camille stayed on the divan another minute, her lips still burning from the way Randall had kissed her. From the way she'd kissed him back. But she didn't smile the way he had as she got up and slipped onto the bed behind the divan. She was already thinking of Oscar. Of their night together in Port Adelaide when he'd been a gentleman as well. Camille couldn't smile because she couldn't determine which encounter trumped the other.

She didn't want to love two different men. But Randall's visit to her room had put an end to her doubt. Camille knew it was already too late.

TWENTY-SIX

*S*he'd forgotten her boots. Camille had gone to sleep wearing only her red silk wrap, and now the soles of her bare feet punished her for it. She opened her eyes to the giant mouth of the ice cave, shivering, her feet melting the hoarfrost on the ice beneath her. The first thing she heard was the hollow moan of the cave. It was like pressing a conch shell to her ear and supposedly hearing the ocean inside. The cave sounded deep, its walls marbled with color and its entrance fringed with dripping icicles.

The second thing Camille heard was breathing, husky and wet. She closed her eyes and tried to wake up. Tried to command herself to be inside her hotel room. Terror froze her when she opened her eyes, perhaps even more so than the ice and wind. The ice cave was still there, her room in Cairo so far away it didn't even exist anymore.

Paralyzed, she listened to the breathing close behind her. The cold air burned inside her chest. She held her breath and turned to see the wolf less than ten feet away. Its white fur, fluffy and thick, looked like something Camille would have loved to run her fingers through. Its bleached brightness made it glow against the slate of the sky, a gathering of misty clouds coming in from the distant sea.

"Uma?" Camille asked, her voice shaky. The wolf's black lips sealed tight at the sound of the name. It cocked its head to the side. The silver tufted ears rotated toward her, piqued.

"Are you Uma?"

The rush of blood in her veins warmed her enough to forget her bare feet as she concentrated on the white wolf. The animal whined an answer Camille irrationally translated as yes. But then, its black lips peeled back, baring teeth, and its wet snout shriveled under a growl. A wall of wind battered Camille head-on, and with it sprang the wolf. Its front paws struck her square in the chest, slamming her down onto the ice. Camille barred herself with her arms, expecting another strike — but the wolf only retreated a few steps, its head low and still growling.

"What do you *want*?" Camille asked, fear twisting with frustration.

She pushed herself up onto her elbows and slid backward on the ice. Her elbow bumped against something solid. She looked behind her and saw the paring knife she'd dropped in the last dream. The ebony handle and steel blade were frozen to the ground, a glaze of frost and ice covering it. It had been there long enough to gather ice? Camille had not dreamt of the tundra for weeks. Were these dreams happening in real time, matching her own reality?

She pounded on the ice to try to free the knife. The ice didn't even crack. The wolf's lower jaw trembled as it growled. Saliva oozed from the corners of its mouth.

"If you kill me here, I'll never get to the second stone," Camille said to the wolf, feeling ridiculous for pleading with an animal. "Isn't that what you want? For me to take the Death Stone from Domorius?"

The wolf's ears flattened at the mention of the gatekeeper's name. It hunched down on its legs and leaped forward, nipping at Camille's feet. Its mouth left spit on her toes, but didn't break skin. She scrambled backward over the ice, hardly feeling the cold cutting into her as she got up and ran into the cave, toward the hollow moan of wind or water or whatever lay inside the recesses of the cavern.

The white wolf followed intently. Its ears were still flat against its head, its black eyes turning a dusky blue in the strange light of the cave. Camille's skin took on a bluish tinge, her red wrap a pale pink. The cave's walls painted everything in variations of their true colors, though they didn't quite make sense. Camille pushed stray pieces of her hair from her face as she backed up, farther inside the cave, away from the pursuing wolf. In the light, her black hair had streaks of silver.

The wolf lunged at her and raked its claws across her legs. Camille gripped her knee, shocked. Warm blood wet her hand and dripped onto the polished ice floor.

"I'm not a threat to you," Camille said. But she knew this animal wasn't going to listen. Even if it *was* Uma, it was still going to attack. And then a strange calm overcame Camille.

This animal was going to attack her. It was going to rip her apart and there wasn't anything she could do to fend it off. Oddly, Camille wasn't afraid. Morbidly, she just wanted it to be over and done with quickly.

The wolf pounced again. Its claws tore through the red silk sleeve and pitched Camille against the ice wall. Blood streamed from her forearm, over each finger, and spattered onto the base of the wall where it met the floor. Camille craned her neck, with new pain coursing through her arm. Everything stilled as she saw a row of wide icicles hanging above her. They clung to an overhang of ice and thinned down into needle-sharp tips. An arm's reach above, perhaps — but no farther than an arm's reach and a jump.

The wolf paced back and forth, its dusky blue eyes never leaving its prey.

"Please, just go away. Please just let me wake up," Camille whispered.

The mass of white fur sprang toward her. The wolf blurred in her vision as she threw herself as high as she could toward the icicle overhang. She heard the snap of the ice, felt the smooth-as-glass dagger in her hand. Her feet slipped out from under her as she landed, and she fell hard on the ice floor. With a twist of her hand, the sharp end of the icicle swiveled outward just as the wolf took its leap.

The wide, broken end of the icicle thumped her in the chest as the wolf impaled its throat on the icy spear. The white wolf bleated and writhed as it gagged a wet hiss, and then fell forward onto her.

Camille's wounded arm seared with pain as she struggled to shove the massive animal off. She finally rolled the wolf to the side and pushed it away with weak, desperate thrusts. Blood sprayed from the animal's throat, matting its fur and speckling Camille's bare feet as she crawled deeper into the cave, away from the dying wolf. Her blood, and the animal's blood, covered her wrap, darkening the red silk into streaked black patches.

Camille held her torn arm tight against her stomach as she stared at the wolf's body, her breathing sharp in her lungs. A shivering mist hovered above the wolf's furry shape, like a wall of heat radiating off a desert floor. Camille stopped gasping for air and watched as a whiter-colored mist whorled out from around the icicle embedded in the wolf's throat, twisting and weaving into a helix of silver vapor.

Camille blinked, and in the fraction of a second it took to reopen her eyes the ice cave was gone. The darkened space of her Cairo hotel room fell in around her, the heavy, brocade draperies shut to the sun. Shaking uncontrollably, Camille forced herself from the soft feather bed to the window, where she batted back the draperies. Sun streamed inside and shone on the blood covering her bed.

The air glistened with frost and her head swooned. She needed to bandage her arm; a mess of gashes started at her elbow and ended at her wrist. Pulling aside the torn panel of her silk wrap, Camille saw a lesser wound across her kneecap. Camille made it to the edge of her bed, and then it seemed to rush at her. Cheek down on the mattress, Camille hugged her arm close to herself again and pictured the white wolf. The strange mist rising from it.

She'd killed the wolf.

She'd killed Uma, the goddess of the immortals.

Desert sand drifted against the Cairo wall, a westerly wind drying the last damp locks of Camille's hair. She stood against the wind, awestruck at the vision greeting her from across the wide reaches of the Nile.

The tips of three pyramids stuck out above the hazy layers of pale sand, lush vegetation, and sparkling water.

On each bank of the great river strips of farmland thrived, fed by the flooded plains. Abruptly, the vegetation stopped and sand dunes took over. Camille had never seen anything like it. The pyramids were ancient beauties. No painting, however well done, would ever do them justice.

Oscar's hand snuck up on her, gently touching the sleeve of her dress.

"Why won't you tell me what happened?" he asked once again. Once she'd come to, Camille had staggered to their room for help bandaging her wounds. The silk wrap had been ruined, but at least her lavender dress was still intact. The sleeve hid her linen dressing.

"Because it's nothing that makes sense," she answered Oscar without looking at him.

"My heart doesn't beat, Camille. You think that makes sense?"

They'd taken one look at her bloodied arm and leg and jumped to the conclusion that Starbuck and Hardy had attacked her in her hotel room. Randall had seemed angry with himself, perhaps for leaving her alone in her room. But he hadn't said anything about his visit earlier while Samuel thoroughly disinfected and dressed her knee and arm.

"Listen, my dreams have been taking me someplace strange, okay?" Camille now explained. "And what's worse, what happens there seems to happen to me here, too, in real life."

The three men stared at her, as if she, not the Great Pyramid to the west, were the ancient wonder of the world.

"What happened to you there?" Randall asked. Camille waited for doubt, for amusement. He didn't show it.

"An animal," she answered, keeping silent about it being a wolf. She didn't want to draw any connections between Uma and the wolf that had attacked her. If she told them, she knew Randall or Oscar would never let her continue on to find the second stone. Domorius was out to stop her, as had been Uma. So why was she even still going? *Oscar. Ira. Maggie.* She repeated the names to herself as she purposely ignored Oscar and Randall overcoming their disdain for each other long enough to exchange a glance of concern.

"I'm fine, really. Can we just concentrate?" she asked. Randall sighed, still looking worn-out. She guessed he hadn't slept after all, just as he'd expected.

"The hieroglyphs said the gates are visible at the eventide hour through a statue of snakes. It's nearly sunset now," he said.

Camille took out the leather scroll and untied the red string. The familiar flash of amber light and sparking embers burned her eyes.

Oscar looked out over the eastern bank of the Nile. "A statue of snakes found where?"

The map rippled with an abundance of golden dust, which indicated sand. A sparkling sapphire arc undulated in a magical current defining the Nile, and emerald strips of farmland bordered each side of the river. The other markings were three coal black flagpoles, each flanked by two slanted rectangular stones. These were situated on the eastern bank of the Nile, right where Camille and the others stood.

She ran her finger along the drawings, black as volcanic ash. "I saw these symbols in the book we borrowed from Starbuck."

Randall took a look, his musky scent still present. "If I deciphered those correctly, they stand for a cemetery, or a necropolis."

Camille glanced up. The only thing in front of them, before the sand switched into verdant pastureland, was a city of ancient tombs. The monuments were massive and ornate, many topped by cupolas raised on pillars.

Randall inspected the map, then the mausoleums. "I guess I did get it right. Should we have a look?"

Oscar adjusted the strap of a bag holding canteens and food over his shoulder, and started down the slight dip in terrain toward the necropolis. The distance he'd kept since she admitted her feelings for Randall was worse than the distance he'd forced between them on the *Eclipse*. It wasn't volatile, or intriguing, or confusing in any way. She knew the root of this bitter, sad distance. Though she knew it wasn't wholly her fault, she still hated to hurt him.

Sand ghosted into her boots as she walked toward the first line of monuments dedicated to the dead. The *wealthy* dead. The intricate carvings and reliefs on the blocks of limestone and thick columns would only have been done for those who could pay for it.

Samuel ran his hand along the sand-pitted surface of a column. "So, a statue of snakes."

Oscar disappeared behind one of the monuments, his eyes roaming over the etchings.

"The snake hieroglyph looks as if it could be on every one of these," he called.

Camille stepped in and out of the shade cast by the columns over the sand, across flat stone platforms and walkways dusted with grit. The common snake hieroglyph couldn't be what the map was pointing to. Maggie would have known what to look for.

"It's not evening for another half hour." Oscar came out from behind a triangular-topped monument. "We're wasting our time."

"Is there something else you'd rather be doing, Kildare?" Randall asked.

"Instead of standing like targets in a maze of sand and tombs? Yeah, I can think of a few things. How about using some of that fortune of yours to buy us weapons?"

Randall snorted a laugh and turned his back, dismissing him. "A gun isn't going to protect you from a Courier."

Camille dug her fingers into her hair and rubbed her scalp. She breathed in the delicious scent of bath oils, but they failed to calm her. Those two would probably spend the entire half hour bickering.

"I know how to protect myself from a Courier. It's not them we need weapons against," Oscar said as Camille walked toward another monument.

"Is that so? Then who *do* we need to protect ourselves against?" Randall asked.

Camille rounded the sharp edge of a mausoleum. Her feet trampled on someone else's toes. She jumped back, her eyes traveling up a pair of narrow legs, past a muscular chest and square shoulders, up to a sun-blistered face rimmed by loose, light copper waves of hair.

Camille parted her lips. "Starbuck."

TWENTY-SEVEN

*C*amille backed up as Hardy appeared at his captain's side. The bruises rimming each eye and the bridge of his nose made him look even more terrifying than before, and to top it off, his beefy hand gripped a short pistol.

"You travel fast." Starbuck's voice bounced off the stones and echoed around them. "But not fast enough."

He kept his own pistol low at his waist, and trained it on Randall and Oscar. Not her. He couldn't risk her, just as Hardy hadn't been able to in Suez.

"Nice necklace," Hardy muttered as he circled Camille, moving back toward Randall and Oscar. Camille reached to her neck, where the sailor's throttling hands had left a ring of bruises.

Camille dropped her hand. "Nice glasses."

Hardy twitched one of his black eyes.

"And where has Margaret run off to?" Captain Starbuck glanced around. His gaze settled on Samuel. Her brother stood just beyond Camille, his expression frozen with alarm.

Looking back, Camille saw that Starbuck wore an expression of injury. She'd expected fury. He'd been wronged by someone he'd trusted, someone he'd probably seen as a member of his crew. Mutiny shouldn't have inspired such a look of sadness.

"Maggie didn't make it," Randall answered. "Sandstorm."

The nose of Captain Starbuck's pistol dropped a centimeter. "My brother adored her."

Oscar looked past Starbuck and Hardy. "Where's the rest of your crew?"

They didn't answer, and Camille assumed they'd all mutinied back in Suez. Captain Starbuck turned his attention to Camille, keeping his pistol aimed at the men. The desert crossing had raised red boils on his fair skin. A few of them had burst open and begun to scab, greatly diminishing his handsome features.

"Mr. Hardy," he said. Hardy pulled back the hammer on his pistol and brought the tip of the barrel to Randall's temple. Randall's arms stiffened at his side.

Captain Starbuck chuckled. "Now, Camille. The stone?"

The tip of Hardy's pistol pressed against the tawny hair at Randall's temple. She couldn't look at anything but the pistol, Hardy's poised hand, and Randall's locked jaw.

"Show me the stone," Captain Starbuck repeated.

Camille shrugged off the knotted strap of the burlap bag and reached inside. Heat seared her palm when she touched the stone. The temperature had doubled, if not tripled, but it wasn't the same kind of heat it bore when she and Oscar made contact. This heat was more severe, agitated.

She brought the stone out of the bag, the base of the triangular rock flat against her open palm. Umandu rippled with amber light. Long-fingered beams reached out of each rugged plane of the rock. Quickly, she looked at Oscar, who seemed just as perplexed. Before, it had only lit like this when both of them were touching it.

"You'll retrieve the Death Stone and bring it back here to me," Captain Starbuck said as the sun slipped lower behind the pyramids.

"You aren't coming?" Camille was surprised he'd omit himself from such a discovery.

"Enter the Underworld? There's no call for that." He motioned to Randall with a careless flick of his pistol. "Especially when I can easily lure you back to me. It's simple. You return with the stones and hand them to me, or your fiancé dies. Forgive the melodrama. It just happens to be effective."

The last crescent of sun disappeared below the horizon and the chill of the desert immediately set in. Camille's hot skin flashed over with gooseflesh, her only bit of warmth coming from Umandu.

She turned her head to the sound of a low hiss.

"What was that?" Hardy's thick voice muted out the hiss. "Was that a snake? Where is it?"

Camille raised her hand to silence him. The hiss became clear again. It *did* sound like a snake. She followed the delicate noise, her ears leading her instead of her sight. The hiss was long and steady, too constant to actually be coming from a reptile. It sounded more like cold water continuously dripping onto a sizzling griddle.

"Where are you going?" Starbuck asked.

"The statue of snakes," she whispered.

An easy wind picked up around them, stirring the top layer of sand and threatening to scratch out the hiss altogether. Camille closed her eyes, directing all her attention to her hearing. With every step, the hiss grew louder. She stretched her free hand in front of her, the imaginary snake so close it could have been coiling around her leg.

Camille's hand brushed something solid and she opened her eyes. She stood in front of a monument. The pale sandstone radiated heat, sighing a long hiss from the sudden drop in temperature. She stepped back and raised her chin to take in the entirety of it. This was not a statue of snakes at all.

Two feline-faced statues sat side by side on matching thrones. Each held ornamented staffs and wore warrior headdresses. Their stone eyes stared straight ahead, toward the Nile. Their bodies looked human, the stone chiseled to show them in simple tunic dresses, belted at the waist and draped to the ankle. Sandals covered their feet, each exposed toe twice the width of Camille's whole foot.

She ran her hand along one of its shins. The statue had not been in the necropolis when they'd first descended upon it. She would never have overlooked something so colossal.

"But where is the gate?" Randall asked.

Starbuck stood behind Oscar and gave the statue a wary inspection. He explored a burst blister on his chin with a few absent strokes of his fingers. The barrel of Hardy's pistol dug deeper into Randall's temple, his hand a vice around the back of Randall's neck.

"There ain't no gate," Hardy said.

Samuel walked in between the two pairs of giant sandaled feet. He spread his arms to his sides, his hands reaching the left leg of one catlike statue, and the right leg of its twin. He stood directly in front of a slim, carved arch that reached up to the statues' knees. The narrow indentation was not the same pale shade of sandstone, but dark and shadowed. Camille held her breath as her brother reached a tentative hand into the space. His fingers hit stone.

He retracted his hand. "I thought it might be . . . never mind."

There were no other openings on the face of the monument, and when Camille and Samuel circled it they saw the back also held nothing.

Umandu burned in her palm, the sting of her skin familiar with it now. Instead of pain, her hand felt charged with a trembling strength. It climbed through her, down her back, and into her legs. Her muscles were flexed without aching, solid and sure. The soles of her feet stuck firmly to the ground, centered and strong. Coming to stand once again in front of the hissing statue, a new depth filled the slim arch dividing the two cat-faced figures. Her brother's hand had met stone when he approached it, but now the space mixed with black, gray, and brown shadows. It moved with them.

Umandu trembled, sending out a command to her legs to move forward, toward the archway. Her mind held no sway at all.

"Camille." Oscar was suddenly right behind her, splitting Camille from the gravitational pull toward the swimming shadows. "You're not going in there alone."

"Exactly." Captain Starbuck nodded to Oscar with his blistered chin. "I certainly don't want you staying here with us. Two against two seems a bit more even, don't you think?"

Randall crossed his arms tightly over his chest. He

rolled his eyes toward the pistol jammed into his head. Hardy's fingers were tensed, his look of concentration severe.

"Don't wear yourself out," Randall said. Hardy gave the pistol a thrust.

That left Starbuck to guard Samuel. He'd once whispered a vow to never harm him. As baffled as it had left her, Camille had believed him.

Samuel stepped up onto one of the sandaled feet, striking a pose a brave explorer might take. "I'm going with them. Fewer for you to look after."

Silence and a long, contemplative gaze passed between him and Captain Starbuck. Camille watched their silent conversation with envy, wondering what was passing between them unsaid. She and Samuel never exchanged looks like that. Starbuck at last dismissed Samuel with a jerk of his pistol.

Her brother leaped off the big toe of the foot and straightened the lapel of his coat. Randall uncrossed his arms and reached inside his own coat. Startled by the sudden movement, Hardy socked him in the gut.

Randall doubled over and held up his hands. "Easy. It's for Camille."

He slowly reached back inside his coat and took out the folded sheet of paper onto which he'd translated the hieroglyphs. She went to him and took it. Randall held on to her hand.

"Just in case," he said. Camille folded and stored the paper inside the burlap bag.

"If something happens," she whispered, though no matter how quietly she spoke, all the ears surrounding them would hear.

If she could only have a moment alone with Randall to say an appropriate good-bye. Once she stepped into those murky shadows between the statues, she'd be gone, in some new place. Her hands shook. Randall covered them with his, subduing the tremors.

"Nothing will happen. Oscar won't allow it. I trust that," he said.

She stared at Randall's hands. Bleak light fell over the city of tombs, and she hoped it shielded her wet eyes. She glanced up and caught the tail end of a hard look Randall had passed over her shoulder, toward Oscar.

He nodded. "Go."

Camille slipped the straps of the bag over her shoulders, trying to maintain the calm his touch had given her. Oscar and Samuel waited between the two statues. They stood aside as she approached, the stone still pulsing in her hand. Each pulse matched the rapid thump of her heart. Nerves attacked her throat so fiercely she thought she might be sick all over the sand.

Oscar took one arm, and her brother the other. Together, they approached the veil of shadows. The strange, shuddering draw of the archway overcame everything else. It pulled her again, and with her final step forward, Camille drew in a full breath. She tasted a sour tang on her tongue. Frosty film climbed the leather upper of her boot as she lifted it through the archway. It mounted her legs, aggravating the new wounds on her knee from her dream, and finally encompassed her whole body as she entered the gates.

She hadn't closed her eyes, having wanted to meet the darkness head on. Crusted by frost in the darkness, she became aware that her eyes had shut anyway. Panicked by the loss of such simple control, she split her eyelids apart.

The brown and black mud of shadows had changed over to a wide, empty sky. The gray, colorless hue made it look overcast, but there wasn't a single cloud above. No clouds, no sun, no moon or stars. Nothing. Samuel's and Oscar's gazes spun in all directions. Each direction looked the same: the flat gray of a never-ending sky.

They stood on the peak of a prominent hill, the ground a single shade darker than the bland sky and bare rock. Theirs was the only rise of land in sight, a good four stories in height. The rest of the terrain below was flat and barren. Not a blade of grass, or a single shrub or tree grew. It was worse than the desert. At least that had had sand and dunes and a fraction of color. It was even worse than the ice of her dreamscape, if that was possible.

Samuel stepped to the edge of the ridge and peered down the impossibly smooth slope. No natural erosion would have ever made a slope so flawless.

"This is the Underworld?" he asked. "I expected brimstone and fiery pits."

Camille extended her fingers, and then curled them one by one. A hair-thin layer of hoarfrost cracked and whitened at each knuckle.

"These are the Forelands." Camille's voice sounded as if it had traveled a great distance, instead of from her mouth. Samuel had sounded distant, too. Muffled and muted, though not a single wind disturbed the air. *The air.* That was what made this place feel more like a dream than even the frozen tundra. Her dreams had wind and rain and sound. These Forelands had nothing real at all.

"And the entrance to the Underworld?" Oscar asked in the watered-down version of his voice. A layer of frost tinged his skin a purplish blue.

Camille didn't have an answer. She thought of Randall's translations and took off one of the straps to reach inside the bag. Her foot slipped on the smooth ridge coated in an invisible sheen of ice, and she landed on her side. Oscar and Samuel reached for her, but she slid from their fingers and down the slippery slope. Camille hugged Umandu to her chest, and floundered with her other hand for a ledge or bump or divot to grasp or slow her descent. She found nothing except a resurgence of pain from the wolf scratches on her flailing arm.

Her feet slammed against the base of the hill. She spun out, twirling in a dizzying circle until she lay flat on her stomach. Oscar and Samuel whirled past her a second later, their weight casting them even farther from the base of the hill.

Samuel slipped trying to get up. "It's like a skating pond."

Camille's ribs ached from landing facedown on Umandu, and her cheek was cold against the ground. Sitting up, she shoved Umandu into the bag and tried to stand.

Oscar helped to steady her, the soles of her boots unable to find purchase on the slick rock. He kept his hand pressed into the small of her back and urged her forward. Their feet coasted over the rock, unable to form normal steps. The ridge had a clear beginning and end. It rose up out of the ground like the upper half of a moon or sun.

The three of them shuffled toward the easternmost edge. Camille had already seen the other side from the peak of the hill. It held nothing but more rock and sky. But as they skirted the base, all three pairs of legs suddenly skidded to a stop and banged off one another.

Crouched at the base of the slope, ankles tucked up beneath him as a seat, Ira Beam sat and stared into the endless distance of the Forelands. He pressed his lips together and a phantom, melancholy whistle drifted past Camille's ears.

"Ira?" she said.

He quit whistling and chewed on a thumbnail instead. Camille stepped toward him and fractured the film of ice on her cheeks and chin with a shocked grin.

"Ira?"

He pushed his hunched shoulders back as if something had caught his attention. He still didn't turn to see her, though.

Camille slipped along the icy ground as she half ran, half fell, toward him. Slowly, Ira turned his head. He stared at her, cocking his head to the side and parting his lips.

"Ira, my God. It's Ira!" Camille screamed back to Oscar and Samuel, also approaching at a slip and run. Her shout echoed off the mound of rock beside her, tickling her eardrums.

Camille reached Ira's side and fell to her knees. She gripped the sleeve of his jacket, the leather cold and inflexible.

He stared at her with a placid expression. "Hello, love."

"Ira, you're all right! I don't believe it. Maggie said you'd be here, but God, I'd almost lost hope."

He pressed his eyebrows together, white and thick with frost crystals. The frost coated his lashes, too. "How long's it been?" he asked.

He rubbed his palms together, still crouching. He didn't pay Oscar or Samuel any attention as they slid in front of him. Oscar dropped to one knee and came level with his blank face.

"You were taken months ago," Camille answered. "By the Couriers. That's what the things were that attacked us in the harbor."

Ira's palms rubbed back and forth, back and forth, shaving off curls of frost. Camille grabbed his hands and forced him to stop. His skin was so cold it burned her.

"Months?" Ira's familiar face, his accent, filled her with joy. But there was something changed about him. She let go of his hands.

"Nothing changes," he said. "It's never dawn or dusk, night or day. Just this."

There was no humor in his eyes, once a constant sparkle. The sparkle had been replaced by a hollow, sober sadness. Her friend had been sitting in these desolate Forelands for nearly three months. Alone, scared, confused, cold. It would be enough to drive anyone mad.

"Ira, we have to find the second stone. Do you know where the entrance to the Underworld is?" Oscar asked. His gentle question turned Ira's attention away from the colorless sky.

The Australian's pupils were nothing more than small pinholes in each blue iris, his lips pale and nearly translucent. Camille winced when he looked at her.

"An entrance. Yeah. Yeah, I think so." He groaned, and grunted, and she realized he was trying to stand.

Camille forgot the searing cold of his skin, and lent him a hand. His knees snapped with the sound of breaking peanut brittle. The frost had built up around the perimeter of his boots, sealing him to the rock. Two hard yanks freed him, though a rim of ice clung to the edges of his boots.

"Where is it?" Samuel asked, a little less delicately than Camille would have preferred. Ira's state of mind, his body, worried her.

"Love, your hand's warm." Ira raised it to his cheek and pressed it against his solid ice skin.

The intimate gesture might have earned him a jab to the ribs back in Australia, but here, in this horrible landscape he'd endured for so long, Camille let him soak in her hand's comparative warmth. He closed his eyes, enraptured. His eyelids were two blue disks of skin covering the bulge of his eyes. The skin was so pale Camille thought she could see blue irises and black pupils through them.

Oscar peeled back Camille's hand, separating it from Ira's cheek. "We need the entrance, Ira."

Ira released her hand. A red, palm-shaped blotch colored his cheek.

"Over here," he said, unable to mask his despair over losing the source of heat.

He trod easily over the icy rock, though she, Oscar, and Samuel continued to lose balance. They rounded a corner and saw a gash in the rocky hill. It stretched from the base to three-quarters up the slope. Umandu's crazed beat pounded through the burlap. It wasn't like before, when it sent out the rhythm of a beating heart — a heart at rest, a heart excited. This was different. This beat felt frantic.

A pool of water lay at the foot of the gash. A fragile sheen of ice crystallized its black surface. Two small, wooden boats sat stiffly in the water, tied off on a metal stake driven into the rock. The boats were thin and curved at each end, widening in the middle just enough for two people to squish inside. Each had a pair of gold painted oars, and on the very tip of the bow, a lantern.

Camille slipped over to the boats. They were strung together with a length of triple-braided rope. She and Samuel climbed into one, and Oscar took the next, urging Ira to get in when the Australian simply stood by. Her brother's knees dug into her back, and her own legs were crammed into her chest.

She reached for the oars, but Samuel already had them.

"You can navigate," he said, and plunged the blades through the ice to heave them forward. The ice splintered and melted beneath the water.

Behind them Oscar also manned the oars, helping Samuel propel both boats forward. Ira sat inert, shoulders slumped forward. The panicked beat of Umandu's pulse increased as the bow's lantern pierced the entrance and darkness consumed them all. Instantly, the stone's pulse sputtered to a halt. The lantern flashed, suddenly aflame, brightening the inside of the cave. They glided over dark, languid water, and underneath arching stone walls.

Ira started to whistle. The acoustics of the tunnel warped it, turning it shrill. Camille recognized the tune, though; he'd taught her the song on their trek through the Grampians. The melody of "Bold Jack Donohue" ricocheted from stone to stone, into her ears, and straight through to her teeth. The flamboyant performances he'd given back in Australia had made the tune fun, but he was whistling it too slowly now. The beat was off, winding down like a music box about to click off.

The whistling stopped. A low, droning hum took over.

"Don't look into the water," Oscar whispered.

Camille immediately did the opposite. The inky river popped with lighter shades, swirling forms, and outlines. She gripped the edge of the boat as the white ripple of a dress and the undulating whirl of long, pale hair rose to within an inch of the surface. The figure flipped onto its back, and a pale-faced woman stared up into Camille's wide eyes.

"Oh my God, they're *people*," she said, as another figure rose into sight. Its arms and legs were not moving, but being carried by the current.

Camille shot a glance out to the other side of the boat. More figures: an overweight man in a sleeping gown, a young boy with shorn trousers and suspenders.

Samuel muttered a curse and stalled the oars. Their boat continued forward without slowing.

Camille looked over her shoulder, past her brother's pale face. Oscar had quit rowing as well. The current was carrying them, just as it was the people in the black water. The hieroglyphs had said something about water. *River feeding on fear.*

"Try to ignore them." Her voice quivered. How were they not supposed to be frightened? Camille wished Umandu would pulse again, and send another stream of heat through her. Her bones ached from the cold. Her teeth started to chatter.

"What are they?" her brother asked. The young boy in the torn pants lifted his face to the sound of Samuel's voice. The boy's eye hung from its socket, his skin bubbled and burned. The cartilage of his nose was exposed, as well as the lower half of his jawbone. Camille suppressed a scream and turned away, tucking herself into the belly of the boat.

"They're the dead," she answered. The droning hum that had replaced Ira's whistling reverberated through the wood beneath Camille's feet. It was coming from *under* the water.

"Are we the dead, too, then?" Samuel asked.

The answer seemed split between the two boats. She knew she and her brother were very much alive, but as for Ira and Oscar . . . she wasn't sure.

"If we were dead, we'd be in the water with them," Oscar answered.

Camille liked that theory. She sat up straighter. A blur of light filled the tunnel ahead: a shapeless, undefined spot. Their boat coasted toward it, the oars still at rest in the notches. Why even have the oars, then?

The blurry spot bellied out, expanding toward them like the fire cloud of an explosion. Camille held up her hand to shield her face. In a single beat, the smoke cloud receded, and when Camille lowered her hand, she saw the frost that had coated her skin and clothes had vanished. She was no longer cold or in the middle of a barren land. Their boats were drifting in the black water of an ocean bay. Ahead was a gray silt beach. The beach rolled up into an endless horizon of sand dunes, the crests scorched black. Beyond the crests was not a wall, or a landscape of any kind. If there had been stars twinkling there, Camille would have guessed it to be the night sky. But it was flat and black, and its emptiness had a terrifying depth.

Where the sky should have been was a craggy ceiling of pointed stalactites, forming upside-down mountains and valleys. The sharp points reminded her of the ice cave and the enormous icicle she'd plunged into the wolf's throat. *Uma's throat.* Camille's gaze dropped back down and fastened on the black void beyond the scorched sand dunes. The void swirled with a curtain of ashen mist. There was something finite about that void. Finite and eternal. The boat continued moving toward the unnatural coastline. Another boat, identical to theirs, lay lilting on the beach.

"Why do you think there's another —" she started to say, but just then the figures that had been traveling beneath the water beside them broke the surface.

They came up standing, so still it seemed as if something beneath the water was lifting them. Not an inch of their clothing or hair was wet or dripping water. Camille didn't want to see the boy with his ruined face, but betrayed herself and looked. He moved through the shallow water without any real motion. Each pale leg stayed side by side, closed together, and his arms were immobile at his hips. His eye drooped from the pink and red flesh of its socket, his other eye trained on the scorched sand dunes.

Samuel took the oars and jammed them through the dark water.

"I can't stop the boat," he said with evident panic. Camille's breathing grew shallow and quick. *Deliver yourself to the highest power.*

She had to deliver herself to Domorius.

The two boats scraped along the beach at the same time. The four of them sat frozen to their benches, Samuel's grip on the oars so tight his hands whitened. The fairhaired woman, the overweight man, and the disfigured boy arrived on the beach, too. Only then did their legs begin to move. In unison, and as slowly as a wedding march, they passed the extra beached boat and ascended the sand dune in front of them.

Camille watched in horror as they crested the dune. Their feet made no imprint in the sand. Without hesitation, they plummeted over the other side, through the white misty curtain. The billowing curtain shuddered violently, and then returned to its lazy sway.

Tremors rocketed through Camille. The others probably saw her shake as she got to her feet.

"I have to follow them."

"No." Oscar rocked the boat as he stood. "That's the real entrance to the Underworld. You go through there, and you might not come back."

"I have to get the Death Stone. It's through there, Oscar. The hieroglyphs said I had to deliver myself to —"

"Domorius. I know." He stared at the white hazy curtain at the top of the dune.

Two more figures broke the surface of the water behind their beached boats. They were older women, and as they glided toward them, their vacant stares saw only the dunes. They hit the beach and moved up a dune the same way the others had.

For as far as Camille could see, both left and right along the endless expanse of coastline, people broke the surface of the black bay and climbed the dunes. They were the dead, all of them crossing over to the other side.

The prospect of getting out of the boat and touching the gray silt beach with her feet frightened her almost as much as walking up the nearest blackened dune and plunging through the swirling curtain of mist.

"We can't just stand here," she said. It was the complete opposite of what her mind was screaming for her to do.

"Samuel, Ira, stay here." Oscar got out of the boat. His feet buried deep into the silt. The two older ladies who'd just plunged through the curtain had not left a single footprint in the sand, the same as the previous three. Camille lifted her foot over the edge of the boat and stepped down. Her feet also made imprints. The dead left no mark, but the living did. A good sign.

Ira sat hunched over, blankly watching the dead rise from the surface. Samuel got out of his boat and pulled it farther up onto the sand, behind the other beached vessel.

"I think I should come with you," her brother said.

Oscar took Camille's hand. The comfort of his touch only made her greedy for more. Right then, she couldn't imagine ever getting enough comfort from Oscar.

"My priority will be to Camille. It will be safer for you here, Samuel."

Camille let go of Oscar's hand. "Neither of you are coming with me."

Oscar stared at her, openmouthed. "Not a chance. I'm not about to let you leap over that dune alone."

She stepped backward, up the dune a few feet. The silt was so fine it slipped out from around her. "You *can't* come with me. Don't you remember? Maggie explained why. Domorius wants your soul, but he'll gladly accept your body."

Oscar came up the sand dune to stand before her. He cradled her cheek in his palm, pressing his fingertips hard against the line of her jaw. His touch was as tender as it was possessive.

"I can't let you go alone," he said.

"If you cross over that dune with me, the Underworld will claim you." She slid off the straps to the burlap bag while Oscar's other hand came up to cup her cheek. "It will claim the stone, too. You have to keep it."

But Oscar didn't move to take the stone. He kissed her instead. He parted her lips with his and kissed her more deeply, more hungrily than ever before. Oscar kissed her like he was saying good-bye.

Camille clung to him, forgetting the sand dune and the dead, forgetting her brother and Ira and the ashen mist waiting for her. This was why she'd traveled so far. He was why. Camille loved him. As Oscar kept her lower lip locked between his for one last, lingering moment, Camille knew she could never love anyone more.

Oscar took the burlap bag from her limp hand. "How do you know Domorius can't claim you as well?"

Another question to add to the queue of others, like to where would she fall, and for how long? And once she landed somewhere, how would she know where to look for the second stone? What if she were in the Underworld for ages, alone and wandering? Oscar and Samuel left on the coastline of the dead to twiddle their thumbs for eternity.

"I don't know," she said. Oscar ground his teeth. It was not the answer he'd wanted. "But I know I have to go. And that you can't."

Samuel raised his hand to interrupt. "My soul is still intact. Does that mean I can come?"

Oscar swallowed hard and turned away, furious.

"No. I can't let you," Camille said. She was surprised at how quickly she shot down the offer. She didn't really want to go alone, but Samuel . . . He was her brother. She couldn't let her fear chain him to her.

"But, Oscar's right, you can't —"

"I can." She pushed up the dune. "Trust me. I *can*."

Oscar quit his pacing and came up after her. "All right. An hour. If you don't come back out in an hour, I'm coming in. I don't care what it costs me."

He stared her down, even though to be precise, he was looking up at her. It wasn't a threat. He meant it.

"Two hours," she countered. "Give me at least that. I don't know what's beyond there —" She nodded toward the curtain of mist, swirling again in a breath of wind that did not extend to them. "Or how long it might take to find the stone. Just please don't do anything heroic because you're worried. Okay?"

He shifted his jaw side to side, and nodded with a slight lift of his chin. He didn't say anything. A spoken good-bye was not going to enter this bargain.

"Be careful, Camille," Samuel said. He seemed to realize the absurdity of his parting words and shrugged them off himself.

Before she could revolt against her own mock bravery, throw herself back down the dune, and huddle into Oscar's safe arms, Camille whirled around and ascended the rest of the scorched sand. The black void behind the gossamer mist made her heart drum faster. All the dead along the beach walked toward it without qualms, and yet violent quakes rumbled through her as she mounted the crest.

The mist fluttered like ragged scraps of fabric, again in a wind that did not reach Camille. Impossible, considering she stood within inches of the billowing shroud. The small hairs on the nape of her neck prickled as she heard a sigh through the mist. *Come.* Domorius knew she was there. He was waiting for her.

"I am," Camille whispered. She stepped off the dune and fell through the mist.

TWENTY-EIGHT

Camille's feet landed on something soft. Her knees bent into a crouch in a surprisingly graceful impact, and her fingers pressed into the thick tuft of a carpet. When she opened her eyes, she saw an Oriental design of black and gold and red. Camille drew back her hand. She knew this pattern.

Straightening her legs, Camille stumbled back and turned in circles. The floral wallpaper, the tallcase clock ticking softly in the corner, the frosted oval glass of the front door, the carpeted stairwell leading to the second floor. She stood in the foyer of her home in San Francisco, unable to breathe.

Camille stepped across the carpet and ran her hands over the flat wood of the clock, needing to feel it. Needing to know it was real. But it couldn't be. She couldn't possibly be home. Though the clock skipped beneath her hand, the house was too silent. Everything was there, every detail fulfilled, right down to the scent of breakfast cooking and of coffee percolating in the kitchen. But there was something missing.

Camille backed away from the clock, her hands fumbling for the pocket doors that led into her father's study. She shoved them aside and barreled in. A fire leaped in the hearth, and above it was her mother's oil portrait. The same half smile, the same brush strokes she'd memorized as a child. Camille ran her hand over the leather of her favorite chaise. She rushed from object to object — the low table where she and her father had eaten breakfast the morning the *Christina* set sail, the rows of leather-bound books lining the built-in shelves, the glass cart holding decanters of port and cognac and sherry, and the tigerwood box of cigars her father had cherished. She touched everything as she circled the room, feeling the loss of each and every object even though they were right there in front of her. Because they weren't. These things couldn't possibly be there.

Camille hurried to the picture window behind her father's desk. The damask curtains were closed to the view of Portsmouth Plaza. She reached for the trimming to pull aside the curtain, but as soon as her hand got within an inch of the window, she was right back beside her father's desk, a few feet away. She walked forward to try again, but her fingers never touched the curtain. Without even blinking, she was back beside the desk. Camille ran toward the window once more, but again found herself where she'd started.

Frustrated, she screamed and swiped a solid glass paperweight from her father's desk. It landed on the floor with a thud. The orange flower, trapped inside the glass, was undisturbed. Camille picked it up, recognizing the paperweight as a Christmas gift she'd given her father one year. Just like the flower, Camille was trapped. No matter how many times she might attempt to peel back the curtains, or even open the front door, she was certain whatever illusion holding her there would not allow her to leave.

She set the paperweight back on the desk and again smelled the delicious scent of flapjacks and sausage. Her hunger drew her out of the study and down the hallway toward the kitchen with visions of a full breakfast like Juanita used to prepare. The hash and eggs, sliced melon and tea. Camille hurried into the kitchen but found the stove unlit. The tile counters and wooden shelves all bare. There was no food for her to eat, just the tempting scent of it to remind her how hungry she was.

She backed out of the bleak kitchen and up the hall toward the foyer. What was she doing here? The hieroglyphs had said she needed to deliver herself to the highest power, but this house was empty. What if Randall had translated incorrectly? What if going over the edge of the scorched dune had not been what she'd needed to do after all?

A rash of sweat broke out on her back and chest, her hungry stomach churning some more, this time with dread. With a sweaty hand, she gripped the banister and lowered herself to the stairwell's bottom step. She buried her forehead in her clammy palms.

A creak in the stairwell behind her fired a jolt up her back.

"My Camille. I thought you'd never come."

Her chest burst with the rapid thump of her heart. She sprang from her seat and stared up at the top of the stairwell.

Her father stood with his hands tucked inside the pockets of his silk vest, his round belly stretching the mother-of-pearl buttons. He smiled down at her as he descended the steps, letting one of his hands run smoothly along the polished railing. Tears threw her vision into shiny blurs.

"Father," she said, her lips trembling.

He stood at the landing, a few steps away from her. If she wanted, she could climb them in one bound and fling herself into his arms. To feel his secure embrace, breathe in his salty sea scent . . . if only she could pretend.

Camille released the hand railing and retreated. This wasn't her father. Just like this wasn't her home. Just like the Courier in the Suez marketplace hadn't been him either. This place — this man in front of her — was an illusion. He wouldn't feel the same, or smell the same, and even the smile he gave her now was not the one she'd loved. He was showing too much gum, and there weren't enough wrinkles etched around his temples.

"Who are you?" she asked.

"What sort of question is that? I'm your father." The false William Rowen ventured the rest of the way down the steps. Camille positioned herself farther away, in the doorway to the dining room.

"You're not my father. And this isn't my home. Where am I?"

He took a cigar from the silver case Camille's real father had used, and produced a flame with a mere snap of his fingers. He puffed a few times until the end glowed red, and then the fire between his thumb and forefinger was extinguished.

"You are exactly where you want to be."

He stepped forward and the facade of her father's image melted away. A tan, well-muscled man evolved before her. Kohl rimmed his onyx eyes and lips. His gold nose hoop brushed the defined peaks of his upper lip, his hair shaved close to his scalp. *Domorius.* It had to be.

"When my pilgrims leap from the dunes, their heart brings them to the place they know as home. There, they stay for eternity."

His deep and thunderous voice rumbled the floor beneath her.

"But I'm not dead," Camille said, hoping it was true. If she'd already died, then at least she hadn't known or felt it.

"No. You are worse. You are an intruder."

The cigar vanished as Domorius curled his hand into a fist. He wore little clothing: a knee-length skirt, leather sandals laced around his calves, a gilded breastplate, and shoulder coverings fringed in leather strips and golden discs. He pounded his breastplate.

"You dare enter my realm with intentions of stealing the Death Stone?"

His lips pulled back from his teeth, stained indigo as if he'd just drunk from an inkwell.

"I had to." Camille's voice was weak compared to the bone-crushing sound of his.

Domorius entered the dining room. Her thighs knocked against the table as she backed away some more.

"You stole a soul that was rightfully mine." His unrelenting stare seethed abhorrence for her. No one had ever looked at her with such pure hatred.

"It wasn't my intention to steal from you. I didn't even know you existed," she said.

Domorius growled and his nostrils flared. The dining room walls wrinkled and dimmed, an ice blue light brightening around them. The table she braced herself against shook, and her hands fell through the wood as if it were sand. Domorius silenced his growl and the walls smoothed over, shutting out the blue light. The dining room table was solid wood again, able to support her.

"Death does not heed the ignorant," he said, moving around the opposite end of the dining table. Where was she going to run? She knew this home by heart, every nook and cranny, how many strides each room took to cross, that there were twenty-nine steps leading to the second floor. But Domorius had imprisoned her. He controlled everything she saw.

"It's one soul," she said. "Just the one. Please."

"And the one leads to two, then four, then eight, until the population of immortals grows exponentially. I have dealt with this epidemic before, and will not do so again."

His tan skin glistened with what looked like sweat. The oil lamps on the table caught a swath of his skin. He sparkled like the gold dust on the map.

"His soul is past due," Domorius said. "There is nothing you can do to save him now."

He raised one of his abnormally long fingers. The overgrown, yellowed nail curved toward the pad of his fingertip. "However, I will allow you to save yourself. Simply give me the Life Stone."

"You mean Umandu," she said.

He sealed his lips and exhaled, the sound of expelling breath hollow from the core of his throat. The punched tin ceiling of the dining room flashed over with another wave of ice blue light. The gatekeeper's flaring temper seemed to reduce the illusion he'd created for her.

"I do not speak its name." The floor rumbled again as he spoke.

Of course. Uma. The goddess he'd once loved, but betrayed. The goddess Camille had quite possibly killed in her last visit to the icy dreamscape.

"And if I don't give *Umandu* to you?" Camille said, wanting to see the illusion of her town house flicker once more. It did.

Domorius held out his hands, palms up. The muscles of his arms were more impressive than Oscar's. And that was saying a lot.

"Then you have a choice for your confinement. This . . ." He flexed his fingers and the entire dining room blew away under a burst of blue fire. The walls melted, the table and chairs dissolved like sugar in boiling water. The carpet disintegrated under her feet, and the foyer beyond the dining room entrance blasted into shards of crystal blue glass.

The illusion of her San Francisco home was gone, and Camille stood on the dark banks of a wide, lethargic river. Her toes were out over the slippery edge. She teetered forward before finding her balance and throwing her weight back. A rocky surface met her backside roughly.

The water was an arctic blue and flowed thick like syrup. Though everywhere around her was like nighttime in a jungle, the water was somehow lit from the depths. A procession of dead glided along the surface of the river — men and women both wizened and youthful, young boys and girls, and even infants, still as stones riding the current on their backs. Camille's heart ached with the sight of the youngest ones: a small girl with scraggly blond hair and soot on her cheeks; a naked baby, its bowed legs splayed out at its sides. Her stomach churned and Camille had to turn away.

Only then did she notice what was behind her. A barren and black hill immediately rose up from the banks of the river. Torchlight lit a series of wide, flat steps leading to an overlook. There, she saw a large throne looking as if it, too, had been carved out of the rocky hillside.

Camille's eyes caught on a notch carved into the base of the throne. Inside, an object shimmered with dark ruby light.

"Or this," said Domorius, whom she could no longer see. He started to replace the illusion as swiftly as he'd taken it away. But when it sealed over, completely rebuilt, Camille was not inside her town house anymore.

Camille breathed in the scent of wood and salt, of tar and wind. She blinked her eyes hard, but when she opened them again, found the room around her had only grown stronger with detail. The dip of the floorboards beneath her was even more severe.

Her cabin on the *Christina* was just as she'd left it the night the storm hit in the Tasman. In the corner of her cabin, the lantern lay in shattered pieces, a puddle of melted and dried wax sealing in the shards. Her pillow was on the floor, her blanket hanging off her bunk. Pale yellow light streamed in through the porthole, so bright Camille's eyes watered when she looked full-on.

She stepped to the doorway with caution, fearful Domorius would greet her in the corridor. But the length of the corridor was empty, though unreasonably bathed in the same pale yellow light as her cabin.

"Camille?"

She clasped the frame of her cabin's entrance. Oscar! She turned toward the companionway. His voice had sounded like it was coming from on deck.

"Camille, where are you? Are you here?"

The illusionary ship rolled starboard and Camille stumbled for the companionway.

"Oscar?" she whispered, but then halted.

No. No, it couldn't be him. Domorius was just taunting her with Oscar's voice.

"I'm sorry, Camille. I couldn't just stand there waiting for you to come back over that dune."

She closed her eyes and tried to shut out Oscar's voice. God, it was so real. So real that it hurt not to answer.

"Please, tell me you're here." Oscar's voice had traveled further away, growing softer. "I shouldn't have let you go."

Camille barely heard the last sentence it was so soft. Illusion or no illusion, Domorius had her trapped. She rushed to the companionway and climbed the rungs, the ropes real enough to leave tiny hemp slivers in her palms.

Salt spray slapped her in the face as soon as she emerged on deck. The warm sunset light of belowdecks was gone, replaced by angry black waves spooling around the *Christina.* Camille held on to the companionway overhang as the ship pitched sideways and then crashed backward. Just like the moment she'd come out on deck with her father in the Tasman's storm, her eyes swept across deck, searching for Oscar in vain. She hadn't seen him that terrifying night, and to no great surprise, she didn't see him now. But she heard him still, his voice screaming her name again and again above the reverberating claps of thunder and the deafening roar of the ocean.

Not an ocean. Not an ocean. Camille squeezed her eyes shut to the imaginary storm and felt her way back down the rungs belowdecks. Even with her eyes still closed, she knew something had changed. The air was cool and damp, heavy with the odor of mold and bracken. She stepped off the last rung and opened her eyes. The hemp rope her fingers were curled around was slimed black and draped with seaweed.

Camille yanked her hand away and turned to face the galley. Her lips parted with astonishment. Every surface of the galley — the tables and benches, the shelving and stove — was coated in iridescent green mold. Coral and barnacles crusted the galley in pink and gray patches; the liquid inside jars on the shelves swam cloudy and clotted; and black, lacelike mildew hung low from the beams like giant tongues dripping saliva.

"Camille!" Oscar's voice shouted once again. This time it came from the farthest reaches of the darkened corridor.

Camille threw her hands over her ears, unable to stand the panic and worry in his voice. A trickle of water slid off the deck and down the companionway rungs, splashing her neck and back. She shivered and stepped forward, out of the path of another surge of water. She turned and watched as the trickle slipping down the companionway accelerated into a steady current. It splashed around her feet and soaked her hem, the fast current blocking off the rungs altogether.

"I'm over here, Camille! Can't you hear me? I need you to answer me!"

The splash of water escalated into a cascade, pouring inside the galley without pause. The water rose around her ankles as Oscar again screamed for her to answer him, to go to him and let him know she was all right. Camille backed up through the now shin-high water, following Oscar's voice even though she knew it could not be him.

But the water . . . it was real. She felt its icy chill creep up her calves and billow her silk dress.

She entered the darkened corridor, the lanterns unlit. The deluge of seawater raced up her thighs and submerged her hips.

"Please, Camille, where are you?" The desperation in his plea equaled her own as the water started to lift Camille's feet from the planks. Seawater buoyed her up, but her sodden dress was weighty and pulled her right back down again. Salt water leaked into her closed mouth and choked her as it slid down her throat. She slapped at the water and kicked to keep herself afloat, but her head dipped under and panic coursed through her.

"Camille!" She heard Oscar shout one last time as her head bobbed above the surface.

She lifted her chin for one final gasp of air and cried, "Oscar!"

Sudden light flooded the blackened corridor and Camille crashed down onto her hands and knees. The frigid water was gone as soon as she opened her eyes. Beneath her was the lush carpet of her San Francisco town house. Slowly, she rose to her feet, shaking from cold and fear, and gasping for air.

She saw Domorius standing in the far corner of the dining room. He walked toward the table and extended his enormous hand.

"If you give me the Life Stone, I will spare you the curse of reliving that scene again and again, for all of time."

Something inside Camille fissured at the thought of going back to the sinking *Christina*, hearing Oscar's desperate pleas as she drowned in the rushing water — and then waking up to do it all over again. Forever. But to give

Domorius the stone would be to hand over Oscar's soul. Even if she did have it, it was something she would never relinquish.

"Your strength surpasses my own tenfold," Camille said. She took fast steps toward the foyer before Domorius could reach her. "Why don't you simply take the stone from me?"

He lowered his hand. The room shifted under his flaring temper. She'd made him angry. Why *didn't* he cross the room and search her for the stone? He could have assaulted her right from the start. Why this game of cat and mouse?

Camille's trembling muscles ironed out flat as the answer came to her. Without Umandu, Domorius could rule only over the dead inside his realm — not the living.

"You can't touch me," she whispered.

The floor rolled violently and the carpet disappeared into the rock of the black riverbank.

"You have no real power over me, do you? You just have this illusion. Your magic."

The walls and ceiling thinned to a fragile shell. The furniture and decor turned lucent. Camille's beating heart, her soul, her very life, was her own magic against him.

The gatekeeper parted his black-rimmed lips into a grotesque void and screamed before bashing the table before him into a pile of dust. The blue flames ate away the illusion in a single chomp, and the rocky hillside and bright blue river of dead filled back in around her. The procession of dead gliding by was deaf to Domorius's wild howls.

And standing to the left of her on the banks of the river was Maggie.

"Camille?" she whispered. Maggie was even paler than her usual snowy complexion, her lips quivering.

Another illusion. Another trick.

"Camille, what's happening? I . . . I was in my father's classroom. He was there! He was alive, and he was teaching me all about the legend of the immortals. It was real. *He* was real."

Camille peered at this illusion of Maggie. There was something different about it than the one of her father. Maggie slipped on the slick rock as she spun to view the peak of the mountain and then the river. She stifled a scream at the sight of the dead.

"The Underworld." Maggie's chin trembled. "Oh God, we're dead. Are we dead?"

Her catlike eyes searched Camille for an answer. "Well, are we?" she demanded again. She started for Camille, reaching out a hand to help her up.

Domorius slid into Maggie's path, taking shape out of a golden mist. Maggie stumbled back, and Camille leaped to her feet. It really *was* Maggie!

"You've been keeping her in an illusion, too, haven't you?" she asked Domorius as he stalked her backward, looking ready to pounce. Something he couldn't do.

Camille craned her neck and looked up to the throne set into the mountainside. The onyx rock, luminous with ruby flames, was still in the notch carved into the left side of the throne.

"Maggie, follow me! He can't touch you if you're alive, and you *are*."

Camille tripped over the slick rock toward the wide, flat steps lit by torchlight. Domorius howled again. She lifted the hem of her skirts and climbed the twisting staircase.

"What's happening?" Maggie asked from just a few steps behind.

The walls of Camille's town house began to rise around her again, all rippling wallpaper and bowing wood planks. Camille looked down, concentrating on the steps, but already she saw patches of carpet and gleaming wood floor. Maggie grasped Camille's hand as she ascended to the same step, and pulled her forward through what was starting to look like her father's study.

"I see it!" Maggie screamed, apparently unimpeded by any sort of illusion. Domorius must have been concentrating on Camille.

Maggie jammed her to a halt. The illusion of her father's study faded with another shriek from Domorius. The onyx stone was right in front of her, set inside the carved shelf in the throne. Domorius tried to rebuild his illusion to shield her from the stone, and the throne began to morph into a section of bookshelves.

"The Death Stone," Maggie breathed, still holding Camille's hand tight in her own. "Hurry, take it!"

Camille reached through the spines of a few volumes and grasped the dark stone before it became lost behind the illusion. It didn't sear her hand with heat as she'd expected. The Death Stone was the polar opposite of Umandu. Her skin ached with cold, icing her fingertips the same way the Couriers had iced her body. A shattering cold tore through her. Ruby flames filled her sight, drowning her vision.

The strobes of amber and ruby brilliance receded, paved over by a craggy silver light. Camille opened her eyes and saw the stalactites of the black bay above her. She had made it back and was lying on the beach where she'd left Oscar and Samuel.

"Camille!" The echoes of Domorius's warped scream distorted into a voice she knew. She lifted her head, gagging on a mouthful of sand.

"Oscar."

A ring of metal brushed her lips and cool water cleared the grit in her mouth. Her arms were still wrapped around the Death Stone, pressed awkwardly against her bosom.

"Are you hurt?" Oscar lifted her up and cradled her against him. Umandu was in one of his hands, free from the burlap bag. All of a sudden, Oscar's body convulsed. An explosion of ruby and pearl light flared around them on the beach. Mirroring Oscar, Camille's entire body flexed and released. The polar temperatures of the sister stones splintered through her like lightning traveling just beneath her skin.

The onyx stone flew from her hand and landed a few feet away. The light and heat and cold subsided. Oscar still held her, though both of his hands were now free. Umandu and the Death Stone were sitting on their flat bases, side by side in the sand. One black, the other golden amber, and they radiated a strange luminosity. They gleamed, buffed and polished. Complete.

"Are you hurt?" Oscar repeated.

"I don't think so." Her voice echoed in her head, her ear pressed up against Oscar's chest. But there was something else there, throbbing against her temple.

Camille pulled away, too frightened to even hope it might be true. She placed her hands against his granite chest. There, beneath his skin, Oscar's heart thundered with life.

TWENTY-NINE

*C*amille wanted to see his face, but the blurry shield of tears wouldn't let her. He covered her hands with his, warm and damp with perspiration. The shield of tears collapsed so that she could finally see him.

"You did it," he said, his lips close, his breath hot and glorious. She couldn't resist the pull of them.

Camille kissed him. Oscar drew her tight against him as they knelt in the sand. She curled her fists into the collar of his shirt, wanting to sink into him and never resurface. His lips moved with hers in a hypnotic rhythm.

"No! Camille, watch out!" Maggie's shout ripped her from the tranquil haze. Oscar's eyes snapped open. He moved Camille aside and jumped to his feet.

"What are you doing?" Oscar shouted, rushing down the dune toward the glassy black water.

Camille gathered her senses in time to see Samuel dragging the small boat that had already been on the beach — the one Maggie must have taken from the Forelands — to the edge of the bay. Maggie ran after Samuel, too, and he shoved her hard as she caught up to him. She crashed to her side on the beach.

"Samuel?" Camille asked. Why had he done that? She reached out to pick up the two stones. Her hand combed the silt. They weren't there.

Cold panic seized her and she threw her attention back to the edge of the black bay. Samuel had the tiny boat in the water when Oscar reached him.

"I asked what you were doing —"

Samuel swiftly spun around with one of the oars in his hands and flogged Oscar on the side of the head. Oscar's legs crumpled and he fell, his body limp. Maggie sprang toward Samuel again, and again he hit her hard enough to send her back into the sand.

"Samuel! No!" Camille shot to her feet and rushed down the dune where Oscar lay unconscious.

"What were you *thinking*?" Camille screeched at Samuel as she reached Oscar's side. Rivulets of bright crimson trickled from Oscar's temple and into his ear. He didn't respond when she shook him.

"I'm — I'm sorry." Samuel tripped over the side of the boat as he climbed in.

Camille got to her feet, livid. From that vantage point she saw not only the glowing amber and pulsing onyx in the boat, but the burlap bag, too. "Samuel, what are you doing?"

Ira sat in solemn silence in one of the other boats. He watched, but made no move to help.

Maggie stood up cautiously. "He's taking them to my uncle."

Samuel stabbed the oar into the beach to propel his little boat into the bay. "I have to," he said. "It's what he asked me to do, and I won't fail him."

Camille lunged for the wide, flat end of the oar. Samuel brought it across her shoulder with a sickening crack. It knocked her clean off her feet and onto her side. She grasped her smarting shoulder and stared after him.

"Why?" The word broke on its way from her mouth. Camille hated the weak sound of it.

Samuel had pushed himself a few yards away, but he'd yet to take a solid row toward the blurry silver dot from which they'd entered the bay.

"You risked everything, Camille, all of it, because you love him." Samuel flicked his eyes toward Oscar, still unconscious on the sand.

"You forsook your own father, you offered up your own life for love." Her brother shook his head. He combed his fingers through his tangle of black hair. "I'm sorry, but I have to do the same."

She squinted at him, unable to understand. What did all this talk about love and sacrifice have to do with taking the stones to Starbuck? Samuel's boat drifted back toward the beach in the current.

"I don't have a choice," he said, drifting ever closer. "Just how you didn't have one. You would never have given up on saving Oscar."

Camille's aching shoulder ebbed under a sick swell in her throat.

"This isn't the same thing at all," she said, the tip of Samuel's boat drifting closer. One lunge and she could grab the lantern. "Starbuck's life isn't in jeopardy. He's using you, Samuel."

She couldn't comprehend what she was saying, or what her brother had just revealed. *Love, love, love.* The word bounced around her head and refused to stick.

"I don't expect you to understand," Samuel said, his skin splotchy. "I know what you must think of me now, that I'm warped and revolting and disgraceful. Don't you think I've thought the same things about myself?"

The lantern inched closer. Samuel wasn't paying attention. Oscar stirred on the sand and muttered a profanity. Samuel jolted, suddenly aware of how close he'd allowed himself to come. She couldn't risk waiting another second. Camille lunged for the lantern and grabbed hold, pulling the prow of the boat into the black water.

Her knees splashed through the surface, her legs engulfed by the piercing sting of ice. Samuel crashed onto his backside as the boat dipped forward. Umandu and the Death Stone tumbled on their straight planes toward her, but the burlap bag got caught behind a bench seat. Camille released one of her hands and grabbed the cold black stone. She chucked it over her head, toward the beach, just as Samuel pried her hand from the lantern and threw it aside.

Camille's other hand came back from tossing the Death Stone and latched on to the sleeve of his jacket. He wriggled his arms free of both sleeves and Camille crashed into the water with nothing but a wool coat turned inside out.

More than just biting cold besieged her as water rushed up her nostrils and into her ears. The sensation of hands and fingers and gnashing teeth clipped at her skin and dress, tugging at her, gluing her to the shallow sandy bottom of the bay. Her eyelids froze open, forcing her to watch as white tendrils of water swirled around her, taking shape out of the blackness. The dead plowed through the water toward her. Camille parted her lips and her scream bubbled into the water. Two hands closed around her thrashing ankles and ripped her from the imprisoning sludge. Black water gushed from her mouth and nostrils as Oscar dug his heels into the sand. He dragged her from the rim of the bay.

Samuel was already halfway toward the blurry silver dot, rowing madly against the current. The oars were for getting out, Camille realized, not getting in.

"You . . . you *traitor!*" Her scream rebounded off the stalactites above, and slammed back into her ears.

She couldn't understand why he was doing this. It all seemed so pointless. Camille had Oscar back. She had Ira and Maggie, too, and now Starbuck could have the stones if he wanted them. Why abandon them on the beach like this?

"The stones have been joined," Camille said as Oscar helped her to stand. "What could Starbuck gain from them now? He hasn't been the one to join them."

Maggie started for the two remaining boats, still hitched together by the thick rope.

"They're joined, but not *officially* joined. Not yet," she answered, and to the rapid sinking of Camille's heart, continued, "We have to hurry! Without Umandu we can't exit the Forelands. It's our lifeline to the world above, just like it was your key to the world below."

Oscar pulled Camille toward the boats. "We might still be able to catch him."

He leaped into the boat with Ira and took up the oars. Maggie and Camille took to the other boat, each of them reaching for the same oar.

"Give it to me!" Camille tugged on the waist of the oar, the handle firmly in one of Maggie's hands.

"You take the stone, and I'll row." Maggie pushed the onyx stone into Camille's chest and let go. Camille dropped the oar in order to catch the stone.

"But I can row faster!"

The blurry silver orb exploded and swallowed Samuel. The hazy orb flashed back to its smaller size and the bay was once again smooth as glass.

"We don't have time to argue!" Oscar shouted.

Camille sat on the front bench with a huff, the stone like a block of ice in her lap. Her *dry* lap. She ran her hand over it to be sure, and realized her sleeve was also dry. Her hair, her dress, even her boots. The water hadn't left an inch of her drenched.

Oscar rowed in reverse, his thrusts propelling the two hitched boats toward the orb. Maggie's feeble rows hardly did a thing at all to help them.

"I don't understand," Camille said, itching to go faster. "How could he do this? How could he choose Starbuck over me? I'm his sister!"

You forsook your own father. For love. Neither Maggie nor Oscar answered. The truth, the reasoning, was not something any of them wanted to admit to understanding.

A howl of wind rolled over the crest of the scorched dune as they neared the blurry silver orb, and blew the misty curtain aside. The current of wind cut across the surface of the black bay and knifed through the ruined silk of Camille's dress. The wind hadn't reached beyond the mist before, but as it raked her tangled hair she smelled its stinking rot. The wind from the Underworld smelled of cabbage decomposing into soft flesh and vinegar, and raging shrieks spawned on the foul wind. And yet Domorius didn't emerge from the misty veil. Perhaps he couldn't. He must have been bound to the Underworld, forced to make Couriers do his bidding on earth. Still, the water's glassy surface erupting into a spontaneous popping boil didn't bode well.

Camille twisted to see Maggie. "What's happening?"

"It's him," Maggie said, her rowing finally gaining speed. "He's going to try to stop us."

THIRTY

*I*n the other boat, Ira winced as steam bubbles burst around them. The steam burned Camille's skin in stealthy licks and pinches, and must have been doing the same to him. Ira looked utterly oblivious, and yet he flinched at the danger around them. What was going on inside his head?

"Faster!" Oscar ordered as the stalactites broke from the craggy ceiling and speared the sizzling water. At last their boats reached the hazy, steel gray orb and the silver explosion of light engulfed them. They were swept away from the heat and into the dark stone tunnel, their boats floating in the dead-infested water.

"Switch off!" Oscar ordered. *It's about time*, Camille thought as she dropped the onyx stone into the bottom of the boat and grabbed the oars from Maggie. Camille shifted forward facing and sliced the water. Camille searched past Oscar and Ira, but saw only midnight and narrowing stone walls. The lantern on Oscar's boat sputtered but gave off little light. Samuel might have already made it to the mouth of the cave.

Camille plunged the blades of the oars into the water, her body heat melting the frosty layer of Forelands ice that had immediately built back up on her skin into beads of cold dew.

"I have the Death Stone still. That has to be good for something."

"You don't understand, Camille. The Death Stone is nothing like Umandu," Maggie replied. "In the world above, it needs the balancing power of Umandu. Joined, the two stones work together. By itself, the Death Stone is . . ." Maggie hesitated, the muted drone of the dead seeming to heighten. "Volatile. It's dangerous."

Oscar looked over his shoulder. His skin was also wet from melting frost. His body was hot; his blood pumping and heart beating. She had him back, whole and complete. She'd succeeded. Samuel hadn't needed to abandon them now that Camille's task was complete. Starbuck could go get his immortal power and Samuel could join him for all she cared. All she wanted was to go home. Go home with Oscar. But then, Randall . . . What about Randall?

The rising hum from underneath the water stopped her from making a decision. The drone had reverberated against the bottom of the boat before, reaching up into the soles of Camille's feet. But now, the tiny vessel shook, drilling into the bones of her hands and wrists as she rowed.

The oars slowed until it felt like they were rowing through a stream of pudding. The length of rope tying the two boats together pulled tight, slowing Oscar. What was happening? She turned to see if Maggie knew, and instead saw the problem.

A pair of pale hands had latched on to the edge of the boat. Before Camille could scream, another pair broke the surface of the water and grabbed the side of the boat right next to her. The small hands pulled the boat to a dangerous angle, bringing Camille face-to-face with a dead woman.

Maggie screamed and jammed her foot against the woman's hands, but the woman continued to hold fast. Her bloodless face dipped below the surface, pulling the edge of the boat under with her. The stone slid toward the black water. Camille dropped the oars and snatched up the stone.

"Camille!" Oscar shouted from his boat. "Kick the hands off!"

Another pair of hands shot from the depths and gave their teetering vessel a final tug. Her and Maggie's screams were cut short as their boat capsized, slinging them both into the black, dead water.

Camille's legs thrashed through a substance more viscous than liquid, her skin aflame with coldness. Pain streaked down her arms, legs, and back. When she dared open her eyes, she saw why. The dead had encircled her. Their fingers clawed at her dress and skin, their billowing hair and clothes blotting out everything beyond. Two women, three men, all with eyes clouded over with white film. Maggie. Where was Maggie? *The river feeding on fear.* They were feeding on her. But how could she *not* be frightened?

Camille struck back, kicking at the bodies pressing in on her, pulling her down. The dead moaned through translucent lips sealed like tight seams. Their moans pitched a notch, and then the white tangle of dead bodies split apart. Maggie swam into Camille, nearly causing her to drop the stone.

Maggie's warm hands wrapped around Camille's elbows and hauled her up, thrashing to fend off two women who groaned with lament. Another pair of warm hands reached into the water and latched on to Camille's arm. Oscar, kneeling on the keel of their capsized boat, brought both girls out of the water and onto the surface of the keel. Camille gasped for air, her body completely and impossibly dry.

"Get into the other boat!" Oscar shouted as he pounded the heel of his boot into the neck of one of the dead grappling for him.

Two more bodies slowly rose from the depths, their faces half-submerged as they glided toward the capsized boat. The stern of Oscar and Ira's boat bumped against their overturned one, and Maggie carefully climbed in. Camille hesitated, the stone clasped against her chest.

"I said go," Oscar repeated. But the boat . . . it was so small. Three people would be pushing it. Four would be out of the question.

"It won't hold us all. Let's flip this one over, and we'll —"

"You can't get back in that water, Camille. Get in with Maggie and Ira. I'll stay here on the keel."

The two dead women reached the rise of the keel and started to climb. Their dresses were drained of any telling color, their hair limp and eyes filmy like the others.

"Here!" Maggie tossed Oscar one of the oars from the first boat. He caught it and swept the two women away with a single swing of the blade.

Oscar then picked Camille up around the waist and set her into the other boat. She tripped over Ira's feet, and the boat dipped dangerously lower in the water. Ira raised his head to look at her, saw through her, it seemed, and then he turned away to gaze at the water.

A break of dim light fell over them.

"The mouth of the cave!" Maggie's elated shout did nothing to excite Camille. The dead were still climbing the keel, Oscar's attempts to kick them off taking longer to achieve.

"Give me an oar," Camille said, and took one from Maggie's hand. She stood to jump back onto the keel and help.

Oscar shot a hand toward her. "No! Stay there, and keep rowing!"

But his boat was sinking below the surface.

"You have to get in with us!" Camille shouted.

"He can't," Maggie said. Panic and anger bubbled up into Camille's mouth.

"What do you mean, he can't?"

"There isn't room, and his weight will send us all in!"

But then Camille saw Oscar tugging on the rope between the two boats to pull himself closer. Thank heavens. He'd come to his senses. Camille prepared to help him in, but when he reached their boat he grasped the metal ring in the prow and started to undo the slipknot.

"What are you doing?" She watched his fingers deftly loosen and release the knot. "Oscar —"

"I'm going to try and flip it back over," he said. "But I don't want you attached to me if I can't."

Camille dove past Ira's slumped form and grabbed Oscar's arm. "Don't!"

At least a dozen white hands were hooked on, submerging it. To flip it back over, Oscar would have to get into the water.

"You have to get to Samuel before he leaves the Forelands. Get yourself out of here. I'll catch up to you — if I can." Oscar eyed the black water creeping up the overturned boat. "I have to do it *now*, Camille."

"Take this!" Maggie shouted, and again tossed one of her oars to Oscar. He'd need it to row himself out of the tunnel and fend off the dead.

Oscar softened the fierce pinch of his lips as he stared at Camille. "I love you. I should never have made you believe I didn't."

He threw the rope into the water, his quickly sinking boat detached from theirs. Maggie's uneven rows jerked them farther away from Oscar.

"No! Maggie, stop. Stop!"

Maggie shut her eyes to Camille's shrieks echoing off the tunnel walls. Maggie's face crumpled as a streak of tears rolled from the corner of her clamped eyelids, her rows never slowing.

Camille turned back to Oscar. He gave her a brave, crooked smile and then dove into the river of the dead.

THIRTY-ONE

*C*amille collapsed, watching the surface of the water. Waiting for the boat to right itself and Oscar to reappear. But the keel slipped under the black water completely and Oscar didn't emerge. Camille counted Maggie's rows, her thrusts having improved since earlier. They were close to the mouth of the cave, the light scattering the dead that had started to follow.

Camille reached ten solid rows and still Oscar hadn't resurfaced.

Ira hunched over, whistling his melancholy tune as if all was right and well, as if Camille's heart wasn't splitting and smoldering inside her. She finally buried her face in her hands and choked on the sobs she'd held at bay. *She'd had him back. . . . She'd had him back.*

The lantern wheezed and snuffed out as their overburdened boat slugged into the ice-covered Forelands. The boat stolen by Samuel lay tied off at the stake. A thin crust of ice already sealed it into the water. Her sweaty hands frosted over and stuck to the edge of the boat as she lifted herself up to get out of the boat. Camille pulled them free, tearing at her skin but not feeling a thing. She was numb, both from the cold and from the sight of Oscar diving into the infested waters. Would he die? She couldn't bear it. She couldn't begin to comprehend the idea of never seeing him again.

"Come on. We need to get to Samuel," Maggie urged her.

"No, I have to stay. I have to wait for Oscar." Camille jerked her arm out of reach when Maggie tried to grab it.

"We don't have time to wait!" she cried. "If Oscar gets the other boat turned back over, he'll follow us. But we need to go, now."

Camille stood at the edge of the pool of water, staring into the mouth of the cave. Oscar would succeed. He'd get the boat flipped and he'd follow them. He had to. And she had to believe he would.

Camille turned her attention, her whole consciousness, toward Ira, who still sat in the boat.

"You have to get up, Ira. Use your legs." She picked up the onyx stone and took his arm.

His body was heavy as she helped him stand, a solid block of ice. The curls of frost had melted from his eyebrows and lashes. Upon a second look, Camille thought there was something different about his eyes, too. Change was good. Maybe all her friend needed was a little thawing.

They followed Maggie around the foot of the hill, hoping to see her brother attempting to scale the icy slope. There had been no divots, or jutting rocks, or any kind of texture at all to latch on to as she'd slid down. Getting back up would be next to impossible.

"How did you not see Ira when you first arrived here?" Camille asked Maggie.

"We wander 'round the hill. Don't always stay in one place." Ira's voice, so long dormant, caused Camille to trip. She caught herself with Ira's sleeve. The glassy rock was easy and concrete for him. He picked her back up and held on to her shoulders.

"We?" Maggie asked. "What do you mean by 'we'?"

Ira closed his eyes to half slits. His fingers fastened around Camille's arms. "You're so warm, love. So warm."

And he was so cold. Camille could see through his translucent skin, to the outline of his bones.

"Come on, let go, Ira." She gave him a moment to get a hold of himself. He trembled, pulling Camille's hands to his cheeks as he had before. Her skin burned.

"I need it," he whispered. Relief and bliss crossed his face. A pale, bloodless face, similar to the dead from the river. Yet his eyes weren't filmy white. They were still blue enough to penetrate the skin of his closed lids.

"Camille?" Maggie stood a few feet away from her and Ira's awkward embrace. "What's he doing?"

The chill of Ira's hands was beginning to travel deeper under Camille's skin, into her bloodstream. Just like a Courier. Only her mind wasn't turning foggy as Ira pressed closer, his need for heat turning him into a human leech.

"S-Samuel." Camille's teeth chattered. "Can you s-see him? Can you reach him?"

Ira wasn't letting go and they were losing time. Maggie slipped as she moved farther away from the foot of the half-moon hill to look.

"No! I don't see him. We're too late!" Maggie wailed, slipping back toward them. She tugged at Ira's arms. "Let go of her, now!"

Ira flung out his arm and hit Maggie in the chest. She flew backward and sprawled out on the icy rock.

"Ira, stop! Maggie! Maggie, are you all right?" Camille tried to see, but Ira only pulled Camille closer, his body trembling.

"We're so cold," Ira whispered into her ear. "So cold. Lost. We need to get warm."

Ira nuzzled her neck. Not intimate, but desperate. Needy.

"Camille?" Maggie whimpered. She hardly heard it in the muddled way sound traveled. "Someone's coming toward me. Don't come any closer, don't —!"

Ira lifted Camille's feet from the ground in his unrelenting embrace. Over his shoulder, she saw Lucius Drake pry Maggie from the ice and crush her into the same strangled hold.

"Lucius?" Camille rasped. Lucius held Maggie tight to his chest. She tried to push him away, but Lucius's muscles seemed to be made of foot-thick ice, like Ira's.

Lucius! He'd been taken by the Couriers, too. How had she forgotten that? Ira hadn't been the only one in the Forelands all these months, frozen and lost.

"Ira," Camille whispered, her breath hot on his ear. He had to listen. He had to thaw out and come back to her.

"Ira, I know you're still in there. Please, you have to help me. It's me, Ira. It's Camille. I'll give you all the warmth I've got, I promise, but you have to help me first. Let me go. Help me, Ira."

He rubbed his cold cheek back and forth against her neck. His arms, wringing her around the ribs, didn't loosen.

Maggie's lips were turning blue, her eyes red-rimmed and bugged out. She couldn't breathe. Lucius was crushing her with his greed.

"Ira, you saved my life, do you remember that? You saved me from the beasts, and you rescued Oscar —" Her voice broke over his name. *"Oscar and me* from the Hesky brothers."

Camille tried to take a breath. Her ribs and lungs screamed in agony.

"And you make horrible tea, and lewd jokes," she gasped.

Ira lifted his cheek from her neck.

"And your personal hygiene is atrocious. You really should bathe more often than you do."

Camille's ribs popped as his hold on her loosened.

"And you can make me laugh like no one else. No one since my father."

Her feet touched the rocky ground, and when she looked up, she saw Ira's blue eyes staring at her. Recognition fired them.

"Help me," she whispered. He blinked twice, and slowly turned his head toward Lucius and Maggie.

In a single pounce, Ira peeled Lucius's arms back and released Maggie from her cage. Camille helped her stand, coughs and gasps wracking Maggie's petite frame. Lucius's howl as he batted Ira off of him was neither muted nor human.

He stalked toward Camille and Maggie, his skin worse than Ira's. Every bone comprising the structure of his face, every tooth set in his jaw, was visible as if nothing but a single sheet of tracing paper covered them. He reached for

Camille and Maggie. His hands showed the same level of deterioration, the jointed finger bones wrapped in sinewy muscle and ethereal skin.

"Camille!"

The distant voice came from behind them. A voice Camille newly despised. She turned to see Samuel sliding down the slope of the hill, and Starbuck slipping along after him.

Ira piggybacked Lucius and twisted him off course. Maggie and Camille slipped over the icy rock toward Samuel.

"What's happening?" Samuel's eyes took in the chaos. "Where's Oscar?" His words reached her ears a second or two after his lips had finished forming them.

"Where's Oscar?" Camille screamed, shaking as she remembered his final smile, meant to reassure her. Everything had always been for her. "He's gone! Gone! Because of you, you wretched traitor!"

Camille left Maggie and pounded on her brother's chest. "How could you do it? How *could* you?"

Samuel threw off her fist and pushed her back. She crashed to the ground and the stone tumbled from her hand. Starbuck lunged for it, but his legs were unsteady like a sailor on a first voyage, and he fell down, out of reach. Maggie slid in and claimed the Death Stone as Starbuck struggled back to his feet. In his hand, he held Umandu. Camille's body reacted to the sight of it — the stone that held Oscar's soul.

"If you have any sense at all, Margaret, you'll give that stone to me." Starbuck's eyes never wavered from the gleaming onyx.

Maggie helped Camille to her feet, and then placed the stone into her hands. "Then I guess I'm senseless after all."

Starbuck blinked rapidly, his impatience growing. He held up Umandu. "You know you can't leave this place without my help. Give me the Death Stone and I'll take you both safely to the necropolis. You have my word."

Behind them, Ira and Lucius's struggle was getting closer. Camille shuffled to the right, taking small steps. Her brother and the captain mirrored her so that their positioning slowly turned like a dial, putting Starbuck and Samuel closer to Lucius and Ira. Camille saw Lucius slam Ira against the rock floor. He was stronger than Ira; he'd deteriorated faster. The real Lucius might have been in there somewhere, too, but deeper. Too deep.

"You're wasting time, Camille. Mr. Hardy is more than ready to take care of your fiancé should we be delayed," Starbuck said. Samuel bowed his head, unable to look at her.

She held the onyx stone closer as Lucius noticed Starbuck and Samuel. *Fresh warmth.* Lucius started toward them.

"I'll give it to Samuel," Camille said quickly. "If you promise to take us out of the Forelands, I'll hand it over to him. *Only* him. It seems fitting, considering he took Umandu from me, too."

Her brother shifted his jaw from side to side, either annoyed or ashamed.

"Passage out of this charming land is granted." Starbuck nudged Samuel. "If you'll go get what we came for."

Her brother took a step forward. Camille reached out and pulled him toward her just as Lucius threw himself upon Starbuck's back, locking the young captain's neck into a choke hold. Starbuck dropped Umandu and used both hands to try to free himself.

"Lionel!" her brother shouted. Camille and Maggie latched on to him, holding him back with all their strength. Still, their feet slipped forward.

Ira walked with sure, mechanical footing over the rocky ground toward Lucius and reached to pull him off Captain Starbuck.

"No! Leave him!" Camille shouted.

Ira complied. He stepped around Lucius, who was blissfully sucking the warmth from Starbuck's body and choking the air from his lungs.

Samuel shoved his captors aside and made a dash toward Captain Starbuck.

"Ira, stop him," Maggie ordered. Like a string puppet Ira shot out his hand and caught Samuel's shirtsleeve.

"Let go!" Samuel tried to yank free, but without success.

"It's only to save you," Camille said, though she knew her brother wouldn't see it that way. Oscar had made her go into the safer boat for the same reason, and yet her own safety had not even crossed her mind. She hadn't cared about it. She'd only cared about his.

Camille crouched and picked Umandu up from the ground in front of Starbuck, who was now on his knees, his lips blue and eyes glazing. Maggie stared at her uncle with a cross expression of regret and satisfaction.

"Up. We have to get to the top of the hill," she said, breaking her stare and taking Camille's arm.

Camille resisted, staring back the way they'd come, toward the entrance to the dark tunnel.

"We can't leave yet!" Oscar could still be coming. If she left with Umandu, the key out of the Forelands, he'd be trapped.

"He's not coming, Camille." Maggie didn't say this harshly, or carelessly just so Camille would hurry and climb the hill. She said it, voice cracking, with sincere sadness and regret. And truth.

Camille's tears burned her eyes as she took one last look in the distance, and then turned toward the hill. Ira started up the slippery slope. With one outstretched arm, he dragged Samuel's thrashing body effortlessly. Ira kicked the toe of his boots into the ice slope, creating fissures for Camille and Maggie to climb by. Other divots were in the hillside, too, perhaps made by Samuel jamming the pointed crest of Umandu into the rock to help him climb.

Camille clutched both stones tight to her, but climbing with the stones, without use of her arms or hands, was difficult.

Maggie extended her hand. "Give me one."

Camille should have been able to hand one over easily, without thought. But she wasn't sure which one she could part with. For so long, Umandu had felt like an extension of her own body. Its draw magnetic. But the onyx stone, even though it was cold, felt good in her hand. Steadying. It made her feel capable.

"You'll be able to climb faster," Maggie said, still waiting.

Camille gave her the Death Stone, parting with its steadying weight. She held on tightly to Umandu as she climbed.

"We can't leave him!" Samuel cried. "Go back! I promise you, Camille, if you don't go back, I'll —"

"What, Samuel? Betray me again? For what you've done I should leave you down here in the Forelands with him!"

Ira pulled Samuel atop the hill and held him there in the same silent obedience. It still wasn't Ira. He'd joined them, but it wasn't him.

"Good. Do it! Let me go, Camille."

Let him go. Let him go be with Lionel Starbuck. He'd choose the Forelands and death by Lucius's fleshless, frozen hands, just to be with Starbuck? Camille reached the top of the hill, her pulse rapid, unable to look her own brother in the eye.

"I'm sorry," she said. "I don't think our mother would forgive me if I did."

Camille held Umandu outward, not sure what to do with it or how Samuel had ejected himself from the Forelands the first time on his own. Maggie, her hand still linked with Camille, grabbed hold of Ira's other arm so that they were all connected.

"How does this thing —"

Camille's throat filled with a whoosh of cold air as darkness fell over them. The rocky terrain fell away from the bottoms of her feet and was replaced by something warmer. Softer.

Sand.

She opened her eyes to the pink light of dawn glinting off sand and limestone. Camille climbed the slight rise of the crevice between the two feline-faced statues, and then collapsed onto the sand. Samuel darted away as soon as Ira released him, slipped on the sand, and nearly fell, too.

The weight of the air — *real* air — pressed on Camille's shoulders and bent her at the knees. The unfiltered sunlight breaking over the necropolis blinded her, and even the silence of the sandy graveyard deafened her now that the muted, underwater sound of the Forelands was gone. Camille stumbled over the foot of the statue and landed against its colossal shin. She took short breaths, Umandu in her palms. But the pulse she wanted to feel, the pulse she and Oscar had given the stone, wasn't there.

If one of you were truly dead, the stone would fall dormant, Maggie had explained to Camille. Tears stung the inner corners of her eyes. *Oscar.*

"What the hell . . ." Hardy's voice made Camille suck back her tears and steady herself on the stone foot of the statue.

Hardy got to his feet, yanking Randall up from where they'd been resting against a mausoleum. He still held the pistol. They both appeared ragged, their hair disheveled and cheeks stubbly. But Randall's glimmering smile, his sheer joy over seeing her, harnessed Camille's complete attention.

"Randall." Camille tried to stand free of the statue, but her legs were spent, her muscles weak.

He stepped forward to go to her, but Hardy reminded him of the pistol with a jab to the side. Randall stopped and stared at Camille, his relief crossing over to alarm. "Camille, what's wrong? Where's —"

Hardy waved his pistol at them, cutting Randall off. "Captain Starbuck. Where is he?"

Maggie came to Camille's side, her face filthy and streaked from the melting layer of parchment-thin ice. Camille could only imagine her own face looked the equivalent.

"My uncle has been detained," Maggie answered. "Indefinitely."

Hardy's grimace slowly changed over into a budding smirk. Before Camille could say anything, the sun's rays slanted taller and lit the crown of the statue. As the night-chilled stone warmed, the hiss of snakes returned. Camille and Maggie leaped off the massive sandaled foot.

Sunlight slid down the statue, reducing the stone into a torrent of white sand and spilling into a pyramid-shaped heap. The gate to the Forelands vanished with the burgeoning rays of sunlight. Camille lowered herself to kneel in the transformed sand as the hissing sound fizzled. She swept her fingers through the grainy remains of the statue. Her way back to Oscar was gone.

She'd lost him once before, but this wasn't the same. He wasn't going to appear beside her in a magic swirl of light; he wasn't going to come back to her, even if her heart longed for him more than anything else. Not this time.

Samuel got to his feet and surged toward Camille, his face contorted with the same pain and suffering that rendered her motionless.

"You killed him!" He bent low to scream into her ear. "He would have brought you out of the Forelands if you'd just given him the chance. Instead you left him there, you left him to die! Give me the stone. Give it to me; I'm going back in."

Maggie helped lift Camille to her feet and shoved Samuel back at the same time. His weakened legs gave no resistance.

"You can't get back in. The entrance is gone." Maggie slipped the Death Stone into Camille's other hand. Both stones at once were heavy. Too heavy. Camille let them drop into the sand. She didn't want them. All she wanted was to go back home. But she couldn't see past leaving the necropolis, let alone how she could sail back to San Francisco and live the rest of her life without Oscar.

Her brother sniffled. "Then I'll wait until sunset when the hissing sound starts again. The statue will reappear if the stone is nearby, won't it?"

He bent and reached for the two stones. Maggie swept her foot into a mound of sand and sent it straight into his eyes. Samuel yowled and stumbled back, covering his face.

"That's for pushing me down." She picked up a handful of sand and threw it into Samuel's open mouth. "Twice."

Hardy pulled Randall forward, his finger on the trigger. Camille had the barest urge to pick up the stones, but it wasn't strong enough to send strength back into her. Instead her eyes wandered, searching for Ira. She found him sitting in the sand against a tomb farther away, his chest heaving for air.

"Give me the stones," Hardy said.

Maggie crossed her arms over her chest. "These stones are the keys to the Vale of Ice. All of my training, all of my *life*, has been devoted to reaching the Vale." She stood steadfast. Hardy shrank an inch under Maggie's vicious stare. "As soon as Camille reaches the Vale with the stones, she'll release Uma from —"

"You don't have to tutor me on Uma and the immortals." Hardy grimaced against the new sun. "You think I'm just some urchin sailor, don't you? You're so full of yourself and your bloody *destiny* that you never even stopped to wonder if maybe — just maybe — your family line wasn't the only one with a responsibility to the stone."

Camille's vision focused. She sharpened it on Maggie's slackened expression. Randall, too, looked at his captor in astonishment. Hardy reveled in the reactions he'd inspired.

"This is priceless," he said with a gruff laugh. "Your dear old daddy never told you about your dissenting cousins, I take it. The *other* line of Firstborns. The disgraceful ones. The ones to whisper about."

Maggie stood speechless, immobile, her bewildered stare locked on Hardy.

"You mean you . . . you're a Firstborn? The same as Maggie?" Camille asked.

Hardy answered without taking his eyes off Maggie. "I'm a Firstborn, but I ain't like her. She wants to give Uma her kingdom back. Me and the rest of my ancestors have always wanted something different."

Maggie pushed her tangled golden hair out of her face and finally spoke. "Uma *is* your ancestor."

"Uma is a power-hungry thief," Hardy retorted.

Maggie gasped, genuinely insulted. "What do you want with the stones, then?"

"To return them to their rightful owner," he answered. "And I'm going to be the honored one to do it. The stone doesn't have a pulse anymore, so the gates are gone. I'll just have to wait for the next Courier to come and get me."

Samuel looked at Hardy through red-rimmed eyes and sand-coated lashes. "I'll come with you."

Hardy snorted. "Sure, come along — if you want to take up permanent residence inside the Forelands. The two stones are going back to Domorius, so you won't have your key out, back to the world above."

Randall, whose arm was still firmly in Hardy's grasp, asked, "And what about you? You'll just stay? Sacrifice yourself?"

Hardy looked hard at Maggie. "That's my destiny." He clicked back the pistol's hammer. "Give me the stones."

Randall's chest expanded as he took a breath and held it. The toes of Camille's boots nudged against the two stones, still at her feet in the sand.

"Maybe we should give them to him," Camille said to Maggie. Uma couldn't rebuild her kingdom if she weren't even alive.

"Absolutely not!" Maggie hissed. "Do you want to see Oscar again?"

Camille's heart wrenched at the thought of it. "Yes."

"Do you want to see your father? Your mother?"

"Yes, but —"

Maggie cut her off. "But nothing. If you give him the stones, any chance you have at seeing them again will be destroyed. Trust me, Camille. I admit to not knowing anything about Mr. Hardy's family line before now, but I do know that Uma is not what he thinks she is."

Camille noticed Ira lifting himself from his position against the tomb, but no one else paid him any attention.

"If I don't give him the stones, he'll hurt Randall. I can't let that happen," Camille said.

Maggie shook her head. "He won't shoot Randall."

Hardy huffed a laugh through his nostrils. "That right?"

A sudden, deafening crack shivered through Camille's ears and down her spine. She screamed and crouched low to the sand for cover. Randall cried out and collapsed to the sand, gripping his shoulder. The echo of the pistol shot cleared and a stain of blood bloomed on Randall's sleeve, spreading to his chest.

"Convincing enough?" Hardy readied the pistol for another shot. "The stones. Now."

THIRTY-TWO

*R*andall clutched his bleeding shoulder and struggled to swallow his cries of pain. Camille brought both stones close to her, her heart swelling too big for her chest. Heat fired up one arm, and cold shuddered up the other. Give him the stones? After he'd just shot Randall? Hardy had probably hoped to scare her. But he had done *nothing* to scare her.

She tightened her fingers around the stones as Ira, still unnoticed by the others, slunk up behind Hardy and Samuel. The ice that had turned him into a solid block in the Forelands had melted, drenching him and making the sand stick to his clothes. His expression was still hard, his shoulders tight, and Camille was willing to bet his strength was still abnormal. She prayed his reflexes were as well.

She drew back an arm with Umandu in her hand. Ira's unnatural blue eyes — piercing, even from a distance — saw the raised stone.

"You've convinced me," Camille said, and let her arm fly forward. She hurled the stone into the air, over Hardy's head, and straight to Ira. He caught it with extraordinary precision, and the Death Stone, too, as she sent that sailing toward him next.

Hardy spun around, raising his pistol toward his new target. But he was too slow. Ira flipped the triangular Death Stone in his hand and smashed one of the ridged edges against Hardy's head. He crumpled and lay motionless on the desert floor.

Samuel rushed toward Ira, who readied the stone for another strike.

"No!" Camille screamed. Ira lowered the stone. Instead, he swung out his arm and effortlessly flung Samuel ten feet away, onto the stone floor of a mausoleum's entrance.

Camille stumbled to Randall. Blood darkened the sand, clotting it in clumps and sticking to his shirt.

"How bad is it?" she asked, ripping the small bullet hole in his sleeve wider. Blood covered his skin, leaving it slick and red and difficult to see the wound. She reached under her skirt, tore the hemming of her petticoats, and pressed the bundled cloth to his shoulder.

Randall winced and swore under his breath. "I'll be all right. What happened? Where's Oscar?"

Maggie helped Camille to lift him. Ira passed by without a second glance and dropped the stones at Camille's feet. He bent at the waist, hooked Hardy's leather belt with his hand, and dragged him toward the mausoleum.

"Oscar . . . he's . . ." Maggie trailed off, unable to look at Camille. And Camille was unable to look at Randall. She didn't want him to see the devastation she knew her eyes would show.

She let Maggie rig a sling for Randall's arm out of her own petticoat hemming, and started after Ira instead. He dropped Hardy's unconscious body on the smooth floor of the crypt's entryway. Samuel rolled to his knees and held the back of his skull.

"Camille, you're making a mistake."

She stepped onto the stone floor. "The only mistake I made was believing you were better than your father."

Ira reached for the curved brass door handles of the windowless mausoleum. The two stone doors moaned and sucked in the air as he pulled them open. Camille's hair billowed forward into the current of stale wind.

"My father was your enemy, yes, but I'm not. Lionel wasn't, either." The corners of Samuel's mouth pulled down. "You're putting your trust in the wrong people."

Ira disappeared with Hardy into the dark cavern of the crypt. Maggie came up to the entryway with Randall, his arm tied close to his chest, his hand pressed to his wound to staunch the blood.

"My uncle manipulated you. What did he claim? That only he could rule the immortals responsibly? That Uma wasn't fit for the job?" She laughed her flowery twitter of a laugh. "All he's ever wanted was to be a Firstborn. Since that wasn't possible, he decided to go after something of a greater importance."

Ira exited the crypt with Hardy's leather belt and Camille's burlap bag, which had been strung around Hardy's shoulder. Ira caged Samuel with his arms and dragged him to the double stone doors. Camille nearly shouted for Ira to stop, to let her brother go. Samuel was in torment just the same as Camille. Whether she understood or agreed with his reasons or not, he was still her little brother.

But what was he besides that? He wasn't a friend or confidant. And even though she wanted him to be, he wasn't someone Camille could trust.

She stared at the mausoleum doors as Ira disappeared inside with Samuel. Each stone slab had been carved with a relief of a massive tree. The bare branches bent and stretched until they took the shape of human arms and hands reaching for the edges of the door. The thick trunk gave way to a tangle of sharp and twisting roots that evolved into legs and feet at the base of the doors. It was grotesque and beautiful all at once. The hairs on Camille's arms stood on end as she heard her brother shouting from inside.

"I know more about the stones than you realize! I won't let you join them!"

She cringed as she heard the air being punched out of her brother's lungs. Ira exited the crypt, and with fearful calm, he shut the massive carved doors. The tips of the branched fingers on each stone slab came tightly together. Another gust of stale air breathed over Camille, and then settled. She hung her head, grieving. She'd failed her brother, too. He hadn't been able to find it in him to love her, and she was certain it was her own fault somehow.

Samuel's muffled voice was hardly audible through the thick stone of the mausoleum. "I swear on our mother's grave, I'll stop you!"

Ira looped Hardy's leather belt through the aged brass handles, and chose the tightest fitting notch. Camille didn't think it mattered. Those doors must have weighed a ton each. Samuel and Hardy wouldn't be following them any time soon, but she did hope someone heard their cries for help before nightfall.

Ira leaned his forehead against the stone relief. His back rose and fell with deep breaths. Camille reached for him, but then hesitated. Ira had changed so much. She wasn't sure who, or *what*, he was now.

"Are you all right, Ira?"

He let his hands fall from the brass handles and turned to her. His skin, no longer translucent as it had been in the Forelands, had returned to the scruffy, rough color she was used to. Other than being soaked through and through, and the newly amplified blue of his eyes, he at least looked like the old Ira.

"I'm all right, love," he answered, winded.

She chanced a step closer. "Do you need help?"

Her brother continued to shout from inside the crypt, but Camille had to close her ears to it. She had to get away from the mausoleum before she changed her mind and let him out.

"I do need help," Ira answered. He surprised her by sliding his arm around her shoulder and leading her away from the stone doors. "It comes in the form of brown liquid."

Camille smiled, the frigid chill of his touch now gone. "Whiskey?"

He winked at her. "Whiskey."

It *was* Ira. She threw her arms around his neck and hugged him tight.

"Whoa, there. I'm feeling a bit odd." He rubbed his neck and rolled his shoulders.

Camille threw her palms up against his chest. "Please tell me your heart is . . ." She felt its steady rhythm and sighed. "Never mind."

He slipped off the strap to the burlap bag and handed it to her. His eyes hitched on Maggie and he hiked up one of his golden brows. Camille could only imagine what he was thinking.

Randall approached them, giving a slight nod of thanks in Ira's direction. His sleeve was bloody, his faced pinched with pain.

"Tell me what happened down there," he said.

Camille concentrated on the sand, on breathing. Maggie changed the subject quickly.

"The map. It's in the bag still?"

Camille undid the clasp and reached in. The aged leather was soft under her fingers, the string tied in a bow.

"Well . . ." Maggie prodded. "Take it out. Don't you want to know where it leads now?"

Camille's fingers glided over the smooth furled scroll once more, and then let it go.

"No." Camille latched the bag and tossed it to Maggie. She caught it, her pale brows arched. "Take it if you want. Take the stones, too. I'm finished with all of this."

Camille wrapped her arm lightly around Randall's waist. "We need to find a doctor and get your arm taken care of."

Randall smiled down at her, the disbelief in his eyes significantly different from the disbelief in Maggie's.

"You can't be *finished*." Maggie scooped up the two stones that were still lying in the sand. "This is all meant for you, Camille. You're the only one who can join the stones in the Vale of Ice."

Camille leaned against Randall as they walked away from the mausoleum, her eyes hitching on the pyramid of sand.

"I'm not going to the Vale of Ice. There's no reason for me to go," Camille said. "Or for you to go, for that matter. Not now."

Maggie sped up her pace to step in front of Camille and Randall. "Why not?"

Camille let go of Randall and pushed up her sleeve, exposing the bandage on her forearm. She unwrapped the linen, dry blood having stiffened the fabric. Maggie furrowed her brow as she inspected the wound.

"It looks like an animal scratched you." Her fingers traveled over the four long gashes. She drew a sharp breath, no doubt realizing what animal.

Camille met her incredulous stare. "It was the wolf."

The corner of Maggie's lips rose up as if she was actually pleased. "The wolf?"

"Yes." Camille retracted her arm. "And I killed it."

Sunlight reddened Maggie's cheeks and ears, either that or they flushed on their own. "That's impossible." She shook her hair, clumped together and still wet. Her smile faded.

"Trust me. It happened," Camille said, winding the linen back around her wound. "And she's the one who attacked me. Why would she do that if she wants me to join the stones at the Vale of Ice?"

Camille tugged down her sleeve. Maggie continued to shake her head.

"I don't understand it," she whispered. For once, Maggie Starbuck was completely without answers. Oddly, it didn't give Camille an ounce of satisfaction.

Just then, Ira removed his jacket and cranked out the water. He slapped the jacket flat and sparks of water hit Maggie in the cheek.

"I'm Ira. Don't think we've met." He put on one of his coy grins. Maggie wiped the speckles of water from her downturned face as if they were speckles of spit instead.

"No, we haven't met, not officially. Luckily for you, I'm not very good with first impressions either."

Maggie started to trudge through the sand, back toward the gates to Cairo, casting a last glance over her shoulder toward Camille. A cross of anger and fear brimmed in her topaz eyes. Ira followed after Maggie.

"Most people prefer my last impressions," he said. "You know. When I'm leaving."

Maggie didn't laugh. She swung the burlap bag onto her back and kept walking. Ira stayed on her heels, cracking another joke as the two of them walked through the city of the dead. The crypts, fanciful towers, and carved columns were awash with sunlight, the temperature rising.

Camille turned back toward the remains of the feline-faced statues. They were already eroding from the constant desert wind.

"I knew you'd return," Randall said softly, stepping up beside her.

She'd returned, yes, but she still felt as if a part of her was buried deep under the sand, past the Forelands and under the dark waters of the tunnel. With Oscar.

Camille wanted to know what had happened to him. She wanted to know, and yet she didn't. If he'd drowned, if Domorius had taken him . . . If Oscar had become one of the dead gliding along that arctic blue river she'd stood on the edge of . . . Camille bit the inside of her cheek and forced the image away.

"What happened to him?" Randall asked, guessing where her thoughts had gone during her long silence.

Camille knew she would eventually explain it all in detail to him, but not right then. Right then the pain was too fresh and crushing to do anything more than simplify what Oscar had done by detaching their boats and letting Maggie row Camille and Ira safely away from the frenzied dead.

"He saved us."

Randall slipped his uninjured arm around Camille's waist and pulled her against his side.

"Of course he did. Oscar loved you."

She couldn't fight the welling of tears any longer. They spilled over, down her cheeks, and Camille removed Randall's hand from her side.

"He did love me. And I loved him, and I can't believe he's gone. Not yet. I don't want to believe it. I *won't*."

It was the truth, and it was time Randall heard it. Losing Oscar for a second time had stripped Camille of the fear she'd had over whether or not Randall would leave, taking his fortune and Rowen & Company with him. She didn't care. If she had to, she'd start over right there in Cairo, or in Australia, or someplace where she would never have to pretend that she hadn't loved Oscar.

"I know." Randall brushed his fingers against the curve of Camille's jaw, turning her to see him. "You don't have to."

He dropped his hand, but stayed where he was. Randall wasn't leaving. He said as much in the quiet of his stare.

She turned back to the heap of sand. It was no longer the shape of a pyramid, but a plateau. The sand wasn't Oscar. It wasn't even a doorway into the Underworld anymore, and now that the stone didn't have its pulse, Camille couldn't use it as one.

"I'm not asking you to forget him," Randall said. "I'm not asking you to not love him."

Hesitantly, Randall reached for Camille's hand. He laced his fingers with hers. Camille turned away from the plateau of sand. Despite his arm, Randall looked well and strong and certain.

"I'm just asking you to come with me into Cairo. Come help me find a physician who can fix up my arm. And then we'll . . . we'll figure out what happens next."

Camille looked at Randall's hand, at his fingers entwined with hers and the blood and dirt on his knuckles. He meant to take care of her. He always had, even when Camille hadn't been able to give her heart to him. Oscar would always own that part of her. Camille contemplated what Maggie had said about being able to see Oscar again, but let it go. If she allowed Maggie to feed her hope, only to discover it wasn't possible, Camille knew it would destroy her.

For the moment, Camille chose Randall's plan. She liked its simplicity and the way it created no promises or ultimatums. That, at least, she could endure. Camille kept her fingers laced with his and headed toward the city gates.